Praise for the novels of
New York Times Bestselling Author

DEBBIE MACOMBER

"As always, Macomber draws rich, engaging characters."
—*Publishers Weekly* on *Thursdays at Eight*

"A multifaceted tale of romance and deceit, the final installment of Macomber's Dakota trilogy oozes with country charm and a strong sense of community."
—*Publishers Weekly* on *Always Dakota*

"Macomber closes book two with a cliffhanger, leaving readers anxiously awaiting the final installment to this first-rate series."
—*Publishers Weekly* on *Dakota Home*

"Sometimes the best things come in small packages. Such is the case here…."
—*Publishers Weekly* on *Return to Promise*

"Ms. Macomber provides the top in entertaining relationship dramas."
—*Reader to Reader*

"Macomber's storytelling sometimes yields a tear, at other times a smile."
—*Newport News, VA Daily Press*

"Popular romance writer Macomber has a gift for evoking the emotions that are at the heart of the genre's popularity."
—*Publishers Weekly*

"Well-developed emotions and appealing characters."
—*Publishers Weekly* on *Montana*

Dear Friends,

Welcome back to Cedar Cove! Olivia, Grace, Charlotte, Jack, Justine and Seth are eager to continue their stories—and introduce you to a few other residents. Like small towns everywhere, Cedar Cove is a mixture of the good, the bad and the unexpected. That's my way of telling you that a few surprises await you in this story. Yes, you're finally going to discover what happened to Dan. And the Beldons will have a most unusual guest in their bed-and-breakfast.... So along with a visit to small-town America, I've tossed in a bit of mystery. I hope you enjoy it.

My hope, as always, is that you'll feel right at home in Cedar Cove—whether you begin the series with the first or the fifteenth book. Note that you'll always be able to tell where the book appears in the Cedar Cove series by the address. Just look at the first number in the address. (For instance, *204 Rosewood Lane* is the second book.)

If you're wondering if there really could be a town like this, let me assure you there can...and there is. Cedar Cove is based on my own hometown of Port Orchard, Washington. Naturally, my characters aren't based on anyone in town, despite all the speculation over coffee at the Pancake Palace (not the restaurant's real name). You see, I've lived in small towns all my life and I've learned that people really are the same everywhere.

Now, sit back and relax. My friends in Cedar Cove can't wait to fill you in on everything that's been happening. And when you've finished reading this book, please let me know what you think. You can reach me in two ways—through my Web site at www.debbiemacomber.com (write your comments in the guest book) or write me at P.O. Box 1458, Port Orchard, WA 98366. I'd love to hear from you.

Warmest regards,

Debbie Macomber

DEBBIE MACOMBER

204 Rosewood Lane

ISBN 1-55166-929-3

204 ROSEWOOD LANE

Visit us at www.mirabooks.com

Printed in U.S.A.

To Nina Lyman
and
her incredible cats.
What a blessing
your friendship
has been.

September 2002

One

Grace Sherman stared down at the legal form that would start the divorce proceedings. She sat in the attorney's office with Maryellen, her oldest daughter, who'd come with her to offer support. Grace reminded herself that this should be straightforward, that her decision was made. She was ready to end her marriage, ready to piece together her shattered life. To begin again… But her hand shook as she picked up the pen.

The inescapable fact was that she didn't want this—but Dan hadn't left her with any other option.

Five months ago, in April, her husband of almost thirty-six years had disappeared. Vanished without a trace. One day everything was perfectly normal, and the next he was gone. Apparently by choice and without a word of explanation. Even now, Grace had difficulty believing that the man she'd lived with, the man she'd loved and with whom she'd had two daughters, could do anything as cruel as this.

If Dan had fallen out of love with her, she could accept that. She would've found enough pride, enough generosity, to release him without bitterness. If he was that miserable in their marriage, she would've gladly set him free to find happiness with someone else. What she couldn't forgive was the misery he'd heaped on their family's shoulders, what he'd done to their daughters. Especially Kelly.

Dan had disappeared shortly after Kelly and Paul had announced that after years of trying, they were finally, excitedly, pregnant. Dan had been thrilled, and Grace too. This baby was going to be their first grandchild. They'd waited so long.

Kelly had always been close to her father and his disappearance at this critical time in her life had devastated her. She'd pleaded with Grace to postpone the divorce proceedings, convinced that her father would return before Tyler was born. When Dan did return, he'd have a logical reason and would explain everything to their satisfaction.

He hadn't come back, though, and there'd been no further information. Nothing but doubts, questions and a churning, deepening anger that intensified in the endless weeks that followed.

When Grace couldn't stand not knowing any longer, she'd hired Roy McAfee, a private detective and former policeman she trusted. Roy had done an extensive search, certain that Dan had left a paper trail, and he'd been right. What Roy had uncovered was a complete shock to Grace. A year earlier, Dan had purchased a travel trailer, paying cash for it. Grace had no idea where he'd gotten that kind of money, nor did she know anything about the trailer. He'd never mentioned it, nor had she seen it. To this day she had no idea where he'd kept it all those months. Or where it was now.

Given the mounting evidence, she had her suspicions. Grace believed that Dan had used the travel trailer to sneak away with another woman. There'd been one sighting of him and it had come late in May.

It almost felt as if her husband had orchestrated this brief reappearance, as if he was taunting her, challenging her to find him. That day had been a low point for Grace.

A co-worker of Dan's had spotted him at the marina and hurried to the library to fetch her. But by the time Grace reached the marina, Dan was gone. A woman had pulled up to the curb and Dan had climbed into the vehicle and driven away, never to be seen or heard from again.

In retrospect, she'd come to believe that Dan was providing her with the answers she so desperately needed. She could think of no other reason he would mysteriously arrive at the busiest place in town, where he was most likely to be seen—and recognized. The library where she worked was less than two blocks away. Clearly, her husband lacked the courage to tell her there was someone else. Instead he'd chosen another, crueler way to inform her; he'd humiliated her in front of the entire community. Grace knew without being told that everyone in Cedar Cove pitied her.

That sighting had settled the matter in Grace's mind. Whatever love she still felt for Dan died that afternoon. Until then, she hadn't wanted to believe there was someone else. Even when the VISA bill showed up with a hefty charge from a local jeweler, Grace had refused to accept that her husband was involved with another woman. Dan just wasn't the kind of man who would be unfaithful to her. She'd trusted him. Not anymore.

"Are you okay, Mom?" Maryellen asked, touching her arm.

Grace's hand tightened around the pen. "Fine," she

snapped, instantly regretting her tone. She hadn't meant to sound so sharp.

Her daughter looked away. Grace focused on the divorce papers, hesitated a moment longer and then with haste signed her name.

"I'll see that this is filed immediately," Mark Spellman said.

Grace relaxed, leaning back in her chair. This was all there was to it? You could end a thirty-five-year marriage simply by signing your name? "That's it?"

"Yes. Since you haven't heard from Daniel in five months, I don't foresee any legal complications. The divorce should be final in a few weeks."

Almost four decades tossed out the window like so much garbage. The good years, the bad years, the lean ones, the years they'd scrimped and saved. Like all couples, they'd had their share of problems, but despite everything they'd held their marriage together. Until now, until this—

"Mom?" Maryellen whispered.

Grace nodded abruptly, surprised at the emotion that choked her. She'd shed all the tears she intended to. In the months since Dan's disappearance, Grace had deeply grieved the loss of her marriage and the man she thought she knew. The truth of it was, she no longer had a choice; divorce had become inevitable. It was essential that she protect her financial interests. According to the attorney, she couldn't afford the luxury of doing nothing.

Her legal situation was one thing, and she'd dealt with that, but the emotional impact had left her badly shaken. Despite her resolve, the grief hadn't diminished. And the humiliation of what Dan had done was with her constantly. Everyone in town was aware of her circumstances and the fact that her husband had walked out on her.

Slowly, Grace set the pen aside.

"I'll wait to hear from you, then," she said to her attorney, rising out of the chair. Maryellen stood with her.

The attorney, a young man closer to Maryellen's age than her own, escorted them to the office door. He began to say something, then merely looked down and murmured a brief goodbye.

Outside his small home office, the sky had turned a depressing leaden gray. Grace felt a burden of sadness settle over her; she'd known this appointment wasn't going to be easy, but she hadn't expected it to exact such a toll on her self-confidence.

Maryellen glanced at her watch. "I need to get back to the gallery."

"I know," Grace said. Her daughter had offered to go to this appointment with her for moral support. Although she was grateful, Grace had thought it unnecessary. But Maryellen was right.

Her daughter was divorced, too. Maryellen had married young and unwisely, and the marriage had ended in less than a year. The experience had so biased her against men, she'd steered away from relationships ever since. Grace had tried to assure her that she'd meet a wonderful man someday, a man waiting for someone exactly like her. Maryellen had considered that naive and refused to listen and now Grace understood why. Divorce *hurt,* and it was the kind of vicious pain that reached deep inside a person. Grace felt off-balance and guilty, as though she had somehow failed. As though it was all her fault. Maryellen knew what it was like because she'd experienced these emotions herself when she was much younger and without the wisdom or perspective maturity brings.

"Will you be all right?" Maryellen asked, obviously reluctant to leave.

"Of course," Grace said, forcing a smile. She ought to be feeling a measure of relief, after all. She'd finally taken action. She'd given Dan every opportunity, even issued a series of mental ultimatums and deadlines. He would come back when Kelly's baby was born. By the Fourth of July. By their wedding anniversary. First one, then another, until she faced the truth. He *wasn't* coming back. If she hadn't heard anything from him by now, she shouldn't expect that she ever would. Dan had no intention of being found.

"Are you going back to work?" Maryellen asked.

"No," she said, refusing to allow herself to succumb to self-pity. "I'm going to lunch."

"Lunch? It's after four. You didn't eat earlier?"

"No." Grace didn't add that her appetite had been nonexistent for days as the appointment with the attorney grew closer. Then, because she knew her daughter was worried, she added emphatically, "I *am* going to be all right, Maryellen."

Maryellen gazed down the steep hill toward the waterfront, where boats gently bobbed in the protected waters of the cove. Vehicles cruised down Harbor Street, so close together they looked like one continuous line. The Bremerton shipyard workers were out, and traffic filled the roads as husbands and fathers hurried home to their families. The same way Dan once had.

"I'm so furious with Dad I don't know what I'd do if I ever saw him again," Maryellen said between gritted teeth.

Grace knew, though. She was convinced that Maryellen would be grateful, that she wouldn't care what he'd done as long as he came home. And Kelly, their youngest, would shout with joy and tell them all how wrong they'd been. She'd run to her father with open arms, eagerly awaiting the excuse that would explain everything.

"I'm fine," Grace insisted. "Really."

Still Maryellen hesitated. "I hate to leave you."

"I'll get over this." Although that was hardly the way she felt. But if Grace had learned anything in life, it was the importance of balance. For each loss, there were compensations, and she reminded herself to keep the good things firmly in sight. "I have so much to be grateful for. You and Kelly, and now a grandson. I'm so sorry it had to end this way with your father and me, but I'm going to come back stronger than ever." Even as she said the words, Grace knew they were true. The sense of loss was profound, but balance would return to her life and so would joy.

It was Justine Gunderson's lunch break, and all she wanted to do was run home and check the mail. She hadn't heard from Seth in nearly a week. All right, five days, but each one of those days felt like a year. Her husband of little more than a month was in Alaska, fishing the crab-rich waters of the Bering Sea. Seth had warned her when she drove him to the airport that he'd be working sixteen-hour days. He'd assured her that he was crazy in love with her and would be back before she had time to miss him.

Seth had been wrong. Justine was miserable. They'd married, as the old western hit said, "in a fever," unable to delay the wedding even one minute once they'd made the decision. Without telling either set of parents, they'd raced to Reno, gotten the license, found a preacher and afterward headed straight for a hotel room.

They were young and healthy and very much in love. Justine had known Seth nearly her entire life. He'd been her twin brother's best friend—until Jordan drowned at age thirteen. Justine and Seth had been in the same high school graduating class. In the ten years that followed, he'd lived in Cedar Cove but they hadn't been in contact until recently, when they'd both reluctantly joined the committee planning their class reunion.

At the time, Justine had been dating Warren Saget, a local developer. Warren was quite a few years older than Justine; in fact, he was just a little younger than her own father. Warren liked having a beautiful woman on his arm and Justine suited him perfectly. It helped that she was willing to keep his little secret—while he might be successful in the boardroom, his powers didn't extend to the bedroom. When they were together, she often spent the night at his plush hillside house overlooking the cove, but that was more for show than anything. She had her own bedroom in Warren's home. Justine knew very well what people thought, but she'd never much cared.

However, her mother did. Olivia Lockhart shared the general assumptions about her arrangement with Warren and had plenty of opinions on the matter. Justine didn't enlighten her, because it was none of Olivia's business. This disagreement between them had put a strain on the mother-daughter relationship. Her grandmother hadn't been particularly pleased, either, but Charlotte wasn't nearly as open in her disapproval.

No doubt hoping to distract her from Warren, her mother had encouraged Justine to date Seth—although even Olivia had been shocked when Justine phoned to tell her she'd impulsively married him.

The marriage was practically as big a surprise to Justine as it was to her family. After a spat having to do with Warren, Seth had walked away from her. Justine couldn't let it end like that, not with Seth, and she'd gone to him, hoping to make amends. To say they'd settled their differences was something of an understatement.

After the wedding, they'd only had that one weekend before Seth had to return to Alaska. In the weeks since, she'd heard from him intermittently, but he couldn't call—or receive calls—while he was at sea, so their communications were few and far between.

Justine glanced at the time and tried to decide whether she should drive home and check the mail or not. If there was no letter, she'd feel depressed for the rest of the afternoon. On the other hand, if Seth did happen to send her a message, she'd be walking on clouds for days afterward. She needed a letter, a phone call, *anything* that would remind her she'd made the right choice in marrying him. Getting married was the only impulsive thing she'd ever done in all her twenty-eight years. She liked her life orderly and precise. The need for control had always ruled her choices—until she fell in love with Seth.

This commitment to order was one reason she fit in so well at First National Bank, rising quickly to the position of manager. Numbers made sense; they added up neatly; they were unambiguous. To the best of her ability, that was the way Justine lived her life—with strong convictions and with exactness, leaving little room for frivolity and impulse.

Out of habit, she looked up when the bank's double glass doors swung open and watched as Warren Saget walked in, bold as could be. He moved directly toward her desk, his manner confident. Justine hadn't seen him since her impromptu wedding. Unfortunately they hadn't parted on the best of terms. Warren had been angry when he learned she'd married Seth and had made some ugly, spiteful remarks. Frankly Justine wasn't up for a second confrontation.

She rose from her chair. At five-ten, plus her heels, she was as tall as Warren. She wore her straight brown hair long and parted in the middle, just as she had in high school, which emphasized her height. By standing, she sent a nonverbal message that she wasn't about to let him intimidate her—and that she intended to keep this meeting short. She absolutely would not allow him to create a scene in front of her staff and customers. Zach Cox, a local accountant, nodded in her direction as he left the bank. Justine acknowledged him and returned her attention to Warren. "Hello, Warren."

"Justine." He met her eyes and the expression she read on his face told her that her fears were unfounded.

"I came to apologize," he said. "I owe you that."

"Yes, you do." She crossed her arms and shifted her weight from her left foot to her right, conveying impatience.

"Can I take you to lunch?" he asked, then rushed to add, "It's the least I can do. I said some things I shouldn't have, and I've regretted it ever since."

"I don't think being seen together is a good idea."

Warren's pale brown eyes revealed his disappointment. "I can understand that," he said, graciously accepting her refusal. To her astonishment, he sat down in the chair across from her desk.

Unsure what to expect next, Justine sank into her own seat.

"How's Seth?" he asked. "Still in Alaska?"

She nodded. "He won't be home for a few more weeks." Twenty-eight days to be precise, if everything went according to schedule. She crossed off the days on her calendar every night as she slipped into her bed, alone and lonely. They hadn't discussed the future; there hadn't been time. One thing was certain—Justine hated the thought of her husband leaving her for several months each year. Already she dreaded next year's fishing season, which would start in May.

"You're looking good," Warren said with a glint of admiration.

"Thank you," she said, unsmiling.

He sighed. "I know you don't believe me, but all I want is for you to be happy."

Warren had been married and divorced twice and had asked her to be his wife on several occasions. Justine had always refused. She'd never had any interest in marrying Warren.

Aware of her growing attraction to Seth, Warren had purchased a startlingly large diamond ring in the hope of changing her mind. Justine hated to admit that the size of that diamond had briefly weakened her resolve. She knew Warren would have loved slipping the ring on her finger and claiming her as his exclusive property. But the man who'd pampered her was hurt and regretful now. He was asking her to forgive his angry reaction to her marriage.

"Well, perhaps we could go for lunch," Justine said and knew she'd made the right decision when Warren's face instantly brightened. She laughed at the way he bounded out of his chair, not bothering to disguise his eagerness. Seth wouldn't mind her seeing Warren on a social basis now and then; Justine was sure of that. He respected her independence and her good sense, and he realized she'd never abuse his trust.

"Where would you like to go?" he asked. "Any place you want, you name it."

"D.D.'s on the Cove," she suggested, choosing his favorite restaurant.

"Perfect." He smiled approvingly.

Justine reached for her purse and followed him toward the front door, which Warren held open for her. "Shall we walk?" she asked. D.D.'s was only a couple of blocks away, but Warren usually preferred to drive.

"Sure," he said. He was making a real effort to be accommodating. He stopped himself from taking her hand, she noticed, and was grateful. She'd actually missed Warren. Yes, he had his faults, but he could be a good conversationalist and had a sharp mind. There was a history between them, too, a history that had more to do with friendship than romance. In his own way he loved her and she cared for him, too, although not with the same intensity she did Seth. With her husband, the attraction was physical and powerful, but in the few days they'd spent together before he left for Alaska there hadn't been time for much conversation. Their intense hunger for each other had overwhelmed them both. Justine didn't need words to know how Seth felt. His lovemaking proved it again and again.

That weekend seemed like a dream now, and she wondered if what they'd discovered could possibly be real.

At the restaurant, Warren and Justine were seated

outside. The patio wouldn't be open much longer. Already autumn was in the air, but Warren chose to dine alfresco instead of at a table inside, knowing she enjoyed the sunshine.

"I hope we can still be friends," Warren said, smiling as the waitress handed them menus.

"That would be nice." She told herself again that lunch every now and then wouldn't bother her husband. Seth wasn't the jealous type and for that matter, neither was she.

Justine and Warren had a common interest in the financial world, so there was plenty to discuss. Their conversation over lunch went smoothly and the ache in Justine's heart had lessened by the time they finished. She still missed Seth dreadfully, but didn't feel nearly as alone and lost as she had earlier in the day. Warren hadn't asked to see her again, hadn't pressured her at all. After lunch they said farewell outside the bank, she thanked him for the meal and he left.

Later that afternoon, as she drove toward her apartment, Justine's spirits were high, higher than they'd been all week. But when she approached the row of mailboxes outside her building complex, she hesitated, afraid to find out if there was a letter from Seth.

She needed to be reassured of his love because her greatest fear was that he regretted their sudden marriage. Her heart pounded as she unlocked the box and slid out the mail.

No letter.

She sorted through the advertisements, junk mail and two bills a second time, just to be sure. Another Friday night alone in front of the television, she thought. She could phone her mother, but Olivia had been dating Jack Griffin from *The Cedar Cove Chronicle* and was probably busy anyway. Feeling defeated, Justine walked into her apartment and tossed her mail on the kitchen counter, kicking off her heels.

A few weeks ago, she would've relished a Friday night to herself. Warren almost always had plans for them. But all of that was irrelevant now, and feeling sorry for herself didn't serve any useful purpose. If she missed Seth, then she should do something that would make her feel close to him.

His sailboat came immediately to mind. *The Silver Belle* was moored at the marina and Seth had given her the key. When he wasn't fishing in Alaska he lived aboard the vessel. Or at least he had until their marriage. They hadn't even talked about where they'd live when he got back.... That could wait, but right now, she needed the comfort of being in his home, among his things. If she spent the night there, she could wrap herself in his blanket, sleep in his clothes, breathe in his scent. She'd slept there several times and always felt better.

Pleased with the idea, Justine changed out of her business suit and into jeans and a sweatshirt. She collected a novel, a new CD for her Walkman and fresh clothes for the morning. She'd pick up dinner on the way to the marina.

She'd just reached the parking lot when she realized she'd left her cell phone behind. If Seth phoned, he'd call that number. Heading back to the apartment, she unlocked the door and opened it to hear the muted peal of her phone. She lurched for it, pushing the talk button with a sense of urgency.

''Hello, hello!'' she shouted. ''Seth? Seth, is that you?''

Only a dial tone greeted her question. Quickly she

checked Caller ID—the number was unfamiliar, although prefaced by 907, the Alaska area code. She punched it in, letting the phone ring ten times before finally giving up.

Grinding her teeth with frustration, Justine sagged onto the edge of the sofa and rammed her fingers through her hair. It was Seth; it had to be. He must've called her from a pay phone on the wharf.

One minute away from her phone and she'd missed talking to her husband.

"I'm home." Zach Cox let himself in the back door off the garage and stepped into the kitchen. His jaw tightened at the mess that greeted him. The sink was piled high with breakfast dishes, and the milk from this morning's cereal was still on the countertop.

"Who left out the milk?" he demanded.

His two children—conveniently—didn't hear him. Fifteen-year-old Allison was sitting at the computer in their home office, cruising the Internet, and Eddie, who was nine, lay prone on the family-room carpet in front of some mindless television program.

"Where's Mom?" he asked next, standing directly over his son.

Eddie lifted one arm and pointed wordlessly toward the sewing room.

Zach ambled in that direction on his way to the bathroom. "Hi, Rosie, I'm home," he told his wife of seventeen years. "What's for dinner?"

"Oh, hi, honey," Rosie said, glancing up from the sewing machine. "What time is it, anyway?"

"Six," he muttered. He couldn't remember when he'd last come home and found dinner in the oven. "The milk was left out again," he said, thinking it would need to be dumped after sitting for ten hours at room temperature.

"Eddie fixed himself a bowl of cereal after school."

Okay, he figured, the milk might be salvageable.

She lined up the shiny black material and ran it rapidly through the machine, pulling out pins as she went.

"What are you sewing?" he asked.

"A Halloween costume," she mumbled with four or five pins clenched between her lips. "By the way—" she paused and removed the pins "—Eddie's school is having an open house tonight. Can you go?"

"Open house?" he repeated. "You can't be there?"

"No," she said emphatically. "I have choir practice."

"Oh." He'd had a long, trying day at the office and had hoped to relax that evening. Instead, he was going to have to attend this event at his son's school. "What's for dinner?" he asked again.

His wife shrugged. "Call for a pizza, okay?"

It was the third time in the last two weeks that they'd had pizza for dinner. "I'm sick of pizza."

"Doesn't that new Chinese place deliver?"

"No." He should know; he'd had Chinese just that afternoon. Janice Lamond, a recently hired employee, had picked up an order of sweet-and-sour shrimp for him. "Besides, that's what I had for lunch."

"What do you want then?" Rosie asked, busying herself with the cape that was part of the Harry Potter costume Eddie had requested.

"Meat loaf, mashed potatoes, corn on the cob and a fresh salad."

Rosie frowned. "I think there's a meat loaf entrée in the freezer."

"*Homemade* meat loaf," Zach amended.

"Sorry, not tonight."

"When?" he asked, cranky now. It wasn't too much to ask that his wife have dinner ready when he came home from work—was it? As an accountant, Zach made enough money to ensure that Rosie could stay home with the kids. This arrangement was what they'd both wanted when they started their family.

At one time, Zach had assumed that when Allison and Eddie were in school, Rosie would come and work in the office with him. The firm of Smith, Cox and Jefferson often required additional staff. Rosie had always intended to get a job outside the home, but it just never seemed to happen. The school needed volunteers. Then there was Brownies when Allison was eight or nine, and now Cub Scouts for Eddie. And sports, after-school clubs, dance lessons... It soon became obvious that the demands on Rosie's time wouldn't be alleviated as the kids grew older. Because they both believed their children's needs should come first, they'd decided Rosie shouldn't re-enter the work force.

"I'm tired," Zach told his wife, "and I'm hungry. Is it unreasonable to expect dinner with my family?"

Rosie took a deep breath, as though she was struggling to hold on to her patience. "Eddie's got open house at school tonight, Allison's coming with me to practice with the junior choir and I've got to finish this Halloween costume before Friday. Eddie needs it for his soccer team's party. I can only do so much."

He could hear the annoyance in his wife's voice and resisted asking her what she'd been doing all day while he was at work.

Rosie glared at him. "If you want me to stop everything right now and fix you dinner I will, but I have to tell you, I think you *are* being unreasonable."

He considered her words, and then feeling defeated and a bit guilty said, "Fine. I'll order pizza."

"Be sure and tell them no green peppers," she said, refocusing her attention on the costume.

"I like green peppers," he muttered, not realizing Rosie could hear him.

"Eddie and Allison hate them—they prefer black olives. You know that. Now stop being difficult."

"All right, I'll order sausage with olives on one half and green peppers on the other."

His wife rolled her eyes expressively. "I'm not all that fond of green peppers myself, you know."

So, in addition to being unreasonable, he was selfish. Well, at least he was batting a thousand. "Sausage and black olives, then," he said.

"Great." He walked over to the kitchen phone, having memorized the number for Pizza Pete's. He placed the order and made his way to the master bedroom.

"Where are you going now?" Rosie asked as he passed the sewing room.

"To shower and change."

"Do you have to?" she muttered.

"What's wrong with that?" he demanded.

She pushed away from the sewing machine and stood up. "I thought you might wear your suit to the open house."

"Why?" He'd been waiting all afternoon to remove his tie.

"It'll make a better impression if you meet Eddie's teacher wearing a suit. Mrs. Vetter will know you're a professional." She coaxed him with a smile, then brushed a piece of lint off his shoulder and smoothed away a wrinkle. "You look so handsome in your suit," she said, smiling. "Maybe you should shave, though."

Zach ran his hand down his face, feeling the bristle scratch against his palm. She was right. "If I shower and shave, then I'm changing out of this suit."

Rosie's frown deepened. "I don't know why you have to be so difficult."

"If I had a decent dinner every once in a while, maybe I'd be more inclined to do as you ask," he snapped. He couldn't help remembering how pleasant lunch with Janice had been. She'd joined the staff the first of the month and had already proved herself as far as Zach was concerned. She was a quick learner, competent, cooperative. Twice she'd gone out of her way to make sure he had what he wanted for lunch. Only that afternoon she'd insisted on driving over to Mr. Wok's for the shrimp dish.

Sitting on the end of the king-size bed, Zach yanked off his jacket and laid it beside him. Unfastening the buttons at his wrist, he rolled up his shirtsleeves and headed into the bathroom.

He was running hot water for a shave when Rosie came into the room. "Do you have enough cash for the pizza guy?"

"I think so," he said. "Check my wallet."

His wife met his gaze in the mirror. "I'm sorry about dinner."

"You're busy."

"It was crazy today," Rosie said, sitting on the edge of the Jacuzzi tub. They'd special-ordered it when the house was built three years earlier and it'd taken months to arrive. Rosie had wanted it badly enough to give up using tile on the hallway and kitchen floors. Zach would have opted for the tile floors but he hadn't been able to refuse his wife this small luxury. Yet he couldn't remember the last time Rosie had actually used the tub. Like him, she was in and out of the shower, rushing from one obligation to the next.

She went on to tell him about her day, the committee meetings, Allison's dental appointment and some library function she'd agreed to coordinate. "I don't know how mothers who work outside the home get everything done."

"I don't either," Zach said, although he suspected that his associates' wives put dinner on the table at night and still managed to work forty hours a week. He also suspected those other wives were better organized than Rosie.

"I'll cook dinner tomorrow night," she promised.

Zach spread shaving cream across his face. "Meat loaf and mashed potatoes?" He didn't hold out much hope, but it sounded good to hear the promise.

"Whatever you want, big boy."

Despite his irritation, he grinned. Maybe he *was* just being difficult.

Two

The credit card must belong to the woman who'd sat across the restaurant from him last Monday, Cliff Harding decided. He'd noticed her. It wasn't like he could have missed her; they were the only two people in the Pancake Palace that afternoon. The lunch crowd had left and it was too early for dinner.

She was attractive and about his age, but she seemed distracted, caught up in her own thoughts. He'd be surprised if she even remembered he was there. They'd paid for their meals at about the same time and that was when it must have happened. His bill was correct, but it was Grace Sherman's credit card he'd slipped back inside his wallet. She apparently had his.

All week he'd gone about his business, oblivious to the fact that he was carrying someone else's VISA card. If an attentive clerk at the pharmacy hadn't pointed it out, he might not have noticed for that much longer.

As soon as he was home, he'd looked up Grace Sherman in the phone book with no luck. However he did find a listing for a D & G Sherman at 204 Rosewood Lane, Cedar Cove. The voice on the answering machine was that of a woman, so he left a message and waited for her to return his call. Thus far, no one had phoned and he suspected he had the wrong Sherman.

What he should probably do was give the credit card to the manager at the Pancake Palace and request a replacement for his own.

Lately Cliff had found plenty of reasons to drive into Cedar Cove. Charlotte Jefferson had called him in June regarding the grandfather he'd never known. Cliff certainly didn't have any warm feelings toward Tom Harding, even if he was the famous Yodeling Cowboy, popular from the late thirties to the mid-fifties. Tom Harding had deserted Cliff's father and grandmother in his quest for fame. Toward the end of his life, Tom must have regretted the pain he'd caused his family but by then it was much too late. Cliff was his only grandson and—at least according to Charlotte Jefferson—the old man had intended to contact him.

Charlotte had to be in her seventies, but she was a woman with plenty of spunk. She'd befriended his grandfather while doing volunteer work at the Cedar Cove Convalescent Center and had taken a liking to the old man. They were friends, Charlotte explained.

Old Tom had lost his ability to speak after a massive stroke, but apparently Charlotte was able to communicate with him just fine. She told Cliff that Tom had given her a key shortly before he died. Upon investigation, she'd found his personal effects in a storage unit and concluded that Tom was the onetime movie and television cowboy star. As Tom's only surviving relative, Cliff was entitled to these mementos.

In the beginning, Cliff wanted nothing to do with the old man, but Charlotte wouldn't hear of it. She'd made it her mission to make sure Tom's things, which included posters, scripts and his six-shooter—were delivered to Cliff, whether he wanted them or not.

Once he met Charlotte, Cliff understood why his

grandfather had felt so comfortable with the older woman, and over the course of the summer, they'd become quick friends.

He made a habit of stopping in to see her or giving her a call every couple of weeks. She appeared to enjoy these visits and bragged proudly about her two children and her grandchildren. Her son, William, lived somewhere in the south, if he remembered correctly, and a daughter, Olivia, was a family court judge right here in Cedar Cove. Cliff had yet to meet Olivia, although he did wonder if any woman could live up to everything her mother had said about her.

Now that Cliff had spent some time studying the items Charlotte had rescued from the storage unit, he'd come to appreciate what she'd done. He could think of no better way to thank her than by giving her one of the movie posters, which he'd had mounted and framed. Charlotte had genuinely loved Tom Harding and that was *before* she'd identified him as the Yodeling Cowboy.

Cliff parked his truck on the steep hill above the cove, angling his tires into the curb. Carrying the unwieldy poster, he walked up the few steps that led to the large family home. As usual, Harry, her ''guard cat,'' was curled up asleep in the living room window. Even before he had a chance to ring the bell, Cliff heard Charlotte turning the door locks.

He'd never had the opportunity to count how many locks Charlotte had, but he suspected Houdini couldn't have gotten inside. He wasn't sure what she had hidden that was so valuable; he did know that anything precious was likely to be buried underneath a pile of panty hose. He was also aware that at some point in their conversation Charlotte was likely to ask him about his bowels.

''Cliff,'' she said happily, unlatching the screen door, first one and then a second lock. ''This is a pleasant surprise. I wish you'd let me know you were planning to stop by. I would've baked you a batch of cookies.''

That was exactly the reason he hadn't phoned ahead. The woman was intent on fattening him up. Cliff didn't need any assistance in that area—he already had a paunch that had come with middle age and he was trying hard to lose it. So far he was down ten pounds from the first of the year, although he swore it would've been easier to chip away rock. Until retirement, he'd never had to worry about his weight.

''I brought you a little something,'' he said as she swung open the screen door for him. Harry raised his head, stared at him and apparently decided Cliff was a friend. The cat closed his eyes and resumed his nap.

''Sit down and I'll make us a cup of tea,'' Charlotte said. ''And I've got some pound cake.''

''Don't go to any bother.'' He knew it wouldn't do much good to protest, but he tried anyway. He was only going to stay for a few minutes. After leaving Charlotte's, he'd drop off Grace Sherman's credit card at the Pancake Palace. He might ask Charlotte if she knew Grace, since the older woman seemed acquainted with nearly everyone in Cedar Cove.

''You must be hungry,'' Charlotte said, sounding hurt that he'd refused her offer.

''Charlotte,'' he insisted, ''open your gift.'' It wasn't wrapped, but the frame shop had slipped it inside a cardboard container.

Charlotte looked up at him quizzically. ''This is for me?''

He grinned and nodded, enjoying her flustered reaction. Charlotte was the kind of person who was constantly giving to others but felt uncomfortable receiving anything herself.

She opened the cardboard, and Cliff helped her remove the frame. He held up the poster and heard the soft gasp when she realized what it was. She covered her mouth with one hand as her soft gray eyes flooded with tears.

''Oh, Cliff, you shouldn't have,'' she said, blinking furiously. ''This is far too valuable to give me.''

''Nonsense. I'm sure my grandfather would've wanted you to have it. If it wasn't for you, I wouldn't even have any of these things.'' Nor would Cliff have known anything about his grandfather, other than what his father had told him. He now saw Tom as more than a selfish, fame-obsessed bastard; he saw a regretful old man who would've liked to turn back the years and make different choices.

''You were a difficult nut to crack,'' Charlotte reminded him, frowning.

He had to agree. She'd been persistent in calling and writing. If he hadn't arrived on her doorstep when he did, Cliff figured she would've brought everything to him herself, venturing onto the freeway in a car he was sure had never been driven over forty miles an hour.

Charlotte reached for a lace-trimmed handkerchief in her apron pocket and blew her nose loudly. ''I don't know what to say.''

''Would you like me to hang it for you?''

''Oh, please.''

He'd come prepared to do that, assuming the task would require his assistance.

"Do you think it would be inappropriate for me to hang it in my bedroom?" she asked.

"I think that would be a perfectly fine choice," he assured her. He followed her into the long hallway to the master bedroom at the far end of the house. The double bed against the wall had a plain curved headboard. An old-fashioned dresser with a large mirror sat on the opposite side of the room. She had a comfortable chair with worn green upholstery and a table with a reading lamp. Cliff guessed she did most of her reading there, gauging by the pile of books on the table.

"How about here?" Charlotte asked, pointing to a bare space on the white wall across from the bed.

Several pictures crowded the dresser top, but Cliff didn't have a chance to study them. One did catch his notice, however. Charlotte saw what he was looking at and reached for the frame. "This is Olivia when she was six months," she said, pointing to the picture of a baby. "She was an exceptional child even then."

Cliff swallowed a smile. Six-month-old Olivia was sucking on her big toe and grinning with toothless delight. Cliff could only imagine what the judge would say if she knew he'd seen the photograph.

"Mom?" Almost as if the picture had conjured up Charlotte's daughter, he heard a woman's voice call from the living room. "Are you all right? The front door's open and—"

"Oh, dear..." Charlotte rushed out of the bedroom. "Olivia?"

"The door was unlocked and you never—" Olivia said, meeting Charlotte in the hallway. She stopped abruptly when Cliff walked out of the bedroom.

Olivia stared at her mother and then Cliff.

"Hello," he said, enjoying the perplexed look. Olivia had matured into a strikingly attractive woman. Now probably wasn't the time to ask if she was still agile enough to lift her foot to her mouth. He couldn't keep from grinning, though. The resemblance between mother and daughter was most apparent in the eyes, although hers were more blue than gray. If he hadn't known Olivia was a judge, he would have guessed she held some responsible position from the dignified way she carried herself. She was medium height, close to his own age, and her hair was still a lustrous brown.

"I'm Cliff Harding," he said, stepping forward and offering his hand.

"Tom's grandson," Charlotte explained. "He was just hanging up a poster of the Yodeling Cowboy for me."

Olivia frowned as they shook hands. "Oh, my goodness, you're Cliff Harding!"

"That's what I just said," Charlotte murmured.

"He has Grace's credit card."

Actually Cliff saw Grace as the one who had *his* VISA card. "You know Grace Sherman?"

Olivia nodded. "We've been friends for years. She was planning to return your call this evening."

Charlotte glanced helplessly from one to the other, as if she'd somehow missed hearing the punch line to a good joke.

As best he could, Cliff explained the situation.

"You'd better take care of that right away," Charlotte advised. "Personally, I don't use credit cards. It's like carrying Monopoly money."

"I'd hoped to get my own card back," Cliff said. "Do you think I could drop in on Grace?"

''She works at the library,'' Charlotte told him. ''You could leave your truck parked here and walk over there. It's only a few blocks away and I don't expect we're going to have many more of these sunshiny afternoons.''

''I think you should meet Grace,'' Olivia encouraged. She shifted her gaze from him and Cliff wondered if *he* was missing something.

''Oh, yes,'' Charlotte agreed. ''Olivia's right, you should meet Grace. She could use a male friend after what Dan did to her.''

''Dan,'' Olivia added quickly, ''is her husband, correction...*was* her husband. He disappeared earlier in the year.''

The two women became engaged in a discussion about Dan's whereabouts and their own suspicion—that he'd left Grace and run away with another woman.

''Grace filed for divorce last Monday,'' Olivia told him.

The same day as the credit card mishap. No wonder she'd seemed distracted and preoccupied. No wonder she'd been alone. Although Cliff would've noticed her if she'd been in the middle of a crowd.

Grace Sherman was like...like a mountain wildflower. He wasn't normally poetic and couldn't really say why he thought of her in those terms, but that was the image that came to his mind. A flower that bloomed despite cold, wind and hardship. He'd tried not to be obvious, but she'd attracted him and he'd wondered about her. It'd been a very long time since he'd looked at a woman, any woman, the way he had Grace.

''I think I will take a walk over to the library,'' he muttered.

''Good idea,'' Olivia said brightly.

Charlotte's daughter seemed eager to send him off. Perhaps she was trying to encourage him to meet her friend. If that was the case, Cliff didn't need any prompting. After saying goodbye to Charlotte and Olivia, he left and strolled down the steep incline toward the waterfront. This was his first visit to the library and he stopped to admire the mural painted on the outside. The town sported several other murals, as well, which he'd often admired.

Grace Sherman stood at the front desk when Cliff entered the library.

She glanced up when he approached the counter. "Can I help you?"

"I'm Cliff Harding," he said and waited.

It obviously took a moment for his name to register. "Oh, hi—you're the one who has my credit card and I have yours. I'm sorry. I should have recognized you. If you'll wait a moment, I'll get my purse." Grace took a deep breath, then said, "I was going to call you back this evening."

"That's what Olivia said."

"You know Olivia?"

"We met this afternoon at Charlotte's."

Again she hesitated, as if needing time to connect all the dots. "You're Tom Harding's grandson. Charlotte's often mentioned you. I apologize, I didn't immediately realize who you were. If you'll excuse me, I'll just be a moment."

"Of course."

She disappeared into a small office directly behind the counter and returned with her purse. His credit card was tucked inside a small white envelope. They exchanged credit cards, laughed about what had happened, then stood gazing at each other for an awkward few seconds.

It was now or never, Tom decided. "I was thinking maybe we could laugh over this at dinner one night." It'd been years since Cliff had asked a woman out on a date, and he felt a little uneasy. When she didn't respond, he was sure he'd bungled the invitation.

"Dinner?" Grace finally echoed. "The two of us?"

Cliff spoke rapidly. "I've been divorced for the last five years. I haven't dated since my wife left and... well, I think maybe it's time I did."

"I see," she said, staring at him again. "I mean..." She paused and took another deep, audible breath. "Thank you." She raised her hand to her throat. "You don't know how flattered I am that you'd ask. Unfortunately, I'm not ready just yet."

That was a fair reply. "When do you think you might be ready?"

"I...can't say. I recently filed for divorce. I don't feel it would be right for me to see anyone else until I'm legally free to do so." She looked away. "I take it you heard about my husband?"

Cliff nodded slowly. "I'll be waiting, Grace, and I'm a patient man."

Her eyes met his and he saw the beginnings of a smile. That was something he hoped to see again. Soon.

"You'd better tell me what's wrong." Jack said, his stocking feet propped up against the ottoman in front of Olivia's large-screen television. Tuesday night was their date night. Olivia had invited him over for dinner and *The New Detectives* on the Discovery Channel. Lately they'd taken turns supplying the meal. This week it had been Olivia's turn and she'd baked a chicken casserole that was worthy of a cooking award. He generally brought takeout.

"What do you mean what's wrong?" she countered.

"You've barely said a word all night."

Olivia sighed and rested her head on his shoulder. It'd been his lucky day, that morning nine months earlier when Jack had strolled into her courtroom. New to Cedar Cove and the newspaper, he'd visited the divorce court, jaded by his own experience and expecting to hear what he always did.

But Olivia was different. A young couple, Ian and Cecilia Randall, had stood before her, accompanied by their attorneys. Another divorce, two people with broken hearts pretending they were above the pain. Only it radiated from both of them. Jack saw it and wondered if anyone else did. He assumed all those involved in the legal process had become blind to the human wreckage that appeared before these judges. Couples walked in battered and broken, emotionally crippled by the pain husbands and wives so often inflicted on each other.

The Randalls had lost an infant daughter, Jack recalled, and were asking Olivia to rescind their prenuptial agreement so they could file for divorce. Olivia denied the petition and, in essence, had denied their divorce. Jack's column that weekend had praised her courage.

Olivia hadn't appreciated the unwanted attention, but she'd forgiven him. In the months since, he'd gotten to know Olivia Lockhart. They'd grown close, and he was beginning to hope this relationship had a future.

"Are you going to tell me?" he asked, wondering if he was reading more into her silence than he should.

He'd had his own bit of troubling news this afternoon, but he wasn't ready to disclose it.

"I'm worried about Justine," Olivia said after a moment.

"How so?" As far as Jack knew, Olivia's daughter was deeply in love with her fisherman husband.

"She was seen having lunch with Warren Saget last Friday."

"Warren?" Jack had never understood what Olivia's daughter saw in the land developer. Now that Justine had married Seth, he'd hoped Warren would move on to greener pastures—which in his case probably meant an even younger woman.

"You heard it or Justine mentioned it?"

"I heard it," Olivia said and gnawed on her lower lip. "Justine doesn't share much with me." She gazed at him with wide anxious eyes. "I think...she regrets marrying Seth."

Jack removed his feet from the ottoman and leaned forward. This was serious. He frowned, trying to think of something reassuring he could say. But he was hardly an expert on the parent-child connection. His relationship with his own son was on rocky ground and with good reason. As a child, Eric had suffered from leukemia. Jack had turned to the bottle for solace, and for years he'd emotionally abandoned his wife and son. Following the divorce, Eric hadn't wanted anything to do with his father. Jack couldn't blame the boy; nevertheless, it stung. Now after several years of sobriety and with Olivia's encouragement, he'd made a determined effort to reestablish contact.

Olivia and her daughter struggled with their relationship, too, but on an entirely different level.

"Just ask her," Jack advised. "She'd probably be willing to tell you."

A quick shake of her head dismissed that idea. "I can't... Justine will resent the intrusion. I don't dare say a word unless she brings it up. Besides, I don't want her to know I heard about her lunch with Warren. She'll accuse me of listening to gossip." Olivia dropped her feet and bent forward. "How is it," she asked, "that I can make judgments in a courtroom that affect the future of our community and yet I can't speak openly with my own daughter?"

It was the same question he'd asked himself with regard to his son. Each week Jack editorialized in *The Cedar Cove Chronicle.* He was never at a loss when it came to expressing his opinion. But talking to his only child—well, there his confidence disappeared. He was afraid of saying too much or not enough, of sounding either judgmental or indifferent.

"Eric phoned this afternoon," Jack said bleakly. "He was upset and I didn't know what to tell him. I'm his father, he came to me with a problem and I should've been able to help him."

"What's the problem?" Like Jack, Olivia knew it was a breakthrough in this difficult relationship for Eric to contact him at all. When he didn't immediately answer, Olivia ran her hand down the length of his back. "Jack?"

"The girl Eric's living with is pregnant."

"They weren't using birth control?"

"No. He didn't think it would happen."

Olivia laughed softly. "I don't understand why any couple would take chances with birth control."

"You don't understand." Jack said, turning to face Olivia. "Since Eric had cancer as a youngster, the drugs and the different procedures left him sterile. The doctors told us that years ago."

Olivia frowned. "You mean the baby isn't his?"

Jack rubbed his hand over his eyes. "It can't be, and Eric knows that."

"Oh, dear."

Jack had wanted to say something helpful to Eric, but he had no words of comfort or advice. He'd hung up feeling that once again he'd failed his son.

The Harbor Street Gallery was quiet for the moment. Taking advantage of the respite, Maryellen slipped into the back room to get herself a cup of coffee. Weekdays tended to be slow, especially in the fall. During the summer months, the gallery was a drawing point for tourists and constantly crowded. As the manager, Maryellen welcomed the lull that came with autumn, especially since the Christmas rush would soon begin. Already they were gearing up for it.

At some point today, Jon Bowman would drop by. She'd last seen him in June and remembered their meeting with embarrassment. Jon was a reserved, perhaps shy man, who had little tolerance for small talk. She'd hoped to engage him in conversation; instead she'd babbled on about all manner of irrelevant things. By the time he left, she'd wanted to kick herself for falling victim to her own eagerness.

No sooner had she poured her coffee than she heard footsteps on the polished showroom floor. After a quick, restorative sip, she set the mug aside, and hurried out front, prepared to greet her customer.

"Welcome," she said, then brightened when she saw who it was. "Jon, I was just thinking about you." His photography had long been her favorite of all the art they sold. The gallery carried work in a variety of artistic media: oil and watercolor paintings, marble and bronze sculpture, porcelain figurines and one-of-a-kind pottery. Jon was the only photographer represented at the Harbor Street Gallery.

His photographs were both black-and-white and color, and his subjects included landscapes and details of nature, like a close-up of some porous stone on a beach or the pattern of bark on a tree. Sometimes he focused on human elements, such as a weathered row-boat or a fisherman's shack. He never used people in his compositions. Maryellen was impressed by the way he found simplicity in an apparently complex land-scape, making the viewer aware of the underlying shapes and lines—and the way he revealed the com-plexity in small, simple details. This was an artist with true vision, a vision that made her look at things dif-ferently.

It was through his work that she knew Jon. As she'd discovered, he wasn't a man of many words, but his pictures spoke volumes. That was why she wanted to know him better. That, and no other reason. Even if she found his appearance downright compelling…

Jon Bowman was tall and limber, easily six feet. His hair was long, often pulled away from his face and secured in a ponytail. He wasn't a conventionally at-tractive man; his features were sharp, his nose too large for his narrow face, hawklike in its appearance. He dressed casually, usually in jeans and plaid shirts.

He'd started bringing his work into the gallery three years ago—a few at a time, with long lapses in be-tween. Maryellen had worked at the gallery for ten years and was well acquainted with most of the artists who lived in the area. She often socialized with them, but other than to discuss business, she'd rarely spoken to Jon.

She found it odd that her favorite artist would resist her efforts at friendship.

"I brought in some more photographs," he said.

"I was hoping you would. I've sold everything you brought me last June.

That news produced a small grin. Jon's smiles were as infrequent as his conversations.

"People like your pictures."

Praise embarrassed him. Whenever customers had asked to meet him, he'd refused. He didn't explain why, but she sensed that he felt the public's focus should be on the art and not the artist.

"I'll get the photographs," he said brusquely, disappearing out the back door.

When he returned, he held an armful of framed photographs of varying sizes. He carried them to the back room, placing them on Maryellen's work table.

"Can I interest you in a cup of coffee?" she asked. She'd offered before and he'd always declined.

"All right."

Maryellen was sure she'd misunderstood him. She told herself it was absurd to feel this elation that he'd finally agreed. She poured him a cup and gestured toward the sugar and cream. He shook his head.

They sat on stools across from each other, both staring into their coffee. "Your work is gaining recognition," she finally said.

He ignored her remark. "You're divorced?" he asked bluntly.

The question caught Maryellen off guard. She'd certainly realized he wasn't much for small talk, but this verged on rude. She decided to answer him, anyway—and then turn the subject back to him.

''Thirteen years.'' She hardly ever mentioned her marriage. She'd been young and immature, and had paid a high price for her mistake. As soon as the divorce was final, she'd reverted to her maiden name and chosen to put the experience behind her. ''What about you?''

Jon apparently had his own agenda because he answered her question with one of his own. ''You don't date much, though, do you?''

''No. Do you?''

''Some.''

''Are you married?'' She didn't think he was.

''No.''

''Divorced?'' she asked next.

''No.''

He certainly didn't bother with sharing, nor did he feel obliged to offer much personal information in exchange for hers.

''Why don't *you* date?'' he asked next.

Maryellen shrugged, choosing a nonverbal reply instead of a lengthy explanation.

Jon sipped his coffee. ''Don't you get asked?''

''Oh, sure.'' She preferred parties and other social events to individual dates. ''Why the interest, all of a sudden? Would you like to ask me out?'' she asked boldly. If he did, she just might be tempted. Then again, maybe not. Dark, mysterious men were dangerous, and she'd already learned her lesson.

''What did he do to you?'' Jon pressed.

Maryellen got off the stool, uncomfortable with the way he continually parried her questions with his. Each question dug a little deeper, delving into territory she'd rather leave undisturbed.

"Tell me something I don't know about you," she said, challenging him with a look.

"I'm a chef."

"You mean you enjoy cooking?"

"No, I'm a chef at André's."

The elite seafood restaurant was on the Tacoma waterfront. "I...I didn't know."

"Most people don't. It's how I pay the bills."

Kelly's voice rang from inside the gallery. "Anybody here?"

Her sister couldn't have chosen a worse time to visit and Maryellen glanced regretfully toward the showroom. "That's my sister."

"I should be going." Jon took a swallow of the cooled coffee, then put down the mug.

"Don't leave yet." She reached out impulsively, touching his forearm. "I'm sure I'll only be a moment."

"Come to André's one night," he said. "I'll make you something special."

Maryellen wasn't sure if he meant she should come alone or if she should bring a date. But it seemed inappropriate to ask. "I'll do that," she said as Kelly walked into the back room. Her sister stopped suddenly, her face filled with surprise and delight at finding Maryellen with a man.

"I'm Jon Bowman," Jon said into the awkward silence. "I'll leave you to visit. Nice seeing you again, Maryellen."

"Bye," she said, her feelings a mixture of surprise and regret. Anticipation too, she admitted privately. And that was something she hadn't felt in years.

Kelly watched him go. As soon as Jon was out of earshot, she asked, ''Was that anyone special?''

''Just one of our artists,'' Maryellen returned, not elaborating.

Kelly claimed the stool recently vacated by Jon. ''How's Mom holding up?''

''Better than I expected.'' Making that first attorney's appointment had been difficult, but her mother's resolve had seen her through.

''Dad's coming back, you know,'' Kelly said.

Maryellen didn't argue, although she'd long since abandoned hope that he would.

''You don't believe me, do you?'' Kelly challenged.

Maryellen had, in fact, given up. For whatever reason, their father had disappeared. When it came to men, she didn't expect much, even from her own father.

Could Jon Bowman be any different? She wasn't going to think about that now, she decided.

''Daddy *will* come back,'' Kelly insisted again when Maryellen ignored the question.

''Time will tell, won't it,'' Maryellen said and reached for her coffee.

Three

She must be in the grip of some insanity, Justine decided as she stepped off the small commuter plane in King Cove, Alaska. It'd been almost two weeks since she'd heard from Seth and she couldn't stand waiting another day.

She'd contacted the cannery where Seth and his father sold their fish and crab, but they didn't have any information about the boat's schedule. Justine had left a message with the frazzled secretary, although there was no guarantee Seth would ever receive it. She'd asked the woman to please let Seth know Justine would be arriving that weekend. She could only hope he'd gotten word of her impending visit.

Walking carefully down the steps of the ten-seater aircraft, Justine looked up expectantly, longing for Seth and praying he'd be at the small airport waiting for her. The wind stung her face, shocking her with its chill. The last weekend of September, and already there was evidence of winter's approach in this cold Alaskan wind.

"Is someone meeting you, miss?" the pilot asked when Justine reached for her overnight bag in the cart outside the plane.

"My husband—I think." But Seth wasn't at the airstrip. She took a taxi into town and listened with half an ear while the driver droned on about life on the Alaskan coast. He dropped her at a waterfront motel with a partially burned-out neon sign that read TEL.

The room was small and plain and dreary with its utilitarian beige carpeting, stained in several places. The curtains and bedspread were a faded floral pattern that wouldn't have been attractive even when they were new. She sat on the edge of the thin mattress, feeling sad and lost. Coming here had been crazy, a sign of how truly desperate she was. Now that she'd arrived in Alaska, she had to accept that this trip was a waste of time.

Her marriage had seemed right and perfect only a few weeks earlier, but now she was overwhelmed by doubts. She couldn't believe she'd actually *married* Seth. She sighed, a long, heartfelt sigh. Quite simply, she needed to know he loved her. And since she'd only heard from him a handful of times, she was beginning to think he didn't. Or rather, that his love was just a temporary passion, a desire he'd now satisfied.

Well, she could spend all weekend in the motel room feeling sorry for herself or she could try to find out where he was. Determined to locate her husband, she dressed in her warmest clothes and asked Betty, the lady at the front desk, for directions to the cannery. She was on foot, but it was only a short distance from the motel to the docks. The wind whipped her long hair about her face as she walked toward the water, her hands buried deep inside her pockets. Because it was late in the fishing season, plenty of boats were tied along the pier.

Justine talked to several fishermen. They were all familiar with Seth and his father, but no one had any information to give her. Disheartened, she headed back to the motel.

As she left, she noticed a large commercial fishing vessel preparing to dock, its huge boom reaching toward the sky. The smaller picking booms stretched out like thin steel arms on either side of the vessel. A large muscular man with a blond head covered in a blue knit cap had his back to her; he resembled Seth in coloring and stature. Was it possible? Could she be this lucky?

Increasing her pace, she hurried down the dock toward the fishing boat. "Seth!" she called, but the wind carried his name away. Still, the man must have heard something because he turned. It *was* her husband. When he saw her, he took one gigantic leap from the vessel to land with both feet on the dock.

Justine ran down the wooden pier and with a joyous shout, hurled herself into his embrace. He grasped her tightly about the waist, lifting her several inches off the ground. He was kissing her and every doubt, every question, vanished with that one frenzied kiss.

Justine heard men chuckling somewhere nearby, but she barely noticed and apparently neither did Seth.

"What are you doing here?" he asked, brushing the hair from her face. His eyes were warm with love. "How'd you know we were coming back in?"

"I didn't—I just prayed you'd be here."

He lowered his mouth to hers once more and murmured something about prayer being highly underrated just before his lips claimed hers.

"I have a motel room," she whispered.

Seth glanced over his shoulder. "Wait here." He hurried back to the boat, leaped aboard and quickly disappeared belowdecks. Justine was beginning to wonder what had happened to him when he reappeared with a dark duffel bag draped over his shoulder. Even though he needed a shave and a shower, he was the most handsome, thrilling, incredible man she'd ever seen.

"How long do we have?" he asked.

"Two days." She slid her arm through his and leaned her head against his shoulder. "We need to talk, Seth."

"We will," he promised, but any conversation would come second if she read the glint in his eyes correctly.

"I see you found your husband," Betty said as they approached the motel.

"I did," Justine said, her voice light with happiness. By the time they reached her room, Justine had the key out and ready.

Seth hauled her into his arms the instant the door was unlocked and carried her inside, flicking on the light as they entered. What had seemed plain and ugly only an hour ago felt like a honeymoon suite just now.

Her husband set her on the worn carpet, and his hands delved into her hair, angling her mouth toward his. Their kiss was long. Passionate. "I need a shower," he muttered impatiently when it was over. "Wait right here."

"Okay," she murmured, eyes closed, still consumed by his kiss.

"Are you hungry?" he asked.

Justine opened her eyes and gazed into his. Seth was stripping off his coat and had started to unfasten the buttons of his shirt. "I'm starving," she told him, but they both knew she wasn't talking about food.

"Oh, Jussie, me too."

He was the only person in the world who dared to call her that.

"I can't believe you're here," he said. He rapidly discarded his clothes, sitting on the far edge of the bed to remove his boots. He stood before her unzipping his pants. Even in his rush, he took time to drape his clothes over a chair. Then he stalked naked into the bathroom.

The shower had to be the fastest one on record. Justine had just slipped out of her shoes and pulled the sweater over her head. She'd started to unbutton her blouse when he returned. The intense look in his eyes stopped her, and her fingers froze on the last button. It was ridiculous to feel so shy with him. They were married and had already spent one glorious weekend together as husband and wife. But that had been weeks earlier and already seemed as distant as a dream.

Ever sensitive to her moods, Seth seemed to know her thoughts, to sense her apprehensions. With a tenderness that made her weak in the knees, he gently drew her to him. His mouth was warm and moist and there didn't seem to be any part of her that he didn't want to kiss. Soon her blouse was on the bed next to her sweater.

Their kisses appeared to have the same knee-weakening effect on him because he sank to the bed and wrapped his arms about her waist. He kissed her belly, then reached up and released her bra, freeing her breasts. He moaned and she lowered her mouth to meet his.

Not long afterward, he urged her onto the bed with him and they were caught in a sensual tumult that lasted until Justine was breathless and spent. Wrapped in her husband's embrace with only a sheet covering their legs, she rested her head on his chest, one arm flung about his waist.

Half inclined, his back against the headboard, Seth ran his hand along the length of her hair. Justine had closed her eyes, but not because she was sleepy. These moments needed to be savored, especially if they had to last her another few weeks.

"I don't know what brought you here," Seth whispered. "But whatever it is, I'm grateful."

"I had to know," she said, her voice more breath than sound. "I had to ask if you were sorry we got married."

"No." He was adamant. Tilting her chin up, he studied her eyes. "Are you?"

Her smile developed slowly. Feeling deliciously relaxed and sated, she had no problem giving him the answer he wanted. "I'm so in love with you it's driving me crazy. I want us to be together, Seth. I hate having you so far from home."

"It's been hard on me, too," Seth told her, his hand continuing its soothing motion. "I've always loved fishing, but my heart's been with you from the moment I left."

Justine stroked his shoulder, delighting in the smooth skin there. "I didn't tell anyone at home what I was doing. I knew if I told my mother or grandmother I was flying up to find you, they'd tell me it was impossible, that I was taking too big a chance."

"You've always had an incredible sense of timing," Seth teased.

"I do, don't I?" She rubbed her cheek against the hard muscles of his chest, loving the feel, the sight, the scent of this man. She eased her leg over his.

"When do you have to leave?" he asked.

"Late Sunday afternoon."

His hands were in her hair again. "In that case, we'd better make up for lost time, don't you think?"

Justine was in full agreement.

Grace woke early Monday morning, feeling more contented than she had in a long while. Buttercup, her golden retriever, who slept on the floor beside her, got to her feet, tail waving vigorously as Grace folded back the covers and climbed out of bed.

"Good morning, sweetheart," she said, reaching for her robe. She wondered what Dan would think if he learned that she'd replaced him with a dog.

Buttercup ambled behind Grace into the kitchen and then let herself outside, through the pet door. While the dog did her business, Grace brewed a small pot of coffee. Humming softly to herself, she showered and chose a red plaid blouse and jean jumper to wear to the library. She slid her feet into a pair of matching red shoes, and then popped two slices of whole wheat bread into the toaster for breakfast.

When it was time to leave, Buttercup followed her to the car. Grace rubbed her companion's ears, grateful that her dog would be waiting for her when she returned.

Buttercup was the perfect housemate: loving, obedient, reliable. She'd return to the kitchen through her dog door as soon as Grace left. And then, when Grace got home, Buttercup would come out to greet her again.

The sun was out, but rain was forecast for the afternoon. Grace loved the autumn months; she remembered that Dan used to feel the same way. Having worked as a logger most of his career, he'd always been at home in the woods. Only in recent years, with much of the forest land closed to lumbering, had Dan taken a job with a local tree service. He'd never complained, but she knew he'd hated it and longed to return to the woods.

The sadness was back, and Grace forced her thoughts away from her soon-to-be ex-husband. Wherever Dan was now and whoever he was with, she wished him happiness. She'd never been able to give him that, even in the early years. They'd married young. Grace was pregnant with Maryellen by the time they graduated from high school. She'd married Dan and he'd enlisted and gone off to Vietnam, but the man who returned wasn't the same man who'd left. Almost forty years later, he still suffered from nightmares and memories he refused to share. She never knew what had happened in those dark jungles and Dan always said it was better that she didn't.

As usual, Monday morning at the library was slow after the heavy weekend activity. Grace decided to change the bulletin board and brought out the packet with a scarecrow, a black cat and a pumpkin patch. They had sets of cardboard cutouts for every season and holiday; Thanksgiving would be next, followed by Christmas. She was busily working on it, when she heard a male voice behind her.

"I'd like to apply for a library card," Cliff Harding told her assistant, Loretta Bailey.

"I can help you with that." Loretta pulled out a form and set it on the counter. She paused when she saw Grace watching her.

Cliff looked over his shoulder. "Hello, Grace."

"Hello." She hoped her voice didn't betray how flustered she felt.

"I thought it was time I got a library card, since I'm in Cedar Cove practically every week."

"We have the highest percentage of people with library cards per capita of any town or city in Washington State," Loretta informed him proudly as she handed him a pen.

"I'm impressed," Cliff said as his gaze moved back toward Grace.

She tried to ignore his appreciative stare but couldn't. All at once she found herself fumbling and a tack fell and rolled across the floor. Bending to retrieve it, she nearly bumped heads with Cliff Harding as he, too, bent down. He was dressed in the same western style as he had been earlier, complete with a Stetson and boots. She even thought she detected the scent of hay on him.

"Are you ready to have dinner with me yet?" he asked in a stage whisper while both of them were crouched.

She glanced up at Loretta, who was carefully studying some paper or other, but Grace wasn't fooled. Her co-worker was keenly interested in Grace's answer, perhaps more so than Cliff.

"I...don't think so." She could feel the heat radiate from her face. His interest left her uncomfortable and out of her element. Her last date had been with Dan, when they were both teenagers. That was almost four decades ago—in a different century! The world was a vastly different place now.

"Would you consider having coffee with me, then?" Cliff asked.

Before Grace could respond, Loretta stood on her tiptoes, leaned over the counter and smiled down at them. "You can take your break now if you want."

Grace resisted the urge to groan out loud.

"The Pancake Palace?" Cliff suggested, grinning boyishly. He seemed thankful for Loretta's encouragement, even if Grace wasn't.

"Five o'clock," she said, none too pleased.

His smile broadened as he stood. "I'll be there."

Grace came to her feet and glared across the counter at Loretta. Cliff, meanwhile, had started toward the door.

"What about your library card?" Grace called out.

Cliff didn't break his stride. "I'll fill out the form next time I stop by," he told her.

By five o'clock, Grace still wasn't sure she'd meet Cliff Harding. Good manners won out. She might be nervous about seeing him, but she'd agreed to be there, and Grace believed in keeping her word.

Cliff slid out of a booth at the restaurant and stood when she approached. "I wasn't sure you'd come," he said quietly.

"I wasn't sure I would, either," she admitted and got into the red upholstered bench across from him. She righted the beige ceramic cup.

Cliff raised his hand in order to catch the waitress's eye.

"I'm coming," Goldie announced from behind the counter. The elderly waitress had been with the Pancake Palace for as long as Grace could remember—as far back as her high school days. It was a new employee, not Goldie, who'd confused the credit cards.

Bringing the glass coffeepot, Goldie poured Grace's cup first, then refilled Cliff's. "You two planning to stay long?" she asked Grace. "The Chamber's coming here for dinner."

This was Goldie's subtle way of informing Grace

that if she didn't want the entire business community to know she was having coffee with Cliff, she'd better cut this meeting short.

Grace wanted to kiss the older woman's hand. "We won't be long."

"Up to you," Goldie assured her with a wink.

"Thanks," Cliff said.

"Yes, thank you, Goldie."

Now that he had her attention, Cliff stared down at his coffee, avoiding eye contact. "I have a fairly good notion of how you're feeling just now."

Grace sincerely doubted that. "You do?"

"You're nervous, a little agitated and your stomach's full of butterflies. Am I close?"

Actually, he was. "Close enough. How'd you know?"

"Because I'm feeling the same way."

"You said you'd been divorced five years?" Did that mean this state of tension in the presence of the opposite sex went on indefinitely?

"Yes."

"Do you want to discuss it?" It'd help if he talked about himself because she had no intention of spilling out the private details of *her* life.

"Not particularly."

"Children?"

"One daughter. She's married and lives on the East Coast. We talk every week, and I make a point of flying out to see her once or twice a year."

At least he kept in contact with his child, unlike Dan who'd abandoned both Grace and their daughters.

"Susan—my wife—fell in love with a colleague from work," Cliff said. His hand tightened around the mug and she noticed a spasming muscle in his jaw.

"According to what she said at the time, she'd never been happy."

"Is she now?"

"I wouldn't know. After the divorce I retired and moved to Olalla," he said, mentioning a local community ten miles south of Cedar Cove.

"The locals call it Ou-la-la," Grace told him.

"I can understand why. It's beautiful there. I have forty acres and raise quarter horses."

"It sounds lovely."

"It is, except for one thing." His eyes locked with hers. "I'm lonely."

That was something Grace understood far too well. Her marriage had never been completely happy, but over the years Grace and Dan had grown content with each other. There was a lot to be said for contentedness—conversation over dinner, a night out at the movies, a repertoire of shared experiences. Dan had usually been there to greet her when she walked in the door after work. Now there was only Buttercup.

"I'm looking for a friend," Cliff told her. "Someone who'd be willing to attend a concert with me every now and then, that's all."

The idea appealed to Grace, too. "That would be nice."

"I was hoping you'd think so." His tone was gentle and encouraging.

"But," she hurried to add, "only after the divorce is final."

"All right," Cliff said.

"One more thing." She met his eyes again. "I'll call you next time. Agreed?"

He hesitated. "Agreed, but does that mean you don't want me going into the library?"

"You're always welcome," she told him. "Just as long as it's on library business."

"Sure." He reached for his mug and raised it to his lips, but not before Grace saw a smile lift the edges of his mouth.

She had the sneaking suspicion that he was about to become a frequent library patron.

Things had been strained between Rosie and Zach ever since the night of Eddie's open house at school. Rosie blamed her husband for that. Zach simply didn't appreciate how much she did. He seemed to think she sat around the house and watched soap operas all day while he was at the office. He didn't understand how complicated her life was. She was so busy she sometimes left the house before he did and didn't return until late in the evening. Now Zach expected her to cook a four-course dinner on top of everything else, she thought angrily.

She'd asked him to attend Eddie's school function and he'd been annoyed with her for days afterward. Eddie was Zach's son, too, and meeting his teacher was a small thing. Yet Zach had complained the entire evening. First about ordering pizza for dinner, then about the green peppers, and he hadn't wanted to wear his suit to the school meeting, and... Later that night, despite her best efforts, their discontent with each other had escalated into a full-blown argument.

They hadn't resolved it in the days that followed, either.

After two weeks of this nonsense, one of them had to make a conciliatory gesture. Despite the fact that she'd been up past midnight reading over the committee report for the PTA planning meeting scheduled that evening, Rosie rose at the crack of dawn and fried bacon and eggs. She used to take the time to cook a real breakfast for her family. She hoped Zach would realize she was trying and that would appease him.

Rosie broke the eggs into the pan once she heard Allison stir. The kids were on different schedules now that Allison was in high school, which made coordinated meals more difficult. But if it was important to her husband that she spend half the morning in front of a stove, she'd do it in order to maintain the peace.

"I have eggs cooking for you," she told her daughter when Allison stepped into the kitchen.

"I hate eggs," Allison said, slamming her backpack onto the table.

"Since when?"

Her daughter eyed her as if Rosie were mentally lacking. "Since forever."

"I forgot." Vaguely Rosie could recall long-ago battles over breakfast. "What about some bacon then?"

"Yuck." Her daughter opened the refrigerator and pulled out a soda.

Rosie was appalled. "You can't have that!"

"Why not?" Allison looked at her with disdain. "I have a pop every morning. Why can't I now?"

"Fine, if that's what you want." It wasn't worth a fight. All the books Rosie had read about raising teenagers recommended carefully choosing your battles. Giving in on the soda seemed minor compared to not letting Allison pierce her nose.

Rosie turned off the burner and slid the fried eggs onto a couple of plates, together with the fast-cooling bacon. Walking down the hallway she knocked and opened Eddie's bedroom door. His room was an environmental disaster area, and as much as possible, she averted her eyes. Her son was sprawled across his bed, comforter on the floor.

"Are you interested in breakfast?" she asked.

Eddie lifted his head and blinked at her. "Mom?"

"Do you want breakfast?" she repeated.

He sat up, suddenly wide-awake. "Yeah," he said with enthusiasm.

This was more like it.

"The chocolate ones are my favorite."

"Chocolate what?"

"Pop-Tarts."

"I fried you bacon and eggs."

Eddie wrinkled his nose as if she'd suggested he dine on slugs. "No, thanks." He flopped back on his pillow and reached for the comforter on the floor.

All right, so much for that. Venturing toward the master bedroom, she found Zach just as he was coming out of the walk-in closet, dressed in his suit and tie.

"I cooked breakfast," she said, a bit stiffly.

He nodded as though he approved.

"Are you ready to eat?"

"I can't now," he said, looking down at his watch. "I've got an early-morning appointment."

That was just great, dammit! No one appreciated her efforts or the fact that she was functioning on less than five hours' sleep. Whirling around, Rosie returned to the kitchen, dumped the congealed bacon and egg in the garbage and forcefully opened the dishwasher. She shoved in the plates.

Zach entered the kitchen. "I'm leaving now."

"Have a good day," she muttered under her breath.

"You, too."

Her husband stopped in front of the door leading to

the garage. "Would you like to meet for lunch this afternoon?"

So Zach *did* realize what she was doing. Now he was making an overture, too. "I think that's a lovely idea." She offered him a grateful smile and he smiled back.

"Eleven-thirty?"

Rosie nodded and he walked over to her and kissed her cheek.

"Dad," Allison called, racing into the kitchen. "Can I get a ride with you?"

"Only if you hurry."

"I'll just be a minute."

"Meet you at the car."

Allison dashed toward her bedroom and returned two seconds later with her sweater, grabbing her backpack from the table as she went.

"Do you have your lunch money?" Rosie asked.

"Duh? Of course I do." Allison kissed her cheek in the same fashion Zach had and was out the door.

No sooner had they left than Eddie appeared in the kitchen doorway. "Is my Pop-Tart up yet?"

"Almost," she muttered and searched the cupboards until she located a box of her son's favorite breakfast food.

An hour later, Eddie left to catch the school bus and Rosie straightened up the kitchen, turning on the dishwasher. Still in her ratty, ten-year-old housecoat, she went to the bedroom and pulled open the dresser drawer to take out fresh underwear.

It wasn't until she was in the shower that she remembered she had to be at the school by noon as a lunch volunteer for Eddie's class. She groaned and raised her face to the water. She'd be away tonight, too. As it was, Zach didn't approve of her chairing this PTA committee. She'd taken the position a year earlier and had promised to serve until the end of term and no longer. But last June not a single parent had stepped forward to volunteer. Rosie had no choice but to continue as chair.

She dressed and was about to call Zach's office when the phone rang. A half hour later, she was rushing out the door, about to ward off an emergency concerning the new choir robes at church. Somehow their order had gotten switched with that of another church, somewhere in Florida. It was imperative that the correct robes show up before the end of the month. At the church, she painstakingly repackaged the robes, made half a dozen phone calls and took the boxes to the post office to return to the company. Not until eleven-thirty did she realize she still hadn't called Zach. Taking out her cell phone, she punched in the number to her husband's office.

"Smith, Cox and Jefferson," came the pleasant—and unfamiliar—female voice.

Rose eased to a stop at a red light. "This is Rosie Cox. Could I speak to my husband, please?"

"Hello, Mrs. Cox, this is Janice Lamond. I don't believe we've met, have we?"

"No, we haven't," she said. The light changed to green and she sped forward.

"I'm sorry, but Mr. Cox left the office. I understand he was meeting you?"

They hadn't agreed to meet anywhere, at least not that she remembered. Where the hell would Zach go? *Think, think,* she ordered herself.

"Did he bring his cell phone?"

"I'm sorry, he didn't. Mr. Cox said he didn't want to take any calls."

Rosie groaned. "Did he tell you where he was headed?"

The woman hesitated. "I believe he mentioned D.D.'s on the Cove."

Of course. It was her favorite and Zach always took her there for her birthday.

"Are you going to be late?" Janice asked. "I could phone the restaurant and let him know, if you'd like."

"I can't make lunch at all," Rosie muttered, truly regretful. Zach would never forgive her. Especially when he learned she had to cancel because she was volunteering yet again.

"Is there anything I can do?" Zach had never mentioned how helpful this new employee was. Rosie liked her already. She pulled into the school parking lot and cut the engine.

"You wouldn't mind phoning him for me?"

"It would be my pleasure."

"Thank you so much."

"Would you like me to tell him where you can be reached?"

"No," she said quickly, not eager to have Zach call her in the midst of a volunteer activity. "Tell him I'll explain everything once I'm home."

"I'll see to it immediately," Janice said.

Rosie appreciated that the firm's new assistant was so friendly and accommodating.

If Zach was upset with her for skipping out on lunch, he didn't give any sign of it when he walked into the house that evening. Rosie was thawing hamburger in the microwave for spaghetti, Eddie's favorite dinner, when her husband came in. As usual, she was in a hurry to get out the door.

She tried to gauge his mood. "I'm so sorry about lunch," she told him.

Zach shrugged as he flipped through the mail. "It was fine."

"I should've checked my calendar. Did the assistant reach you?"

"Actually she joined me."

"You had lunch with your secretary?" Rosie wasn't sure she liked the sound of that.

"She's not my secretary, she's my assistant," he explained, his back to her. "I left the office early because I wanted to get a table by the window. When Janice called with the news, I said it was a shame to let that table go. I was only joking when I suggested she come over since you couldn't, but she took me up on it."

"Oh." Rosie was silent for a moment. "Did you have a nice lunch?" She'd eaten a candy bar out of a machine.

"It was all right," he muttered and headed toward the bedroom for a shower, but she noticed he was whistling.

"I can meet you for lunch any day next week," she called after him.

"Sorry, honey," he said as he strolled past her. "I'm booked solid."

Four

Having her nails done every other week was Maryellen's one luxury. Although beautifully manicured fingernails were an extravagance, she couldn't make herself give it up. Even more than that small pleasure, though, Maryellen enjoyed her friendship with the "girls" at Get Nailed. They were close to her age and single, but unlike Maryellen they wanted men in their lives.

Every second Wednesday morning, Maryellen listened while they bemoaned their fates. She was often amused by the crazy schemes they devised for meeting men. Frankly, she couldn't understand why Rachel, her nail tech, hadn't found a decent man. Maryellen considered her attractive and savvy.

The third Wednesday in October, Maryellen arrived for her appointment. Rachel was, as usual, ready for her. As soon as Maryellen was seated, Rachel doused a cotton swab in nail polish remover and reached for her hand.

"How's it going?" Rachel asked.

"Great, how about you? Meet anyone last weekend?"

"I wish," Rachel returned with a long sigh. "I'm not getting any younger."

Maryellen knew that Rachel had made it her goal to

find a husband by age thirty, and her birthday was only a few months away.

"I read something interesting this week," Maryellen told her. "It's about a town in Ireland named Lisdoonvarna. Every September and the first week of October, eligible men come to town looking for wives. Apparently it's a tradition that's been going on for years."

"This is a joke, right?" Terri asked from across the room.

"No, I swear to you this is real."

"Where do these women come from?" Rachel asked.

"All over the world. According to the article, a woman flew all the way from Australia to find a husband—and she did."

"I can't afford to go to Ireland," Rachel muttered.

"No, but maybe we could hold our own festival," Terri suggested.

"You could do that," Maryellen said, wanting to encourage the other women. She didn't want to get involved herself, but she did hope the crew of Get Nailed would do something with the idea.

"A Marriage Fest?" Terri's voice picked up speed with her excitement.

"Yeah, but who'd come?" Rachel asked. "I can see it now. We'd make headlines 'cause we're throwing a party in order to meet potential husbands, and not one man would show up."

"Maybe you're right," Terri said with a discouraged sigh.

"If I want to get out of a relationship, all I have to do is mention the word *marriage* and the man drops me like a hot potato." Rachel frowned as she concentrated on Maryellen's chipped thumbnail.

"You're right about that," Jane, another tech, added. "Men in America have got it too good." There was a chorus of agreement.

"I've given up on Prince Charming. I'd be happy to meet the guy who grooms his horse," Rachel said.

Maryellen smiled, and so did petite, blond Jane.

"Actually, forget about the guy grooming the horse," Rachel went on, "I'd settle for a man who knows how to change the oil in my car."

"I dated a guy like that once," Terri told her. "Larry's head was constantly under the hood of a car. He was far more interested in listening to an engine purr than me. It's too bad, because he was basically a nice guy."

"Why'd you break up?"

"He got grease on my white silk blouse."

"You broke up with a great guy because he ruined your blouse?"

Terri nodded. "What can I say? That blouse cost me seventy bucks, and Larry didn't seem to think it was any big deal. The way I figure it, if a guy can't appreciate a seventy-dollar blouse, then I don't want anything to do with him."

"I'd like to meet a man who has his head screwed on straight when it comes to money," Jane said. "Everyone I've ever dated expects me to pick up the tab because they're constantly broke."

"I met this rich guy once, but he was dead boring," Jeannie said, leaping into the conversation. "We dated for three months and I broke up with him because I had more fun washing my hair."

"I'll take a boring guy over a user any day of the week," Jane informed her.

"What about you, Terri?" Maryellen asked. Terri,

who dressed in bold, bright colors, was tall and big-boned, with soulful dark eyes. "What kind of man interests you?"

"I want a man who appreciates good food and isn't afraid of a woman who likes to eat," she said without hesitating. "I'm sick of men who want skinny women. I want a man to take me to a fancy restaurant and ask me to order an appetizer and suggest I save room for dessert. Better yet, I'd like a man who did the cooking himself." She glanced around the shop. "Does anyone know someone like that?"

A sudden silence cut off the lively conversation. "Well, actually, I do know someone who cooks," Maryellen said slowly, thinking of Jon Bowman. "Jon's a chef at a truly wonderful restaurant."

"Why'd you break up with him?" Rachel asked.

"We've never, uh, actually dated." Nor would they, despite her curiosity. Maryellen loved Jon's work and he intrigued her as a person, but her interest in him wasn't romantic. No men in her life, no matter how attractive: that was her Number One rule. "I'd be willing to introduce you, Terri, if you wanted."

"You would?" The other woman's voice lifted with enthusiasm.

"So what do we do next?" Rachel asked, glancing around the shop. "It looks like we've all dated a man who meets someone else's criteria, which is great but isn't helping any of us right now."

"We could throw a party," Jeannie said. "Sort of drag out our discards for the others to sort through."

"A rummage sale of old lovers," Terri suggested. Her client laughed, and the other women at the shop joined in.

"I'll wear my black blouse," Rachel said decisively.

"I don't care if Larry ruins that." Then, looking at Maryellen, she added in a whisper, "I can't afford to be picky. My car's in sad shape."

Jane reached for the calendar. "We could make it a Halloween party," she announced. "What do you think?"

The immediate consensus was that a Halloween party was a good idea.

"That'll give us a little more than two weeks to come up with some fun ideas. Let's get this organized."

"Yeah."

"You bet."

"Count me in."

Maryellen wasn't sure how it happened, but despite her original reluctance, she soon found herself involved.

"How are we going to get the guys to come?" Jane, the most practical of the group, asked. "I don't think Floyd would be interested in dating me again."

"Larry could be married for all I know."

"Ask," Maryellen said. "And you need to be upfront with them. Explain to the guy that you're bringing him to the party as your guest, but he'll be meeting other women once he gets there."

"I'll let Larry know that someone's dying to meet him," Terri said.

"Perfect!" Rachel sounded absolutely delighted.

When Maryellen left Get Nailed, her head was spinning. She really hadn't meant to become part of this scheme, although she'd started the conversation.

She didn't know how the others planned to handle this, but she certainly wasn't going to wait for the last minute to mention the party to Jon. When Terri had talked about wanting to meet a man who enjoyed food, he'd come instantly to mind. In retrospect, Maryellen regretted mentioning his name. She didn't know what had prompted her. It was probably because he'd been in her thoughts ever since their last meeting. This latest group of photographs was some of his best work to date, and she'd been almost sorry they'd sold so quickly.

Considering that she'd suggested the direct approach to the others, she felt obliged to follow her own advice. She waited a week, and then dialed the phone number listed in her Rolodex.

Jon answered on the second ring. "Hello."

"Jon, hello, this is Maryellen Sherman." She hesitated, waiting for some kind of acknowledgment. "The manager of Harbor Street Art Gallery," she added.

"Yes, I know."

She'd swear he sounded amused, which only served to fluster her more.

"I've been invited to a Halloween party," she said, rushing to explain the reason for her call. "Everyone's supposed to come with a date—well, not a date exactly. We've been asked to bring someone, a man, to introduce to someone else. I have this friend who's really lovely and she likes to eat." She grimaced, thinking that sounded kind of dumb, but plunged on anyway. "She enjoys her food and well, her biggest wish is to meet a man who likes to cook and naturally, I thought of you." She realized she was rambling and stopped abruptly.

There was no response.

"Would you be interested in attending the party?" she finally asked. "You'd be under no obligation." She wanted that understood. "Basically, you'd be doing me a favor."

"By meeting this friend of yours."

"Yes."

"The one who enjoys a good meal."

"Yes. Her name's Terri, and she's a lot of fun. I think you'd like her."

"You'd be there?"

Maryellen sighed. "Yes, of course. I'd introduce you to Terri. So—what do you think?"

"Can I let you know later?" he asked after another long pause.

"Of course." She figured she should feel encouraged that he hadn't rejected her outright.

"Then I'll be in touch."

"Great."

"Listen, before you go, did you get a chance to look over my pictures?"

"Oh, yes, and they're fabulous! I've sold every one of them already. I was hoping you'd be bringing me more."

"I'm working on it."

"That would be great." This was by far the longest and most involved conversation of their three-year working relationship.

"You haven't come into André's," Jon said. "I was looking forward to cooking for you."

"I appreciated the invitation, really I did, but I'm worried about giving you the wrong impression. Like I explained, I'm divorced and I'm not going to remarry and this party is just a friends thing.... If you came, that would be fabulous but only because I want you to meet Terri. Oh, did I mention we're holding it at The Captain's Galley, in the bar?" She managed to get all that out in a single breath. "Halloween night," she added.

"I'll get back to you."

Maryellen thought that was fair enough.

After two glorious days and nights with her husband, Justine no longer had any doubts about her marriage. She was more in love than she'd dreamed possible.

Flying up to Alaska on the spur of the moment like that, without making any arrangements, had been preposterous, and yet she'd found Seth. Justine considered it a sign. Seth was truly meant to be her husband.

In a few weeks he'd be home, and they could discuss the future and make the necessary plans for their lives together. There had been so many pressing questions she'd wanted to ask him. But once they were together, none of them had seemed all that important. The only thing that mattered was lying in Seth's arms, sharing their love.

Justine vowed that if Seth asked it of her, she'd live aboard his sailboat for the rest of her life. But she suspected he'd probably want to move in with her. Staying in her apartment was more practical than living at the marina.

She'd told him about sleeping on his boat at her most desperate moments, seeking to feel closer to him. From his reaction, she knew he'd been touched by her fears. He'd kissed her again and again as she described her doubts, all the while whispering reassurances and promises. Justine had left Alaska feeling deeply loved.

The following Friday night, Justine dropped by her mother's house on Lighthouse Road. She hadn't been avoiding Olivia, but she hadn't sought her out, either.

By the time Justine pulled up in front of the large

two-story house with the wide wraparound veranda, her mother was at the door, waiting for her.

"Hi, Mom."

"Justine! I'm so glad to see you," Olivia said, hugging her tight. "You haven't come to the house in ages."

"I've been busy—in fact, last weekend I flew up to Alaska to see Seth."

"You were in Alaska? You might've let someone know." The disapproving edge was back, but Justine chose to ignore it.

"You're right, I should have," she agreed mildly. She wasn't here to fight with her mother.

"Come inside," Olivia insisted, wrapping her sweater more snugly around her. "It's cool this evening."

Justine obediently followed her mother into the house. The kitchen was the most comfortable room and it seemed natural to sit there. "Tea?" Olivia asked. It was one of their long-standing rituals.

"Please."

Her mother turned away as she put water on to boil. "How is Seth?"

"Wonderful. He'll be home soon. I miss him so much. That's the reason I flew to Alaska—I just couldn't stand being so far away from Seth and I had all these air miles from my credit card. I called the airline, got a seat and off I went—without even knowing if I'd find him or not. I was afraid to tell you what I was doing for fear you'd try to change my mind."

"You went through all that to be with your husband?" her mother asked.

"Oh, yes. I really am in love with him, Mom."

Justine expected this news to be exactly what her mother wanted to hear. Instead Olivia was frowning.

"What?" Justine asked.

Olivia pulled out a chair and sat across from her. "Does Seth know you had lunch with Warren?"

So that explained it. Her mother knew. For that matter, so did Seth, and while he hadn't asked her not to see Warren again, she could tell he wasn't pleased that she'd accepted his invitation to lunch. Justine had been a bit surprised by that, but she wouldn't do it again.

"Warren wants you back, doesn't he?" her mother said when she didn't immediately respond.

"Did I mention that Maryellen Sherman and I met for lunch earlier this week?" Justine said, pointedly changing the subject. Warren was off-limits as far as she was concerned. "She wanted to congratulate Seth and me."

Her mother set the bowl of tea bags in the center of the table. "So you'd prefer not to discuss Warren."

"That's right."

Olivia squared her shoulders and nodded firmly. "Then we won't. Tell me about Seth. When will he be back?"

Justine filled in the details. The longer she spoke, the more relaxed her mother became—and Justine understood why. Her mother finally had complete confidence in her love for Seth. Olivia now knew that nothing Warren said or did was going to change the way Justine felt about her husband.

"How is Maryellen?" Olivia asked as she poured them each a second cup of tea. "I see Grace every week at our aerobics class, but we seldom have a chance to talk." She laughed. "Actually we need all our energy just to breathe. Did Maryellen tell you Grace filed for divorce?''

Justine nodded. ''By the way, what happened with Maryellen's marriage?'' It'd never occurred to her to ask before. Justine had only been fourteen at the time. All she remembered was her mother and Grace, her best friend, talking on the phone a great deal. Maryellen had moved home for a while, and she'd taken back her maiden name as if she'd never been married at all.

Her mother stirred a teaspoon of sugar into her tea. ''I don't think anyone really knows, not even Grace. When Maryellen got married, I remember Grace telling me she didn't feel Clint Jorstad was a good match for her daughter.''

''Apparently she was right,'' Justine said. Then a frightening thought occurred to her. ''What do you feel about Seth and me?'' she asked, raising hopeful eyes to her mother, trusting her judgment and wisdom.

''Oh, Justine, I think the world of Seth. I couldn't be more pleased for you both. Seth's perfect for you.''

Justine smiled. ''I think so, too, Mom, I really do.'' For the first time in a while, she thought about her brother. Seth and Jordan were best friends, and then Jordan had drowned the summer they were all thirteen. Seth was in Alaska with his father and hadn't learned of the accident until he'd returned home. Justine had been with Jordan that dreadful August day. She'd held his lifeless body until the paramedics arrived. He was her twin, her best friend and her brother. Her entire world had changed that summer. Only a few months afterward, her parents had divorced and within a shockingly short time her father had remarried. Her younger brother, James, seemed oblivious to the uprooting of their security, but Justine had felt it all, lived it all.

"What are you thinking?" her mother asked, a slight frown on her face.

Justine shook her head. "Nothing important," she said, which wasn't true. But she didn't want to bring up the one memory that would never stop hurting. The one death her mother could never recover from. Drinking the last of her tea, she carried the cup and saucer to the sink and said, "I'd better get home."

"Thank you for coming by." Olivia touched Justine's cheek. "I'm thrilled about you and Seth. Honestly."

"I *am* happy, Mom," Justine said and impulsively hugged her mother. "Next time I won't wait so long to visit."

"Good." Olivia walked her to the porch and waved as Justine drove off.

When Justine got back to the apartment complex, she found a note from the manager taped to her door; it said she'd accepted a delivery on Justine's behalf.

After dropping off her mail, she hurried down to the manager's office and learned that a huge flower arrangement had arrived. The large crystal vase was filled with an array of carnations, pink lilies, irises and a handful of others she couldn't name, as well as artful sprigs of greenery. It could only be from Seth.

Justine could hardly wait to read the card. Seth loved her, missed her, and her sweet, wonderful husband must have realized she'd need an emotional boost to get her through the next few weeks.

Justine discovered almost immediately how wrong she was. Only one word was written on the card.

Warren.

She groaned with disappointment and tossed the small card onto the kitchen counter. She set the vase carelessly on the table, cringing every time she looked at it.

An hour later, while she was scrounging around her refrigerator, seeking out something easy and edible for dinner, the doorbell rang.

She answered it to find Warren Saget standing there, wearing a flashy thousand-dollar business suit and an even flashier smile. ''Hello, Justine.''

''Hello, Warren,'' she said without enthusiasm.

''Did you get my flowers?''

She didn't invite him inside. ''I did, but I wish you hadn't.''

''I wanted to thank you for having lunch with me.''

She'd guessed as much. ''It was very thoughtful.''

He met her eyes, then stared at the handle on the door. ''Can I come in?''

She shook her head. ''I don't think that's a good idea.'' If her mother had heard about their lunch date, Justine wondered how many other people in town already knew. She had no intention of adding to the gossip by having Warren's visit to her apartment reported next.

''All right,'' Warren said, looking hurt and a little confused. ''I didn't mean to intrude.''

''You didn't, it's just that...'' She stopped herself from saying more. Warren was far to clever when it came to getting his own way and she wasn't going to make it any easier.

He waited for her to continue and when she didn't, he asked, ''Do you have any plans tonight?''

She certainly wasn't telling him that the most exciting plan she had was a rerun of *Nash Bridges.* ''Why?''

''I was hoping you'd have dinner with me. No pressure. It's just that I figured you might be lonely with

Seth gone for so many weeks. I thought you might enjoy a night on the town."

"No thanks, Warren."

He shrugged. "No harm in asking," he said with a forced smile.

"Actually I think there might be."

He arched his eyebrows as if she'd surprised him.

"The two of us shouldn't be seeing each other. It's...inappropriate. In fact, I'd appreciate it if you didn't visit me again—either at work or at my apartment."

The hurt-little-boy look was back. "Justine, you don't think I'd purposely do anything to jeopardize your relationship with Seth, do you?"

"It doesn't matter what I think. I mean it, Warren, stay away from me."

"You told him, didn't you?" Warren's eyes narrowed. "That big Swedish oaf is jealous." He laughed, although the sound was humorless.

She refused to defend Seth or make excuses for him. Her husband was uncomfortable with her seeing Warren and that was the end of it. Her relationship with Warren was over; it had been for a long time, regardless of their recent lunch date. Nothing he said or did was going to change her mind.

"The next thing I know," he said bitterly, "you'll be telling me that big oaf got you pregnant."

"Warren, please." She dragged out his name, implying that this conversation was boring her. "Just go." She wasn't willing to stand in the doorway and argue with him. She started to close the door, but Warren's words stopped her.

"You *are* pregnant, aren't you?" he demanded. "Don't you see what he's doing to you?"

"Warren..."

"Don't let it happen, Justine. I'd hoped you'd come to your senses before—"

She was through listening and shut the door with a resounding bang.

Leaning against it, Justine felt weak with relief. He was gone. She'd been an idiot to go out for lunch with him that day. She saw now that it was disloyal to Seth; furthermore, Warren was too competitive to ever be a friend, as she'd naively thought. Not only that, Cedar Cove was a small town, and perceptions mattered. She couldn't risk humiliating her husband by allowing people to think she was seeing Warren—her supposed former lover—behind his back.

Warren had brought up an interesting point, though. Pregnancy. Shortly after Jordan's death and her parents' divorce, Justine had decided she didn't want children. But now that she was married, she realized her views had changed. She could only hope Seth felt the same way.

Jack Griffin slapped cologne on his freshly shaved cheeks and blinked at the sting. He caught his reflection in the spotted and foggy mirror and wiggled his eyebrows a couple of times.

"Tonight," he said aloud, reminding himself that this could very well be the evening he lured Olivia Lockhart into his bed. Their relationship had been progressing nicely—*very* nicely. But they were both mature adults, and with those years had come a certain...patience. A kind of caution. They weren't twenty-year-olds at the mercy of their hormones. Still, he was a man in every sense of the word, and he'd like nothing better than to take their relationship to a physical level. Beyond kissing and cuddling... He was ready to make the leap and hoped she agreed.

The divorced family court judge wasn't like other women he'd known. Olivia had class and culture, and he was a no-account drunk who remained sober one day at a time.

Grace Sherman had told him about Olivia's upcoming birthday and he was grateful. This was exactly the occasion he'd been looking for, a chance to show her exactly how much he cared. Jack had searched long and hard for the perfect birthday gift. His quest had been to find something that would let her know the message of his heart. Something that suited a woman who was both sophisticated and unpretentious. The diamond tennis bracelet was it.

Choosing a clean shirt, he reached for the gray velvet box and examined the bracelet. It was stunning, if he said so himself. He'd never bought anything as beautiful as this, not even for his ex-wife. The jeweler had sold him on the quality, and had then shaved off an extra ten per cent when Jack showed more than idle interest. Nothing wrong with being practical, he figured. The extra cash would go toward a fancy dinner at The Captain's Galley. He enjoyed imagining Olivia's reaction when she opened the box. Twice now he'd wrapped it, and then because he wanted to be assured it was as lovely as he remembered, he'd unwrapped it just to take another peek.

Whistling, Jack finished dressing. *Tonight,* he said again, his blood already heating at the thought of Olivia lying in his arms.

A sound came from the direction of his living room and he stuck his head outside the bedroom door. "Anyone here?"

No response.

Jack frowned, then checked his reflection one last time.

"Dad?"

Jack froze. Eric was here? *Now?*

"Eric?" Jack stepped out of the bedroom to find his twenty-six-year-old son standing in the middle of his living room, a suitcase in his hand.

"You were on your way out?" Eric asked.

"I'm not expected for a while," Jack assured him. The boy looked dreadful, his complexion pale with pain. His shoulders were hunched and his misery was evident in every line of his body. "What's wrong?"

Eric shrugged.

Experience had taught him that only a woman was capable of bringing a man to this point. "Did you and Shelly have a fight?"

Eric's returning snort was devoid of humor. "You could say that."

Glancing at the suitcase in his son's hand, he assumed this was more than the usual disagreement. "She kicked you out?"

Eric nodded.

His son slumped onto the sofa and gazed pleadingly up at Jack. "Do you have time to talk, Dad?"

Jack's relationship with his son was tenuous at best. For almost his entire life, Eric had lived with his mother. Even after Jack became sober, Eric had rejected every effort he'd made to establish a relationship. This year, this past spring, was the first time Eric had agreed to see Jack. Afraid he might inadvertently say or do something to distress his son, Jack had invited Olivia along for the initial meeting. They'd all had dinner on the Seattle waterfront. Buoyed by the success of that outing, Jack and Eric had gotten together every month or so since.

Jack was thrilled with the prospect of having a good relationship with his only child. He had a lot to prove, both to Eric and himself. He didn't want anything to injure this fragile beginning.

"Of course I have time. Tell me what's on your mind." Jack sat down across from his son, leaning forward so Eric would know he was interested and that he cared.

"It's Shelly and her pregnancy," Eric murmured.

That much Jack had guessed, but he didn't say anything.

"The baby *can't* be mine. I told her that and she blew up at me. She said if I seriously think she's pregnant by someone else, then I should get out of her life."

"I'm sure she didn't mean it," Jack murmured. "Women say things like that when they're upset."

"She meant it enough to throw me out of the apartment."

So much for *that* pearl of wisdom, Jack mused. He cursed himself for not being better at this.

Eric looked as if he was about to weep. "She said she never wanted to see me again."

"I'm sure she didn't mean that, either."

"I think she did."

"Perhaps she did when she said it, but she'll have a change of heart later." Jack winced at his own glibness. "Soon," he added. "She'll ask you to come home soon."

"I hope she does," Eric said emphatically. "The apartment's leased in my name," he added, "but I don't want her to move. She can have the apartment if she wants."

"What about you? Where will you go?"

Eric hesitated, then glanced up. "Would you mind very much if I stayed here with you? Just for the time being."

"Me?" Jack echoed, and was instantly sorry. "Me—well, I guess we won't get in each other's way too much, if it's only for a few days." So much for romantic evenings with Olivia anytime in the near future.

"It probably won't be for long." Eric sounded hopeful.

"Of course not," Jack said, his voice as confident as he could manage. "My guess is that Shelly will call tomorrow, wanting you to come home."

"You think so?" Eric's eyes brightened.

"Sure thing."

Eric shook his head, his expression grim. "I doubt it, Dad. First of all, I didn't tell her I was coming here and secondly..." He paused and rubbed his face. "Do you think the doctors might've made a mistake about me?" The appeal in his eyes was painful to see.

"You mean about being able to father children?"

"Yeah. Is there any chance?"

Jack looked at him thoughtfully. "It was a lot of years ago. There are ways of finding out about these things, you know."

"Yes, but Shelly says..." He sighed deeply. "I wouldn't suspect her of being with another man, but a little while ago she mentioned this new guy she's working with and they seemed to be real buddy-buddy. They were doing a lot of overtime together—and now she turns up pregnant. What else am I supposed to believe?''

Jack glanced at his watch. Olivia was expecting him to pick her up in five minutes.

''You have somewhere to go, don't you?'' Eric asked. ''You should leave,'' he urged, but if anything, he sounded worse than when he'd first arrived.

''Let me see what I can do,'' Jack said, his own heart sinking fast. He couldn't leave Eric like this. The boy was hurting and needed to talk. For so many years, he hadn't been any kind of father to his son, and he wasn't about to fail Eric again.

''Let me call Olivia,'' he said. ''She'll understand.''

''You're sure?'' Eric asked.

''Of course.'' Disheartened, Jack sequestered himself in his bedroom and dialed Olivia's number.

She answered almost immediately, and seemed surprised to hear from him.

''I have to break our date.''

''Our date tonight?'' She sounded as disappointed as he was.

''Eric's here,'' Jack explained.

''Oh.''

''Shelly kicked him out and he came to me. He needs to talk. And he may end up staying here for a few days.'' He sighed. ''I hate to do this to you, but you understand, don't you?''

''Of course,'' she said softly. ''He's your son.''

''Thank you. I'm sorry about this.''

''I'll call Mom and keep the reservation. I'd rather have dinner with you, but I understand. Children—regardless of their age—always need to come first. You know how strongly I believe that. Thanks for telling me, Jack, and good luck.''

Jack understood that she was praising his effort to communicate with his son—and with her. The one thing Olivia hated above all else was secrets, a lesson he'd learned early on in their relationship when he'd tried to hide the fact that he was a recovering alcoholic.

"I'll talk to you later," she said.

"Later," Jack repeated and then because he'd almost forgotten, he added, "Olivia?"

"Yes?"

"Happy Birthday."

Five

"Do you have plans for tonight?" Grace phoned to ask Olivia late Friday afternoon, the following week. It was a clear, crisp day toward the end of October, and Olivia had been waiting to hear from Jack ever since his phone call on her birthday.

"Plans? I wish..." Olivia said. "Do you have any suggestions?" she asked with a little more enthusiasm.

"How about taking in a football game?" Grace said. "We could go to dinner afterward. It's been ages since we had a chance to catch up."

Olivia was delighted that Grace had called her. During the months since Dan's disappearance, Grace had closed herself off from almost everyone. She'd kept her conversations brief and superficial, clearly unwilling to disturb the bedrock of pain and grief that had become the basis of her life. Again and again she'd found excuses to postpone visits or social plans. Olivia was concerned, but she respected her friend's need for privacy. It was no reflection on their long and very solid friendship. Grace was dealing with the loss of her marriage. Olivia stood by her, encouraged her with notes and cards and called frequently, just to maintain communication and to let Grace know she was there. This was the first time in a long while that Grace had called her to suggest an outing.

"I'd *love* to take in a game," Olivia told her friend.

"I thought you would," Grace said. "Have you heard from Jack yet?"

"Not a word."

"Damn."

Grace had that right. Olivia was tired of making excuses for him, even in her own mind. He'd been absent from her life all week. He hadn't called once. Nor had he shown up for their usual Tuesday night get-together. She couldn't help being disappointed that he'd had to break their date on Saturday; she certainly understood. But at the same time she'd hoped he would, at the very least, leave a brief message telling her how Eric was doing—and maybe saying he missed her. He could've called to make a tentative plan for next week or even the week after that. Instead, he'd ignored her.

"Meet me at the football field at seven," Grace said.

"I'll be there."

Olivia was grateful to have somewhere to go and something to do. Especially with her best friend, who seemed to be emerging from her self-imposed isolation. Her social life had revolved around Jack for months. Almost always, they spent part of a weekend together.

At seven o'clock, Olivia met Grace just outside the chain-link fence at Cedar Cove High School's football stadium. The field was ablaze with lights and the stands on both sides of the field were quickly filling up. Grace had dressed in gray wool slacks with a blue-and-green plaid wool jacket. She wore her thick salt-and-pepper hair shorter these days, and it suited her. Dan had always preferred a shoulder-length style, reminiscent of her high-school appearance, but Grace didn't need to please Dan anymore.

"You look great," Olivia commented as they stood in line to purchase their tickets.

"Of course I do. The only thing you ever see me in these days is my sweats for aerobics class."

Olivia smiled because it was all too true.

"Remember in high school when we used to come and cheer on the team?" Grace asked as the line moved slowly toward the ticket counter.

"Do I ever. Bob Beldon and Dan were our football heroes—" Olivia paused. She regretted bringing Dan's name into the conversation.

Grace touched her arm. "I was thinking the same thing. Dan was a wonderful athlete when he was young. I still remember the year he scored the winning touchdown that put Cedar Cove in the playoffs for the first time in a decade."

"So do I," Olivia said, glancing at her friend. "It doesn't hurt to talk about Dan?"

Grace gazed into the distance. "Not really. But it's easier to think about the early years, before Vietnam." She was silent for a moment. "I don't know why he left me the way he did. I've gone over it a thousand times and can't come up with an answer. I just don't understand how he could do this. I realize I might never know. All I can say is that this was his choice. I have my own choices to make, and I need to move forward with my life."

"You always were a strong woman," Olivia said, not hiding her admiration, "but you're stronger now than ever."

"I wish that was true," Grace murmured and then she changed the subject, looking up at the night sky. "I love this time of year."

"Me, too." The weather in the Pacific Northwest

had taken a decided turn in the last couple of weeks. Soon the autumn rains would start, and the clear bright evenings would become storms of wind mingled with a steady drizzle.

After paying for their tickets, they purchased a program from one of the drill team members hawking the small booklets just inside the field. Making their way toward the stands, Olivia paused to see what seats were still available.

"Olivia! Grace!" Charlotte's voice rang out from the home field section.

Olivia glanced around until she found her mother waving her right arm high above her head. Charlotte sat next to Cliff Harding about halfway up. Her lap was draped with a small red quilt and Cliff was wearing a fringed leather jacket and his ever-present cowboy hat.

"Do you mind sitting with Mom?" Olivia asked, although her real question had to do with Cliff Harding.

"No it's fine." Grace's eyes were on Cliff and she gave a slow smile.

Now, *that* was an interesting development, Olivia mused as they climbed the steps.

Olivia hugged Charlotte as she edged past her mother. Moving down, she left plenty of room for Grace. Cliff sat on the outside of the row, closest to the stairs.

"What a pleasant surprise to run into you two," Charlotte said, sounding positively delighted. "Cliff's never been to a Cedar Cove football game. My column in the newspaper this week was about supporting our youth, you know?"

"I read it, Mom, and it was a great piece." Her mom

derived real pleasure from writing the Seniors' Page for the *Chronicle.*

"Cliff read it, too, and I told him he'd never be part of the community until he's cheered for our football team."

Cliff was studying the program and seemed impressed with all the community advertisement that supported the team. "The last time I was at a high school football game was when I was in high school myself."

"This town takes its football seriously," Olivia told him.

"I can see that." The game was about to start and there was standing room only. In addition to the football team itself, the school band, the cheerleading squad and drill team were all present.

"Do you two have plans for after the game?" Cliff asked, but Olivia noticed that he directed the question at Grace.

"Olivia and I are going to dinner," Grace explained.

"Cliff invited me out, as well," Charlotte said. "Why don't you two join us?" She glanced from one to the other.

"Sure, that sounds like fun," Olivia said. From Grace's reaction to seeing Cliff, she knew her friend wouldn't object.

The game was close, and at halftime the score was tied. Olivia was, once again, amazed by how many people her mother knew. Not a moment passed without Charlotte calling out to one person or another. Her weekly column had increased her recognition among the townspeople, and she was obviously well-loved for her charitable activities, including her volunteer work at the local convalescent center where she'd met Tom Harding.

Cedar Cove High School won in the last five seconds with a field goal. The mood was festive as the stadium emptied. Since the Pancake Palace would definitely be crowded after the win, Cliff suggested The Captain's Galley in the downtown area.

They met there and were quickly escorted to a table for four. Olivia noticed that Cecilia Randall still held the position of hostess, but there wasn't time to chat with the young Navy wife. Once they were seated, conversation was light and flowed smoothly both before and after they ordered.

Try as she might, Olivia found her thoughts wandering to Jack, and that distracted her. Without being obvious, she'd searched for him throughout the game. He generally wrote the sports articles for the high school teams, simply because he loved going to the games. Olivia had given up counting the number of sporting events they'd attended together. But if he was at the game tonight, she hadn't seen him.

Of course, she could phone him. They weren't fighting, although she had to wonder why he hadn't called her. Perhaps Eric was still with him, but his son couldn't possibly take up *every* minute of Jack's time. Olivia was getting downright irritated.

Conversation ceased as their meals arrived and then it resumed. They'd moved from the football game to the state of the local economy. Olivia added a comment every now and then as she nibbled at her crab salad, but her spirits weren't high and she struggled to keep her thoughts away from Jack.

Even though she'd dated occasionally since her divorce, she hadn't gotten close to another man the way she had with Jack. Because their personalities and backgrounds were so different, he brought balance and spontaneity to her rigid schedule. With him she was free to laugh and shed the formality that had taken over her life after she was elected to the bench. Jack was unconventional, witty, fun—and, damn it all, she missed him.

The bill came, and before anyone could argue, Cliff reached for it. "My treat, ladies," he insisted.

Olivia objected. She'd never have agreed to join them if she'd known Cliff was buying. "I can't let you do that," she said.

"Hey, how often does a man get the chance to be seen with three beautiful women?"

"This is very thoughtful of you," Charlotte said and patted his hand, sending Olivia a sharp glance. Sighing, Olivia decided to accept graciously and murmured her thanks.

Grace chuckled. "Are you sure you're not using *my* credit card?"

They all laughed and after savoring the last of their coffee, they parted for the night.

"Is everything okay?" Grace asked as they strolled to the parking lot next to the library. "You've been quiet all evening." Olivia had hoped for a few minutes to speak privately to Grace, but with her mother and Cliff present that hadn't been possible.

"Who can get a word in edgewise with my mother?" Olivia joked.

"Is everything okay between you and Jack?" How like Grace to care about her friend's petty concerns when *she* was the one whose life was in upheaval.

"I think so," Olivia told her, and then added. "I hope so."

"So do I."

They parted with promises to talk soon, and Olivia

drove home. As she walked into the hallway, she saw that the message light on her answering machine was flashing. She stared down at it for a few hopeful seconds. Pressing the button, she waited and was rewarded by the craggy sound of Jack's voice.

"Olivia, hi. Sorry I haven't been in touch lately, but I've had my hands full with Eric. I was hoping you'd be home so we could talk. You're not out with some other guy, are you?" There was a forced laugh. "Listen, I'm really sorry about last week, but I hope to make it up to you. Phone me back, all right? I've got a special birthday gift for you. Can we get together soon?"

Olivia checked her watch. It was close to eleven and too late to return his call. Anyway, he'd kept her waiting all week; she'd keep him guessing until morning. As she readied for bed, Olivia was smiling.

Maryellen wanted to kick herself for coming up with this ridiculous "swap meet for men" idea. It'd all started out innocently enough with her mentioning the article she'd read about that town in Ireland. Next thing she knew, she was part of the party-planning. By her following nail appointment, this Halloween get-together had gathered momentum to the point that she'd lost count of how many people were attending.

"You're still bringing that chef friend of yours, aren't you?" Terri asked. Maryellen had barely sat down when Terri started grilling her with questions she couldn't answer about Jon.

"Like I said, he's just a friend—no," she amended. "Jon's more of a business acquaintance. And he hasn't given me an answer yet."

"Oh." Terri sounded disappointed. "So you don't know if he's coming or not?"

"I can't say for sure." She hadn't talked to him since that initial conversation a week ago. "If he's not there, I'll make sure you get introduced some other time."

Terri's dark eyes lit up. "Great."

The following evening—Halloween night—Maryellen stood in the darkest, creepiest corner of the decorated bar with a fake spider dangling from the ceiling directly above her. More than ever, she felt convinced that this had all been a mistake. The room was crowded with maybe a hundred men and women, some in costume, some not.

Then without warning, without her seeing him arrive, Jon was standing next to her. He held a frosty mug of beer. "Hi," he said, looking out over the crowded room.

"You came." Now that was brilliant. Nothing like stating the obvious. "I mean...you didn't call me back and when I didn't hear, I assumed you wouldn't show up."

"I should've phoned, but I wanted to make sure I could get the evening off first."

"It's all right—don't apologize." He hadn't but...

"Between the restaurant and my photography, I've been working a lot of hours. Sometimes I lose track of time."

An artist's working habits weren't new to Maryellen. "I understand."

He took a sip of beer. "Can I get you anything?"

"I'm fine, thanks." Then, glancing around the room, she saw Terri, who'd dressed as Cleopatra complete with heavy eye makeup and black wig. "There's the woman I wanted you to meet."

"All right," Jon said, following as she wove her way through the crowd.

"Terri," Maryellen said, interrupting the other woman's conversation with someone—male or female?—dressed as a wizard in voluminous robes. "This is Jon, the man I was telling you about."

"Hello, *Jon,*" Terri returned, as though she'd waited her entire life for precisely this moment. The wizard, having lost her attention, drifted off.

"Pleased to meet you, Terri," Jon said.

"I hear you're a chef." Terri edged closer to him, and Maryellen could see she'd already had more than enough to drink. She bit her lip, wanting to suggest that it might be best if they talked another time. "I know my way around a kitchen, too. Want to stir up something together?"

"That might be interesting." Jon took another sip of beer, and Maryellen could see he was trying hard to disguise a smile.

"Maryellen said you also take pictures."

"I do a little of that on the side."

"Actually, Jon's a brilliant photographer," Maryellen rushed to explain, mortified at what he must think.

Trying not to be conspicuous about it, she wandered away and eventually returned to her protective corner. She wasn't there long before Jon joined her.

"So, Terri's the woman you wanted to set me up with?" he asked.

"Have you ever done something you regret?" she asked. "I'm afraid this is one of those situations."

He nodded, but didn't respond, and they stood in silence for a few minutes.

Someone put a bunch of quarters in the jukebox, and the music started. Several couples formed an impromptu dance floor. Jon made a sweeping gesture. "Shall we?"

Jon didn't give her a chance to object. He put his beer aside and gently pulled her into his arms.

He felt strong and solid against her, but Maryellen was having none of it. "I don't think we should," she said, her posture rigid. She didn't want Jon to hold her, didn't want this relationship to be anything but professional. Yet she recognized that she'd broken her own rule in calling him, inviting him here—in acknowledging her attraction to Jon Bowman.

"Relax," he whispered close to her ear.

"I can't."

"Why not?"

She sighed. "It's a long story. Jon, I'm serious, this isn't a good idea."

"One dance," he said. "Okay? Think of it as your penance for setting me up with your friend."

Refusing would be ungracious. "Okay," she agreed, but reluctantly. She tried to keep her distance, although it was difficult with Jon's arms around her, urging her closer. The song was that slow-dance classic, "Cherish," and she couldn't help feeling affected. If Jon wasn't so gentle and warm and considerate, it would've been easier to maintain her reserve. She began to relax in his embrace.

"Better, much better," he whispered, leading her across the floor. He stroked her back in a slow circular motion that was doing crazy things to her pulse. The music ended long before she was ready to stop.

"That wasn't so bad, now was it?" Jon asked.

She blinked up at him, not realizing she'd closed her

eyes. "No." It was scary and wonderful, both at once. She didn't *want* to feel any of this. Warning bells were clanging in her head. Nevertheless, when the next song started—even before he asked—she slipped her arms around his neck and swayed toward him.

Jon didn't say anything, but she could feel his smile. To her own amazement, she was smiling, too.

They danced for what seemed like hours, danced to song after song. They didn't talk, but the communication between them was unmistakable. The way he held her close told her he'd been interested in her for some time. And the way she responded to his touch told him she found his work brilliant and beautiful, and that he intrigued her—as an artist *and* a man.

She wanted to know why he answered every question with a question. Did he have secrets? She suspected he must. After all, she had her own. Secrets that had remained buried since the early days of her marriage. No one knew, not even her mother. Not her sister. No one. Perhaps it was this that drew them together. Perhaps this was what he sensed in her and she felt in him. Of one thing Maryellen was sure. Secrets could be dangerous.

The Halloween party was breaking up and Jon suggested he walk her to her car. Maryellen agreed. Knowing that parking would be scarce, she'd used her space behind the art gallery. It would be dark and deserted, and she was glad Jon had offered to escort her.

"I had a good time," he told her as they entered the alley.

"I did, too." Darkness swallowed them up no more than two feet from the street.

"I forgive you for wanting to pawn me off on your friend."

Maryellen's face instantly went hot, and she felt grateful there wasn't enough light for Jon to notice. "That was all a misunderstanding."

He chuckled. "If you say so."

As she fumbled in her purse for her car keys, Jon stopped her. "I've wanted to know you better for years," he said in a low voice.

Maryellen couldn't have muttered a word had the fate of the world depended on her reply. She envisioned herself thanking him in a flippant, matter-of-fact way, then whirling around and unlocking her car door. Instead she stood rooted to the spot, staring up at him. He was going to kiss her. That couldn't happen; she simply couldn't allow it. Yet, all the while objection after objection marched through her mind, she found herself slowly—against every rational dictate—leaning toward him. Her head was raised, her eyes half-closed.

When his lips met hers, it wasn't the slow, seductive kiss she'd anticipated. Jon lifted her from the pavement until she stood on the very tips of her toes. His mouth was hungry, urgent, needy as his lips seduced hers. She tasted his passion as his tongue swept her mouth and swallowed his moan as it went on and on and on until she was sure she'd faint.

No man, not even her husband, had kissed her so thoroughly, so passionately. When he broke it off, Maryellen was breathless and speechless. Had he released her, she would've crumpled into a heap on the ground.

"Oh, no." When she could manage to speak, these were the first words that emerged.

"No?" Jon asked.

"Oh…no."

"My ego's taking something of a bruising here. Can't you do better than that?"

"Jon." She gave herself a moment to gather her composure. "That was—"

"Pretty damn wonderful if you ask me."

"Yes...it was." Maryellen couldn't begin to explain to him why this was such a mistake.

"I've been wanting to do that all evening," he said in a satisfied tone.

Arms dangling at her sides, Maryellen slumped against her car. It was still hard to breathe, and for some reason, she felt as if she was about to cry. "I think we need to talk."

"We'll talk," Jon promised, kissing her again. She'd been half expecting it, and even though she was prepared this time, his touch devastated her, left her gasping with shock and pleasure.

"Soon," he said as he eased his lips from hers. "All right?"

"Okay," she agreed hoarsely, although she couldn't recall *what* was going to happen "soon."

Once secure and inside her car, she placed her hands on the steering wheel. She was trembling so badly she found it impossible to insert the key into the ignition. What had she done? What had she unleashed on them both?

Dressed in jeans and a sweatshirt, Grace started outside to look around the house and garage. She couldn't delay winterizing her home any longer. Dan had always taken care of such chores; now, for the first time in her marriage, Grace would need to complete these unfamiliar tasks herself.

Thankfully, her son-in-law had stepped in whenever

she'd required help. He'd shown her how to change the furnace filter, fixed a leaking faucet and repaired the dryer, but Grace couldn't continue to rely on Paul, dear as he was. She had to learn to cope with these situations on her own.

The first thing she did was stare at the open garage door. For the last two weeks, the automatic door had refused to budge. Grace had managed to open it manually, but last evening it had stuck in the open position. It needed to be fixed before someone saw it as an invitation to rob her.

Standing in front of the garage, wearing Dan's oversized gloves, hands on hips, Grace regarded the garage door like a dragon ready to roar down sulfur and fire upon her.

"Get a grip," she muttered under her breath. "You can do this. You've done everything else—you can tackle a garage door, too." Okay, first she had to find the manual and the necessary tools. Dan was always so proud of his workbench. He had every gadget imaginable. Yet he hadn't taken a single one with him when he walked away. Like everything else about his disappearance, this baffled her.

Was this other woman so incredible, so amazing, that she provided for his every need? Or did the things that used to matter to him no longer mean anything? He'd left behind his clothes, his tools, even his wedding band. He'd taken nothing more than the clothes on his back.

Grace didn't know where she'd find the manual. She thought Dan kept his various instruction books in a box somewhere in the garage. She saw a stack of boxes piled beneath the workbench; she slid the top one out. Kneeling on the concrete floor, she opened the lid. Instead of the manual, she found the thick woolen shirt she'd bought him last Christmas. She lifted it and gasped. The shirt had been shredded. It looked as though Dan had taken a pair of scissors to it and systematically cut the fifty-dollar shirt into strips. All that remained intact was the collar and cuffs.

Grace remembered asking Dan about the shirt, remembered him telling her it was his favorite, but she'd never seen him wear it. After a while, it had completely slipped her mind.

Another box revealed a second ugly surprise. Kelly had given Dan a highly touted book on World War II for his birthday. He'd thanked her profusely and said he'd read it. But he hadn't. Instead it, too, had been destroyed, the pages ripped from the binding. Grace discovered two more boxes of his carnage. It was as though he'd planted them there for her to find. Dan couldn't have shouted his hate more loudly had he been standing directly in front of her.

Shaken to the core, Grace discarded the boxes in the garbage and sat down on the back porch steps. Her first reaction was anger. How dare he do such a thing. How dare he! Then she felt the overwhelming urge to weep. Tears stung her eyes, but she refused to give in to them. She refused to hand her husband the power to reduce her to a sniveling, spineless weakling.

Buttercup joined her and seemed to sense Grace's distress.

"What would make him do this?" she asked her golden retriever.

Buttercup looked up at her with big, soulful eyes.

"I don't know either, girl. I just don't know." Needing to hold someone, Grace put her arms around the dog's neck and buried her face in Buttercup's fur.

She wasn't sure how long she sat there, feeling intense anger, regret and simmering emotion. After a while she got to her feet. The garage door wasn't going to fix itself.

In the process of digging through the neat stack of boxes, she eventually happened upon the manual. She flipped through it and quickly read over the information. The book offered suggestions for troubleshooting, which she studied in detail. Again and again she reminded herself that she could handle this.

She'd just positioned the stepladder when a pickup truck pulled into the driveway. Grace recognized Cliff and hesitated, her feet on the fourth rung up.

"Hi," he called, climbing out of the truck. Buttercup trotted over to greet him. While friendly, the golden retriever was protective of Grace and wasn't keen on letting strangers into the yard. To Grace's surprise, Buttercup greeted Cliff as if he were family.

"Hi," she said, wishing now that she'd worn a newer pair of jeans and a less faded sweatshirt.

"Charlotte mentioned that you had a problem with your garage door," he said, bending down to scratch her dog's ears.

Grace blinked, unsure how Olivia's mother had known about her problem, but then Charlotte always did have a way of finding out things.

Cliff straightened and seemed to await her invitation. "I came to see if I could give you a hand."

At this point, Grace wasn't about to refuse help. "I'd be grateful if you'd look at it. I've been reading the manual but I haven't had a chance to check out the mechanism yet."

"I have a knack for stuff like this." He glanced

around. "I'm gifted at cleaning leaves out of rain gutters, too."

Grace laughed. "You must be an angel in disguise."

"I don't think so." He helped her down from the ladder and even before Grace could get inside the house to brew a pot of coffee, he had the garage door working again.

"What was wrong?" she asked, astonished that it had been so easy.

"The wheels jumped out of alignment. I just put it back on track. Nothing to it."

While Cliff carried the ladder over to the house, Grace reached for the rake and started gathering together a huge pile of oak leaves. When she'd finished, Cliff helped her pack them inside plastic bags.

"Are you ready for that coffee?" she asked, when they'd tied the last bag.

"That'd be great."

She welcomed him into her kitchen and set out two big mugs. "I don't know how to thank you."

He studied her a moment, then grinned boyishly. "I'll think of something," he teased.

"I'll bet you will." Grace laughed—and suddenly realized that just a couple of hours earlier, she'd been fighting back tears. The contrast was all the more apparent when she saw the way Buttercup had warmed to Cliff.

"Buttercup normally isn't friendly with strangers," she told him.

Cliff petted the dog. "She probably smells the horses."

Grace propped elbows on the table. "I'd forgotten you raise quarter horses."

"They're a big part of my life. Do you ride?"

Grace shook her head. "I haven't been around horses much."

They chatted for a while, the ebb and flow of their conversation completely natural. Rarely had Grace felt more at ease with a man. More than once, she had to remind herself that legally she was still married to Dan. While he might have run off with another woman—or at any rate, run off—she intended to remain true to her vows.

As he was getting ready to leave, Grace saw Cliff glance toward the living room. A framed family photograph stood on a bookshelf. "That's Dan?" he asked.

She nodded.

Cliff walked over to the bookcase and picked up the photograph, which had been taken almost twenty years earlier. Both girls were teenagers then, and Kelly was in braces. Dan's gaze had been somber as he stared straight into the camera, not revealing any emotion.

After an extraordinarily long moment, Cliff replaced the faded color photograph.

"I don't know why he left," Grace whispered. "I just don't know."

Cliff didn't say anything.

"It's the not knowing that's dreadful."

"I can only imagine."

She swallowed tightly.

He brushed the hair from her cheek. "I don't want you to feel guilty about me being here this afternoon. This wasn't a date."

Grace smiled tremulously.

"If you're going to suffer pangs of remorse, then you should worry about how much I want to take you in my arms right now. If you're going to feel guilty, then do it because I'm having one hell of a time not kissing you."

Grace closed her eyes, knowing that if she looked at him, Cliff would realize it was what she wanted, too.

Sighing, he stroked her cheek with his knuckle before he turned away.

Eyes still shut, she heard him open the door and leave.

Six

Janice Lamond had been a valuable addition to Zach Cox's office staff. She'd taken on more and more duties and had developed an excellent rapport with his clients. He appreciated her attitude and her strong work ethic. When it was time for her six-month evaluation, Zach called her into his office.

"Sit down, Janice," he said, gesturing toward the chair across from his desk.

Janice sat on the edge of the chair and met his look with a tentative smile, almost as if she were nervous about what he might say.

"You've been with the firm half a year now."

"Has it really been that long?"

It felt as though she'd always been part of his office team. She was well-liked and fit in smoothly with the firm's other employees. Eager to please, she wasn't quick to rush out the door at the end of the day. He appreciated the effort she took to make the clients who visited the office feel welcome.

"As you know, we review employee performance twice a year."

Janice squeezed her hands between her knees. "Is there an area where I can improve?" she asked.

If there was, Zach didn't know what it would be.

She was about as perfect an employee as he could find. "No, no. You've done an excellent job."

"Thank you." Her eyes shone at his praise. "It's a pleasure to come into work each day. I like my job."

She made it a pleasure for Zach to come into the office, too. Janice was organized. Her desk was orderly and she kept his appointments running like clockwork. When he arrived at the office in the morning, Janice was there to greet him, the coffee was made and the mail was on his desk. It was a stark contrast to his life at home. With so many committee appointments, Rosie often left the dinner dishes on the table or stacked in the sink overnight. The house was a continual mess, and even the most mundane tasks just never seemed to get accomplished. Still, Rosie was his wife and he loved her.

"I'd like to give you a ten-percent raise," Zach told Janice. "The other partners are in agreement."

"Ten percent?" she repeated as if she'd misunderstood him. "After just six months?"

"We've learned that if we want to keep good employees, we need to compensate them adequately. We're happy with your work here at Smith, Cox and Jefferson. We hope that you'll be part of our team for many years to come."

"I'd like that very much."

Zach didn't have anything more to add. He stood, and Janice did, too. He walked her to his office door.

"I can't thank you enough," she said.

"I'm the one who should be thanking you."

"A ten-percent raise," she added excitedly, covering her mouth with both hands. "This is just *great.*"

Before he could react, Janice threw her arms around his neck and gave him a hug. As soon as she realized what she'd done, she blushed and hurriedly left. Zach figured it was just an impulsive gesture from a warm, emotionally generous woman.

But Zach enjoyed that little hug, and found himself smiling for the next few minutes.

At five-thirty, when the workday was technically over, he remained behind to finish up some paperwork. He wasn't in a hurry to get home these days. Rosie was generally busy with some volunteer project or other, and Allison and Eddie were involved with their own friends and activities. Janice was closing down her computer as he walked out of his office at six o'clock.

"I didn't know you were still here," he said, glancing at his watch.

"I wanted to review these numbers one last time before I put the Mullens Company report in the mail."

He smiled at her. It was exactly this attention to detail that had earned her the raise. "Good night, Janice."

"Good night, Mr. Cox, and thank you again."

As Zach turned off Lighthouse Road and headed toward Pelican Court, the smile left him. It was doubtful Rosie would have dinner ready. In all likelihood, she was preparing for some function outside the house. She never seemed to plan ahead for such events, and as a result she went into panic mode, shoving something that passed for dinner onto the table. Most likely, the meal would consist of some packaged crap she'd bought at the grocery store, something that could be slapped together without any effort. Some nights she brought home dinner from the deli. There was nothing he liked less than Chinese food that had been sitting under lights all afternoon. The deli-roasted chicken wasn't half-bad, but he was as tired of that as he was of pizza.

Zach parked the car in the garage and loosened his tie as he entered the kitchen.

"You're late," Rosie said, rushing to place silverware in the center of the table. "Dinner's ready."

"What are we having?"

She reached for a container on top of the garbage can and read the label aloud. "Lasagna."

"Is it cooked all the way through this time?" The last entrée she'd served was still frozen in the middle.

"It should be. I had it in the microwave for twenty minutes." Then without a pause, she turned her head and yelled for the kids. "Dinner!"

"Are you going out?"

"I told you this morning I have my book club tonight."

"Did you read the book?"

"Who has time? But I want to hear what everyone else has to say." There was a decided edge to her voice, as though she disapproved of him questioning her about her activities.

Zach picked up the mail and sorted through it. He stopped at the VISA bill, which he'd paid off a month earlier. Slipping his finger under the flap, he slit it open. To his dismay he found a three-hundred-dollar charge from Willows, Weeds and Flowers.

He asked Rosie about it.

"Oh yes, I forgot to tell you. I used the card to buy flowers for the ladies' auxiliary luncheon at the hospital."

"Three hundred dollars for *flowers?*"

"The committee's going to reimburse me."

"When?"

"Don't take that tone of voice with me, Zach," she snapped. "I'm sure I'll have the check by the end of the week."

"That card is for emergencies only."

Rosie glared at him, her hand on her hip. "That *was* an emergency. The lady delivered the centerpieces for the banquet, and the treasurer hadn't arrived yet. She had to be paid. Surely even you can understand that?"

"So *you* volunteered?" Zach didn't know why his wife found it necessary to leap in and rescue the world.

"Someone had to. Why are you so upset about this?"

"It's more than just this one incident," Zach said. "It's everything. I'm sick of the dinners you throw together because you're in a hurry to go somewhere else. I'm sick of you rushing out the door every night, sick of the house being a mess."

Tears filled Rosie's eyes, and her cheeks turned a deep shade of red. "You have no appreciation for everything I do around here."

Zach glared right back. "Everything you do? Tell me, exactly what is it you do all day, except race from one unpaid venture to another? In the meantime, your family's eating garbage. Our home is a mess and I haven't seen you for more than ten minutes all week."

"Are you suggesting I care more about my committees than I do my family?"

"I'm suggesting nothing. I'm saying it outright."

"You don't get it, do you?"

"Wrong," he shouted. "I'm definitely getting the message and so are our children. The kids and I are running a distant second in your life. You fill up your days with volunteer work so you'll feel valued and important, and frankly I'm sick of it."

He suddenly saw that Allison and Eddie had walked into the kitchen and were standing frozen in the doorway. Zach hated fighting in front of the children, but these negative emotions had been corroding inside him far too long.

Rosie looked at him as if he'd physically struck her, then burst into tears and stormed into their bedroom.

For a stunned moment Zach stood there as his children accused him with their eyes. He didn't understand why his home life was in constant turmoil. It was little wonder that he preferred being at the office with its well-organized environment.

Needing time to clear his head, Zach removed his tie and headed toward the garage.

"Where are you going, Dad?" Eddie called after him.

Zach didn't know. "Out."

Neither of his children said anything to stop him and the truth was, Zach didn't want to be delayed. Once in his car, he drove around for a while until his stomach rumbled. It'd been a long time since lunch, and returning home to a half-cooked frozen entrée held no appeal.

It was nearly eight by his watch. Zach stopped at the Taco Shack on the outskirts of town. The Mexican restaurant was better than scarfing down fast food, but at this point he didn't much care. Zach decided he'd order a couple of tacos and eat them in the car.

As he stepped up to the counter, he noticed a woman sitting by herself at a table. He didn't think anything of it until he realized she looked familiar. Turning, he gave her a second glance.

"Janice?"

"Mr. Cox, what are you doing here? I mean—I didn't know you ate here."

"I do every now and then," he said. The teenage girl working the counter hurried over to take his order. Zach examined the menu and decided on a chili relleno and a cold drink. While he waited for his meal, he sauntered back to where Janice sat.

"What brings you to the Taco Shack on a Tuesday night?"

She looked sweet and pretty when she smiled up at him. "I'm celebrating my raise."

"By yourself?"

She nodded. "My ex-husband has our son on Tuesday nights, and I was too excited to go home and sit in front of the television all by myself."

Zach's order came a few minutes later, and he went to collect it. "Do you mind if I join you?"

"No. I mean, that would be great."

Zach lingered over his dinner and they both ordered coffee afterward. The tension that had been with him all evening dissolved and he found himself laughing and enjoying this visit.

When Zach finally returned to the house it was almost ten. Rosie was in bed, pretending to be asleep. She lay on her side, her back to him. He stared at her for a moment and debated whether he should apologize. No, he mused, he was finished apologizing to his wife. She was the one who needed to make amends. But if she wanted to give him the cold shoulder, that was fine with him.

Jack sat at his desk at *The Cedar Cove Chronicle* and stared at his computer monitor. The cursor blinked accusingly back at him from a screen that was almost blank. This article about the bond issue for the local park should have been finished two days ago. Jack didn't lack an opinion on the subject. He had plenty to say, and he'd write it out in fine form, just as soon as he chased Olivia from his thoughts.

It'd been almost a month since he'd canceled her birthday dinner. These had to be the longest thirty days of his life. The fact that Eric was living with him had complicated everything. His routine, his hard-won peace of mind, his productivity had been shattered all to hell.

This was what Jack got for dwelling on life's regrets. He wanted to be a good father to Eric; he longed to make up for the lost years, and here was the opportunity. Unfortunately, the timing couldn't have been worse.

Naturally Eric would decide he needed a father at the same time Jack was falling in love and wanted to spend every spare moment with Olivia Lockhart. The first week Eric was with him, Jack had spent hour after hour listening to his son's woes. It seemed Eric had at least fifteen years of hurt and doubt that he needed to release. Patiently Jack had listened and when he could, he offered comfort and advice.

When Jack eventually did have a chance, he'd phoned Olivia, dying to see her, dying to take a break from his son's troubles. He'd hoped that an hour or two with Olivia would rejuvenate his spirits. Instead he'd hit rock bottom when she wasn't home. He waited around all night for her to return his call. She didn't until the next morning, and by then he'd left to cover the Christmas Bazaar for the newspaper's Neighbors Section.

They finally did connect, early the following week, and Jack noticed that her feelings for him appeared to be cooling. It wasn't anything she said, exactly. Her son-in-law was back from Alaska, and she was working with Charlotte on putting together a wedding reception for Seth and Justine.

Every time he'd talked to Olivia since then, she was busy. Too busy to see him. Even their Tuesday night get-togethers had fallen by the wayside. Just how much trouble could a wedding reception really be? It seemed Olivia constantly needed to run somewhere or talk to someone. Someone other than Jack.

The hustle and bustle of this wedding reception aside, what worried Jack was her changing attitude toward him. Yes, there was a decided cooling. Whenever they managed to chat, Jack braced himself, half expecting her to suggest they break it off. It was this expectation—the feeling that she was looking for a kind way to tell him to take a hike—that prevented him from giving her the bracelet. He was afraid she'd view the expensive gift as a means of manipulating her and so he'd held on to it, not knowing what else to do.

The cursor on his screen continued to blink, and Jack wheeled his chair around, gazing out the window. This wasn't going to work. He needed an AA meeting and a talk with his sponsor.

He found a meeting near Bangor, but because he was in unfamiliar territory, he sat at the back of the room and listened to the speaker, who had over twenty years of sobriety. At the end of the session, when the group stood, joined hands and said the Lord's Prayer followed by the Serenity Prayer, Jack's voice rose and blended with the others. These people were family. They might be strangers but they all shared a problem that bonded them.

On the drive back to the office, Jack stopped at Thyme and Tide, the bed-and-breakfast on the waterfront owned by his sponsor and friend, Bob Beldon, and his wife, Peggy.

Bob was busy tinkering in the garage with one of his woodworking projects when Jack pulled into the driveway. Bob came out of the garage to meet him.

"How's it going?" Jack asked, not quite ready to launch into his reason for visiting.

"Good. How about you?"

Jack shrugged.

Bob smiled knowingly. "I figure if you're coming by to see me in the middle of the day, something's up. Want to talk about it?"

Jack sighed, grateful he didn't need to lead into the subject delicately. "Have you got a few minutes?"

"Sure. Come on in. Peggy's visiting her sister, but I'm sure there's still coffee in the pot."

Jack was grateful. He was feeling unsettled, and even after ten years without a drink, the urge still came, especially at times like this. The meetings helped, but talking to Bob would give him a sense of perspective. It'd been a long while since the cravings had hit this hard.

"How are things with Eric?" Bob asked, heading into the kitchen. He paused on the back porch and removed his sweater, which he hung on a hook there. Then he led the way into the large, spacious room. Despite its size, the kitchen was warm and inviting, with its oak table, its woven rug on the polished floor and bunches of drying herbs by the window.

"Eric's still with me. He doesn't like it any better than I do, but he's stuck until he can work out this mess between him and Shelly."

"What's going on with him and the girl?"

The hell if Jack knew. Twice now, at Jack's suggestion, Eric had phoned Shelly. Jack had made himself scarce, but it didn't take a psychic to figure out that the conversations hadn't gone well. Within minutes the calls were over, leaving Eric more depressed than ever.

"I didn't come to talk about Eric," Jack told his friend. "I've got a problem with Olivia."

"What's up?" Bob silently offered him coffee, which Jack refused. Apparently Bob thought better of it himself and reached inside the refrigerator for a cold soda. Jack declined that, as well.

"I'm crazy about Olivia," Jack admitted, although this wasn't news to Bob, who'd encouraged the relationship from the first.

"I know." Bob opened the soda and leaned against the counter as he waited for Jack to continue.

Jack remained standing, too. Soon he was pacing. "I used to think she felt the same way about me."

"What changed her mind?"

"That's just it," Jack said. "I don't *know*. I had to break our dinner date on her birthday when Eric showed up unexpectedly. She seemed to understand, but lately..." He shook his head, unsure how to put into words what he sensed. "I keep thinking she's had a change of heart and is looking for the right moment to tell me to take a flying leap into some cow pasture."

Bob considered his words. "So you're waiting and wondering and making yourself insane, anticipating the end—even though she hasn't actually said anything about it."

"Yeah, I guess I am," Jack conceded.

"Wouldn't you rather know what she's thinking?"

Jack let the question roll around in his mind, and decided that, in all honesty, he didn't. He wanted to hold on to Olivia as long as he could because, dammit, he was falling in love with her. "She's preoccupied with Justine's wedding reception," he said, offering an excuse.

"You didn't answer the question. In fact, you're skirting the issue entirely and I know why. You don't want to face the truth, in case it isn't what you want to hear."

"She might want to end it, and I don't. Like I told you before, I think I'm in love with her."

"You're right—Olivia might decide to call it quits. But if she does, you'll deal with it."

Bob had more confidence in him than Jack did. "I don't want to lose her."

"Wouldn't knowing be better than all this doubting?"

Well...yes, he supposed so. "Maybe," he muttered. The only way to find out was to ask Olivia outright. He might not like the answer, as Bob had said, but this anxiety was damned hard to cope with. If she was going to reject him, he might as well get used to it. "Okay, I'll do it. I'll talk to Olivia." He stopped pacing and nodded at his friend. "Thanks."

Bob nodded solemnly in response, then downed the last of his cola and walked Jack to his car.

Now that he'd made up his mind, Jack decided he had to take immediate action. He checked his watch: four-thirty. Olivia should be home from the courthouse. He drove directly to her house on Lighthouse Road. He hadn't phoned her all week because he was afraid of what she might say; she hadn't called him, either. Parking in front of her house, he cursed his own weakness, his own need. This would be a lot easier if he didn't care so much. One thing he knew—if she told him to get lost, he wasn't going to reach for a drink.

He rang the doorbell and waited.

The next millennium came and went before Olivia opened the door. She held the phone to her ear, but when she saw it was Jack, she smiled, unlatched the screen door and gestured him inside, still talking.

"I'm sorry Marge can't make it, Stan, but I'm sure Justine will understand."

Ah, so she was speaking to her ex-husband. Jack had met Stan several months earlier, just before he'd gotten serious about Olivia. Her ex was a pompous SOB as far as Jack was concerned.

"Can you get here before three?" She smiled apologetically at Jack, who sat down on the sofa.

"Of course your aunt Louise is invited." She rolled her eyes and made a wind-it-up motion with her hand, as though eager to get her ex off the line. "I have to go—I have company…Jack. You remember Jack, don't you? You don't?"

Liar, Jack thought. Her ex knew exactly who he was.

She laughed but Jack couldn't tell what was so funny. No doubt old Stan had made some derogatory remark about him.

"I have to go, Stan," she said again, a little more loudly this time. "I'll see you next weekend with your aunt Louise. Give Marge my best. Bye."

A second later, she clicked the off button on the portable phone and sank onto the sofa next to Jack. "Were we supposed to meet this afternoon?"

"Ah…no, but I hadn't seen you in a while. I've missed you."

"I've missed you, too. I swear this reception is going to be the death of me. But Justine's my only daughter and I want it to be perfect for her and Seth. She frowned slightly. "You did get the invitation, didn't you?"

Jack nodded. He was beginning to feel better already. "You look worn-out," he told her. Maybe she'd noticed that he was emotionally spent himself, but he didn't plan to drag Eric into the conversation. This was about him and Olivia, not their families or their obligations.

"I *am* worn-out," she agreed. "I can't believe how much time and organization a simple wedding reception requires. I hope both you and Eric will come."

It felt good to be invited. "If you want."

"Of course I want you there. I'm going to need all the moral support I can get." The phone in her hand rang and she pushed the Talk button and raised the receiver to her ear. "Mom, sorry, I'm on my way. Yes, yes, tell the caterers I'll be there in ten minutes." She clicked off the phone, then leaped up from the sofa and started toward the kitchen.

"You're busy." Jack stood, thinking it would be best if he left.

"I'm sorry, Jack." She turned abruptly to face him. "Can we meet later?"

His heart sank. "I'm covering a school board meeting tonight."

She nodded, although he doubted she'd heard him.

"Wait," he said, and took her by the shoulders.

She seemed mildly startled but smiled when she realized he intended to kiss her. Her arms slipped around his neck and she met his mouth with her own.

Slowly, after their kiss had ended, he eased his mouth from hers. "I needed that."

All too briefly, she pressed her head to his shoulder. "So did I."

* * *

Justine was exhausted but jubilant as she held open the apartment door while Seth unloaded the last of the wedding gifts from the car. The reception had been wonderful—she couldn't believe her mother and grandmother had pulled it off. The entire afternoon had been as close to perfect as she could imagine. The food was incredible, the music lovely, the atmosphere festive. She'd met Seth's relatives and he'd met all of hers. His were easy to locate in a crowd; they were the big, husky, outgoing Swedes, while hers were comparatively restrained and tended to group together.

"I don't know how Mom and Grandma did it." Justine said, sitting down on the pale-blue sofa and propping her feet on the matching footstool. "I think this was the most magical day of my life, other than our wedding day, of course." She found their elopement wildly romantic.

Seth sat beside her and leaned his head against the sofa back. His large feet, crossed at the ankles, joined hers on the footstool. He seemed as exhausted as Justine.

"I feel so spoiled," she whispered.

Seth slid his arm around her. "I didn't know I had that many relatives," he muttered.

"It's been years since I saw my dad's aunt Louise."

Seth kissed her neck and drew her closer against him. "Second thoughts?"

Justine smiled. "Not a one. You?"

"None," Seth vowed. "I love my wife."

Seth had been back from Alaska for almost three weeks and their lives had been a whirlwind from the moment he stepped off the plane. Preparing for the reception had taken up some of their time and adjusting their lives to each other's had been more of a challenge than she'd anticipated. Seth worked at the marina and his hours changed from week to week. Slowly, he'd started moving his personal items into her place. Living together involved all kinds of accommodations, some of them delightfully easy and some more difficult, since neither of them was used to sharing decisions or routines with another person.

Still, every time Justine woke up and realized the man in her bed was her husband, she became so giddy with happiness she couldn't go back to sleep. They found ways to amuse themselves in those early-morning hours. Unfortunately that made for extra-long days at the bank and she arrived home exhausted, her eyes stinging from lack of sleep.

"Who was that man with Grace Sherman?" Seth asked.

"Cliff Harding," Justine told him and giggled. "She went out of her way to tell me they weren't dating, but I think they must be."

"Has anyone heard from Dan?"

"Not that I know of. Mom said the divorce will be final the Monday before Thanksgiving."

"That's next week."

"I know."

The idea of divorce had a sobering effect on Justine. Her father had been at the reception, but Marge wasn't. She wondered if there was anything wrong between her father and his second wife. If so, she didn't want to know about it. Maybe Marge had purposely stayed away, realizing the situation would be awkward. Jack Griffin had been one of the first to arrive and then stood in the background while her mother and father took center stage. It must have been difficult for him, since Olivia had barely had a moment to spend with him.

"You're frowning."

Justine looked at her husband, and all she could see was his love. She didn't want that to change, not ever. "I hope you'll always love me, Seth," she whispered.

"Jussie, how can you say such a thing?" he asked, "I'll draw my last breath loving you."

"Promise?"

"With my very heart," he said, gathering her into his arms.

"I don't want what happened to my parents to happen to us."

Seth kissed her brow. "It won't. We won't let it."

Her parents' divorce had taken place a long time ago; nevertheless, Justine remained affected by it. She knew she must sound insecure and emotionally needy, and blamed the fact that she was so tired. Seeing her parents together, laughing and chatting with their guests at the wedding reception, had reminded Justine of the happy life they'd all shared before Jordan's death.

"I miss my family," Justine whispered.

"I'm sorry James couldn't be here."

Her brother was in the Navy, stationed in San Diego, and had been unable to attend the reception. "I wish he could've come, too."

"But it wasn't your brother you were talking about, was it?"

"No. I so badly want everything to go back the way it was before the summer of 1986." She paused, swallowing hard. "I remember how furious I was at Jordan that morning for reading my diary. And...and then that afternoon my twin brother was dead and my parents—

my entire family was never the same again.'' Justine turned to look at her husband, tears in her eyes. ''None of us ever got over it.''

''I know.'' Seth rubbed her cheeks softly with his thumb, catching the first tears. He continued to hold her close. ''I'll always love you,'' he promised again.

Raising her head, she sought his mouth. Their kisses quickly deepened, taking on an urgency that was growing familiar.

Seth lifted her into his arms as though she weighed next to nothing. He carried her into the bedroom and helped her remove her dress before stripping out of his own clothes.

Their lovemaking was slow and emotional, and they clung to each other for a long time afterward.

''Will it always be this good?'' she asked, kissing her husband's shoulder.

''I hope so,'' Seth teased.

''Seth?''

''Hmm?''

''What do you think about children?''

''Children? You mean, as in us having a baby?''

''Yes.'' That was exactly what she meant.

''Now?''

''Well...soon.''

''How soon?'' he asked.

She took a moment to mull over the question. ''I was hoping very soon, say in nine or ten months. If you agree.'' She let her smooth, silky leg stroke his.

''You once told me you didn't want children.''

''I changed my mind. How do you feel about a child—or two?''

''I'd be thrilled, but only if you're sure.''

''I'm sure.''

Seth kissed her neck and let his lips travel over her collarbone and then lower. Justine arched her back and moaned softly as he gently sucked her nipple.

Seth moved from one breast to the other, pausing in between. "One question."

"Anything," she whispered, panting and eager for him to make love to her again.

"Do twins run in your family?"

Justine laughed. "Every generation."

Seth gave an exaggerated groan. "I was afraid of that."

"If we happen to have a boy..." she murmured as he continued to explore her body. She ran her hands over his broad shoulders and sighed at the exquisite sensations she experienced.

"Hmm..."

"I'd like to name him after my brother."

Seth raised his head so that their eyes met in the moonlit room. "So would I."

"I think Jordan would be honored to have our son carry his name."

Seth's eyes seemed to glisten. "I think we should start on this baby project now, don't you?"

A moment later, he moved over her, and Justine opened her body and her heart to receive his love. Her life could never return to the way it was before that summer afternoon sixteen years ago. Yet for the first time since that day, she felt truly free to create a new happiness. Hers and Seth's.

—

Seven

Now that Justine and Seth's wedding reception was over, Olivia could concentrate on Thanksgiving. Sitting in chambers after a day spent working out legal solutions in family court, she flipped the pages of her calendar and was dismayed to see that the holiday was almost upon her. Where had the days gone? She could barely remember when she'd last seen Jack. Was that her fault or— No, he was the one avoiding her, she decided. Olivia shook her head; she didn't want to dwell on her on-again, off-again relationship with Jack Griffin.

There was a polite knock on the door. A tap Olivia instantly recognized as her mother's. Charlotte enjoyed sitting in Olivia's courtroom from time to time. She claimed she got her best knitting done while listening to Olivia's cases. Only rarely did she visit Olivia while she was in chambers, and then it was usually because she had a strong opinion on one of her daughter's cases. Charlotte usually managed to convey her views in a direct and unequivocal manner.

"Come in, Mom," Olivia called.

"How'd you know it was me?" Charlotte asked, stepping into the room. She carried her knitting bag, which was twice as large as her not insignificant purse.

Her mother gazed approvingly at the dark mahogany bookcases, which lined three walls.

Olivia swallowed a smile. "What's on your mind, Mom?"

Charlotte set her knitting bag on the green leather sofa and sank into its thick cushions. "Do you realize it's almost Thanksgiving?"

"Just now. I swear I don't know what happened to this month."

"I was just thinking we should invite Jack over this year. How do you feel about that?"

Actually, Olivia felt fine about it. Regardless of who'd been avoiding whom, an invitation to Thanksgiving dinner might go a long way toward healing the breach. "That's a marvelous idea."

Her mother glowed with pleasure.

"His son is still living with him, so we'll want to include Eric, too," Olivia reminded her.

"Of course," Charlotte readily agreed.

"What about Cliff Harding? Will he be alone?"

Charlotte picked up her knitting bag and rested it on her knees. "I talked to him just the other day, and he's flying to the East Coast to join his daughter and her family."

"How nice." Olivia was fond of Cliff, and she especially liked the patient way he dealt with Charlotte—and with Grace, too. She was pleased that he'd accepted the invitation to attend Justine and Seth's wedding reception. His presence had obviously made the event that much more pleasurable for Grace, especially since he'd spent most of the afternoon at her side. Grace seemed more like her old self when Cliff was around. It was touching to see her respond to a man's attention. When Dan disappeared, Grace had assumed she must be lacking in some way. For months, she'd blamed herself, although Olivia was certain the blame couldn't be hers.

"I'll do the pies," Charlotte said. "Mincemeat, apple, pumpkin and pear. I do love a good pear pie."

"What about the dinner rolls?" Olivia asked hopefully. Her mother's homemade rolls were a treat not to be forgotten.

"Of course. That's understood."

They completed the menu—who'd be bringing what. Olivia was responsible for the turkey, dressing and all the trimmings. Olivia would ask Justine to provide the fruit salad and whatever else she wanted to contribute. Jack and Eric would be their guests.

As soon as her mother left, Olivia reached for the phone and punched in Jack's number at the newspaper office. She was connected to his line right away.

"Griffin," he barked, sounding preoccupied.

"Lockhart," Olivia returned.

"Olivia." His voice softened. "Hi."

"Hi, yourself. What are you doing?"

"Tell me what you're wearing first." That teasing quality was back in his voice.

"Jack! I'm at the courthouse."

"Okay, what do you have on under your robe?"

"Would you stop?"

He sighed as if restraint demanded a lot of effort. "What's up? Miss me, do you?"

"I called to invite you and Eric to Thanksgiving dinner with Mom, Justine, Seth and me."

"You are? I mean, sure. Great. We'd love it."

"You didn't have any other plans?"

"Nope," Jack told her. "Well, I was going to get a frozen turkey-in-a-box out of the freezer department and bake that. This'll be something to look forward to. It'd be perfect if only..." He hesitated.

"If what?" she asked.

"Would you mind inviting one other person?"

"Who?"

"There's this other woman I've been dating for the last few weeks who's lonely and—"

"Jack!"

"You don't believe me?"

"Not for a moment." Olivia was having a hard time not laughing out loud. She'd been worried about their relationship, but everything seemed back to normal.

"I'm serious about inviting someone else," he said, and the teasing left his voice. "Would you mind terribly if I asked Shelly Larson to join us?"

"Eric's girlfriend? The one he thinks is pregnant with someone else's baby?" Olivia frowned.

"I'm desperate for those two to reconcile," Jack told her. "My son is miserable without her. He loves Shelly, and I think if they were to meet on neutral ground they just might be able to patch things up. Yes, it'll take some adjusting on Eric's part, but he's willing if Shelly is, too."

Olivia didn't want to get caught in the middle of this conflict, but she realized that Jack was at his wits' end. Eric and Shelly were obviously at an impasse—and Eric showed no sign of moving out of Jack's house.

"Would you do that, Olivia?" Jack pleaded. "For the sake of my sanity."

And their relationship, Olivia added silently. "On one condition." She said. "I don't think it's a good idea to spring this on Eric, or on Shelly, for that matter. You have to tell Eric I'm inviting her."

"Done," he promised. "But will you talk to Shelly

for me? Please? I don't want to sound like I'm meddling."

"But you are," Olivia pointed out.

"Yes, but I don't see any other alternative. They can't seem to resolve this on their own."

"All right, give me her phone number," she said with a sigh. She wrote it down and then made little squiggly lines around the numbers while they continued to talk.

"You doing anything exciting tonight?" Jack asked, and his voice dipped to a sexy growl.

"I don't know. What have you got in mind?"

"The Chamber of Commerce is having an open house. Wanna go?" Jack's suggestive tone implied a night of passionate lovemaking, not a rather dull business event.

"I just might be able to fit it into my busy social calendar."

"Can I pick you up at seven?"

"Seven's good."

"Wear something sexy."

"For the Chamber of Commerce?"

"No, Olivia," he said blandly, "for me."

The smile lasted a long time after the conversation had ended.

As soon as Olivia got home, she called Shelly Larson. After a lengthy explanation of who she was and why she'd phoned, she waited for a response to her invitation.

"Does Eric know about this?" Shelly asked.

Her voice was soft and well-modulated. Olivia tried to match it to the photograph Eric had once shown her. As she recalled, Shelly was a petite brunette who worked for a Seattle-based advertising agency. She'd been living with Eric for almost two years.

"Jack suggested I invite you," Olivia said. "I agreed on the condition that neither of you walked into this blind. He's hoping you and Eric can settle things once and for all."

Shelly didn't respond; apparently she was still considering the invitation.

"Do you have family in the area?" Olivia asked, wanting to get some idea of Shelly's support system.

"No—my mother died when I was a baby and my dad hasn't really been part of my life. I was raised by my grandmother, but she's been gone for three years now."

"So you're on your own."

"Yes." She didn't seem interested in continuing with that theme. Instead, she burst out, "I just don't understand why Eric doesn't believe the baby is his. It's an insult to me and to everything I stand for."

Olivia certainly didn't want to take sides. According to Jack, his son was incapable of fathering children, but stranger things had happened. "Men are just dense sometimes," she said, hoping she sounded sympathetic.

"I very much appreciate the dinner invitation," Shelly said, her voice gaining strength and conviction, "but I have to refuse. Eric and I are finished."

"Not if you're carrying his child," Olivia reminded her. "In that case, the relationship is far from over."

"It doesn't matter. Eric doesn't believe me, and as far as I'm concerned, the courts can deal with this. I don't want to put a damper on your Thanksgiving—that wouldn't be fair to you or Jack or your other guests. It was very thoughtful of Jack to want to include me, but it just won't work."

Olivia didn't feel comfortable ending the conversation just yet, now that she knew Shelly was alone in the world. "I'd like to keep in touch, Shelly, if you don't mind?"

"I guess that would be okay. Jack has a right to know his grandchild."

They hung up shortly afterward, and Olivia stood there, thinking over what had been said. The young woman had shown extraordinary wisdom in declining the invitation, in Olivia's opinion. She could sense how badly Shelly wanted to be included in the festivities, yet she'd refused, knowing that the others would be made uncomfortable by the situation between her and Eric.

Jack arrived promptly at seven. "Well?" he asked hopefully. "Did you talk to Shelly?"

"I did, and she turned us down."

"No." Jack groaned and ran all ten fingers through his hair in abject frustration.

"What did Eric say?"

"He'd come to dinner if Shelly came, but otherwise he was thinking of joining a few of his friends over in Kirkland where he works."

"Maybe that's for the best," Olivia said.

"Not for me," Jack cried.

And not for them either, Olivia supposed.

"Damn, I was counting on better news than this." He slumped onto her chair, then reached inside his jacket. "I've had this for weeks and was waiting for the right time to give it to you." He took out a gaily wrapped package. "It's your birthday gift."

She stared at him in complete astonishment.

"Go ahead," he urged. "Open it."

Olivia took the gift, sat down next to Jack and untied the ribbon.

"I'm sorry it's late," he said, watching her anxiously.

She peeled away the paper and lifted the lid of a gray velvet box. The instant she saw the diamond tennis bracelet, she let out a gasp.

"Do you like it?" he asked.

"Jack, I...I'm not sure what to say."

"I wanted you to know how important you are to me, Olivia."

"Oh, Jack..." She struggled to tell him how thrilled she was and then decided that words weren't necessary. With great care she set the box aside and slipped her arms around Jack's neck, kissing him in a way that would leave him in no doubt of her appreciation.

Thanksgiving would be a quiet day for Grace with just Maryellen for company. The divorce had been declared final on Monday. She didn't have to appear in court; Mark Spellman had phoned her late in the afternoon with the news that everything had gone smoothly. As of Monday afternoon, she was no longer married to Dan. All the paperwork had been signed, sealed and notarized. She was a single woman again.

Thanksgiving morning, Grace woke early. Just as she had a year ago. But last Thanksgiving she'd bought a twenty-pound turkey. While she stuffed the bird and prepared it for roasting, Dan had bantered with her and then gone outside to cut firewood. Later, Kelly and Paul had come to dinner and Maryellen did, too. It had been a pleasant day, a family day, full of laughter and warmth.

This year, Kelly and Paul were driving to his parents' home, Dan was gone and the twenty-pound turkey had been replaced by a small turkey breast and a store-bought pumpkin pie.

Grace found it impossible to contain her emotions. The house had never felt so big and empty. Sensing her mood, Buttercup stayed close to Grace as she wandered aimlessly from room to room.

Shortly after she'd filed for divorce, Grace had cleaned out Dan's side of the closet. Although she'd searched his clothes before, desperate for some hint as to why her husband had disappeared and where, she'd gone through each shirt and pants pocket a second and even a third time. Then she'd folded up his clothes and set them aside to donate to charity. They were neatly piled in bags and boxes, which she'd left in one of the empty bedrooms for the moment.

The phone rang, and glancing at her watch, Grace saw that it was barely seven.

"Hello," she said, wondering who would phone this early.

A burst of static answered her.

"Hello," she said again, more loudly this time. An uneasy feeling came over her when the line was suddenly disconnected. She hung up but kept her hand on the phone for a few seconds. How…strange. This was just the kind of stunt Dan would pull. Dear God in heaven, *could* it have been him?

Was he, too, thinking about their Thanksgiving just a year ago? Perhaps he missed her; perhaps he'd read about the divorce in the paper's legal announcements. Dear God, this was craziness! Sheer absurdity. She *had* to let go of Dan, she had to stop thinking about him.

Her marriage was over, and she had to move on to the next stage of her life.

Maryellen got to the house around noon. By then, Grace had the potatoes on to boil and the turkey breast was baking, browning nicely. She planned to mash the potatoes with garlic and serve broccoli and a small salad. "It smells good in here," her daughter said as she let herself in the kitchen door.

She set a small pot of bronze chrysanthemums in the middle of the table and kissed Grace on the cheek.

"I made that orange-cranberry relish you like so much," Grace said.

"Oh, Mom, that's great. It just wouldn't seem like Thanksgiving without your relish." She opened the refrigerator and peeked inside. "My goodness, how much did you make?"

"Just what the recipe calls for." Maryellen's question was yet another reminder that it was only the two of them this year. "Take whatever you want home with you."

"Okay." Maryellen moved restlessly around the kitchen. "Do you need me to do anything?"

"Everything's pretty much under control."

Her daughter walked down the hallway to what had once been her bedroom. She returned a couple of minutes later. "I see you've got Dad's stuff packed up."

Tears clogged Grace's throat. She nodded. "The divorce was final on Monday."

"I know." Maryellen gently squeezed her arm. "How are you handling this?"

"About the same as you did when your divorce came through."

Maryellen sighed deeply. "That bad?"

Grace looked away, determined not to allow this day of giving thanks to become a day of grief and anger.

The phone rang and Grace motioned for Maryellen to answer, fearing that if she spoke now, her voice would crack.

"Hello," Maryellen said, then frowned. "Hello? *Hello?*" After a moment, she hung up the receiver. "That was weird. There was no one at the other end."

"I got a call like that earlier," Grace said. "No one answered then, either."

Maryellen stared at her with stricken eyes. "Do you...think it was Dad?"

Grace had already guessed exactly that, but she had no way of knowing for sure. Cutting back on expenses had been important, and soon after Dan's disappearance, she'd cancelled Caller ID and the other extras the phone company offered.

"Why would he do such a thing?" Maryellen demanded, sounding angry now. "Why can't he just stay out of our lives instead of playing these sick games?"

"I suppose he misses us," Grace said. It was the only reason she could think of.

"If he misses us so much, why doesn't he come home?" Maryellen shouted. "I'm going to tell him that." She reached for the phone and started punching in numbers.

"Who are you calling?" Grace asked.

"Star 69."

"It won't work," Grace said, her voice tight. "I couldn't afford all those extras.... Dan must've known that. He must've figured out that I wouldn't be able to trace the call." She closed her eyes in a futile effort to regain her emotional balance. "Sometimes I think I hate him for doing this to us."

"Mom, it's all right. We can't let him ruin our day...."

"Your father and I were married for more than thirty-five years." Her legs felt shaky and she sank into a kitchen chair.

The phone rang again.

"Don't answer it!" Grace said. "Don't give him the satisfaction. Let it ring, just let it ring."

On the fifth ring, the answering machine came on, and once more the only sound they heard was static.

Maryellen pulled out a chair and sat down across from Grace. She took her mother's hands, clasping them tightly. "I don't know why Dad left," she whispered, "but whatever the reason, it wasn't because of anything you did or didn't do. You're a wonderful mother and you were a good wife."

Grace hung her head, watching as her tears dripped onto the quilted place mat. "Thank you, sweetheart." She wished she could believe Maryellen, but she didn't think men walked away from long-term marriages if they were content.

She sniffled and made an effort to put the phone calls out of her mind. Maryellen released her hands, passing her a tissue to wipe her eyes.

"I wish Cliff Harding was here," Maryellen said forcefully. "That would shake Dad up, wouldn't it? It'd serve him right if a man answered the phone."

Grace smiled shakily. "That it would."

The potato water had begun to boil over, and Grace leaped up to turn down the burner. She used those few seconds to compose herself and when she returned to the table, she was smiling.

"Mom," Maryellen said hesitantly. "What about

you and Mr. Harding? Are the two of you going to start dating now that the divorce is final?''

Grace had been thinking about this for weeks, unable to arrive at a firm decision. In fact, she'd put Cliff off once already. ''Probably not,'' she told her daughter.

''You should,'' Maryellen urged. ''I like him. I know Kelly might have a hard time accepting another man in your life, but she'll get used to it.''

''It isn't because of what Kelly will say—or you or anyone else, for that matter,'' Grace confessed. ''Don't misunderstand me, I like Cliff, but I'm not ready to enter the dating world.''

''But Mom...''

''It's too soon. I still feel too raw. I thought...I hoped I'd find some closure when the divorce became final, but I can see now that isn't going to happen. I have to *know,* Maryellen. I need answers. Where's your father? Why couldn't he tell me where he went or why? What deep, dark secret is he hiding from us?''

Grace knew very well that life didn't always supply the answers. Perhaps one day she'd find peace. But for now there was none. Instead, the uncertainty and the anger and grief raged inside her, as strong as they'd been the day her husband disappeared. Not that her life was devoid of happiness or that she didn't still have plenty to be thankful for. She had her daughters, her friends, her job, but—

''You *have* to, Mom. You have to.''

Her daughter said this with such urgency Grace didn't know how to respond.

''If you don't, I'm afraid you'll end up like me.''

''And what exactly is wrong with you?'' Grace asked sharply.

''Look at me!'' Maryellen cried. ''I'm thirty-five and

I'm terrified of falling in love again. I don't trust my own judgment. I practically have a panic attack if a man wants to kiss me. I'm so afraid of what might happen that I refuse to allow any man close to me. I look at Kelly and Paul, and they seem so happy and so normal. Why couldn't my marriage have been like that?"

"Oh, Maryellen..." Grace had no idea what to tell her daughter. Maryellen so rarely spoke of her marriage that she felt at a loss as to how to comfort her.

"I love little Tyler so much. But I'm never going to have a child of my own."

"Don't say that. You're still young," Grace insisted.

Maryellen shook her head. "Don't let your divorce do to you what mine did to me," she repeated. "Please, Mom. You have a lot of good years ahead of you. If you get another chance at love, take it! Promise me you'll take it—and that you'll be happy. Otherwise I don't think I'll ever find any kind of contentment myself."

Thanksgiving with her mother had been one of the most disturbing days of her life, Maryellen thought as she opened the gallery first thing Friday morning. She still felt emotionally drained from it. If she could've taken today off, she would have. But she expected to be swamped with customers in what was traditionally the biggest shopping day of the year.

With so many people stopping by the gallery, it was almost two before she had a chance to eat her leftover-turkey sandwich. The only reason she had a moment to herself then was due to her assistant, Lois Habbersmith, who'd agreed to work the afternoon with her. The gallery's absentee owners, the Webbers, lived in

California and trusted Maryellen to handle all aspects of the business.

Sitting on a stool in the back room, Maryellen crossed her legs and had just taken the first bite of her sandwich when Jon Bowman entered the room.

"Jon..." She hadn't expected him. Already her heart was hammering wildly. He'd phoned twice since the Halloween party and she'd managed to avoid speaking to him both times.

"Still running away?" he asked.

"I don't know what you mean," she lied.

He grinned, letting her know she hadn't fooled him. "Could you use some more pictures?"

"Yes," she said, eager for as much of his work as he was willing to let her have. "That last group completely sold out."

"Can I get them to you this evening?"

She wondered why he hadn't brought them now. "Yes, that would be fine. What time?"

"Seven."

The gallery closed at six. "I can wait for you here," she told him. She'd hang the photographs right away so they'd be ready for sale tomorrow.

"I want you to pick them up at my house," he said matter-of-factly. "I promise you, the drive will be worth your while."

Maryellen frowned. How clever of him to make sure she didn't have a previous commitment. "I'd prefer to have you bring them here." That was how their arrangement had worked in the past.

"I know you would, but not this time. I'm making dinner for you. If you want the pictures you'll be at my place at seven."

She started to argue, to tell him she wouldn't be

blackmailed, but he didn't give her the opportunity. He simply walked away. If she was going to argue, she'd have to follow him into the crowded gallery, and he knew she wouldn't do that.

Twice that same afternoon, Maryellen had inquiries about Jon's work, and she found herself promising they'd be available the next day. His pictures sold almost as fast as they appeared on the walls. If she wanted more, he'd made it plain she'd have to come and get them herself.

At seven, muttering under her breath, Maryellen drove down a dark country road, using a flashlight to check addresses on mailboxes, searching for Jon's driveway. When she finally located the proper drive, she turned into the dirt-and-gravel lane and drove another mile. Just when she was about to give up, the two-story house came into view.

She parked in the back, climbed out and stopped to look over the dancing lights of Seattle twinkling on the other side of Puget Sound. His home must be close to the waterfront. A ferry, with lights blazing, glided across the water in the distance.

"I wondered if you'd come," Jon said from somewhere in the darkness. He emerged from the shadows to welcome her.

"You didn't leave me much choice." She wasn't happy about this and she wanted him to know it.

"No, I didn't," he agreed. "Come inside."

"I...I can't stay for dinner. I hope you didn't go to any trouble."

"I went to a tremendous amount of trouble. I'd like you to stay. Please."

"But..." He left her no option but to follow him into the house.

The interior was only partially finished, she noticed. Pieces of furniture were positioned on bare floors. The walls were mostly framed in although unpainted. The kitchen had new appliances and white-tile countertops, but only a plywood sub-floor. A linen-covered table with candles sat in what must be the living room. The light was dim, coming entirely from a couple of small table lamps and what spilled through from the kitchen. Large picture windows revealed a staggering view of the Seattle skyline.

"Let me take your coat," Jon said.

Maryellen wanted to resist, she really did. Instead she slipped the coat from her shoulders. Jon took it and walked over to a closet without doors and placed it on a hanger.

"Would you like to see my home?" he asked.

She nodded. "Who's the builder?"

"Me," he said with a chuckle. "I'm doing everything myself."

She remembered Jon telling Terri he was a jack-of-all-trades. Now she realized how accurate that statement was. He led her through the house. The only room with a door was the bathroom. The master bedroom was upstairs and had a balcony facing the water.

"I sit out there in the summer with my morning coffee," Jon told her.

Maryellen could imagine it—the peace and silence, the clear, fresh beauty of Puget Sound in early morning.

"I have five acres here," he continued. "Before you wonder how could I afford this property, I should tell you the land belonged to my grandfather. He purchased it back in the 1950s for practically nothing. When he died he left it to me.'' A timer rang in the kitchen. ''Dinner's ready.''

He helped her down the stairs, leading the way and clasping her hand in his own. Once back in the main part of the house, he escorted her to the table and pulled out a chair.

''Can I do anything?'' she asked.

''No,'' he assured her.

First he lit the candles. The he poured the wine, a spicy Gewurztraminer. After that, he brought out a salad—lettuce with sliced fresh pear, shaves of Roquefort cheese and wonderful honey-coated roasted walnuts. The dressing was a delicate raspberry vinaigrette.

''Oh, my,'' Maryellen whispered after one taste. ''This is incredible.''

''It's only the beginning,'' Jon promised.

They had one glass of wine with the salad and another before the entrée of baked salmon with a dill sauce so creamy Maryellen closed her eyes to savor the first bite. Dessert was an apple-and-date torte.

Between courses, Jon filled her wineglass again, opening a second bottle, and when they'd finished dinner, Maryellen was warm and slightly dizzy. He brought her to a comfortable sofa. A classical CD—she recognized Vivaldi's ''Four Seasons''—played in the background.

''I'm going to need lots of coffee,'' she told him.

''It's already brewing.''

She could smell the rich aroma. Feeling flushed and utterly content, she leaned her head against the back of the sofa and looked out over the astonishing view. Lights twinkled like fireflies in the distance, and the dark water reflected a three-quarter moon. Jon had turned off the lights, so her own image wasn't mirrored in the glass. There was nothing to interfere with the view.

He sat down next to her. ''That wasn't so bad now, was it?'' Then as if she might misunderstand the question, he added, ''Being here with me, I mean.''

''It's been very...nice.''

''Admit it. I'm not so frightening, am I?''

She shifted sideways to look at him and smiled. ''You can be.''

''When?''

''When you kiss me.'' It must be the wine talking, yet it was the truth.

Jon took her hand and examined her long, tapering fingers. ''This might come as s surprise, but your kisses frighten me, too.''

''I frighten you?'' This didn't surprise so much as amuse Maryellen.

As if to prove his point, he bent forward and pressed his mouth to hers. It was a gentle, undemanding kiss but one that promised so much more.

''See?'' he said in a low voice, sounding unlike himself. He flattened her hand against his chest. ''Feel my heart.''

''Yes... It's beating hard.'' Her own heart was pounding, too. Wanting to reveal what his kisses did to her, she leaned toward him and placed her mouth over his. The kiss was deeper, longer, more involved. By the time it ended, Maryellen's head was swimming. ''Feel *my* heart,'' she whispered.

Jon laid his large hand over her chest, but then as though he couldn't resist, he cupped her breast. He gave her ample opportunity to stop him, but she couldn't. The feelings his touch produced in her were too exciting. Too enticing. His fingers fumbled with the buttons on her blouse as he continued to kiss her. Even before he'd finished, she reached behind and released her bra, letting her breasts spill forward. Jon caught them with both hands and groaned when she leaned closer and ran her tongue along the inner edge of his ear.

After that, everything happened so fast, Maryellen lost track of who undressed whom. All she knew was that they were on the sofa and Jon was about to make love to her. His eyes held hers as he positioned himself above her.

"Do you want this?" he asked.

She closed her eyes and nodded, so eager for him that she wrapped her arms tightly around him and urged his mouth back to hers.

"Say it," he insisted.

"Yes, please."

Their lovemaking was long and slow. And it was exquisite, unlike anything she'd ever experienced. At some point during the night, they moved upstairs to his bed. Exhausted, Maryellen fell into a deep sleep with Jon's body curled around hers, his arm over her waist, his hand pressing her close.

Shortly before dawn, with morning just beginning to light the sky, she stirred. Startled, barely aware of her surroundings, Maryellen woke and abruptly sat up. "Where am I?" she asked.

"You're with me," Jon said and brought her back into his arms. He kissed her again and she turned to face him.

The second time they made love, she sat atop him, her long hair streaming over her shoulders and onto her breasts.

In the morning, Maryellen woke first and lay quietly

in his arms for several moments, considering what she'd done. Jon Bowman had seduced her—and she'd let him. He'd wined and dined her and then he'd lured her into his bed—and she'd let him. She'd been a willing participant, without a thought to birth control or any form of protection. This was insanity.

Careful not to disturb him, she slipped out of the bed, mortified to find she was completely nude. Tiptoeing down the stairs, she gathered her clothes piece by piece and held them against her breasts. She'd put her underwear on and was stepping into her wool slacks when Jon appeared at the top of the stairs, naked from the waist up.

"You're sneaking away?" he asked.

She didn't answer. Her intentions were obvious, and they didn't include breakfast over coffee and a newspaper, either. "That shouldn't have happened."

"But it did. Are you going to pretend it didn't?"

Her face burned red. "Yes."

"Maryellen, be reasonable."

"No—we have a professional relationship. It can't be anything else."

"Why not?"

She didn't have any answers without launching into explanations she didn't want to give. "Because it can't. I'm sorry, but this is the way it has to be."

"You owe me more than that."

"I owe you nothing." She continued dressing as fast as she could, zipping up her pants. "You planned this little seduction. The wine, the dinner, the music..."

"The hell I did! You wanted me as much as I wanted you. If you're going to be angry, fine, but at least be honest."

"Yes, I wanted you, but I would never have slept

with you if you hadn't blackmailed me into coming out here. You had everything planned—right down to the three glasses of wine, didn't you?'' She flipped the hair away from her face and grabbed her blouse. She jerked her arms into the sleeves and didn't bother to fasten the buttons before walking over to the closet and grabbing her coat. She yanked it free and left the hanger swinging.

''Maryellen,'' he pleaded. ''Don't leave like this. Don't lie to me, and don't lie to yourself. I didn't plan what happened.''

''It's very clear that you did.'' When she was young and naive and a virgin, Clint had lured her into his bed with wine and promises. They'd taken wild, irresponsible chances with pregnancy, just as she'd done now. In all the years since her marriage and divorce, she'd apparently learned nothing.

''Fine,'' he snapped. ''Believe what you want, but I know the truth and so do you.''

Maryellen stomped out, and it wasn't until she'd driven halfway home that she remembered the photographs.

Eight

Jack didn't know how much longer he'd be able to stand having Eric in his house. His very *small* house. When he went to make breakfast that morning, he discovered an empty bread sack. Eric had eaten the last of the bread. That was just the most recent instance of his son's thoughtlessness. He wondered how Shelly coped with Eric's slovenly behavior, cursing as he shoved plates and cups into the dishwasher.

Doing his best to control his irritation, Jack decided he could go without his morning toast. It would be good for his waistline. However his attitude didn't improve when he discovered that Eric had used up most of the hot water for his own shower and then thrown in a load of wash.

Unaware that the hot water tank was empty, Jack stepped into the stall and turned on the water, only to be drenched in icy spray. Yelping, he slammed open the glass door, scrambled out and grabbed a towel. Unfortunately it was damp from Eric's shower. His son had managed to use both towels, so there wasn't a dry one for Jack.

"That does it!" he shouted, flinging down the towel. When Eric had first come to live with him, it was supposed to be for a few days. This had gone on for weeks now, and Jack was putting an end to it.

His disposition was quickly moving from irritation to outrage as he tried to dress, still wet from the shower. Twice he had to stop and take deep breaths in order to calm his thundering heart. As far as he could see, Eric and Shelly were at a stalemate. Neither one of them was going to budge. Jack had hoped they'd patch things up on Thanksgiving Day at Olivia's. Unfortunately, Shelly had refused the invitation.

Eric had tried to hide his feelings, but they were all too transparent. His son had pinned his hopes on seeing Shelly over the Thanksgiving holiday, and her refusal had left him reeling. He was convinced she was involved with someone else now. That was when Jack had convinced Eric to visit a fertility clinic. Following the visit, Eric had gone into a depression that had lasted for days.

Not knowing what else to do, Jack felt he had no choice but to take matters into his own hands. By the time he reached the newspaper office, he'd formed a plan of action. He was going to call Shelly himself.

Luckily he had her work number, and when they connected, he suggested they meet for dinner. Shelly agreed and they set a time, choosing a place on the Seattle waterfront. Things had to change, and quickly. For his son's sake…and his own.

At six-thirty that same day, Shelly met Jack at the fancy seafood restaurant. She'd already been seated and was waiting for him. She hadn't seen him yet and he took advantage of the moment to study her. Shelly was a pretty girl, petite and fragile-looking, especially now. Jack was surprised to see that she was already wearing a maternity top. Easy enough to guess that she was pregnant.

"Hello, Shelly," he said, kissing her on the cheek before sitting across from her.

"Mr. Griffin."

"Please," he insisted, "call me Jack."

"All right." She lowered her gaze, apparently reading the menu, but Jack had the feeling she already knew what she wanted to order. He knew what *he* wanted. The crab cakes were excellent. But this meeting wasn't about crab cakes or any other menu item.

"I imagine you're wondering why I called you," Jack said as he set aside the menu.

"I assume it has to do with Eric." Then, as if she couldn't help herself, she asked. "How is he?"

"Not great," Jack told her. "He misses you."

Shelly looked toward the pier and the expanse of black inky water beyond. "I miss him, too." Her voice was soft.

"Was my son always such a slob?" Jack tossed in the question, hoping for a lighter mood. Eric could well have come by it naturally. His own lack of orderliness had never bothered Jack much, but Eric's drove him to distraction. Besides, Eric far surpassed him in any slob competition.

"Always," Shelly said with the beginning of a smile. "I'm the organized one. Is he eating all right?"

It probably wasn't a good idea to admit his son was eating him out of house and home. "He seems to be doing just fine in that department. How about you?"

Shelly smiled a little more, and Jack noticed how pale she was. "I'm constantly hungry. I've never had an appetite like this in my life. I have breakfast and then by midmorning I'm so ravenous I have a second breakfast."

That explained why she was already into maternity

tops. The poor girl had turned to food to help her through this difficult time. Jack wished he knew what to say.

"Have you talked to Eric recently?" he asked, carefully broaching the subject.

"No...we haven't spoken since a week before Thanksgiving."

"Then you don't know." Jack's heart fell. So Eric hadn't told her.

"Know what?"

"I convinced Eric to visit one of those fertility clinics and have his sperm tested. You claim this baby is his and Eric says it can't be because of something a doctor told us years ago."

Shelly brightened immediately. "That was a great idea. Then he knows the baby is his."

"Unfortunately, no." Jack glanced around, surprised they hadn't seen a waiter yet. As if on cue, the man stepped forward. Jack asked for coffee and the crab cakes; Shelly ordered the garden salad, with extra ranch dressing on the side, chicken fettuccini Alfredo, plus an order of garlic-and-cheese bread. Jack suspected that if desserts had been listed on the main menu, she would have ordered that, too.

"Explain what you meant about Eric. If he went to the clinic, then he *must* know he's the baby's father," Shelly pressed. She spread the linen napkin over her lap and smoothed it out vigorously, as if a wrinkle were cause for disciplinary action. Her face was tight with anxiety.

"According to the report, the likelihood of Eric fathering children is highly improbable." Jack hated to be the bearer of bad news, but he assumed Eric had told her. He'd figured their subsequent conversation, more than the report, was the cause of his son's depression. "I read the clinic's report myself. His sperm count is very low. There *is* a minuscule possibility he fathered the child, but he doesn't see that. All he read were the words *highly improbable.*"

Shelly lowered her eyes and Jack wondered if she was struggling not to weep. "That explains a great deal," she whispered.

"Oh?" Jack didn't mean to pry, but if she was going to volunteer the information...

"It explains why he hasn't called me. He doesn't believe the baby's his. He obviously thinks I cheated on him, and I resent that. His lack of faith in me is very hurtful, Jack." She stared down at the table. "But despite all that, he's continuing to make the rent payments. He knows I can't handle them with what I'm earning."

Jack wanted to groan out loud. While he appreciated the fact that Eric was generous, it also meant it could be years before he moved out on his own. Jack was stuck with his son.

"I told Eric not to, that I'd make the payments on my own, but he's still covering the rent." She paused, shaking her head. "I'm grateful. I don't know what I'd do if I had to manage rent plus everything else."

"Forgive me for being blunt here," Jack said, "but I need the truth. Is Eric the father of your baby?"

For the first time Shelly's eyes met his. "This baby is your son's. As soon as he or she is born, I'll be able to prove it without a doubt. Until then, I don't think it would do any good for Eric and me to see each other again."

That answered Jack's other question even before he had the opportunity to ask. "I see."

"Thank you for your concern, Jack," she said quietly. "I appreciate it. But it doesn't matter what that clinic told Eric. Because I know differently. I'll be giving birth to the evidence in less than five months."

By the end of dinner, Jack didn't feel any closer to a solution. When he arrived home, Eric was sitting in front of the television eating from a large bag of potato chips.

"You're late," his son said, keeping his gaze focused on the television.

"I had dinner with Shelly in Seattle."

Eric reached for the remote control and turned off the TV. "You were with Shelly?" He frowned at Jack, as if waiting for him to elaborate. "Did she call you?" he finally asked.

"I called her." Jack shrugged off his raincoat and considered the best way to approach this dilemma.

"Did you tell her about the sperm test?" Eric demanded. His son was on his feet now, outrage flashing from his eyes.

"There wasn't any bread left this morning," Jack said, "and the hot water was used up and then both towels were wet and—"

"You broke my trust because I ate the last stale piece of bread in the house? Is that what you're telling me?"

"No... I was hoping that if I reasoned with Shelly, we might clear this up once and for all."

"If you want me out of here, all you have to do is ask." Eric stormed into what had once been the spare bedroom.

"I didn't say I wanted you to move out," Jack said, but his words held little conviction.

"Not a problem, Dad," Eric said, rushing out of the

room a minute later with his duffel bag. Clothes spilled out from all sides. "I'm out of here. You weren't much of a father when I needed one as a kid. I don't know what made me think you'd be any different now."

Jack groaned in frustration. He'd made a mess of this when all he'd been trying to do was get their lives back to normal. "Eric, listen, I'm sorry."

"Sorry?" Eric repeated as if this was the most ridiculous comment he'd ever heard. "It's a little late for that. Don't worry, I won't bother you anymore."

With that, he was gone and Jack wondered how long it would be before he heard from his son again.

Cedar Cove was a wonderful place to be at Christmastime, Maryellen mused as she opened the gallery the first Friday in December. Evergreen boughs were strung along both sides of Harbor Street and large festive candy canes hung from each of the streetlights. The gallery itself was decorated with tiny white lights and elegantly draped swags of spruce that scented the air. It was the smell of Christmas to Maryellen, the smell she associated with childhood holidays—and with her father. She had a sudden sharp memory of him, bringing in a fresh Christmas tree, stamping snow from his feet. Maryellen blinked back unexpected tears.

For some reason, she found herself thinking of Jon. It'd been two weeks since Maryellen had last seen him, but, she suspected it wouldn't be long before he arrived at the gallery with more of his photographs. Especially since she hadn't brought them with her when she'd left his house. Maryellen had done her best to prepare emotionally for this next confrontation. She couldn't allow what had happened to taint their business relationship. A thousand times since that night she'd wanted to kick herself for giving in to her baser instincts. She had plenty of excuses to justify her actions, but time and truth had knocked down every one of them. It wasn't the wine or the moonlight, nor could she blame Jon for seducing her. She'd been fully involved.

Almost as if Jon was aware that she was thinking of him, he showed up shortly after the gallery officially opened for business. Maryellen was busy with a customer when he came into the large open studio. She noticed that he had two framed photographs with him and guessed there were more in his vehicle.

Maryellen was still waiting on the customer as Jon made a second and then third trip, carrying photographs into the back room.

"I'm going to think it over," Mrs. Whitfield said.

It took Maryellen a moment to realize the doctor's wife was referring to the watercolor she'd been considering as a Christmas gift for her husband.

"That'll be fine," Maryellen said. Then, with far too little warning, she was alone in the back room of the gallery with Jon.

"Hello," she said stiffly, doing her best to remain cordial and polite. Before leaving his house, she'd told him their relationship, from that point forward, would be strictly business. She'd meant it.

"Hello." His eyes probed her with such intensity she looked away.

"It's a lovely morning, isn't it?" she murmured.

"The sky's a dull gray and it's threatening to rain."

She smiled weakly. Obviously, small talk wasn't working, but when had it ever with this man? "I see you've brought me a few pictures."

"These are the ones you left at my house. If you hadn't been in such a rush—"

"I appreciate your bringing them by," she said, cutting him off before he could say something else to remind her of that evening.

"I came for another reason," he said. He tucked his hands in the back pockets of his jeans. His pacing was making her nervous, and then she realized he was nervous, too. He stopped abruptly. "Are you free Sunday afternoon? There's a dinner train I've always wanted to take and I was hoping you'd agree to come as my guest."

This was exactly what Maryellen had feared was going to happen. She held her breath so long that her lungs began to ache. "Thank you, but no."

"No?" He sounded hurt and confused.

"I meant what I said earlier. It's important that our relationship not become personal."

He frowned. "A little late for that," he muttered.

She ignored his remark. "I'm not interested in seeing you outside the gallery." She couldn't make it any plainer than that.

"You were the one who invited me to the Halloween party."

"I know, and that was a mistake. The first of several. Listen, Jon, this is all rather embarrassing and awkward, but I'd consider it a favor if you forgot all about what happened."

His frown darkened. "That's really what you want?"

"Please."

It looked as though he was going to argue with her, but then he shook his head. "I don't have any other choice do I?"

"I know. Again, I'm sorry."

"Fine, whatever."

Maryellen wrote him a receipt for the pictures and held it out to him.

An uncomfortable moment passed before he took the slip, turned and walked out of the gallery. As soon as he was gone, Maryellen closed her eyes and released her pent-up tension in the form of a deep sigh. She sagged onto the stool and tried to compose herself.

"Just a minute here," Jon said, bursting back inside the room. "I don't do a good job of pretending. Maybe *you* can forget what happened, but I can't. Dammit, Maryellen, what we had was good. Surely you can see that?"

"No, I can't. Please don't make things any more difficult than they already are." She should've known he wouldn't be willing to drop this.

"I'm not the one making things difficult—you are. Let's meet and talk this out. You decide when and where."

"There's nothing to discuss."

"I don't understand you," Jon said, pacing again. The old boards creaked beneath his feet as he walked around a gorgeous blue porcelain vase she was getting ready to display. "If you want to pretend it didn't happen, fine, be my guest, but I can't. I wish to God I could because I haven't been able to stop thinking about you. About us…."

"Rest assured the matter is out of my mind."

He snorted at that, recognizing her remark for the lie it was. "If you gave us a chance," he argued, "you might discover we have something worthwhile here."

"I doubt it," she said as blandly as she could, wanting him to assume that this conversation was boring her. "I'm afraid you've misread the situation.

He stared at her. "You do this sort of thing on a regular basis?"

She laughed, hoping to sound amused when in reality she felt humiliated and ashamed. "Not in a while... Jon, I'm sorry if you read more into our night together than you should have, but—"

"I know, I know," he said, and raised his hands to stop her. "I get the picture."

She sincerely hoped he did.

"Our relationship is strictly business."

She nodded, forcing herself to smile. It probably looked more like a grimace.

He slowly surveyed the back room of the gallery. "That being the case, I won't trouble you again."

"I appreciate that, Jon," she said gratefully.

"Will you mail me a check once the photographs sell?" he asked.

Maryellen didn't immediately make the connection. "Mail you a check? You mean you won't be in again?"

"I don't think it's a good idea," he said starkly.

"Ah..." He had her flustered now. "That's exactly why I wanted to keep the personal out of this! There's no need to end our professional relationship, is there? I mean, your pictures are wonderful, really wonderful, and— You will let someone else drop off your work, won't you?"

The question fell between them and hung there for several tense seconds. While she waited for him to consider her solution, Maryellen clenched her hands behind her back. This wasn't what she wanted. She was proud to display his photographs. His work brought in customers and paid him well. It was a mutually beneficial relationship. A *business* relationship.

Jon held her gaze, and in him she saw anger and regret.

"I think it's time I made arrangements with another gallery," he said with a shrug that looked anything but casual.

Maryellen bit back words that would ask him to reconsider, that would plead with him to stay. In a small voice she managed, "If this is what you prefer, then I can only wish you the best."

"It isn't what I'd prefer," he told her flatly. "It's what you want. Goodbye, Maryellen."

A thickness formed in her throat as Jon turned and for the second time started to leave. "Oh, hell," he muttered, turning back. He walked quickly toward her. "Don't worry," he said, taking her by the shoulders. "Like I said, I don't plan to bother you again, but I would like one last memory before I go."

"What?" she asked, her voice trembling, reacting to the shock of his touch.

"This," he said hoarsely. Then he kissed her as if it was the only thing that had been on his mind from the moment she'd dashed out of his home. His kiss was hard and hot and unbearably slow. By the time he tore his mouth from hers, the blood was pounding in her ears.

Maryellen tried to prevent herself from giving him the satisfaction of a response, but when he released her, she staggered back two steps and gasped for air. Her hand went to her throat in an instinctive reaction.

Muttering something she couldn't quite hear, Jon left and this time she knew it was for good. Her legs were unsteady and Maryellen felt close to tears. Making her way to the coffeepot, she poured herself a cup and was shocked by how badly her hand trembled as she filled the mug.

He'd kissed her like that because he wanted her to remember him. To remember the night they'd spent together. His ploy had worked far too well. Maryellen shut her eyes, and their slow, seductive lovemaking played back in her mind. She recalled how he'd touched her, the feel of his strong, masculine hands as he'd explored her body, caressing her first with his fingers and then his tongue. She remembered in vivid detail the sensations she'd experienced as he made love to her. She'd wanted him with a passion that was difficult to renounce.

She hadn't set out to hurt Jon, but she could see that she had. In the process she was hurting herself, too. Jon didn't understand why she'd rejected him. He didn't know, and he never would. She'd sent him away for a reason that lay buried deep inside her.

She'd walked this path once before and still bore the scars. Sometimes emotional wounds were harder to heal than physical ones. Sometimes they never healed at all.

Strings of Christmas tree lights were spread out on the living room floor when Zach woke on Saturday morning.

"Hi, Dad," Eddie said when Zach looked in, yawning, on his way to the kitchen. His son sat amid the lights, straightening them and draping the long cords along the back of the sofa.

"What are you doing with those?" he asked. Rosie liked having the outside of the house decorated with Christmas lights, but he'd always found it a nuisance.

He glanced at the clock and saw it was barely seven. Apparently Rosie was already up.

"Mom got them out," Eddie explained, and stuck the plug into an outlet. Lights instantly blazed, nearly blinding Zach.

He suspected this was his wife's less-than-subtle hint that she wanted him to string up the lights this morning. Great, just great. She might've mentioned it earlier, but then they weren't on the best of terms these days. Remaining civil during the Christmas holidays was going to be difficult if Thanksgiving was any indication. Somehow they'd made it through the day without a major blowup—probably because Rosie had spent most of the afternoon in the kitchen with her sister, no doubt complaining about him.

"Where's your mother?" he asked irritably.

"She's gone."

"Gone?" Zach checked the time again. "Where is she now?"

"Christmas Bazaar at the high school."

"What's she doing there?"

Eddie shrugged. "She didn't tell me. Can we go to McDonald's for breakfast? I'm getting tired of Pop-Tarts."

Zach stared at his son. This nine-year-old kid actually believed the alternative to Pop-Tarts was a meal outside the home. Rosie had gotten so lax in carrying out her responsibilities as a full-time wife and mother that their children didn't even know that most families ate meals together around a table.

"Dad?"

Eddie's urgent cry cut into his thoughts. "Look!" He pointed to the television. "That's what I want for Christmas."

Zach studied the screen and watched some remote-controlled monster truck propel itself over a huge dirt mound with a deafening roar.

"Mom said I could have it."

"She did, did she?" Zach would talk to Rose about that. He wasn't forking over a couple of hundred bucks for a stupid toy. Wandering into the kitchen, he discovered that the coffee wasn't on but his wife had taken a moment to jot him a note, which she'd propped up next to the automatic drip pot.

Working until four at the Bazaar. Put up the outside lights, okay? Allison's at a slumber party and will need a ride home. If you have a chance, would you buy the Christmas tree? See you later.

Rosie

His wife had forgotten to mention she'd be working at the bazaar. That was predictable enough. But he'd hoped that for once they'd have a day together without obligations or demands. It used to be that buying the Christmas tree was a family event; they'd go to the lot together and everyone had a say. Decorating it was fun, with music playing in the background and popcorn popping and hot cider. These days, getting and trimming the tree was an afterthought, a nuisance that had to be fitted into the cracks in Rosie's overbooked schedule.

"Can we go to McDonald's for breakfast?" Eddie asked a second time.

Zach didn't answer him.

"Dad?"

"Sure," he muttered, noting that there wasn't any

milk in the refrigerator. Not only had Rosie left him with a to-do list, but the house was devoid of groceries.

Zach was furious all morning about his wife's lack of attentiveness when it came to her family. He remembered what Janice Lamond had told him about the special Saturday she'd planned for her son. She was clearly the type of mother who made her child a priority.

After breakfast at McDonald's, Zach collected Allison from her friend's place, and then, with Eddie's help, tackled putting up the Christmas lights.

"Are we going to buy our tree today?" Eddie asked while Zach stood on the ladder and attached the lights along the roofline of the house. He gazed down on his son, who was looking anxiously up at him.

"Ask your sister if she wants to come," Zach called.

"Okay." Eddie raced into the house. He wasn't gone more than fifteen seconds. "Allison said she'll come if she has to. We don't need her, do we, Dad?"

"Tell her we need her."

Eddie stared up at him, his face a picture of disbelief and disgust. Zach couldn't keep from laughing. With a twinge of regret he realized it was the first time he'd smiled all day. It wasn't his children's fault that Rosie chose to spend her day with strangers rather than her own family. Once she was home, Zach intended to have a very long talk with his wife.

Buying the Christmas tree proved to be one more annoying episode in a day that had started off badly and quickly gotten worse. By the time they returned to the house, the kids were bickering and hungry. When Zach pulled into the garage, he saw that Rosie's car was there.

"We got the tree, Mom," Eddie announced as he rushed into the kitchen.

"Hi," Zach said, determined to put on a happy front until he had a private moment with his wife. "How was your day?"

Rosie sat on the sofa with her feet up. "I'm exhausted. How did everything go at home?"

"Great," Eddie said. "Dad and I got the Christmas lights up. We went out to breakfast at McDonald's and then we stopped at the store and bought milk."

"You got groceries?" Rosie asked, a look of relief in her eyes.

"Just milk and bread." Again it was Eddie who answered. "Dad thought we should make tomato soup and toasted cheese sandwiches for lunch, and we needed stuff for that."

"It sounds like you guys had a nice day."

"Are we going to decorate the tree tonight?" Allison asked, her expression bored.

"Sure," Zach said.

"Not tonight, sweetheart," Rosie answered simultaneously.

Allison glanced from Zach to Rosie.

"I've just spent nine hours on my feet," Rosie said. "The last thing I want to do now is decorate a tree. We can do it tomorrow after church."

"I can't," Allison complained. "The French Club is having their bake sale in the mall, remember?"

"Oh, right." Rosie rubbed a hand over her eyes. "I'm not supposed to help with that, am I?"

"Yes, Mom..." Their daughter sounded both hurt and provoked.

"Okay, okay."

"What about dinner?" Zach asked.

They'd already had pizza once that week and KFC another night. Zach realized this was an especially busy time of year, but it seemed important that they have at least one meal a week as a family.

"Who wants what?" Rosie asked.

"Pizza," Eddie shouted.

"I'm not hungry," Allison insisted.

Zach frowned.

"I suppose you want meat loaf and mashed potatoes," Rosie muttered just loudly enough for Zach to hear.

"That'd be nice," he said, and then added, "for once."

"Are we going to do the tree or not?" Allison asked, slouching on the sofa next to her mother.

"Apparently not," Zach said.

"If that's what your father wants." Their voices mingled as, again, they spoke at the same time.

Allison stood and headed toward the hallway. "You two work it out and when you've decided what you want to do, let me know. I'll be in my room."

As if he, too, sensed that a fight was brewing, Eddie disappeared into his bedroom immediately afterward.

The silence after they left was deafening.

"You might've told me you planned to be gone all day," Zach said, unable to hold back his resentment.

"I did," Rosie flared.

"When?"

"Monday night, remember?"

"If I remembered, I wouldn't be bringing it up now, would I?"

Rosie propelled herself off the sofa and marched into the kitchen. "I don't want to argue about it."

"Good, because I don't want to argue, either. But I'm sick of this, Rosie."

"What is it with you?" she demanded, whirling around. "We can't talk anymore."

"All I said was that I don't remember you telling me you'd be gone all day."

"And I said—"

"I know what you said." He was fast losing his temper. "You might've reminded me."

"Why, so I could listen to you complain about it?"

Ah, so that was it. She saw him as complaining. The finger had been pointed and it was aimed in his direction.

"I'm making up a to-do list for you," he snapped, grabbing a pen and paper. "First, we need groceries."

"You were at the store. You might've picked up more than milk and bread, you know."

"I work forty hours a week."

"And I don't?" she shouted.

"Look around you and answer that question for yourself. If you *are* employed, exactly who are you working for? Not your family. Not me. Not our children. A Christmas Bazaar is more important than a Saturday with your family. A bake sale at the mall outweighs decorating a Christmas tree."

Rosie slammed a pound of frozen hamburger into the microwave. "Don't paint yourself as a martyr in this marriage, Zachary Cox. If you think you're so perfect, then you can start doing more to help around here. Who said it was *my* responsibility to buy the groceries? You seem to think that because I don't have a nine-to-five job, you can rule my days. I have a life, too, you know."

"Don't yell!" Eddie screamed. "Don't yell anymore!'' He stood in the kitchen entrance, tears in his eyes, his hands covering his ears.

''Eddie, I'm so sorry,'' Rosie cried, sounding close to weeping herself. She bent down to hug their son and cast an accusing glare at Zach. ''Now look what you've done!''

''Me?'' Funny how everything got turned around so that he was the one at fault.

Zach waited until after dinner—a pot of chili thrown together in about twenty minutes, but still an improvement over recent meals—before approaching his wife again. ''It's clear we have several issues that need to be addressed,'' he began as she watched a rerun of ''Buffy the Vampire Slayer.''

''Several issues,'' she repeated. ''You sound like an attorney.''

''So, I sound like an attorney. Let's just get through the holidays. The kids are hurting.''

''So am I, Zach.''

''I'm not exactly overwhelmed with happiness myself.'' He walked out of the family room and into the bedroom. A second television was set up there. He put on the History Channel and tried to watch a documentary about Napoleon.

Rosie came in an hour later. ''Do you want to talk this out?''

He glanced in her direction and frankly couldn't see the point of any discussion. ''Not particularly.''

She didn't say anything for a moment. ''That's what I thought. Just remember I tried, Zach. I sincerely tried. But you're impossible.''

If she was trying so hard, then she'd be with her family where she belonged, Zach thought and steeled himself against giving in. Rosie was the transgressor here, and he wasn't going to drop this until she owned up to her faults.

Nine

Grace hadn't been sleeping well since Thanksgiving Day. The more she dwelled on the phone calls, the more she came to believe it'd been Dan on the other end of the line. For some sick reason, her ex-husband felt it was necessary to destroy what little peace she'd found in the months since his disappearance. It had occurred to her that he might even have someone feeding him information about the details of her life. That would explain the timing of the calls.

During the last three weeks, she'd consistently awakened about four in the morning, when the night was its darkest. She was unable to return to sleep and lay there overwhelmed by guilt and fear and pain. She felt anger, too, as she imagined where he was and who he was with—imagined them laughing at her. It had been like this in the beginning, but gradually she'd come to terms with the shock of Dan's actions. Now, following the phone calls, it was bad again, as bad as it had been those first few weeks.

When Grace arrived at the library on Monday morning, her eyes burned from lack of sleep and her spirits were in the doldrums. The only positive feeling she had about the holidays had to do with her grandson. Little Tyler was almost four months old now, and the very light of her life. The problems of the world faded away when she held her grandbaby.

Cliff Harding entered the library just before noon. Grace sensed his presence even before she saw him. He returned a book and then casually strolled toward her desk. He wore a lazy smile that touched her with its warmth.

Grace's mouth went dry, and despite herself, she felt flustered. She knew he'd gone to see his daughter on the East Coast, but she hadn't heard from him since, and for that she was grateful.

"If I asked you to lunch, would you come?" he whispered, leaning against her desk.

Before she could answer, he added, "Charlotte told me your divorce was final Thanksgiving week."

"It was." She swallowed hard, unsure how to tell him what was in her heart. She wasn't ready to get involved in another relationship. And she didn't know when she would be. The divorce might be final but the questions, the doubts and fears, continued to haunt her. Legally she was free, but emotionally she clung to the past.

"Lunch?" he repeated.

"I don't think so.... I'm sorry."

"How about a walk along the waterfront? The sun's out and a leisurely stroll would do us both good."

Grace agreed; it seemed like a reasonable compromise. "Let me check with Loretta first."

Her assistant was more than willing to switch lunch hours. Grace gathered her coat and gloves and met him in front of the library. Cliff was studying the mural when she joined him. The painting was a favorite of hers; the artist had depicted a late 1800s waterfront scene with a family picnicking in the background.

"How was your visit with Lisa?" she asked. From previous conversations, Grace had learned that his daughter was twenty-eight and married to a financial advisor in Maryland.

"Wonderful. She asked me if I was dating yet." He looked meaningfully in her direction.

"What did you tell her?" Grace asked. She buried her hands in the pockets of her long wool coat and matched her pace to his as they walked toward the gazebo and picnic area. The grandstand was where the Concerts on the Cove were staged each Thursday night during the summer. Now, in mid-December, the whole park was bleak and empty. Their only company was a bevy of seagulls who circled above looking for a handout. Their piercing, discordant cries echoed across the waterfront.

"I told Lisa not yet, but I'd picked out the girl." Again he studied Grace. "I'm just waiting for the girl to notice me."

Notice him? Grace nearly laughed out loud. She'd noticed Cliff, all right. But she stood frozen with one foot in her old life and the other unwillingly thrust into a new one.

"Are you going to keep me waiting long, Grace Sherman?"

She wished she had an answer for him.

"Don't say anything," Cliff said. "I promised myself I wasn't going to press you." He exhaled, and his breath created a fog in the cold, crisp air. "You asked about my visit with Lisa and I can tell you it was definitely an experience."

"How so?"

"The day after I arrived, a blizzard hit."

"I heard about that on the news," Grace said, remembering the report of the snowstorm that had struck the East Coast Thanksgiving Week. "Did you lose your electricity?"

"Right in the middle of cooking Thanksgiving dinner. Naturally, the turkey was only partially done. I suggested we serve sushi turkey but no one seemed interested."

"What did you do?"

"What any enterprising soul would. The turkey got barbecued in the middle of a snowstorm."

Grace laughed, picturing Cliff huddled over a barbecue with wind and snow whirling all around.

"How about your Thanksgiving?" he asked.

"It was quiet with just me and Maryellen." She gnawed on her lower lip, wondering if she should mention Dan's phone calls. In the end, she didn't. Then, feeling guilty and uneasy about what she had to say to him, she sank onto the edge of a picnic bench. "Listen, Cliff, maybe this isn't such a good idea."

"What? Us taking a walk?"

"No... Your daughter's anxious for you to get out into the dating world again and you appear to be ready. I want you to start, but I don't think it's right for me just yet."

He frowned as if she'd completely missed the point. "What you apparently don't understand, Grace, is that the only woman I'm interested in dating is you."

Grace shook her head. "Come on, Cliff—I don't believe that. Ask Charlotte to recommend someone. She knows just about everyone in town and once you've met a few other women, you can decide if you still feel the same way."

His frown was back in place. "You're not the jealous type, I take it?"

A year earlier her response would have been automatic. There wasn't a jealous bone in her body, she would've said. She couldn't say that any longer. Until a few months ago, she hadn't viewed herself as possessive. Then she'd learned that Dan had been seen with another woman. Afterward she'd been filled with such rage that she'd torn the bedroom apart and dumped his entire half of the closet outside. Dan's clothes had been strewn across the front porch and the yard.

"I don't know about that," she told him. "I think most people are capable of jealousy. Anyway, I want you to promise me you'll at least consider meeting other women. It'll be good for you, Cliff." Good for her, too, perhaps.

He walked over to the middle of the large gazebo, stood there a moment, then purposefully strolled back. "Okay. I considered it."

Grace laughed, shaking her head. "You're not taking me seriously."

"Oh, but I am." Cliff sat down on the bench beside her. "I don't want to see any other woman, Grace. I'll wait for you. Like I told you before, I'm a patient man. Don't worry, I'm not going to pressure you, but I might give you a gentle reminder every now and then."

Grace didn't know why he remained persistent. She hadn't given him any encouragement. And so far, she'd been the only one to benefit from this relationship—she and her garage door.

"I'd like to show you my place someday," Cliff said. "You and Charlotte can both come. In fact, I'd enjoy it if you would. It'd be completely nonthreatening," he said with a grin. "You can even bring Buttercup if you want."

Grace thought about it. She'd formed an image of his home, and she was curious to find out if the reality matched her expectations. She nodded. "I'd enjoy a tour," she said.

"When you're ready to learn how to ride, Brownie's the one who'll teach you everything you need to know. She's gentle as the day is long, and she's the perfect horse for a beginner."

"She's agreeable to that, is she?"

"Sure is." Cliff's eyes danced. "So, should I schedule an outing this month?"

December was usually crowded with engagements, but in her current frame of mind, Grace wasn't in the mood to socialize. The prospect of visiting Cliff's ranch strongly appealed to her.

"I'm free on Saturday afternoon, if Charlotte is."

Cliff looked pleased. "I'll find out and get back to you."

"You meant that, about Buttercup coming along?" Her dog was an important part of her life and Grace liked the idea of the golden retriever accompanying her.

"Of course."

Cliff reached for her gloved hand, taking it between his own. His eyes met hers, and he smiled. "I keep telling you I'm patient, Grace, and it's true. I'm willing to wait for what I want." Then he turned over her hand and kissed the inside of her wrist.

Grace closed her eyes to savor the moment. She wanted this too. As much as he did—maybe more—but first she had to get Dan out of her head. And out of her heart. Because, despite everything, he still claimed a piece of it.

* * *

Maryellen didn't need the pregnancy test kit to tell her what she already knew. Sitting on the edge of her bathtub, she stared at the little blue stick and felt the numbness spread into her arms and legs. It'd been nearly a month now, and she'd done her best to ignore what was becoming increasingly obvious.

Striking her forehead with the heel of her hand, she closed her eyes. "Stupid, stupid, stupid."

Panic grew inside her until she was sure she was going to faint. Regaining control of her emotions required a monumental effort.

When she could manage it, she stood and studied her reflection in the bathroom mirror. How pale she was. That explained a comment she'd received earlier in the day. A longtime customer had stopped by the gallery, taken a hard look at Maryellen and asked if she'd had the flu.

A bad case of the flu would've been welcome, compared to confronting the truth of her situation.

What should she do? The question rolled around in her mind like a marble inside a tin can. Difficult as it was, she tried for a while to pretend that nothing was wrong. But after heating a frozen entrée in the microwave, she sat at the kitchen table and sorted through her emotions.

One thing was clear. She wasn't telling Jon Bowman. He was completely out of the picture as far as she was concerned. There was no reason to tell him. No reason to see him. Jon's work was now being represented elsewhere. He need never know about the pregnancy until after the baby was born, and then he'd no doubt assume some other man was the father. That was exactly what Maryellen wanted.

The thought that perhaps he had a right to know wasn't something she could accept at the moment. The thought that perhaps he, too, had a responsibility toward this baby—no. She rejected the idea without further consideration.

Another concern arose: the necessity of keeping this news a secret from her friends and family for as long as possible. A year earlier when Kelly was pregnant, her sister had barely showed. Even in her seventh month, Kelly had worn her everyday clothes. Maryellen hoped she might be able to hide her condition until then, as well. She'd wear loose dresses and make a point of staying away from formfitting business attire. Hiding her pregnancy would be a challenge but she'd do it while she could.

She needed to make room in her life for the baby. This unplanned pregnancy was a shock but she'd quickly adjusted to it. In a sense, she was getting an opportunity she'd never anticipated. This child, *her* child, was taking shape within her womb, and for a moment she was almost giddy with joy. Then reality hit.

In a little less than eight months she'd be a mother. Life was giving her a second chance, and this time she wasn't going to repeat the mistakes of the past. This time she wouldn't allow a man to dictate her life—and that of her child.

Overwhelmed by emotion and full of half-formed plans, Maryellen found that sitting at home held little appeal. The Christmas shopping season was in full swing, and if ever there was a night she needed gaiety and fun, it was now.

She headed for the shopping complex on Cedar Cove Drive, next to the six-plex theater. The strip mall held several small businesses, a Wal-Mart, a huge craft store and a hardware outlet. The parking lot was nearly full. Maryellen walked toward the cinemas and glanced over the selections offered, but didn't see any that piqued her interest.

Rummaging around the craft store seemed a far more interesting prospect. It wasn't until she was walking across the parking lot that she saw Jon, coming in her direction. Instinctively, Maryellen froze. Jon saw her and he, too, stopped in his tracks. Each seemed to be waiting for the other to make the first move.

Maryellen recovered before he did and even managed a smile as she continued toward him. "Merry Christmas, Jon."

"Hello, Maryellen." His look was guarded, closed. "Christmas shopping?"

"Browsing." Her shopping had been finished months earlier.

He merely nodded.

"I understand you've taken your photographs into Seattle." The rumor mill had been quick to inform her that his work was now being displayed in a large Seattle gallery. It was a coup for him and she was pleased to hear it, although the Harbor Street Gallery would miss the money his work generated.

He nodded again.

"Congratulations, Jon." She genuinely meant that.

"Thank you."

No need to stand in the middle of a parking lot. "Well, it was nice seeing you." That was stretching the truth, but it would be impolite to say anything else. She started to walk past him when he stopped her.

"Maryellen."

"Yes?" She knew she sounded impatient.

"About that night."

She closed her eyes, not wanting to hear it. "Haven't we already discussed it to death?"

"I didn't plan what happened."

"So you said." She didn't dare look at him.

"What I'm trying to say is that I didn't protect you, if you know what I mean." He shrugged when she failed to respond. "Do you really need me to spell it out?"

"No." An explanation was the last thing she needed. Not when she knew better than he did exactly what the consequence of that night could be—what, in fact, it was.

"Will you be all right? I mean, is there a possibility that...you know." His concern was evident in his anxious frown.

She forced a smile. "Don't worry about it."

"I am worried." His eyes clouded. "I need to know—to be sure."

For one terrifying moment, Maryellen was afraid he'd guessed. "I'm fine, Jon. I appreciate your concern but the situation's under control."

His relief was evident as the tension eased from his shoulders. "You're sure?"

"Positive."

He held her eyes a second or two longer, then abruptly turned away.

Now Maryellen could finally relax. She expelled her breath and hurried into the Tulips and Things Craft Store.

On Friday, five days before Christmas, Maryellen took her lunch break down at the Potbelly Deli, which served wonderful soups and inventive sandwiches. The restaurant was a local favorite, and she went there as often as she could. Enjoying a cup of the seafood chowder, Maryellen sat in the corner by herself, reading an art magazine, when her mother stepped inside.

"I thought I saw you in here," Grace said. "Do you mind if I join you?"

"I'd love it." Although they lived and worked in the same town, a week would slip past without the chance to talk or visit.

Her mother ordered a bowl of the tomato bisque soup and a cup of coffee, then sat in the chair across from her. "I had a visitor not long ago."

It didn't take Maryellen long to guess. "Cliff Harding?"

Blushing, Grace nodded. "He invited me and Buttercup to see his horse ranch. I went out there on Saturday." She stirred her soup and didn't look up. "Charlotte was going to come originally, but she wasn't feeling well, so it was just Cliff, me, Buttercup and the horses. He has magnificent horses." After a slight pause she continued, adding comments about the home, a two-story log house, and the acreage—pastures, woods and even a stream.

Maryellen couldn't remember seeing her mother more animated about anything in quite a while. "That sounds wonderful." It was a step in the right direction that her mother had agreed to this outing with Cliff.

Grace tasted the soup, crumbled a package of oyster crackers and dumped them in. When she glanced up, she stared at Maryellen for a moment, her eyes narrowed. "My goodness, you're terribly pale," she said. "Are you feeling sick?"

"I'm pale?" She tried to pretend this was news.

"You look anemic."

"I'm fine, Mom."

Her mother studied her, frowning slightly. "I want you to promise me you'll make a doctor's appointment."

"I don't need to see a doctor," she said, wanting to laugh off her concern. "The next thing I know, you'll be lecturing me about eating prunes the way Mrs. Jefferson always does."

Grace swallowed another mouthful of soup. "If you don't make the appointment, then I will. I don't remember ever seeing you this pale. If I didn't know better, I'd think you were pregnant."

The words shocked Maryellen so badly that she choked on her soup. She coughed and wheezed, tears springing to her eyes, and her mother leaped up and pounded her hard on the back.

"Are you all right?"

Maryellen reached for her water glass and sipped. "I'm fine...I think."

A minute or more passed, and Maryellen could feel her mother's scrutiny. When Grace finally spoke, her voice was low. "Your father was always closest to Kelly," she said. "You were the one I identified with most. We're quite a bit alike. You realize that, don't you? My hair was once the exact shade of yours. My eyes are the same dark brown."

Maryellen didn't know where this conversation was leading, but she had her suspicions. "You're my mother," she said lightly. "Of course I look like you."

Her mother's voice fell to a whisper. "I was a senior in high school when I discovered I was pregnant with you."

Maryellen swallowed hard. The details of her birth hadn't ever been openly discussed, although she'd figured out in her early teens that her mother had gotten pregnant in high school.

"I told Dan, and we had no idea what we were going to do. It was important that we wait until after graduation before we told our parents, but my mother knew. I never had to tell her about you, and do you know why?"

Maryellen's eyes filled with tears and she picked up her napkin, crumpling it in her hands. "Because you were so pale?"

Her mother nodded. "I was anemic, too. Young and healthy though I was, the pregnancy drained me and I looked deathly pale. It wasn't a severe case, just enough for me to need a prescription for iron tablets." She didn't say anything else, didn't press Maryellen or throw questions at her. Instead she waited.

"Then you know," Maryellen said after a moment, fighting hard not to weep openly in public.

"The father?"

"Out of the picture," she said, not wanting to mention Jon's name.

"Oh, Maryellen..."

"I'll be fine," she said, putting on a brave front, "really I will. Mom, I'm almost thirty-six years old. I can take care of myself."

"But..."

"It took some adjusting, but now that I've accepted this, I'm happy." The joy was decidedly absent at the moment with tears making wet tracks down her cheeks.

"We always had this connection, Maryellen," her mother said. "I knew. Somehow I knew."

"We didn't always, Mom."

Grace looked up at her. "What do you mean?"

"If we had this special connection fifteen years ago, you would've known then, too."

Her mother stared at her with wide, disbelieving eyes.

There, it was out—a piece of the truth that she'd assumed would remain forever buried. Her sin, her pain, the guilt she'd carried with her for all these years.

"You were pregnant before?"

The lump in her throat was so big, she could only answer with a nod.

"Leave it to you to wait until the last minute to put up a tree," Olivia teased Jack as he took the first package of decorative balls from a shopping bag. Actually, Olivia thought it was rather a sweet gesture on Jack's part. Eric had briefly moved out but was back, much to Jack's relief. He'd bought the Christmas tree in an effort to lift his son's spirits over the holidays and Olivia had agreed to help him decorate it. This had entailed buying lights and decorations, since Jack hadn't bothered much with Christmas since his divorce.

Eric had grown progressively more depressed at the approach of Christmas. Jack had done what he could to pull his son out of his melancholy but to no avail. Two days before Christmas, he invited Olivia over to decorate a Christmas tree while Eric was out. They hoped the surprise would jolt him into a more cheerful frame of mind.

"I kind of like this pitiful tree," Jack said, stepping back to examine it. The branches all seemed to be bunched on one side, while the other side was almost bare.

"It's a Charlie Brown tree for sure." In Olivia's opinion, this was the sorriest-looking evergreen in the lot, but she agreed it held a certain appeal. She'd brought some leftover ornaments, along with a CD of Christmas music, and they were in business.

Andy Williams's voice crooned as a small fire blazed in the fireplace. "So?" Jack asked, rearranging the string of twinkling white lights. "Are you doing anything special after this?"

"I was thinking I'd let you take me to dinner."

"The Taco Shack?"

Olivia sighed. Nine times out of ten, that was the restaurant Jack chose. "Do they still owe you for advertising?"

"I can eat there for another twenty years."

"I was afraid of that."

Jack hung a plastic gingerbread man on a drooping tree limb. "You like Mexican food, don't you?"

"Sure—but I enjoy the company more."

Chuckling, Jack grabbed her around the waist, preparing to kiss her. Olivia certainly wasn't objecting, but then the door opened and Jack stopped abruptly. He loosened his grip and Olivia nearly fell to the floor, catching herself just in time.

"Eric," Jack said, sounding startled. "I didn't expect you for a couple of hours."

His son walked into the room, looking about as gloomy as a man can get. He didn't appear to notice that Olivia and Jack had been in the middle of a kiss.

"You picked up the mail?"

Eric nodded.

"What happened?" Olivia asked. The boy seemed to be in shock.

Eric slouched forward and dropped the mail on the coffee table. "I heard from Shelly."

"She wrote you?" Jack seemed encouraged by this development.

"No..." Eric covered his face with his hands. "She sent me a picture."

"A picture?" Jack frowned. "Of what?"

"The baby," Eric supplied. Then he straightened and looked them both full in the face. "Correction, babies. Shelly's having twins."

"Twins!" Jack fell back onto the sofa.

Eric reached for the top envelope and withdrew a folded paper. "See for yourself."

Jack clambered to his feet. He took the paper and examined it, with Olivia glancing over his shoulder. Sure enough, the fuzzy photograph revealed two distinct fetuses. They were positioned in such a way that it was easy to detect the sex. "Both boys from the look of it," Jack announced.

"Shelly didn't include a note with the ultrasound results?"

"No," Eric said, "but when I got this, I thought we should talk, so I drove over to the apartment..."

"And?" Jack pressed.

Eric ran his hand over his face and didn't seem to know where to start. "The thing is, I love Shelly. These last few months have been hell, the two of us being separated like this."

"They've been hell for me, too," Jack muttered, and Olivia elbowed him in the ribs.

"Did you have the chance to talk to Shelly?" she asked sympathetically.

"I told her the truth," Eric said. "I love her, I've always loved her. I don't care if the baby—the babies are mine or not, I want to be with her." He rubbed his face a second time and Olivia thought he might break into tears. "I can't do any better than that, can I? I've already given her my heart. I offered her my forgiveness, too. What more can I do?"

Olivia groaned. "She doesn't need your forgiveness, Eric."

"They *can't* be my babies," Eric cried. "But I'm willing to *make* them mine, if she'd let me."

"She refused?" Jack was clearly outraged. "The woman needs to see a shrink! You both do."

"Jack!" His son didn't need chastisement now; he was already depressed. It wouldn't help to heap more blame and censure on his burdened shoulders.

"Shelly wouldn't talk to me. She threw me out."

"Of your own home?" Jack was practically growling. "The woman is a fruitcake!"

"Jack!" Olivia elbowed him again. He was making matters worse instead of better. "Let the boy tell us in his own way."

"Sorry," Jack said, although he didn't sound it.

"I went to talk things over with Shelly. I wanted her to know that I don't care who the father is. Me, this new guy she works with or some man on the street." His face hardened, and while he might be saying the words, Olivia found it difficult to believe them.

"And she threw you out?" Again it was Jack whose voice rose in disbelief.

"Shelly was crying too hard for me to hear what she said, but she made one thing plain," Eric murmured. "She wanted me out of there."

"Women," Jack muttered. "Can't live with 'em, can't live without 'em."

"Would you stop," Olivia demanded. "Cut the clichés and the unhelpful comments, okay?"

Jack cast her an apologetic look.

''Shelly said it would be best if I was completely out of her life.'' Eric spoke in dull tones, and his misery was breaking Olivia's heart.

''What about the babies?'' she asked.

''She said...it's too late.''

''Too late? What did she mean by *that?*'' Jack shouted.

''She doesn't want anything more to do with me.'' He seemed even closer to tears. ''At least, I think that's what she said.''

''She might've been saying something else,'' Jack said desperately. ''Maybe you didn't understand....''

''I understood the door she slammed in my face,'' Eric told him. ''It's over for us, I know that now.''

''Let's not be hasty,'' Jack said. ''Let's—''

''Eric, sit down,'' Olivia instructed, ignoring Jack. ''I'm going to make a pot of coffee, and then the three of us are going to discuss this.''

''What's there to discuss?'' Eric asked, shrugging hopelessly.

''Quite a bit, actually, because those babies are going to need their daddy and—'' she paused and stared pointedly at Jack ''—their grandfather, too.''

''What more can I do?'' Eric asked again, following Olivia into the kitchen.

''Don't worry,'' she said confidently, gathering him close. ''Life has a way of turning out for the best. If your mother was here instead of in Kansas City, she'd tell you the same thing. It's painful just now, but be patient. Shelly will eventually reach out to you. She needs you, Eric, and she wants you back in her life.''

''You think so?'' His eagerness to believe, made his expression—so vulnerable and expectant—almost painful to watch.

"I do." Olivia nodded, sincere in what she said to him. In her experience, a woman didn't maintain as much contact as Shelly had—dinner with Jack, sending the ultrasound pictures—if she wanted to sever all relations with a man. The things she'd said to Jack, suggesting that she and Eric would see each other after the birth, struck Olivia as promising, too.

"Really?" Jack asked. "How long do you think it'll take?"

"Yeah," Eric echoed. "How long?"

"That I can't answer," she said and wanted to kick Jack for bringing it up.

"You're a very wise person, aren't you?" Eric said, looking at her in admiration. He finally seemed to relax a little.

"She's great," Jack agreed.

"Now, how about helping us decorate this Charlie Brown Christmas tree?" Olivia urged.

Eric hesitated and then gave her a huge grin. "Okay!"

In her heart of hearts, Olivia was convinced that everything *would* work out for Shelly, Eric and the twins—no matter who their father was.

Ten

Over the years, Olivia had given a number of speeches. She tended to shy away from accepting these engagements, but in her position as an elected official, they were unavoidable. This was the first time she'd been asked to speak at the Henry M. Jackson Senior Center, and she was admittedly nervous.

The senior potluck luncheons were held on the first Monday of each month. Last June, Mary Berger had asked Olivia to be the January speaker. Six months had never passed so quickly. Olivia had dutifully written the appointment in her date book and then promptly forgotten all about it. Not until she opened her appointment book for the New Year did the reminder jump out at her.

Naturally, her mother was excited about having "my daughter, the judge," come and speak to her friends. Knowing Charlotte, she'd gloat for a month. Olivia appreciated her mother's support, but found her pride excessive and a little embarrassing. Charlotte took every opportunity to tell friends and strangers alike that her only daughter was a judge; worse, she was prone to detailing Olivia's various judgments, complete with commentaries of her own.

As Olivia dressed for the luncheon, she paused, standing inside her walk-in closet, and frowned as she thought about her mother. Charlotte had overdone it this holiday season, baking for friends, visiting and supervising events at the Senior Center, writing the seniors' column each week.

By Christmas Day, Charlotte was exhausted. It used to be that nothing slowed her down. For the first time, Olivia realized that her mother's age had caught up with her. Charlotte just wasn't her usual self, although she valiantly tried to hide how worn-out she was.

Christmas afternoon, when the family gathered at her mother's house, Charlotte had looked pale and drawn. As soon as they'd finished dinner, Olivia insisted she rest. Charlotte had, of course, resisted. Olivia wondered how she was going to convince her mother to take on fewer commitments in the new year.

Choosing a soft suede dress in a pale tan color with a brown and gold scarf, Olivia arrived at the Senior Center a few minutes early. Charlotte and her best friend, Laura, were at the door waiting for her. Beaming with pride, her mother immediately hugged Olivia as though it'd been months—rather than a few days—since they were last together.

"You remember Laura, don't you?" her mother asked unnecessarily, drawing Olivia into the large room, which was set up with tables seating eight, a buffet area and a slightly raised stage that held the speaker's podium plus the head table.

"Of course I do," Olivia said, smiling warmly at her mother's knitting friend. Charlotte and Laura were the people responsible for inspiring the thriving seniors' knitting group. The enthusiastic Laura was an accomplished knitter and Olivia had always suspected she could convince the whole world that peace was a possibility if everyone took up knitting needles instead of guns.

"I'm so pleased you could accept our invitation," Mary Berger, the center's social director, said as she approached Olivia. "We're looking forward to hearing what you have to say."

Olivia smiled blandly. She was nervous already and hoped she could pull this off without stumbling over her notes and humiliating herself—and her mother—in the process.

"Did you want our guest of honor to sit with you?" Mary asked Charlotte. She leaned close to Olivia and said in a low voice, "Your mother tends to want speakers she knows to sit with her and her friends instead of at the head table."

Olivia recalled that Jack Griffin had spoken to the seniors last year, and apparently her mother had captured him for herself. She'd paid the price, however, when Jack had convinced Charlotte to contribute to the weekly Seniors' Page for *The Cedar Cove Chronicle.*

"Mom? Would you like me to sit with you and Laura and the others?" Olivia asked.

Charlotte stiffened and her chin came up as though the question offended her. "I think you should be at the head table."

"I do, too," Mary said primly. With that, she turned and walked smartly in the direction of the stage. Olivia was about to follow when Charlotte caught her by the arm.

"Get your dessert early," she said in a loud whisper.

"Dessert?"

"If you don't get it right away, everything'll be gone by the time we line up for the buffet. So we help ourselves to dessert first. That's just the way we do things here. I don't approve, mind you, but no one cares what I think about it.''

''All right, Mom,'' she whispered back.

Mary showed her to her seat at the head table, and Olivia reached for her dessert plate as instructed by her mother. The food tables offered a variety that was truly impressive. She chose a piece of lemon sponge cake and returned to her seat just as Mary was about to say a few words of welcome. The social director of the Senior Center made a small huffy sound as Charlotte walked past.

''Your mother might not approve of the practice, but it doesn't stop her from indulging, does it?'' Mary said, leaning down from the podium.

''She knows that if she doesn't get her dessert beforehand, there won't be anything left,'' Olivia said calmly, setting her piece of lemon sponge cake next to her empty plate.

Olivia tried not to smile. In many ways, her mother was a rebel, but a much-loved one. There were days Charlotte drove her crazy, yet at the same time Olivia deeply admired her. Charlotte was fully involved in life; she engaged in plenty of creative activities and had a genuine commitment to the welfare of others. Twenty-five years from now, Olivia hoped to be just like her. The fact that the indefatigable Charlotte seemed to be losing energy distressed everyone in the family, and Olivia resolved to talk to her about seeing the doctor.

As the seniors closest to the wall left their tables to form a long line at the buffet table, Olivia saw Justine and Seth at the back of the room. Her daughter and son-in-law had come to hear her speech. Charlotte got to the newlyweds first, and quickly escorted them to her table. Olivia watched as her mother introduced the young couple to her friends, who were obviously enchanted, especially by Seth. Soon space was cleared next to Charlotte, and they both sat down. Laura urged Seth to his feet a moment later, escorting him to the buffet table to fill plates for himself and his wife.

Justine and Seth weren't the only surprise visitors. Olivia saw Jack slip into the back of the room just as she stepped up to the podium to give her talk. Pausing when she noticed him, she was encouraged by his broad smile and his wink. Smiling too, she launched into her speech—which was about the creativity of older people and how much they contributed to society.

Afterward, Olivia couldn't remember a word of it, but apparently she'd made sense because there was a nice, appreciative round of applause when she finished. Mary announced that Bob Beldon, the proprietor of the Thyme and Tide B and B, would be the February speaker, made a few other "housekeeping" announcements, and the meeting was over. To Olivia's astonishment, a small crowd swarmed toward the head table to thank her for coming.

Charlotte hurried around the table and stood next to Olivia, clutching her arm, telling anyone and everyone that Olivia was her daughter—as if this was news! Mary had announced the fact earlier, but apparently that didn't satisfy her mother.

Justine and Seth waited until her admirers had drifted off. "You sounded really good, Mom," Justine said. "I understand why Grandma's so proud of you."

This was quite a compliment coming from her daughter. For a moment, Olivia was too overwhelmed to speak. Her relationship with Justine wasn't always easy, although God knew she tried. The most difficult aspect of being a parent to an adult child was holding one's tongue, she'd discovered. "It was wonderful of you and Seth to be here."

Seth, her son-in-law, stood a head taller than everyone else in the room. "Great job, Olivia," he said with a respectful nod.

"We came by to ask you to dinner tonight," Justine told her, "And I'm cooking."

This was the first invitation she'd received from her daughter, and Olivia didn't know quite what to make of it. "Thank you. I'd enjoy that." Then, because she thought—and hoped—there might be more to this invitation than met the eye, she asked, "Any special reason?"

Seth chuckled. "Don't worry, we aren't going to ask for a loan or anything."

"Trust me, I'm not worried. Just...curious." She was thrilled to see her daughter this happy. Justine looked more at peace with herself than she had in years, and it was clear to Olivia that this marriage had brought her daughter contentment. She didn't know what had happened to Warren Saget, but he was apparently out of her life. That certainly didn't hurt Olivia's feelings any.

"Then you'll come?"

"Of course."

As Charlotte escorted her to the door, she said, "Laura and I are going to take a trip out to the Silverdale yarn store this afternoon." Charlotte needed more yarn about as much as the desert needed more sand, but Olivia didn't say so. If buying yarn of every weight and color made her mother happy, Olivia could only approve.

"I'll walk you to your car," Jack said, coming up

behind her. ''Hello, Charlotte.'' He kissed Olivia's mother on the cheek, then placed his arm around Olivia's shoulders. ''Excellent speech. I took lots of notes.''

''Jack!'' she cried. ''You're not going to put anything about this in the paper, are you?''

''Sure I am.''

''No, you're not,'' Charlotte said sternly, shocking them both. ''*I* am. Olivia is my daughter and I write the Seniors' Page. She spoke at the Senior Center, so don't traipse on my territory. I don't care if you *are* the editor, this story is mine.''

''Okay, okay.'' Jack raised both hands in mock surrender, but his eyes were twinkling.

Jack kept his arm around her shoulder as they walked outside. ''That wasn't so bad, now was it?''

''Yes, it was,'' Olivia said, ''but I survived.''

Jack checked his watch and grimaced. ''I'm late to report on a City Council meeting. I'll call you, okay?''

''Yes, please do.''

He kissed her and it was more than just a short kiss of farewell. He was saying he missed her, missed their Tuesday-night dinner dates. She told him she did, too. Amazing how much a single kiss could say.

They parted, and Jack reluctantly turned and hurried across the street to his battered car. Olivia hated to see him go. Sighing, she returned to the courthouse for her afternoon session.

By that evening, as she drove to Justine and Seth's apartment, Olivia had begun to wonder again about the reason for this unexpected invitation. Would there be an announcement?

Her daughter answered the door, looking so radiantly happy that it was all Olivia could do not to stare. She'd only been to the apartment one previous time, when it'd been filled with gifts from the wedding reception and boxes were scattered every which way. Her daughter had done a wonderful job of incorporating Seth's things into her utterly feminine home, making it *his* home, too.

Seth brought out a bottle of sparkling wine while Justine hung up Olivia's coat.

"Are we celebrating something?" Olivia asked, sitting on a delicate chair with petit point upholstery.

"We have news," Justine said, smiling warmly at her husband.

Seth set the wine bottle on the counter and then sank down on the sofa next to Justine. "When I returned from fishing this last time, Justine and I decided we didn't want to spend half the year apart."

"It's just too hard on both of us," Justine added.

This was their news?

"You're giving up fishing?" Olivia asked. It was in Seth's blood. The Gunderson family had a long history as fishermen, dating back four or five generations.

"Seth and I are buying a restaurant," Justine announced. "The Captain's Galley has been for sale for a couple of months and we made an offer, which the owner has accepted."

Okay, this wasn't exactly what Olivia had hoped, but it wasn't bad. "That's great!"

"We haven't decided on a new name yet," Justine said. "But we're very excited." She glanced at her husband and he reached for her hand.

Olivia relaxed. "I'm thrilled for you. It's going to be a lot of hard work, but you already know that."

"Seth's been saving for years for something like this." Again her daughter looked proudly at her husband. "I'll keep my job for now, but eventually I'll be working at the restaurant, too."

"Are you keeping the current staff or hiring new people?" Olivia asked, wondering about Cecilia Randall, who worked as a part-time hostess at The Captain's Galley.

"We don't know any of the staff yet," Seth told her. "This is still very new. In fact, we just found out that our offer had been accepted an hour ago."

"Actually, we invited you to dinner *before* we heard from the real estate broker."

"Oh? You mean there's more?"

"Mama," Justine said, leaning forward and gripping both of Olivia's hands.

Her daughter only called her that when she was feeling very emotional; Olivia hadn't heard it in years. Justine's beautiful blue eyes filled with tears as she smiled at Olivia. "Seth and I are pregnant."

Olivia let out a cry of sheer happiness and leaped to her feet. Justine and Seth stood, too, and Olivia wrapped her arms around them as tears of joy streamed down her cheeks. *This* was the news she'd come to hear.

Cliff Harding sat with his long legs stretched out, staring at the television set. The sitcom bored him, but he didn't blame the writing or the acting. He'd been restless all day.

Hell of a way to spend a Friday night. What he really wanted to do was see Grace. He'd purposely not talked to her since shortly before Christmas. He was tired of always being the one to contact her; this time, he decided, she'd have to call him. Ten days into the New Year felt more like ten lifetimes, and his resolve was weakening. He'd told her he was a patient man but that was stretching the truth. He *could* be patient. He didn't like it, though, not one damn bit.

Maybe she was right and he should think about seeing other women. The problem was, no one interested him half as much as Grace. He liked everything about her. Her smile, her laugh, the gentle way she had with children and animals. She wasn't conventionally beautiful, but she possessed beauty in abundance. He liked her salt-and-pepper hair and approved of the shorter cut, preferring it to the longer style she'd worn in the family photograph. Although she'd obviously aged since then, the years had only added depth and maturity.

Cliff believed in the importance of loyalty—a belief his divorce had confirmed—and he didn't want to be with a woman who could easily turn her back on a thirty-five year marriage. But it was now nine months since Dan's disappearance, and from all the evidence, the choice to leave had been his.

Everything he'd heard pointed to the fact that Grace's ex was involved with another woman. The afternoon Grace spent on his ranch, she'd told him a little about those early weeks after Dan had vanished. When she described finding out about a ring he'd charged at a jewelry store, she'd grown tearful. Apparently Dan had bought a ring on their VISA bill. His last paycheck covered the amount of the purchase, and that had been mailed to Grace from his employer.

What hurt Grace was the fact that other than the plain gold band he'd given her on their wedding day, Dan had never purchased *her* a ring. It seemed he'd bought one for another woman, though, and that had cut Grace to the quick.

Walking into his office, Cliff reached for a novel, the latest thriller by an author he particularly enjoyed. But even before he went back into the living room and opened the book, he knew it was useless. His mind was on Grace, not the mindless entertainment of a television sit-com, or even the involved plot of a murder mystery.

Christmas week was the last time he'd seen her. Again, it had been at his own instigation. After the trip to the ranch, she'd written him a brief note. Three lines. A simple thank-you, and yet he'd read that card over and over, looking for some secret message, some encouragement.

He waited until just before Christmas, then dropped in at the Cedar Cove Library with a gift. It was nothing creative or terribly expensive. Just a token gift so she'd known he'd been thinking about her. From her brief note, he saw that she'd used a fountain pen. He preferred fountain pens himself. He'd picked up one of his favorite brands, had the store wrap it and then promptly delivered it to her at the library. She'd seemed surprised and grateful but also embarrassed because she didn't have anything for him.

She couldn't afford it, he realized. Her ex-husband's disappearance had obviously created financial difficulties; she'd worked with a budget that included two incomes and now there was only one. Their conversation was brief, the day he saw her at the library, but he could easily read between the lines. This was a difficult Christmas for her, and not only because it was the first since her divorce became final.

Cliff harbored a secret hope that she'd invite him to Christmas dinner, but she was joining her youngest daughter for the holiday. He'd hoped she might call him on New Year's Eve, perhaps suggest meeting for a drink. But that hadn't happened, either.

Now Cliff was beginning to doubt himself—and Grace. She might never recover from Dan's disappearance. Even if they got involved, he feared she'd always be looking over her shoulder for Dan. Perhaps the best thing to do was walk away and forget he'd ever met her.

It should be easy. They'd never kissed. Okay, once on the cheek. They'd held hands a couple of times, but that was about as sensual as it got. Cliff was more man than saint, and whenever they were together the temptation to hold and kiss her, *really* kiss her, grew more potent.

The phone rang, startling him out of his reverie. He'd never been one for extended telephone conversations. His gruff, unfriendly voice usually turned telemarketers away, which he considered a definite bonus.

"Harding," he barked.

No one spoke, and Cliff had started to hang up when he heard Grace's tentative greeting. He jerked the phone back to his ear.

"Grace?"

"Hello, Cliff. I hope you don't mind me phoning you out of the blue like this."

"Hello, Grace." He kept his voice just a little impatient.

"I wanted to thank you for the fountain pen. I really like the way it writes."

His problem, Cliff decided, was that he was too eager, which was why he'd come up with his wait-and-see strategy, why he hadn't been in touch since Christmas. If he was a bit more standoffish, she might appreciate him more, seek out his company. Apparently, his plan had worked—although only seconds earlier he was ready to forget the entire relationship. Cool Hand Cliff, that was him.

"When you came by the library, you suggested the two of us might go out for dinner one night."

"Did I?" he asked casually, although he knew very well that he had.

"Yes." She sounded pretty certain of herself. "I was thinking I'd take you up on that offer—if you're still interested."

He was interested, all right, and it was becoming increasingly difficult to pretend otherwise. "When?"

"I…I don't know. What's a good time for you?"

"Let me check my calendar." He ruffled through the pages of his book, as though he had to consult a full social calendar. "How about tomorrow night? Seven?"

She sighed, clearly relieved. "That would be perfect."

All day Saturday, Cliff was in a state of nervous anticipaton. Saturday night, Cliff had shaved, showered and dressed by six. He could leave now, but in evening traffic it only took about fifteen minutes to get from his ranch to her house. He'd rather arrive early, though, than hang around at home.

As it was, even after taking his time, he got there a whole half hour ahead of schedule, which he was afraid might give Grace the wrong message. Instead, he was pleasantly surprised to discover that she seemed equally nervous.

"I thought we'd drive into Tacoma," he said. He wanted Grace to feel comfortable, and he wasn't sure that would be possible if she was constantly worried about who might see the two of them together. "There's a nice Italian place I'm fond of on the other side of the bride." The Narrows separated the Kitsap Peninsula from Tacoma and the bridge linked the two communities.

"I love Italian food."

Cliff had called ahead and reserved a corner table. The drive was relaxed, conversation alternating with companionable silence. Their meal took nearly two hours as they lingered first over dinner and wine and then coffee and dessert. Cliff wasn't eager to leave, but the restaurant was filling up and it didn't seem right to hold on to the table all night.

Returning to Cedar Cove, they approached the Narrows Bridge. As traffic slowed, Cliff glanced at Grace and saw she'd leaned her head against the back of the seat, her eyes closed.

"You look very peaceful," he said.

"I feel wonderful." She paused. "It was a lovely evening."

The food was excellent, the merlot some of the best he could remember, but he sincerely hoped Grace was referring to the company and not the meal.

"I feel...free," she said, eyes still closed. "I assumed that if I agreed to have dinner with you, I'd spend the entire night feeling guilty."

"You don't have anything to feel guilty about—yet."

"Yet?" She lifted her head and stared at him.

"I'm going to kiss you Grace," he said firmly, keeping his eyes on the road. "And when I do, you're going to feel that kiss all the way down to your toes."

"Ah..."

"It's going to be a kiss that'll knock you for a loop…and then some."

"Cliff, I—"

"Do you have any objections?" he asked, his voice gruff, fearing rejection.

"Just one," Grace whispered placing her hand on his knee.

"What's that?"

"Stop this damn car and just do it."

Cliff was more than happy to oblige.

Rosie and Zach were tense with each other over the Christmas holidays, and things didn't seem to be getting any better in the New Year. Rosie tried, she honestly did, but Zach was increasingly demanding and unreasonable.

They were constantly bickering, constantly at odds. Some days she was convinced her marriage had been a mistake. Zach didn't want a wife, he wanted a maid. Rosie had tried to live up to his expectations, but when she did manage to juggle her schedule to do these wifely chores, it always backfired. Breakfast was a good example. He apparently wanted her tied to the stove, yet no one was interested in her cooking.

Shortly before Christmas, in a conciliatory mood, she'd made meat loaf and mashed potatoes and even gravy. Eddie hated the meat loaf, and Allison complained about the potatoes. Rosie could have put up with their dissatisfaction if Zach had shown one bit of appreciation for her efforts. Instead, he'd pointed out that real potatoes didn't come out of a box and that his mother had never used canned gravy. Well, she wasn't his mother, as she'd told him. Zach had muttered,

"You can say that again." Rosie found his remark insulting and hurtful.

Today, though, everything was beginning to add up. That morning Zach had forgotten his briefcase at the house. On her way to a meeting with the church library committee, Rosie had brought it to the office.

Seeing Janice Lamond with Zach had opened her eyes. No wonder he was dissatisfied with his home life. Zach and this other woman were involved. They might not be having an affair—or were they?—but there was *something* going on between them.

Rosie brooded about it during her meeting. She skipped her volunteer stint at the school that afternoon. All day she seethed. With an unaccustomed burst of energy she cleared up accumulated clutter in the house, vacuumed and did five loads of wash. She had a casserole in the oven when Zach got home.

Standing by the kitchen door with her hand on her hip, she glared at him as he walked in.

"What?" he demanded when he'd taken two steps into the house.

"We need to talk."

"About what?" He loosened his tie, looking weary.

"I want to ask you about Janice Lamond."

"What's she got to do with anything?" Zach spat out.

As if he didn't already know. Whirling around, Rosie slapped a plate into the dishwasher. "I think it would be best if we talked about this after the children are asleep."

Zach disappeared for five minutes; then he was back. "If you've got a problem I want to hear it now."

"Fine." Rosie yanked open the silverware drawer

and took out the knives and forks for the evening meal. "I was at your office this morning, if you remember."

"Yes." He crossed his arms and leaned against the kitchen counter. "So what?"

"I saw the way your assistant looked at you—and the way you looked at her."

Zach frowned. "You're imagining things."

"The hell I am." The more Rosie thought about it, the hotter she burned. All day she'd been wondering exactly what was happening between her husband and this other woman. She was so hurt, so furious, she could barely think straight.

"There's nothing going on between Janice and me," Zach said after a stilted silence.

"Fine. I want you to get rid of her."

"What?" Zach nearly exploded.

"If what you're saying is true—" which, frankly, she doubted "—then you won't mind getting a new assistant."

"Because you're paranoid about another woman. I don't think so." His jaw was tight and that stubborn expression came over him. "You're jealous...."

"I have eyes in my head, Zach. I *saw* the way she looked at you."

"Give me a break." His hands were clenched now.

"No wonder I can't do anything to satisfy you anymore. You've been picking away at me for months. I'm not a good enough housekeeper and our meals are below your high standards. That's how it started, isn't it?"

"I never realized what an active imagination you have," he said, and while his words weren't insulting, his tone was. "You're so far off-base it's pitiful." He circled the table as though he found it impossible to stand still.

"I want her out of your office."

Zach clutched a kitchen chair with both hands, his knuckles standing out white. "Forget it."

Moving behind a chair, too, Rosie mimicked his posture. She stared across the table at Zach, her eyes narrowing. Looking at him now, his face distorted with anger, she wondered if he wasn't already involved in an affair. Never had she believed something like this would happen to her and Zach.

"You refuse to fire her?"

"Damn straight I do! First of all, this is none of your business. Second, Janice Lamond is organized, efficient and a pleasure to have in my office. I am not going to discharge her because my wife is jealous. If anything, you could take a few lessons from her about keeping this house clean and orderly."

The words hit her as hard as a physical blow. "If that's the way you feel," she said, shocked by how cool and unemotional her voice sounded.

"That's exactly the way I feel."

"Then perhaps it would be a good idea if we separated."

Zach looked at her sharply. "Is that what you want, Rosie? Be damn sure it is before you start anything."

"I'm not putting up with an affair." She wanted that perfectly clear.

"For the last time, I'm not having an affair with Janice Lamond and the fact that you're suggesting I am is an insult to both Janice and me."

"Perhaps you aren't involved physically yet, but you are emotionally. You think I can't tell? Do you honestly believe I'm so blind I can't see what's happening right before my eyes?"

"I don't know if you're even capable of recognizing the truth."

Rosie bit her lip. "You're the one who's blind. I want her fired."

Zach laughed derisively. "Like I said, that isn't going to happen."

"You mean to say you'd rather lose your marriage, your wife, your children and your home in order to keep your assistant? She's that important to you? Guess what that tells me, Zach."

Allison appeared then and stood tentatively in the doorway to the kitchen. "Are you two fighting again?"

"No," Rosie said, softening her voice.

"Yes," Zach countered, nearly shouting in his anger. His eyes were as cold as she'd ever seen them.

Rosie didn't care; she wasn't backing down.

He was being contradictory on purpose, trying to create more havoc and discord than he already had.

"I don't want to argue in front of the children," Rosie said pointedly.

"You started this and we're going to finish it right here and now." He slammed his hand down on the table, rattling the silverware.

"Mom? Dad?" Eddie stood beside his sister.

Rosie turned and said, "Dinner will be ready in ten minutes. Go wash your hands."

Both children stayed where they were.

"Do as your mother says," Zach ordered.

Reluctantly they left the kitchen. Rosie heard them talking as they left. Although she couldn't make out what was being said, the word *divorce* was clear.

"Is this really what you want?" Zach asked.

"Is this what *you* want? To throw your family away for your assistant?"

He ignored the comment. "A separation might not be such a bad idea. I don't want my children subjected to your paranoia."

Rosie tried to swallow the lump in her throat.

"If you want this so badly, then I suggest you consult an attorney," he muttered.

"I will," she tossed back at him. Her heart felt numb and the sensation was spreading. Staring sightlessly ahead, she gripped the chair so hard her nails cut into the wood.

Zach stood there a moment longer, then turned and reached for his briefcase and walked toward the door leading to the garage.

"Where are you going?" she asked.

He hesitated only a second. "If we're planning to separate, then I'll need an apartment." With that he stalked out.

Rosie remained where she was, hardly able to breathe, hardly able to believe that her marriage had come to this.

Eleven

The wind howled and rain pounded the house as Bob and Peggy Beldon prepared for bed. The winter months were slow at the bed-and-breakfast. It was three days since their last guest had departed. This business was their retirement project, but right now Bob didn't object to the scarcity of paying guests. It gave Peggy and him a welcome break and the opportunity to enjoy their home and each other.

The wind rattled the winter-bare branches against the windows as Bob turned off the television after watching the eleven o'clock news. The lights flickered. ''Looks like we're in for quite a night,'' he said. ''Better have some flashlights handy.''

Peggy nodded, picking up their coffee mugs and moving into the kitchen.

Bob was about to head up the back stairs when he noticed a pair of headlights. A car had turned into their driveway. ''We aren't expecting any guests, are we?'' Although he knew the answer, he asked in case Peggy had booked someone and then forgotten to mention it.

''Not until the weekend.'' Peggy stuck the two mugs in the dishwasher.

''Looks like someone might be coming.''

His wife parted the drape and stared out the window over the sink. ''It isn't anyone we know, is it?''

"Hard to tell in this rain, but I don't recognize the car." Bob was halfway to the front door when the bell rang. He turned on the porch light and unfastened the lock. A man stood on the other side, wearing a raincoat and slouch hat. He held a small suitcase in one hand. His head was lowered, shadowed, making it impossible to see his face clearly.

"I saw the sign from the road. Do you have a room available for the night?" he asked in a low, husky voice.

"We do," Bob told him and took a moment to size up the stranger. The man was in his mid-fifties, he guessed, but it was difficult to be sure. He kept his shoulders hunched forward as he stepped into the house. Yet Bob thought he looked vaguely familiar.

Always warm and welcoming, Peggy ushered their guest into the kitchen, where the registration forms were kept. The man glanced at the form Peggy handed him. "I'll pay you now," he said, withdrawing cash from his pocket.

"We need you to fill out the information card," Bob said. He had a funny feeling about this guy, although he couldn't place him.

"I'm Bob Beldon," he said. "This might seem like an odd question, but have we ever met?"

The stranger didn't answer.

"Honey, don't delay our guest with questions," Peggy whispered.

Irritated, Bob frowned slightly. He couldn't help wondering why the stranger had chosen a relatively remote bed-and-breakfast rather than one of the more convenient motels off the freeway.

"Can I get you something warm to drink?" Peggy asked.

"No, thanks." His response was gruff, almost unfriendly.

"What brings you out here on a night like this?" Bob pressed. "We aren't exactly on the beaten path."

"None of that's important just now," Peggy said, glaring at Bob. He could tell she was annoyed by his attitude, but he definitely felt a little uneasy.

The stranger ignored his question. "If you'd show me to my room, I'd appreciate it."

"Of course." Peggy led the way down the long hallway off the kitchen. "You have your choice. We have the Goldfinch room and the—"

"The first one is fine." He seemed impatient to be about his business, whatever that might be. "I'll have the registration card filled out for you in the morning." He opened the door and set his case inside, then with his back to them, said, "I hope you won't mind if I turn in. It's been a long day."

Bob was about to tell him the paperwork had to be completed first, but Peggy cut him off. "Breakfast is served between eight and ten. Sleep well."

"Thank you." He closed the door hard and they heard the lock snap into place.

Bob waited until they were upstairs before he spoke. "I don't like the looks of him."

"Don't be ridiculous," Peggy said as she went into the master bathroom to remove her makeup. "He's a paying guest. You don't have to like him. My guess is he'll be gone early in the morning and that'll be the end of it."

"Maybe," Bob muttered, but he had the sinking feeling that wouldn't be the case.

The storm continued to rage, and Bob stood at the bedroom window that overlooked the inky waters of the Cove. The lighthouse on the point could be seen in the distance, warning ships of danger ahead. An eerie sensation came over him. More than once, he'd wondered about this business of allowing strangers into their home. He didn't like the man in the room downstairs, although he couldn't say exactly why. All he knew was that his gut instinct told him the stranger was trouble.

Peggy was such a warmhearted soul that all she saw was the plight of someone caught in a storm, looking for shelter from the night. Bob wished he felt the same.

"Are you coming to bed?" his wife asked, turning down the comforter and sliding between the crisp, clean sheets.

Maybe Peggy was right. She generally was. The man downstairs was just someone passing through. In the morning he'd be on his way and they'd never see him again. The stranger had already paid in full, and if he was reluctant to fill out the information card, well, that was his prerogative.

The following morning, Bob was awakened by the sun. He jerked into sudden wakefulness, surprised to see that it was light outside. Peggy had already gone downstairs; he could hear her singing along to the radio as she baked blueberry muffins. They were her specialty, and the blueberries came from their own small patch next to Peggy's pride, her herb garden. The aroma of fresh coffee wafted up the stairs.

Bob rubbed his hand down his face, recalling remnants of a familiar nightmare. Not images so much as feelings, impressions, and they hadn't been pleasant. After he'd climbed into bed, he'd fallen into a light, restless slumber, followed by a deeper sleep. Try as he might, though, he could remember nothing of the dreams he'd had.

Normally he was up before Peggy and made the coffee. Feeling guilty for sleeping so late, he hurriedly dressed. As an afterthought, he walked quickly to the window. Sure enough, the white Ford was still parked below. So their guest hadn't sneaked out as Bob had half suspected—and half hoped—he might. Perhaps this morning the stranger would be a bit friendlier than he'd been the night before, and Bob could discover what it was about him that had struck a familiar chord.

Peggy smiled when she saw him. "Good morning, hon. It's ages since you slept this late."

"I know. I don't understand why."

His wife hesitated. "You had another of your nightmares."

"I don't really remember...."

"Are you all right this morning?" Her face creased with worry lines as she studied him.

"I'm fine," he murmured. "I didn't get up—did I?" Twice over the years, Bob had awakened somewhere outside their bedroom. The only explanation had been sleepwalking.

"You were in bed when you woke, weren't you?" she teased.

He nodded and was instantly relieved. He hugged his wife, then poured himself a cup of coffee. Taking his Alcoholics Anonymous "Big Book," he walked into the sunroom and settled in his recliner to read. He had twenty years of sobriety behind him, but he still lived one day at a time. He was a drunk who was one shot glass away from ruin, and he didn't allow a day to go by without reminding himself of that. Twenty minutes later, Peggy took the muffins out of the oven.

Their morning routine was set, and it was almost ten before his wife realized they hadn't seen their guest, although his car was still there. Curiosity led Bob outside to glance through the driver's window. A map lay on the passenger seat and a half-full water bottle was in the drink holder, but he saw nothing out of the ordinary.

"I did tell him breakfast was between eight and ten, didn't I?" she asked Bob when he came back into the house.

"Maybe he's just sleeping in. He said he had a hard day."

"It's after eleven," Peggy murmured a bit later.

"He's an odd duck." Bob wasn't going to change his opinion about that.

A half hour later, Peggy was again concerned. "Maybe we'd better check to see if he's all right."

"Let him sleep," Bob insisted. "For all we know, he could be in his room working. He did have a computer with him, didn't he?"

"I don't remember."

To Bob's way of thinking, if the stranger wanted privacy, he'd give it to him.

His wife sent him a questioning look, then shrugged and went back to the quilt she'd recently started. Bob went to his garage workshop; in retirement, he'd taken up woodwork and enjoyed building furniture. Over the years, he'd created some pretty nice pieces, if he did say so himself. He'd recently finished a chest of drawers and was proud of the workmanship. After he'd added a final coat of varnish, he returned to the house. It was now twelve-thirty. A look out the window revealed the stranger's car parked where it had been earlier.

Bob fixed himself a ham sandwich and resumed his tinkering around the garage. A few minutes later, Peggy sought him out.

"I think we're going to have to go in there," his wife said. "I knocked on his door, but there wasn't any answer."

Bob decided Peggy was right. Following her into the house, he pounded on the bedroom door.

"Are you awake?" he called loudly.

"There's no need to yell," Peggy whispered. She looked nervous, and frankly Bob was starting to feel the same way. Although they'd been in business for more than ten years, it was the first time they'd had an experience—or a guest—like this.

"I have the key," Peggy told him when there was no response.

"Okay."

"Should I call Troy Davis?" she asked.

The sheriff was a good friend, but Bob didn't want to waste Troy's time if there was a logical explanation. "Not yet."

"But something must be wrong."

"Don't leap to conclusions, Peg." He wished now that he'd gone with his instincts and told the stranger to seek some other place for the night.

Peggy handed him the key and Bob reluctantly inserted it in the lock. Slowly, he turned the knob and swung open the door. Their guest was sleeping in the middle of the bed. His coat hung in the closet, with his hat resting on the shelf directly above. The suitcase was open, but it looked as though a surgeon had packed it. Everything was crisply folded and compact. The suitcase appeared to be undisturbed.

"He could just be sick," Peggy said, clinging to Bob's arm.

Bob doubted it. He recognized that smell, and his skin crawled with memories of jungle warfare almost forty years earlier. The scent of death was one a man didn't quickly forget.

Whatever the stranger's purpose for being in Cedar Cove, it would likely remain a mystery now.

Bob moved to the bed and stared down at him. The night before, his face had been shadowed by his hat, which was pulled low over his face. He looked younger now that Bob could see him clearly. Younger and completely at peace.

"Is he...dead?" Peggy asked, her dread palpable.

Although he already knew the answer, Bob felt for a pulse in the man's neck. There was nothing. "I think it's time we phoned Troy," he said.

Fifteen minutes later, the yard was filled with emergency vehicles. EMTs, several officers and the medical examiner tramped through the house. Bob answered question after question, but he wasn't able to provide Troy or Joe Mitchell, the medical examiner, with much information.

"There'll have to be an autopsy," Troy said.

"Are you going to take him out of here soon?" Peggy asked. Bob could tell that she was shaken by all of this. Truth be known, so was he.

The medical examiner came out of the room and peeled off his plastic gloves.

"Do you have any idea what killed him?" Bob asked.

"Not yet," Joe said, frowning. "He's driver's license says his name's Whitcomb. James Whitcomb, and he's from Florida. Mean anything to you?"

"No." Bob could say that with certainty, despite the hint of familiarity last night. "I've never seen the man in my life."

Joe continued to frown. "He's had extensive cosmetic surgery."

Bob hardly knew what to make of that information.

"There's something unusual going on here," Joe said, following the body as it was wheeled out of the room and down the hall.

Maryellen's popularity at Get Nailed had fallen considerably after the Halloween party. Rachel, her nail tech, had met Terri's discarded male friend who enjoyed working on cars. Things had looked promising for a while.

All through November and December, Rachel had been full of praise for Larry and everything he was doing for her car. First, he replaced her failing brakes, and at a fraction of the cost a shop would have charged. Then he got her interior lights working. He even managed to fix her tape deck. Rachel was grateful and managed to convince herself that she was falling madly in love. How could she *not* love a man who was saving her hundreds of dollars?

Then her transmission went out. This was a major repair, but Rachel's hero was confident he could fix it. All she had to do was buy the new transmission. Unfortunately Larry had overestimated his skills. Not only had he bungled the job, but Rachel had to take her vehicle into the shop and pay for the repairs a second time. To add insult to injury, Larry had presented her with a bill for all the labor and parts he'd put into her car. Needless to say, the relationship had taken a sharp turn south.

Jane's experience wasn't much better. She'd been looking for a man with money sense. Jeannie had once dated a very nice but very boring financial advisor whom she'd introduced to Jane at the Halloween party. Jane and Geoff had instantly hit it off. Jane insisted Geoff wasn't nearly as boring as Jeannie had said. But then he'd given her a hot stock tip that was close to being insider information. Sure enough, Jane had invested her entire savings and almost immediately, the stock fell eight percent.

"What I learned from all this," Rachel said, as she finished the polish job on Maryellen's nails, "is that if one of us dumps a man, it's for a damn good reason."

"You can say that again," Jane echoed.

"What about the guy you met?" Jeannie asked Maryellen.

She blinked, pretending not to understand the question. "I didn't meet anyone."

"That guy you brought stuck to you like glue," Terri called from the other side of the shop, where she was working on an older woman. "I had my eye on him big-time, but he wasn't having anything to do with me."

"I'm sure you're imagining it." The last person she wanted to discuss with her friends was Jon Bowman.

"Not likely," Terri muttered, standing in front of the display of fingernail polish. She picked up a bottle and read the name on the bottom. "How about 'More Than a Waitress'?" she asked her customer.

Thankfully, attention was turned away from Maryellen.

"Are you going out with him?" Rachel asked, ambushing her with the question. "You might not have noticed how hot that guy was for you, but the rest of us sure did."

"I haven't seen him since before Christmas, but if I do, would you like me to give him your number?" This was the only way she could think of to convince Rachel that she wasn't interested in dating Jon.

"No way. I've been with guys who're hung up on someone else. It's a real downer, if you know what I mean." Coloring the last fingernail, Rachel set the timer and lowered the light over Maryellen's perfect pink nails.

Once they were dry, Maryellen hurried out of the shop. She was meeting her mother for dinner at the Pancake Palace. Her entire schedule was off, due to a meeting with the gallery owners, who'd flown in unexpectedly. Luckily, Rachel could fit her in for a late-afternoon appointment.

Fearing questions, Maryellen had been avoiding her family. Kelly, busy as she was with Tyler, had readily accepted her excuses, but Grace was having none of it. Given no other option, Maryellen agreed to meet her at the Palace, where the food was plentiful and cheap.

Grace already had a booth by the time Maryellen arrived. She slipped into the seat across from her and reached for the menu.

"How are you feeling?" her mother asked immediately.

"Wonderful." That was a lie, but Maryellen didn't want Grace to overreact to her situation. At this point, only her mother knew about the pregnancy; she hadn't been ready to divulge the news to Kelly or any of her friends, especially while she felt ill. Every day for the last month, Maryellen had awakened with a queasy stomach. Invariably, a short time later, she was hanging her head over the toilet. She didn't recall Kelly having these symptoms when she was pregnant. In any event, if her sister *had* suffered from morning sickness, Paul was there to love and encourage her and then hand her a washcloth. Maryellen had rarely felt more alone.

Grace set aside the menu. "So you're in perfect health? Ha! I don't believe that for a moment."

"Mother," Maryellen said, doing her best to remain cordial. "Don't. Please don't."

"Don't what?" Grace demanded and then seemed to have a change of heart. "Let's start again, shall we?"

"Please. Tell me what's going on with you. Please, Mom, just this once don't drill me with questions I don't want to answer." She bit her lip and prayed her mother was listening.

Grace stared at her, obviously unhappy about her daughter's request. "All right," she said slowly. "There's plenty of other news for us to discuss."

"Like what?" Maryellen asked gratefully.

"Well, for one thing," Grace said, cradling her water glass in both hands. "I went out to dinner with Cliff Harding last Saturday night."

Now, *this* was news Maryellen had been waiting to hear. "Cliff called you?" In her opinion, he'd been patient for far too long.

Her mother blushed and looked down at the menu. "Actually, I phoned him." She said this as if she'd committed some terrible breach of etiquette.

"Mom, that's great!"

"I've never called a man in my life." Even now Grace sounded unsure that she'd done the right thing.

"What convinced you?"

"Olivia," her mother said without hesitation. "And two glasses of wine. She persuaded me Cliff was going to lose interest—and oh, I've been so lonely and miserable."

Maryellen raised one eyebrow. "Wine can certainly loosen one's inhibitions." She was in a position to know.

"Olivia and I were celebrating," her mother went on to explain. "Seth and Justine are expecting. And did you know they bought a restaurant? It's all so exciting for them."

"Yes, I'd heard about The Captain's Galley. I'm sure they'll do well and I—"

A flustered teenage waitress came for their order.

Maryellen waited until the girl was out of earshot. "You didn't mention anything about me, did you?"

"No," Grace murmured. "But I was tempted."

"No one can know, Mom."

"But why—"

"I have my reasons."

"I want to talk to you about this, Maryellen, but every time I try, you clam up and get defensive. I'm your mother. Do you think I don't realize you're avoiding me? I want to know why."

That should be obvious. "I wish I'd never told you… I knew I'd regret it and I do."

"It's more than the pregnancy," Grace whispered. "It's what you said at lunch that day."

"Mom, don't." The lump in her throat was growing thicker. "Please don't. I can't discuss that."

"You said you'd been pregnant before. Fifteen years ago, you said. Was it before you were married or—"

Maryellen shook her head, refusing to discuss the

most painful time in her life. "So what about your dinner date," she said instead.

Her mother gazed at her, eyes dimmed with sadness. "Will you tell me one day?"

Not if Maryellen could find a way to avoid it. Her entire life had changed because of that pregnancy. The woman she was today, and would always be, was a result of having conceived Clint Jorstad's baby. She might never have married him otherwise, never have taken a path she now knew had been so wrong. But as much as she wanted to lay the blame at her ex-husband's feet, Maryellen was well aware of her own failings. It was easy to create excuses, to rationalize what she'd done. She'd been young and vulnerable and so incredibly naive.

"*Will* you tell me one day?" her mother repeated.

"Perhaps." This pregnancy was a second chance—an opportunity she'd never expected. This time she'd follow the dictates of her heart.

"Have you told Kelly?" Her mother insisted on asking questions Maryellen didn't want to answer.

"Not yet, but I will."

"When?"

"Mom... I'll tell Kelly when I'm ready to let other people know." Maryellen loved her sister, but Kelly simply couldn't keep a secret. The moment she learned the news, it would be all over town.

"Tell me about your dinner with Cliff," Maryellen said again, eager to hear the details of her mother's first official date after her divorce.

"We ate at a wonderful Italian place in Tacoma."

"Away from prying eyes." Maryellen nodded. "That was thoughtful. Did he kiss you?"

The warm color that invaded her mother's cheeks

was answer enough. "Yes." She picked up her fork and examined it carefully.

"Mom, you're blushing."

"The only man who's kissed me in the last thirty-seven years was your father. Until Saturday, of course."

"How was it?" Maryellen knew it was wrong to enjoy seeing her mother this flustered. She resisted the urge to laugh outright, but she was genuinely delighted by the fact that Cliff had planned such a romantic evening, and by her mother's innocent reaction to it.

"The kiss was nice. Very nice."

"Are you seeing him again?" Maryellen asked next.

"You're as bad as Olivia."

"Well, are you?" she pressed.

"Probably, although he hasn't asked."

The waitress arrived with two Cobb salads. "Can I get you anything else?" she asked and put down their bill before they could even respond.

Maryellen watched the girl leave. "I guess not."

"I'm afraid you and Olivia are making more of this evening with Cliff than you should." She plucked a napkin from the dispenser. "It was only one dinner and we haven't arranged another."

"But you'd go out again if he asked."

"Yes— Oh, I don't know—dating frightens me. Everyone seems to think it's the right thing to do, but if that's true, then why do I feel so damn guilty?"

"You shouldn't. You're divorced."

Grace sighed. "Both you and Olivia have encouraged me to see Cliff, but I'm not sure I should...."

"Why not?"

"Oh, honey, don't you know?" Her mother's face was drawn with anxiety. "I need to know what happened to your father. There's this knot in my stomach that's been there since he disappeared.'' She began to shred the paper napkin. ''After I went to dinner with Cliff, I felt good. Kind of...liberated. Free. But it didn't last. I could hardly sleep that night.''

''Mom, you're divorced. You *are* free.''

''Perhaps legally, but I still *feel* married. Despite everything, I feel I belong with your father. I don't know if that'll change until I find out where he is and what drove him away.''

''Mom.'' Maryellen's hand covered her mother's. ''We might never know.''

''I realize that, but it doesn't change how I feel.''

Charlotte sat in Dr. Fred Stevens's waiting room, knitting furiously as the minutes ticked slowly by. She'd been seeing Dr. Fred for the past twenty years and she had complete faith in him. He'd been Clyde's physician, and her husband, too, had trusted him implicitly.

''The doctor can see you now, Charlotte,'' Pamela Johnson said, standing in the doorway that led to the examination rooms.

Charlotte tucked her knitting into her bag and followed the nurse. When they stopped at the scale, Charlotte slipped off her shoes and stepped on, eyes closed and breath held. Some information it was better not to know.

''You're down five pounds,'' Pamela announced.

''Really?'' That made sense, though, seeing that her appetite had been nil for weeks. In the beginning, she'd assumed it was all the stress surrounding the holidays. Then Charlotte had noticed how drained she felt at the end of the day. Lately, climbing stairs seemed to strain her heart and there were all those problems with needing to get to a rest room quickly.

Pamela led the way into the first exam room. She asked a few preliminary questions and took Charlotte's blood pressure. After making a notation in the chart, she placed it in a slot on the outside of the door.

"Go ahead and remove your clothes and put on the gown," the nurse instructed before she left.

Charlotte examined the soft blue paper top. It was ridiculous to think such a thing could cover her. She so seldom needed an appointment other than her yearly exam that she couldn't remember from visit to visit if the gown was supposed to open in the front or the back.

"Hello, Lottie," Dr. Fred said, entering the room about five minutes later.

So few people called Charlotte by that name, it shook her for a moment. Naturally Dr. Fred used it because that was what Clyde had always called her.

"Hello, Dr. Fred."

The physician sat on the stool as he read her chart, while she sat higher up on the examination table with her bare feet dangling. Looking down at her toenails, she was embarrassed to see that they needed a fresh coat of polish. Oh my, this was embarrassing. She tried to cover one foot with the other.

"What's the problem?" Dr. Fred asked. He apparently hadn't noticed her toes.

Charlotte described her symptoms. Tiredness, she explained, a lack of appetite and energy and that pesky problem with her bowels. The more she spoke, the more alarmed she became. "It sounds like I should've come in weeks ago."

"I agree," Dr. Fred said sternly.

"I've been so busy and then there was Christmas...." Her voice trailed off. Her excuses all rang false, even to her own ears.

After a routine exam, Dr. Fred had Pamela take several vials of blood. When she'd finished, he returned to the exam room. Thankfully Charlotte was dressed and prepared for the verdict.

"Well?" she murmured, not sure what to think. Perhaps all he had to do was prescribe iron tablets and she could go back to her regular life.

"I won't know anything until I get the results from the blood tests."

"Do you have any suspicions?" she asked, wanting answers.

"I have a few ideas, but I'll wait for confirmation."

"You were like this with Clyde, too," she said impatiently.

"I'd be irresponsible if I indulged in speculation, wouldn't I?"

"Well...I suppose," she said reluctantly.

Dr. Fred chuckled. "I don't suppose you brought me any of your green tomato mincemeat?"

"You're shameless."

"I am!" He peeked inside her knitting bag.

Charlotte slapped his hand and then pulled out a tall Mason jar filled with his favorite pie mixture.

"You're my sweetheart."

"As long as I feed you mincemeat," Charlotte said with a grin.

"I'll give you a call when the test results are in," he told her as he walked her to the door.

Although she didn't have any answers yet, Charlotte felt better during the next few days. For too long she'd ignored her health and now that she'd taken a positive step toward finding out what was wrong, her spirits lifted.

Dr. Fred's office phoned early the next week; he'd ordered a barrage of tests. One, a colonoscopy, required a trip to Harrison Hospital in Bremerton. Not wanting to alarm Olivia, Charlotte had her friend Laura drive her.

"I've had this procedure done myself," Laura told her when she arrived to pick her up. Bess and Evelyn had come along for moral support.

"We're going to pamper you," Bess insisted from the back seat.

"You're making me feel like an old woman," Charlotte protested—but not too loudly. Actually, she was grateful for her friends' presence.

Evelyn snickered. "Charlotte, in case you didn't notice, we *are* old women. Now buckle up and stop complaining."

Although she was given anaesthetic, Charlotte was awake for part of the procedure. She heard the medical staff whispering together, calling over another doctor, pointing to an area on the screen. She wasn't sure what it all meant and anxiously awaited the verdict.

When Dr. Fred joined his associates, she could see from the look on his face that it was serious. When he did speak, she heard only one word and that was enough to send her world into a tailspin.

Charlotte's friends chatted on the ride home, but her head was buzzing and she scarcely heard a thing they said. Laura came into the house with her.

"Do you want me to call Olivia?" she asked.

Charlotte shook her head. "No…I don't want to disturb her. She's so busy."

"She needs to know."

"I'll tell her soon," Charlotte promised.

Laura fussed about her for a few moments and then, being the good friend she was, realized that Charlotte wanted to be alone. She hugged Charlotte before she left.

Sitting in her chair, with Harry on her lap, Charlotte reviewed her options. She didn't expect to live forever, but she felt she had a whole lot of life in her yet. When she was finally ready to talk, it wasn't Olivia she called but her son, Will, who lived in Atlanta.

"Mother!" Will was clearly surprised to hear from her. "How are you?"

"Just grand," she lied. "I imagine you're wondering why I'm phoning you at work in the middle of the day, since this is when the rates are high."

"The thought did cross my mind," Will said. How like Clyde he sounded, her son, the nuclear engineer. How proud she was of him and Olivia, too. Suddenly Charlotte found herself trembling.

"Mom, what's wrong?"

Will always seemed to know when something was troubling her. "I was in to see Dr. Fred last week."

A pause followed. "When I spoke to Olivia, she said you'd been tired lately."

"Yes, well, that's true. I have been."

"Tired enough to decide you needed to visit Dr. Fred."

"Yes. You know how he loves my green tomato mincemeat. Normally I would've baked him a pie, but this time I just brought him a jar. I had plenty of green tomatoes this year."

"Mother, you didn't call me to talk about your pies, did you?"

"No..."

"What did Dr. Fred have to say?"

"Well, not much. He wanted me to have a few tests." She pressed the phone hard against her ear.

"Which you did?"

"Oh, yes, he was quite insistent about that. The most intrusive one was this morning. It was at Harrison Hospital."

"Did Olivia go with you?"

"Oh no, I couldn't bother her on a Thursday, especially at the end of the month. You know how busy her court schedule can get."

"In other words, Olivia doesn't know anything about this?"

"Not yet."

"Did you get the test results?"

Charlotte felt the tears fill her eyes and was grateful that Harry was lying on her lap. Petting him soothed her and just then, with her fears close to overwhelming her, she needed him.

"Mother?" Will said more loudly this time. "Are you still on the line?"

"I'm here."

"What did the doctor say?"

She hesitated. "Will, I know it would be a terrible inconvenience to you and Georgia, but I was wondering if you'd mind making a trip to Cedar Cove in the near future."

"Mother, *what* did Dr. Fred tell you?"

Charlotte bit down hard on her lower lip. "I'm afraid I have cancer."

Twelve

Zach didn't want this separation, but Rosie had taken the choice away from him. His soon-to-be ex-wife was the unreasonable one. He'd been shocked and hurt when she'd had him served with divorce papers. Basically he had twenty-four hours to vacate the family home. He was stunned that she'd resort to seeing an attorney and setting everything in motion. Yes, they'd talked about it, but that had been in the heat of an argument. He certainly hadn't expected her to kick him out of his own home.

Since she was obviously determined to go through with the divorce, Zach hoped they could at least handle the whole process in a civilized manner. Nothing he said or did would convince Rosie that he wasn't involved with Janice. He'd given up reasoning with her. If his wife had so little faith in him, he was better off without her.

Finding an apartment within a reasonable distance of the house, however, had proved to be a challenge. Luckily Janice had been able to help him look; otherwise, he wasn't sure what he would've done. Rosie knew his work schedule better than anyone, and he'd hoped she would appreciate that with quarterly taxes due and the rush of year-end figures he needed to complete for his business clients, his free time was limited.

In that hope, he'd been mistaken. Rosie didn't seem to care.

Zach was trying hard to maintain a positive attitude for the sake of his children. His relationship with Allison and Eddie was the most important thing to him. He intended to remain a large part of their lives, no matter what the terms of the divorce.

"Do you have to leave?" Eddie asked, looking forlorn. His son sat on the end of the bed in the master bedroom while Zach packed up his half of the closet.

"For now that would be best." Zach refused to drag his children into his problems with Rosie. They were innocent. Rosie was the one he blamed. She'd been acting like a jealous shrew for weeks, although he figured that was just a symptom of her insecurity—an insecurity he'd done nothing to cause.

"I want you and Allison to come over to my apartment with me, okay?"

"To stay?"

This was difficult. "Your mother and I need to work that out. Right now I just want you to see where I live."

"Okay." Eddie sounded like he was trying not to cry. "Can I come anytime I want?"

"Of course! My apartment is your home, too."

Eddie shifted on the mattress and sat on his hands. "Do you still love Mom?"

"Of course I do." Zach set a work shirt on the stack already in the middle of the bed, then sat down beside his son. He placed his arm around Eddie's shoulders and struggled for the right words. "Sometime two people who love each other can't agree on certain things anymore. When that happens, it's better if they live apart."

Eddie lowered his head. "Mom said the same thing."

Funny that they could agree on the rationale for divorce more than they could agree on anything to do with their marriage. They hadn't spoken much in the last few weeks. All communication had been through their attorneys, which was ridiculous as far as Zach was concerned, since he'd continued to live at home.

"Allison says this whole divorce is bogus."

Zach noted that *bogus* was currently a favorite word of his daughter's. He didn't bother to respond.

"Will you talk to Mom?"

Not if he could avoid it, Zach mused. They no longer argued, and for that he was grateful. If anything, Rosie went out of her way to be polite. It was almost as though they were strangers. His wife, however, had plenty to say to her attorney. His sins were outlined in legal documents that went on for pages. Knowing it would anger him to read anything more than the title page, Zach left everything to his attorney. He'd known Otto Benson for years and had frequently worked with him, and he trusted Otto to represent him fairly.

"You ready to help me load everything into the car?" he asked his son.

"Okay." Eddie didn't reveal a lot of enthusiasm. He slid off the edge of the bed and paraded behind Zach with an armload of clothes. Zach arranged the starched dress shirts on the back seat of his car and took the stack Eddie had brought out with him.

"Do you want to see my apartment?" he asked Allison when he returned to the kitchen.

His daughter removed her earphones and turned off the portable CD player. She stared at him a moment as though she hadn't heard. Finally she muttered, "Are you *really* going to leave, Dad?"

"I'm afraid so, sweetheart."

"But you vowed to always love Mom."

"I know, and this is hard, but you can see that your mother and I do nothing but argue. That's not good. We're going through this divorce for you kids, to save you from—"

"You're doing this for me and Eddie? I don't think so, Dad. It seems to me you and Mom are doing this for yourselves. Eddie and I just happen to be stuck in the middle, and I hate it. I really, really hate it." She was shouting by the time she finished. Before Zach could reply, Allison slipped the headphones back over her ears, blocking him out.

Zach saw the tears in his daughter's eyes and they twisted his gut. He wanted to tell her that the difficulties between him and Rosie had nothing to do with her or Eddie. This wasn't *their* fault.

Maybe he and Rosie had outgrown each other. That was something he'd read in an article on marriage breakdown that Janice had given him. She'd photocopied it from some women's magazine. Maybe he and Rosie had stopped having anything, other than the kids and the house, in common, as the article suggested. Perhaps because he made a good living and they were now financially comfortable they'd lost that sense of being *partners,* facing the world together, creating dreams together. Lately their marriage had been filled with bitterness and resentment. All they did was make each other miserable, and that was no way to live and certainly not a healthy environment in which to raise their children.

Looking around the house one last time, Zach loaded

up his remaining essentials. For obvious reasons, Rosie had been missing for most of the day. This was no surprise, seeing that she spent the greater part of every weekend with people other than her family, anyway. Nor did it upset him when he noticed the breakfast dishes still in the sink, unwashed. That was par for the course. He had his own list of sins that his wife had committed, but unless she made it impossible, he was taking the higher road and refused to drag her faults into a courtroom.

"You coming to see my new apartment?" he asked Eddie, striving for a bit of enthusiasm.

"I guess."

"You'll have your own room there, you know." The second bedroom was necessary if he intended to have the children stay with him, and Zach did. He couldn't afford beds just yet, but he'd buy them as soon as possible.

"I don't wanna sleep in the same room as Allison," Eddie complained.

"You can sleep in my room if you want."

"I can?"

"Sure thing."

That appeared to appease Eddie for the moment.

Before he left, Zach asked Allison a second time if she wanted to see his new place, but she sat with her earphones on, music blaring, and pretended not to hear him. She was angry and Zach understood how she felt. Eventually she'd come around and they'd be able to discuss this. Allison had always been closer to him than her mother.

The two-bedroom apartment was a little less than three miles from the house on Pelican Court. It wasn't as large, but then he could barely afford to maintain two households. He'd wanted a three-bedroom place, but couldn't find one within his limited budget. He'd chosen this complex so the kids would still be in the same school district. Otto was hammering out a parenting plan with Rosie's attorney.

Once at his apartment, Zach opened the door for his son. Eddie walked into the living room and glanced around, frowning. "Where's the TV?"

"I'm taking the one in the master bedroom." Rosie and he were still in the process of dividing everything up, but most of the furniture had yet to be moved. So far, Rosie hadn't been difficult about the division of household assets, and Zach trusted that would continue. Considering that he was the one who'd paid for everything in the family home, it was only right that he take what he needed for his new place.

Apparently it hadn't occurred to Rosie that she was going to have to find a job. Zach made a respectable income, but he couldn't afford to pay all the expenses for two households. For the first time since the children were born, Rosie would be forced to work outside the home.

"Check out the bedroom," Zach said as he hauled a load of clothes into the larger of the two rooms. The newly carpeted room was stark and empty without a bed, but all of that would be resolved shortly. Soon, Zach told himself, he'd feel just as much at home here as he had in the family residence.

"Hello." A soft rapping was followed by a voice Zach recognized instantly.

"Janice." Zach hadn't expected a visit from his assistant, especially on a weekend. "Hello," he said.

Shyly, she came into the apartment with a boy close to Eddie's age.

"This is my son, Chris," she said with her arm around her son's shoulders.

"This is Eddie."

"Hi," Eddie said, sounding tentative.

"I thought I'd stop by and ask if you have everything you need," Janice said. "I know how much work moving can be and I wanted to see if there's anything I can do."

She'd always been helpful, and Zach appreciated her efforts more than ever. She brought in a sack and placed it on the kitchen counter.

"Eddie, why don't you show Chris the apartment?" Zach suggested. Almost immediately the two boys disappeared into the back bedroom.

"I brought you a housewarming gift," Janice said, then proceeded to unpack a coffeepot, plus grounds.

"You didn't need to do that." Zach remained on the other side of the kitchen, a little uncomfortable with her generosity.

"I know… You can tell me to get lost if you want, but I knew you were moving in today. I know from my own experience how difficult this is and I hope the transition goes smoothly for you and your wife."

"Thank you." Zach preferred to keep his business and his personal life separate, but without Janice's help in this recent crisis, he didn't know what he would've done.

An hour later when he drove back to the house with Eddie, the first thing he noticed was Rosie's car parked in the driveway. Eddie brightened as soon as he saw it. He threw open the car door and raced toward the house. Zach followed with far less enthusiasm. He'd hoped to move all his personal stuff before Rosie returned. There were still books and CDs and…

"Hi," Rosie said, her face tense, but not unfriendly. "I see you're packing up."

Zach nodded.

"I made a new friend," Eddie said, hugging his mother about the waist.

"That's nice. You'll have friends both here and at your dad's place."

"Chris doesn't live in the apartment building. His mother is Dad's assistant and they came over with a gift to warm the house."

Sure enough, his wife's eyes narrowed to thin, angry slits. "I'll just bet," she muttered under her breath, then stormed out of the kitchen.

Zach's shoulders sagged in defeat. This was something Rosie would try to use against him when they went to court. Janice's innocent gesture of friendship and support would be turned into "evidence."

Cliff Harding had a good feeling about this Saturday afternoon date with Grace. It'd been three weeks since their dinner and they'd spoken intermittently on the phone. He could tell that Grace still had reservations regarding their relationship. Something had happened in the past three weeks. He wasn't sure what, but when they did speak she'd sounded shaken and uneasy. When he asked her about it, she made excuses and quickly got off the phone.

Under normal conditions, he would've questioned Charlotte, who was his best source when it came to Grace, but his friend had enough to deal with. She'd soon undergo surgery, followed by chemo, which was hard on a person, physically and emotionally. He'd seen his own father waste away, ravaged by lung cancer. Of course, back in those days they didn't have the effective cancer treatments they had now. Still...

So, no, he couldn't ask Charlotte what was going on with Grace. She had troubles enough of her own.

But Cliff was convinced it had to do with Dan. She wanted answers about what had happened to her ex-husband, and hadn't realized yet that the peace she sought had to come from within.

However, he was encouraged by her invitation to lunch. Perhaps now he'd understand what had caused her to withdraw from such a promising beginning.

It was a blustery, windy day, the first weekend in February, when he drove into town. The sky was leaden, threatening rain.

Buttercup announced his arrival with a sharp bark, then ambled onto the porch where Cliff stood waiting. The golden retriever wagged her tail, and after Cliff rang the front doorbell, he leaned down and stroked the dog's silky fur. At least he'd managed to win *her* over.

"Hello, Cliff," Grace said, sounding stiff and reserved. She unlocked the screen door to let him in. "Typical February day, isn't it?"

He agreed, thinking she looked wonderful in a red turtleneck sweater and tight jeans. The scent of chili simmering in a Crock-Pot on the kitchen counter wafted toward him and he breathed in appreciatively.

"Smells good."

"It's my chili." Her eyes refused to meet his. "Would you like to sit down?" She motioned toward the living room.

"Sure."

She waited until he was seated, then sat across from him. "I've been rude lately and I thought I should explain what's been going on."

"Please." He waited patiently, settling back on the worn, comfortable chair. He noticed she didn't seem to know what to do with her hands. First she clasped them together as though praying, then she slid them between her knees. Buttercup lay down at Grace's feet.

Grace looked sheepish. "Have I done it that often?"

He merely shrugged, smiling a little.

"I don't *mean* to be rude, it's just that every time I'm convinced that seeing you is the right thing, something happens that causes me to question myself." She stared at her hands.

"What was it this time?"

Grace gently petted Buttercup's head. "Do you remember when you came that one Saturday last fall and fixed the garage door and cleaned the gutters for me? I was grateful in more ways than the obvious. For the first time since Dan left, I felt like I *could* go on—that I could let go of my marriage."

Cliff had been encouraged that day, too. He'd hoped it would be the first of many such visits....

"Then shortly afterward—on Thanksgiving Day—I heard from Dan."

Now Cliff was completely confused. To the best of his knowledge, Dan had disappeared last April. No one, not Grace or either of her daughters, and from every indication no other friend or family member, had heard from him since then. There'd apparently been a brief sighting in May, but that was it.

"You spoke to Dan?" he asked.

"No," she clarified. "But he phoned the house. He didn't say anything. He just...let me know he was there."

"How can you be sure it was him?"

"I can't prove it," she said and straightened, clasping her hands again. "It's instinct. Early Thanksgiving morning, the phone rang and there was no one on the other end. It was Dan—I know it was him."

Bad enough that Cliff had to deal with an ex-husband who'd vanished into thin air; now he was stuck with ghosts as well.

"Then after you and I went to dinner in Tacoma, I felt so good about seeing you. I really believed we could have a relationship."

"So do I," Cliff insisted. "We're right together."

"I thought—oh Cliff, that night was magical. I enjoyed everything about it."

"The kisses?" His ego demanded that she admit to enjoying their kisses as much as he had.

"Those most of all," she whispered.

Cliff's reaction had been the same. He'd dropped her off at the house and he'd felt ecstatic, full of anticipation, looking forward to seeing her again. Then silence, followed by various lame excuses. He hadn't known what to think.

"A little more than a week ago, something else happened. This Dan issue refuses to go away."

"Did he phone you again?"

"No—this time I got a call from Joe Mitchell. He's the medical examiner. Recently a man died while staying at the Thyme and Tide bed-and-breakfast."

Cliff remembered reading about that in *The Cedar Cove Chronicle.* It was a strange story, one that didn't make much sense. Apparently the man hadn't been identified yet. "He was carrying false ID, right?"

"Yes. Joe said the dead man had gone through extensive cosmetic surgery, too."

"He'd altered his appearance?"

Grace nodded. "Joe noticed he was about the same

age as Dan and had a similar build. He was playing a hunch when he contacted me."

Understanding came in a flash. "The medical examiner thought it might be Dan?"

She briefly closed her eyes and Cliff realized how traumatized and upset she must've been to receive such a call. "Joe thought I might be able to identify him." She gave a perceptible shudder. "Going to the morgue was awful. Just awful..."

Cliff slipped closer to the edge of the chair cushion. "But it wasn't Dan, was it?"

Grace lowered her gaze and shook her head. "No." She swallowed tightly. "God forgive me, I wish it had been—not that I want him dead but I need answers. I need to know why he left and if he ever intends on coming back."

Her knuckles were white, and it was hard for Cliff to stay where he was. The urge to hold her grew stronger by the minute.

"First the calls on Thanksgiving and now this. It's almost as if—"

"Calls?" Cliff repeated. "There was more than one?"

"Actually there were three, and every time we answered, all we heard was static. I felt the eeriest sensation, and I knew it had to be Dan. It *had* to be. Who else would phone not once but three times and then say absolutely nothing?"

"Wait a second." Cliff raised his hand, his thoughts swirling frantically. "Who else?" he echoed. "What about me?"

"What?"

Cliff cleared his throat. "That was me."

"You phoned—and didn't say anything?" Her voice was raised in accusation.

"Remember the blizzard I told you about? I tried to call you all day, and I did manage to get through on three different occasions. But the first two times, the only thing I could hear was static. The third time no one picked up and I didn't leave a message."

"That was *you?*" Grace pressed her hands to her lips. "But I thought...I believed it was Dan."

Tears filled her eyes, and Cliff didn't care what she thought, he had to hold her. Moving onto the sofa beside Grace, he wrapped his arms around her. "I'm sorry. I would've mentioned it earlier, but I didn't know."

"I felt as if Dan was reaching out to me—as if he was saying how sorry he was. A year ago, we'd had a wonderful Thanksgiving and this year...this year it was only Maryellen and me and..."

Cliff brought her closer still and rested his chin gently on her head. She felt warm and soft in his embrace. More than that, it seemed so right to hold her. He savored these moments, treasured them. He yearned to tilt her face toward his, to lower his mouth to hers, but he didn't want Grace to turn to him in grief. When they kissed again, he wanted it to be in discovery. In mutual passion. In shared affection.

The front door opened suddenly, which shocked them both. Grace jerked away and inhaled sharply. "Kelly..."

Her youngest daughter stood in the room, holding Tyler in a baby carrier, her eyes huge and angry. "What's *he* doing here?" she demanded.

"Kelly, this is Cliff Harding, the man I told you I was seeing," Grace said, recovering quickly. She left the sofa and crouched down to look at her grandson. Little Tyler was sound asleep.

"Your mother invited me to lunch," Cliff added, wanting it understood that he hadn't stopped by without a reason.

Kelly remained tense, standing there, glaring at them both.

"Please, sweetheart, sit down." Although her daughter was clearly furious, Grace remained courteous.

Kelly did as her mother asked, but reluctantly. "Why didn't you tell me about Maryellen?"

Grace sighed and looked away. "It wasn't my decision not to tell you. It was Maryellen's."

"My own *sister* is pregnant, and I'm kept entirely in the dark?"

This was news to Cliff, too, but now didn't seem the time to mention it.

"I suggest you take this up with Maryellen," Grace said. "The last thing I want to do is get between the two of you. I will say that I didn't agree with Maryellen, but the choice was hers."

"She told you, though." Kelly's hurt was evident. "She didn't trust me? She left me to figure it out for myself, like...like I don't matter?"

"I'm sorry, but it was your sister's choice," Grace repeated.

"How many other people know? Am I the only one who doesn't?"

"I guessed she was pregnant," Grace admitted. "She didn't tell me voluntarily."

Cliff could see that Grace and her daughter needed to talk, and his being there wasn't helping. "Why don't I leave for a while?" he said, getting to his feet.

Grace reached for his hand and gazed up at him, her eyes appealing. "You will come back?"

"If you want."

"Give us an hour," she said.

Cliff nodded, and after bidding Kelly farewell, he headed for the front door. He wasn't halfway out when he heard Kelly tear into her mother.

"How could you date again?" her daughter cried. "We don't know what's happened to Dad and already you've got yourself a boyfriend. I can't *believe* you'd do such a thing. First Maryellen keeps her pregnancy from me, and then I learn my mother has a few secrets of her own. What's happened to our family? Nothing's been right since Daddy left. Nothing."

Then it sounded as though Kelly burst into tears.

Sunday afternoon, Olivia stood inside the main terminal of Sea-Tac Airport, awaiting her brother's arrival. She glanced at her watch; Will's flight was due at three o'clock and she had plenty of time. After several telephone conversations, it was agreed that he'd fly in for their mother's surgery, which was scheduled first thing the following morning.

Olivia had a good relationship with her older brother. They'd kept in frequent touch through the years, and he'd lent a willing ear during that terrible summer back in 1986. Will had been as shocked as Olivia when Stan remarried so quickly following the divorce. Lately, though, it seemed that with their busy careers, brother and sister spoke less often. They'd started e-mailing each other, but usually those e-mails were just a means of passing along jokes, news articles and statistics; they conveyed little that was personal.

Charlotte's cancer had badly shaken Olivia. Her

mother had always been healthy, vigorous, full of energy. In the last few months, she'd watched Charlotte decline right before her eyes, but she'd been so caught up in her own life that she hadn't realized the seriousness of what was happening. She'd attributed her mother's growing frailty to old age.

At precisely the time he was expected, Will came through the secure section of the airport. He paused to look around. When he saw her, his eyes lit up and she walked into his warm embrace.

''You're as beautiful as ever,'' he said.

''And you always were a liar,'' she returned. Already she felt better, knowing that Will would be with her on Monday. ''How's Georgia?'' Her brother had been married for more than thirty years. Georgia was a career woman—an advertising executive—and hadn't wanted a family. Will had reluctantly agreed, but Olivia wondered if he regretted that decision. If so, he'd never mentioned it to her.

''Like me, my wife leads a busy life.''

The oddly stilted words bothered Olivia, as did his detached tone. She suspected trouble in the offing, but this wasn't the time to ask him about it. She sensed that Will was not okay, or at least his marriage wasn't.

Once they'd collected Will's luggage and paid for parking, they headed out of the airport and toward the freeway that led to Cedar Cove.

''My, my,'' Will commented when they turned out of the airport parking lot. ''Where did you get that bracelet?''

Olivia had hesitated before wearing the diamond tennis bracelet Jack had given her, fearing it might invite questions. ''It was a birthday gift from Jack Griffin.''

''The newspaper man? Mom told me you were seeing him.'' He glanced at her pointedly. ''From you, however, I've heard almost nothing on the subject.''

Olivia hadn't fully identified her feelings toward Jack and wasn't sure what to say about their relationship. ''Actually I like him quite a bit.'' She felt her brother studying her and briefly let her eyes leave the road in order to meet his.

''If that bracelet is any indication, he feels the same way.''

''I hope he does.'' Feeling more comfortable about discussing Jack, she added, ''His son's living with him just now and that's been a challenge.'' Eric seemed to be in constant turmoil, miserable one moment and elated the next.

''I'm glad Justine is happily married,'' Will said. ''Not so long ago, Justine laughed in my face when I mentioned the word marriage. She claimed she wasn't interested.''

''Not only is she married, she's pregnant.''

''You're joking! As I recall, her laugh got a whole lot louder when I suggested she might want a family one day.''

Olivia beamed at him. ''I've never seen her happier. I love Seth all the more because of that. Oh, Will, I want you to meet him.''

''And James's marriage is going well?''

She nodded. ''Stan and I were shocked at how quickly it all came about, but I've met Selina and she's a good match for him. I'll bore you with the latest pictures of Isadora Delores the minute I get a chance.''

''I'll look forward to it.''

They entered the freeway, and Will reached for his cell phone. He punched in a number, held the phone to his ear for a moment, and then clicked it off. ''I thought I'd let Georgia know I've arrived. She must be out.'' He said it as though he wasn't surprised, but Olivia wondered why he didn't leave a message. Later, when Charlotte's operation was over, she'd talk to him about it.

''Is Mom emotionally ready for this surgery?'' Will asked.

Olivia couldn't tell. Judging by outward appearances, Charlotte was calm and confident. A few days earlier, however, Olivia had gotten a glimpse behind the mask and for a few fleeting seconds witnessed raw fear.

''Did you know Grandma Munson died of the same form of cancer?'' Olivia asked her brother. Charlotte had brought up that fact the day she'd been so worried, and Olivia knew she was terrified that history was about to repeat itself.

''I barely remember Grandma Munson,'' Will said.

''Mom's putting on a good face but she's frightened.''

''She's afraid colon cancer will kill her, too?''

''I think so,'' Olivia told him. ''She wants to be strong. It's funny, but when she first told me about the cancer, I panicked. The crazy part is Mom's the one who comforted *me*. She gave me the information she'd printed off the Internet.''

''Mom goes on the Internet?''

''Occasionally. One of the knitting ladies she meets with at the Senior Center took a computer class. As soon as Bess heard Mom had cancer, she invited her over. The two of them went on a search to find all the information available on colon cancer.''

''Mom's certainly one of a kind,'' Will said. ''Remember all that business with the Yodeling Cowboy—

how she removed his effects and hid them in her underwear drawer?''

Olivia laughed, and it felt good to be with her brother.

''How's Grace doing these days?'' he asked suddenly. ''Any news on Dan's disappearance? He's never come back?''

''A couple of times Grace was convinced he'd returned to the house, but that was early on.''

''How would she know?''

''Working in the forests all those years, Dan smelled like evergreen. Twice when she returned from work, the inside of the house had the scent of a Christmas tree. The only way that could've happened was if Dan had shown up.''

''Anything since?''

''Not a peep. She thought he might've phoned on Thanksgiving, but eventually found out it was Cliff. He's that friend of Mom's Grace has been seeing on and off.''

''A friend of Mom's,'' Will echoed. ''I'd think he was too old for Grace.''

''Oh, no—Cliff's the grandson of Tom Harding, the cowboy actor.''

''Right. I'd forgotten his name.''

There was a silence and then Olivia said, ''You know when we were growing up, I always thought you had a crush on Grace.''

''I did.''

''You never asked her out, though.''

''No,'' he said, ''but that's because I was shy.''

''You!'' Olivia didn't believe it for a moment. ''I know she would've loved it if you had asked her.''

And maybe things would have turned out differently for both of you.

"You're joking." Will sounded surprised. "I think Grace is one of the most incredible women I've ever met."

His admiration was sincere and equaled Olivia's. "I do, too. Even through all this craziness with Dan, she's been solid as a rock."

"Does anyone know what happened to Dan? Any evidence at all?"

Olivia shook her head. "I wish there was, but no."

"What about a calculated guess?"

"The truth?" She glanced away from the road long enough to gauge his reaction. "Everyone assumes there's another woman involved. He bought a ring just before he disappeared and then later he was seen in town with a woman. It was almost as if he was flaunting his affair."

"But that's not what you think?"

"No," she said. "It doesn't add up."

"How so?"

"Well, Dan wasn't exactly Mr. Personality. He was never the same after Vietnam. Sometimes, for no obvious reason, he went into these depressions and closed out the world. He'd be completely unresponsive—sometimes even cruel. When he was like that, he made life miserable for Grace."

"Why did she stay with him all those years?"

Olivia wasn't entirely sure, but she had her own theory, based on her long friendship with Grace. "She's an honorable woman. When she said her vows, she meant them. *For better or for worse.* But Grace got the *worse* a lot more often than she got the *better*—and a lot more often than either of us will ever know.

Still, she loved Dan and in his own way, Dan loved her."

Olivia exited the freeway at the second Cedar Cove off-ramp and drove toward her mother's home. "When we get to Mom's, beware of Harry. He's pretty protective of her."

Will chuckled. "Don't tell me Mom's got a man living with her."

Now it was Olivia's turn to smile. "Wait and see."

Thirteen

While reading the February 7th issue of the Bremerton newspaper, Jack surreptitiously watched his son out of the corner of his eye. They'd just finished a dinner of microwave lasagna and ice cream. Immediately afterward, Eric had begun to pace the small, compact living room of Jack's waterfront rental house as though he found it impossible to keep still. The boy had been getting on Jack's nerves for weeks. They'd had more than one verbal confrontation during the months since Eric had moved in with him. Ironically, instead of driving them apart, their arguments seemed to have cemented their relationship as father and son.

When Eric had first arrived, they'd both been careful, each afraid of saying or doing something to upset the other. That awkwardness soon dissipated when what was supposed to be only a few days had stretched into nearly five months. There was definitely a degree of irritation, but at least it was honest and they'd finally moved beyond the superficial.

"Would you stop pacing!" Jack shouted when he could tolerate it no longer. He closed the newspaper and tossed it on the footstool as Eric glared at him from across the room.

"I can't help it," Eric muttered. "I think better on my feet."

Jack expelled his breath in a rush, his patience in short supply these days. Briefly he wondered how Eric's co-workers handled his bursts of nervous energy. He wished he had Olivia to distract him, but she was busy with her mother. If she wasn't at the hospital, then she was entertaining her big brother. Jack hadn't seen her in almost a week and damn it all, he missed her.

"What's your problem *now?*" Jack barked.

Eric looked mulishly back at him and said nothing.

It went without saying that it had to do with Shelly and the twins. Jack had never seen anyone agonize over a woman more than his son.

"Are you getting her anything for Valentine's next week?" Jack ventured.

Eric whirled around. "You think I should?"

"When was the last time you talked to her?"

Eric glanced away. "A week ago. I called to see how she's doing."

"I thought you'd decided to walk away." Jack didn't agree with that decision, but this was his son's life, not his. He wanted to support Eric in whatever he decided about Shelly and these two babies. But as far as Jack was concerned, it didn't matter if Eric was the biological father or not; these twins were going to need a daddy. After meeting Shelly and getting to know her, he was convinced the children *were* Eric's, despite medical evidence to the contrary. Shelly simply wasn't the kind of woman who'd fool around and it was clear she still loved Eric, regardless of everything that had happened.

"I *tried* to forget about her," Eric snapped. "But I can't stop thinking about her."

Jack felt he had to help his son. "You know, Eric," he said calmly, "those babies *could* be your own flesh and blood.'' He'd pointed it out before; after all, the doctor at the fertility clinic had acknowledged there was a slight—make that minuscule—chance. But it was still a chance.

Eric flopped down on the sofa and buried his face in his hands. ''You think I haven't prayed for that? I wish to hell I'd never gone and had my sperm checked.'' He hesitated, shoulders hunched forward, and when he spoke again his voice was so low Jack had to strain to hear him. ''Last week when I talked to Shelly, I suggested we get married and raise the babies together.''

''That's terrific,'' Jack said before he realized Shelly had obviously turned him down. Otherwise his son wouldn't be moping around, as miserable as he'd ever been.

''It would be terrific if she'd agreed.'' Eric's voice throbbed with pain.

Jack wanted to kick himself for being so insensitive. ''I'm sorry.'' He leaned forward, resting his elbows on his knees. ''Women can be unreasonable.''

''You're telling me?'' Eric asked.

Jack chuckled.

''You and Olivia seem to be getting along okay, though. I like her, Dad. She's good for you.''

''I like her, too.'' They got along exceptionally well—or had until recently. In the last few months, it seemed that life kept getting in the way of their developing relationship.

''Listen, Dad,'' Eric said, straightening. ''It's time I got on with my life. Shelly's made it obvious that we're through. I figured she'd come to her senses and we could settle this, but it doesn't look like that's going to happen.''

"Not for lack of trying on your part." Although Jack liked Shelly a lot, he thought she was being more than a little stubborn. He understood her feeling of betrayal about the fact that Eric had accused her of sleeping with another man, but his son had turned himself inside out in an effort to appease her. Apparently nothing he said or did could satisfy Shelly.

"None of that matters anymore."

Jack studied his son. His voice rang with a determination and strength Jack hadn't heard in a long time. "What do you mean?"

"I've applied within the company for a transfer."

"To where?"

"Reno, Nevada."

Suddenly tense, Jack clenched his fists. "And you got it?"

"Not yet, but I'm first on the list. I should know in the next couple of months. Once I hear, you can have your house back." He said this with a flippant air. "I'm sure that'll be a big relief."

"True—and not true." Jack didn't want any misunderstanding; he craved his privacy but was grateful for this opportunity to know his son better. "I've enjoyed having you around, even though you drive me crazy."

"We drive each other crazy, but it's been good. I owe you a great deal, Dad."

They hugged quickly, and Eric walked toward his room. "I know it isn't going to make any difference, but I think I'll send Shelly flowers for Valentine's Day."

"Flowers," Jack repeated. He'd make sure Olivia received a big bouquet, too. It was the traditional gift.

"I'll leave the card blank," Eric added. "She'll

know they're from me.'' With that, he disappeared into the bedroom.

So Eric would be moving out and from the sound of it, the transfer would come soon. Jack sank down on the sofa, closing his eyes. He decidedly had mixed feelings about this, but there *was* one major benefit. He could get his own love life back on track.

He liked everything about Olivia—her looks, her smarts, her class. He loved the way she laughed at his stupid jokes and how she made him feel when he was with her. Okay, okay, he'd admit he often thought about making love to her. It hadn't happened yet, but…

Excitement flooded him at the prospect of resuming their relationship, picking up where they'd left off. He'd learned a long time ago that Olivia prized honesty above all else. Knowing that, he planned on being completely straightforward; he'd confess his feelings and ask where she felt the relationship was going—and where she wanted it to go.

Standing he reached for his coat. ''I'm heading out for a while,'' he called to Eric.

Thinking about Olivia made him miss her even more. They'd only talked once that week, very briefly. When he'd gone to visit Charlotte at the hospital, Olivia hadn't been there. Jack didn't feel he could press Charlotte about her daughter's whereabouts, but he *was* curious. Then, as he was leaving, he'd run into her in the hospital lobby; she'd been with her brother and had made somewhat perfunctory introductions, her mind clearly on something else.

It probably wasn't proper form to show up unannounced, especially at a stressful time like this, but he did have a good excuse. Charlotte wrote the Seniors' Page each week and did a fabulous job of it. Her friend

Laura had willingly stepped in, but Jack needed to know Charlotte's prognosis and when he could expect her back. It wasn't a question he felt comfortable asking the older woman, so he'd use that as an excuse to drop in on Olivia.

As he drove down Lighthouse Road, Jack whistled, his mood light. The situation with Eric and Shelly wasn't ideal, but his son had done everything possible to salvage the relationship. He didn't blame the boy for wanting to get on with his life.

Jack loved Olivia's big old-fashioned house with the dormers, the square-paned windows and the wraparound porch. Light blazed from the front windows, spilling warmth onto the porch. His heart swelled as he anticipated her opening the door, imagining her smile, her kiss....

Jack parked and hurried up the steps to her door. He leaned against the doorjamb, struck what he hoped was a sexy pose and rang the bell.

Only a few seconds passed before the door opened—and Jack came eye to eye with Stan Lockhart, Olivia's ex-husband. Jack immediately straightened. He'd met Stan last May and had disliked him on sight. From the look the other man gave him now, the feeling was mutual.

"Who is it?" Olivia called from some distance away. She was probably in the kitchen. Music from Credence Clearwater Revival played in the background.

"Your boyfriend's here," Stan shouted over his shoulder.

Jack noticed that he was left to wait on the porch until Olivia arrived. The instant she got there, she threw open the door and greeted him effusively. Grabbing his hands, she pulled him into the house.

"I didn't mean to interrupt your party," he said, feeling like an intruder. He noticed she wore the bracelet he'd given her and that helped ease his mind.

"You're not," she insisted, wrapping her arm around his. "You've met my brother, Will."

Jack awkwardly nodded in Will's direction.

"And of course you know Stan."

Again the brief nod.

"We're celebrating Mom's release from the hospital. She's doing really well, better than anyone expected. She'll be coming home in the morning! The doctors assured us they got all the cancer, which is a huge relief. She's still going to have some precautionary chemotherapy, but everything looks very hopeful."

"That is good news," Jack said. His eyes narrowed slightly as he focused his attention on Stan.

"Stan and I are old friends," Will explained. "This was the only time we could all get together before I fly back to Atlanta."

Jack appreciated the explanation. "I won't keep you," he said. "I just stopped by on the spur of the moment to see how Charlotte's doing."

"Please stay," Olivia urged.

He shook his head, invented an excuse and left as soon as he could. Olivia walked him out to his car but not before he saw Stan watching her. A chill went through Jack, leaving him as cold as ice. In that split second, Jack had read the other man's look.

Stan Lockhart was in love with Olivia and he wanted her back.

Grace grabbed her workout clothes and headed for the YWCA for her regular Wednesday-night class. Because of Charlotte's surgery, Olivia had skipped the last two weeks, but she'd promised to show up tonight. Charlotte had been out of the hospital for a couple of days but she'd been staying at Olivia's; she'd be moving home on Friday. Grace was anxious to see her friend. They'd spoken earlier in the day and Olivia had sounded short-tempered, which was unlike her. Obviously something upsetting had happened, but Olivia hadn't had time to explain. Grace just hoped it wasn't anything affecting Charlotte.

She waited in the parking lot, leaning against her car, until Olivia parked in the space next to hers. Her friend climbed out of her own car and jerked her gym bag off the front seat.

"What happened?" Grace asked.

"Jack and I got into it earlier today," she muttered.

"You and Jack? But I thought—"

"You thought wrong," she said. "I tried to reason with him, but it was impossible." Her face reddened.

"So what happened? What was the argument about?"

"He called me first thing this morning, and you wouldn't *believe* what he said to me."

Grace practically had to run in order to keep up with her as they started toward the gym. "What did he say?"

"He's jealous of Stan. Good grief, Stan and I have been divorced for sixteen years! He's been married to Marge almost that long. But that's not the half of it." Venting her frustration, she shoved open the gym door. Stopping abruptly, she crossed her arms. "Enough! I can't talk about it anymore. Every time I do, I get more upset."

As always, the gym was bustling with all kinds of activities. Weaving through the crowded entry, Grace followed Olivia into the locker room, where they began to change into their workout clothes. Grace sat on the bench and put on her tennis shoes.

Olivia yanked off her sweater and slacks; she wore her leotard and tights underneath. She adjusted the tights, snapping the waistband viciously. Grace cringed. Then Olivia pulled on her sweatband, disarranging her hair.

"How are Justine and Seth doing?" Grace asked, broaching a new subject. She didn't know what else Jack had said, but it must've been a hell of a fight.

Olivia sagged onto the bench. "Poor Justine is worrying herself sick about this restaurant. She's working too hard, and the only person she'll listen to is Seth. I'm absolutely delighted that she's pregnant, but I do think they might have waited a few months."

Grace understood Olivia's concern. They hadn't been married long but they'd already started on their family *and* a new business. To complicate their lives, Justine continued to work at the bank and as far as Grace knew, Seth was still employed at the marina. In addition, they were having extensive remodeling done at the restaurant. Between getting bids and working with contractors, the young couple was run ragged.

"Your mother's doing okay?" Grace asked next.

Olivia nodded. "Mom's weak and she sleeps quite a bit, but she's doing remarkably well."

Grace was relieved to hear that.

Olivia glanced at her and then said, "Cliff sent the most beautiful floral arrangement. He really is very thoughtful."

Grace didn't want to talk about Cliff Harding. She

hadn't seen him since the Saturday they were interrupted by Kelly. Her daughter had been rude and unfriendly and Grace was embarrassed by the way Kelly had treated him. Cliff had returned later that afternoon, but the mood was broken. She'd wanted to apologize, tell him how much she regretted Kelly's intrusion. She'd let it slide, just as she'd allowed so many things to slide during her marriage. Cliff hadn't brought up the subject, either, and now it hung between them like an argument they hadn't resolved.

"When's Will flying out?"

"He left this afternoon. I'm going to miss him." Olivia gave a deep sigh. "Despite the circumstances, this was a good trip. It's been a long time since the two of us had a chance to visit."

"Maybe he'll consider vacationing here more often," Grace said.

"I hope he does. Will's a wonderful man."

"I think so, too."

Olivia stood for a moment, frowning.

"What's that look for?"

"Nothing." She shook her head as though to dispel her thoughts. "Let's get this show on the road," she said, urging Grace toward the room where the aerobics class was held.

Most Wednesdays, Grace enjoyed this class. She'd reluctantly agreed to it when Olivia had asked her a year earlier; she wasn't athletically inclined and had never enjoyed exercising. What made it tolerable was knowing she could count on seeing her best friend at least once a week. But because the class was demanding, the only opportunities they had to talk were before and after the workout. Sometimes they found themselves standing in the parking lot, chatting for an hour or more.

That night, by the time class was over, Grace had worked up a sweat. Thank goodness for the cool-down exercises, she thought; her heart was pounding furiously. Olivia's face was red and her hair drenched. She'd driven herself harder than ever, working out her frustrations over Jack, Grace suspected.

"I needed that," Olivia said as they made their way back to the ladies' locker room. "I'm still so mad at Jack I could spit."

"It isn't just Jack," Grace told her. "It's everything. You're worried about Justine and the baby. Your mother just had major surgery, and there's all the emotional turmoil around that. Now Jack's acting like a hurt little boy because he found you and Will and Stan having dinner one night and he wasn't invited."

Olivia wiped her face with a towel and reached for her shampoo.

"You're being pulled from every side," Grace went on. "Your mother, your daughter and Jack."

"You're right, I am," Olivia admitted. She looped the towel around her neck. "That's exactly the way I feel." She sat down on the bench and sighed. "I really am worried about Justine, but she won't listen to me. She thinks I'm an old fuddy-duddy because I'm concerned that she's doing too much while she's in the early stages of her pregnancy."

"And then there's Jack."

"Ah yes, Jack." Olivia's voice softened somewhat. "I feel bad about our fight. I lost my temper."

"Call him," Grace said. "My guess is he'll be thrilled to hear from you."

Olivia considered the suggestion a moment, then

shook her head. "Not yet. Give me time to calm down and I might reconsider."

"Want to go out for dinner?" She wouldn't have offered, since her budget was tight these days, but she knew Olivia still needed to talk.

"Come to my place. I've got plenty of leftovers. Mom's friends made her enough meals to last a month. There's a huge dish of broccoli lasagna."

"You're on." Grace so seldom cooked meals anymore that anything homemade sounded heavenly.

Two hours later, lulled by a tasty meal, a glass of red wine and the sweet alto voice of Anne Murray, they sat in Olivia's living room. Charlotte was sound asleep in the back bedroom.

Relaxed, Grace accepted a second glass of wine and closed her eyes. "What would you think if I called Jack?" she asked. "We used to do that in high school, remember? If I had an argument with my boyfriend, you'd call and smooth the way for me."

Olivia giggled softly, sitting beside Grace on the sofa. "Of course I remember, but it sounds a bit juvenile, don't you think?"

"And your point is?" Grace asked.

Olivia laughed. "Go ahead. See what he says."

Grace didn't need to be told twice. This was silly, but fun, too. Olivia gave her the portable phone and Grace found Jack's number on speed dial, then waited for the phone to ring.

Just before Jack answered, she changed her mind and passed the phone to Olivia. "I don't know what to say." She was afraid Olivia was going to cut the connection. Instead her friend held the phone to her ear.

"It's me," she said. "I wanted to apologize for blowing up at you this afternoon."

Olivia didn't say anything for several moments, then she slowly smiled. "You're forgiven, too." She laughed at whatever he said. "You can thank Grace. She was the one who insisted I had to patch this up. As usual, my friend was right."

Soon after, Olivia disconnected and looked over at Grace. "Thanks," she whispered.

Grace felt good. "You're welcome."

"Do you want me to call Cliff for you now?"

She shook her head, but Olivia ignored her. "His number?"

"Olivia!"

"Don't make me look it up," she said. "And don't tell me you don't know what it is, either."

"Oh, all right."

To her surprise Olivia didn't immediately hand her the receiver. She waited until Cliff had answered, then said. "Hi, Cliff, this is Olivia Lockhart. I wanted to thank you for the flowers you sent Mom. They're absolutely lovely." After a brief discussion of Charlotte's prognosis, she said, "I have someone here who wants to say hello." She handed Grace the receiver.

Grace drew in a deep breath and tried to relax as she brought the phone to her ear. "Hello, Cliff."

"Grace." He sounded both surprised and pleased. "I thought Olivia was staying with her mother."

"Not exactly— Charlotte's staying here. But once she's back in her own house, her friends want to take turns spending the night with her. I'm here because Olivia and I went to our aerobics class and then had dinner and a couple of glasses of wine."

"Ah, that explains it. You're feeling brave enough to talk to me."

"Something like that."

"We never did finish our conversation that Saturday, did we?"

"No," Grace admitted.

"Are you willing to try again?"

It was as if she really had reverted to being a teenager. "I'd like that very much," she said shyly.

"So would I," Cliff said, and then repeated. "So would I."

Sharon Castor, Rosie Cox's attorney in the matter of her divorce from Zach, had explained that the next step was a settlement hearing. Both parties would meet with their attorneys at a mutually agreed-upon location to go over the final details of the case, including child custody.

They were scheduled to meet at the library in the courthouse. The main problem had to do with the children. If they couldn't agree on custody and division of property, they'd go before the judge in an informal hearing. Sharon had said the judge's decision wasn't binding, but it was most likely what would be decided if the suit went to trial. Meeting with the judge informally would save everyone time and expense, which suited Rosie. She wanted this over as quickly as possible. Now that the process had been set in motion, she was eager to get out of this disastrous marriage.

For the first time since Zach had become a partner in the accounting firm, lack of money was an issue. While they were married, they'd lived on a budget and Rosie had been good about keeping their expenses within the confines of that—admittedly generous—monthly allotment. All of a sudden, she had less than half the money she'd had before, and it was difficult to meet expenses. The financial difficulties she'd experienced since Zach moved out of the house were bad enough. But he'd taken half the furniture and half the linens and half of just about everything else. A dozen times a day she'd reach for something to find it wasn't there. It was a harsh reminder of her husband's absence from the family.

Sharon Castor and Rosie were seated in the library when Zach and his attorney arrived. Rosie had found Sharon's number in the phone book. She'd chosen her without references or anyone's recommendation because she was too embarrassed to admit to her friends that she needed an attorney. She wanted a female lawyer and she liked the name Castor. Rosie wasn't a spiteful woman, but she wanted Zach to feel like he'd swallowed a dose of castor oil by the time she finished with him. He deserved no less after what he'd done to their family.

Rosie and Sharon waited in silence while Zach and Otto sat across from them.

Rosie set her clenched hands on the table and so did Zach. She avoided eye contact with either Zach or his attorney. A sick feeling invaded the pit of her stomach. It'd started earlier that morning and grown progressively worse all day.

"Did you fill out your portion of the parenting plan?" Otto Benson asked Sharon.

"We did." Sharon shoved the paperwork across the table for Zach and his lawyer to review.

What amazed Rosie was how civilized they were all acting. Her life was being ripped apart and for pride's sake she had to sit like a fifty-pound sack of flour and pretend everything was fine.

Zach and Otto put their heads close together and started whispering.

"This isn't going to work," Otto said without emotion. "My client loves his children and he doesn't feel they'll receive adequate attention if they remain in their mother's sole custody."

"You can't possibly believe that!" Rosie exploded. Zach was as much as saying she was an unfit mother.

Sharon Castor placed her hand on Rosie's forearm. "Do you mean your client believes the children would be better off living with him?"

"Yes," Otto answered for Zach.

"In a two-bedroom apartment?" Rosie burst out. This was a joke; it had to be. She was astonished that Zach would even suggest such a thing. Then it dawned on her. Zach wanted the house. He wanted to kick her out of her own home. Move her out and within short order he'd probably install Janice Lamond. The thought infuriated her.

"I could afford a larger apartment if I wasn't forced to pay all your expenses. It would help if you got a job." Zach's voice was close to a snarl.

Rosie glared at him, hardly able to believe that she'd once loved this man. Loved him enough to abandon her career and bear his children. Now just looking at him made her sick.

"That brings up a point I wanted to address," Sharon Castor said, as emotionless as Benson had been. Rosie marveled at the other woman's calm, but presumably she was accustomed to this kind of situation. "Rosie's going to need classes for retraining and updating her teaching skills."

"The hell she does," Zach said and pounded the table so hard the papers nearly slid onto the floor. "Rosie has a college degree. What more does she need?"

Rosie started at the violence she saw in him. It shocked her, but she supposed it shouldn't. She'd never believed her husband of sixteen years would cheat on her, either. While she didn't have proof Janice Lamond was sleeping with Zach, she certainly had her suspicions.

"It's true my client has a degree in education, but it's been a number of years since she was in the classroom. It would be impossible for her to get a position with the school district without some refresher courses."

"Which you want *me* to pay for," Zach snapped. His attorney whispered something to him. Zach seemed to want to argue, but after a moment, he gave a resigned nod.

Rosie could tell he wasn't pleased. Petty though it was, she was glad. She'd never thought herself capable of this kind of emotion, but she hurt so badly that she wanted him to feel just a small part of the agony she'd suffered in the last six weeks.

Otto straightened. "Mr. Cox will agree to pay for the refresher courses, but they must be completed within a predetermined time."

"My main concern is supporting my children and making a new life for myself," Rosie said.

"You have meetings and volunteer commitments every night of the week," Zach taunted. "If the kids live with me, they won't be eating packaged dinners."

"Do you plan to do all this cooking and caring by yourself or will you be hiring your assistant to do it for you?" Rosie was half out of her chair, so outraged she felt like screaming.

"Please," Sharon Castor said, again placing her

hand on Rosie's arm. "Yelling isn't going to solve a thing."

"I want my children with me," Zach insisted.

"Allison and Edward belong with me," Rosie countered.

Sharon Castor and Otto Benson exchanged looks.

"In instances such as this, when both parents have strong feelings about the custody of their children, it's best to work out a joint custody plan." Otto spoke first, laying the suggestion on the table for Rosie and Zach to examine.

"How would that work?" Zach asked, his temper cooling.

Rosie's own sense of outrage was partially mollified, although she hated the idea of her children being exposed to Zach's girlfriend. Joint custody wasn't a new concept by any means, but it wasn't something she wanted to consider. Frankly, she'd assumed that Zach would rather not have the kids getting in the way of his new relationship. She'd also assumed that his arguments to the contrary had been intended as leverage against her.

"I recommend that the children spend four days with Rosie," Sharon Castor said, "then three with Zach."

"And the following week," Otto Benson added, "they'd be four days with Zach and three with Rosie."

Sharon nodded.

"What about child support?" Zach asked.

Leave it to him to ask about money.

Otto explained that in situations like the one described, there would be no child support paid. However, all expenses for the children, such as braces, summer camp and clothing, would be shared.

At first Rosie fumed that Zach would dare to bring

up the subject of support at all, but the more she thought about it, the better she felt. This was an opportunity to prove to Zach that she didn't need him. He'd figure out soon enough that he needed *her,* though; he'd never appreciated everything she did for him. She'd be free to make a new life without having to depend on him for anything and that was the way she wanted it. Perhaps joint custody *was* worth considering.

Fourteen

Grace couldn't afford a single night in a luxury hotel in downtown Seattle, much less two, but she booked the weekend anyway, using a discount coupon. Next she went to see Maryellen at the gallery. Her oldest daughter had been avoiding her since Christmas. Grace wasn't putting up with any more of that.

"Hello, sweetheart," she said, grateful that Maryellen was alone in the gallery.

Maryellen looked slightly apprehensive, and Grace knew she was searching for an excuse to cut this visit short. "Hi, Mother." She acknowledged her with a brief nod. "To what do I owe this unexpected pleasure?"

"I've come with an olive branch."

Her daughter regarded her warily. "Why is that? Have we argued?"

"Not exactly, but lately whenever we've been together, I've tried to ferret out information about the baby's father and your plans. That was a mistake." Maryellen had refused to answer any of her questions, and Grace suspected that whoever had fathered her daughter's child wasn't yet aware of the fact. Her biggest fear was that he was a married man. Maryellen's reaction to her probing led her to suppose exactly that.

Maryellen smiled. She wasn't as pale as she'd been

a month ago and anyone looking at her likely wouldn't guess that she was pregnant. But Grace saw it in a hundred different ways and was amazed that she'd somehow missed her daughter's first pregnancy. Other than that one brief reference, Maryellen hadn't mentioned it again. At times Grace wondered if she'd imagined it.

"I got us a hotel room in Seattle," Grace said, explaining the reason for her visit.

"A hotel room? What for?"

"Our first and—hopefully annual—mother-daughter getaway weekend."

Maryellen raised her eyebrows. "And Kelly's coming?"

"I hope so." Grace knew her daughters weren't exactly on the best of terms. Kelly felt hurt and angry that Maryellen hadn't told her about the baby. Grace made it a practice not to get caught in the middle of their disagreements, but right now that was difficult because Kelly was angry with her, too.

Kelly had always championed Dan. She felt betrayed by her father—and now Grace was dating Cliff Harding, which she viewed as yet another betrayal. Maryellen's decision to keep her pregnancy a secret had been the final offense in Kelly's eyes.

"If Kelly agrees to this, then I will, too," Maryellen told her.

"That's what I was hoping you'd say."

That evening she called her younger daughter. It was no easy task convincing Kelly to escape to Seattle for a weekend, but Paul encouraged her. Her husband, knowing Kelly was miserable, insisted this would be a bonding time for him and their son.

In the end, much to Grace's delight, Kelly agreed.

Friday evening, the three of them took the Bremerton ferry into Seattle and got a taxi at the waterfront. The young driver, clearly a recent immigrant, leaped out of the cab and opened the door for them, then hurried around to the driver's seat.

This was an adventure for Grace, and she was determined to spend a memorable weekend with her two beautiful daughters. "It's a pleasure to have such a gentlemanly driver," Grace told him, her spirits high.

"Thank you, Mrs.," he returned as he drove away from the dock. His English was broken but they all made an effort to understand his comments and questions about the city. He headed to the hotel on Fourth Avenue and pulled alongside the curb, where the doorman stepped forward to open the car door.

Grace paid the driver and added a healthy tip. "Welcome to America," she said.

"Thank you," he said and bowed his head. "God bless America."

"God bless America," she repeated.

The hotel lobby was plush and expansive, with a huge marble pedestal in the center boasting the biggest floral arrangement Grace had ever seen. They walked leisurely to the registration desk and checked in; Grace managed not to wince when she handed over her VISA card. A few minutes later they were escorted to their room by the bellman.

After Kelly had phoned to check on Tyler, she relaxed. This was the first time she'd been away from her son for more than a few hours and she missed her baby.

Sitting on one of the queen-size beds, her youngest daughter wrapped her arms around her knees. "Do you have names picked out yet?" she asked her sister.

There was a tense moment before Maryellen answered. "Not really… Actually, I'm hoping for a girl and if the baby does happen to be one, I was thinking of naming her Catherine Grace."

"That's a beautiful name."

Grace felt tears prick her eyes, but she quickly blinked them away, not wanting to subdue the evening's mood by getting sentimental and weepy. She so longed for this weekend to be perfect. She wanted to laugh with her daughters, to talk and reclaim the closeness they'd once shared.

When Dan disappeared, the three women had lost more than a husband and father; their sense of family and security had been damaged. For herself, Grace needed answers but at this point it didn't matter what those answers were.

In the meantime, it was as if they were holding their collective breath. They'd been left suspended between what they knew and what they didn't. There were no answers to account for Dan's disappearance—just doubts and questions. Because of this, a rift had slowly developed between them. It was that rift Grace was trying to heal.

They woke early the next morning, eager to explore and play tourist. They started with the Pike Place Market, eating hot rolls and drinking exotic blends of coffee on the street. They walked between long stalls, laden with every kind of fruit and vegetable. Grace liked the seafood stands the best. Fish, crab, shrimp, clams and scallops were displayed on beds of crushed ice. They cheered with the rest of the crowd as the fishmongers tossed large salmon to one another.

They ate lunch on the waterfront under gray, overcast skies. Next they toured the Seattle Aquarium and saw the Imax film of the eruption of Mt. Saint Helens, a tourist favorite. By the end of the day, they were giddy with exhaustion. No one was eager to go out again, so they ordered pizza, which was delivered to their hotel room. They sat on the beds, ate with their hands and laughed over paying an outrageous three dollars for a single can of soda out of the room's mini-bar.

Despite being tired, they stayed up, dressed in their pajamas and robes, and talked away the night. Each avoided the subject of Dan and all the conjecture that surrounded his disappearance. Nor did they discuss Maryellen's pregnancy, other than to come up with possible boys' names. Yet both subjects were very much on their minds. Like Grace, neither of her daughters was willing to risk the fragile peace they'd discovered.

Sunday when they checked out of the hotel, Grace was tired, and more than a little regretful that their time had come to an end. Yet she was exhilarated to have shared this special weekend with her daughters. It was everything she'd hoped it would be.

"Let's do this again," she said as they sat in the ferry terminal and waited to walk onto the boat.

"It won't be as easy next year," Maryellen said. "Not for me, at any rate. I'll have the baby."

"Bring her," Kelly insisted.

"Her?" Maryellen joked. "You sound very sure that I'm going to have a daughter."

"It's a girl," Kelly said confidently.

"How can you possibly know that?"

"I just do." She crossed her arms and stretched out her legs, leaning back against the hard wooden bench. "In my heart, I knew Tyler was a boy long before he was born and I have the strongest feeling that you're going to get your little Catherine Grace."

Grace had no idea whether her daughter was guessing or if she did indeed "have a feeling." In any event, she figured Kelly had a fifty percent chance of being right. Most importantly, she saw her daughters laughing and joking together when only a few days ago she'd thought that might never happen again.

When she'd booked the hotel, Grace's rational self had said she couldn't afford this; now she knew it had been worth every penny.

Roy McAfee looked away from the computer screen and glanced down at the Sherman file on his desk, a file that grew thicker by the week. Months earlier, Grace Sherman had hired him to discover what he could about her missing husband. So far he'd struck out. He'd come across a number of potential clues, but they'd all gone nowhere. Roy took this case personally and felt decidedly frustrated by his lack of success.

After twenty years on the Seattle police force, Roy had reached the rank of detective. Following a back injury he'd sustained from tackling a suspect, he accepted early retirement. Timing was good; both their sons had graduated from college and were on their own.

He and Corrie had moved to Cedar Cove, where the cost of living wasn't as prohibitive and property values remained reasonable. Roy had expected to settle happily into early retirement.

What Roy *hadn't* expected was how quickly he'd grow bored with sitting around the house. Within eighteen months of moving to Cedar Cove, he'd started a new business—as a private investigator. Corrie had been around police work her entire life, and she took on the task of being his assistant and secretary.

When he hung out his shingle, Roy had assumed he'd be getting mainly employee background checks and insurance cases, but the surprising variety of business that came his way made life interesting. His most puzzling and difficult case was the disappearance of Dan Sherman. The man had vanished so completely that if Roy didn't know better, he might suspect Dan had become part of the Witness Protection Program.

Corrie walked into the office and brought him a cup of freshly brewed coffee. She nodded at the computer screen. "Dan Sherman?"

Roy shrugged. Corrie didn't say it, but they both knew he just couldn't leave that one alone. The hours he put in these days were without compensation. Grace had given him a budget and the money ran out before he'd found answers.

"Troy Davis phoned," Corrie told him. "He made an appointment for this afternoon."

Now, this was interesting. The local sheriff was only a nodding acquaintance. Roy had spoken to him a few times and their paths had occasionally crossed. Roy liked Davis well enough, but the sheriff didn't seem quite as sure of him. Reserving his opinion, Roy supposed, pending more evidence.

"Did he say what he wanted?" he asked.

Corrie shook her head. "Not really, just that he might have a bit of work for you."

At three o'clock exactly, Troy arrived and Corrie ushered him into Roy's office. Roy stood up to greet the sheriff, who was an inch or two taller than his own six-foot height and had a bit of a paunch. Too many hours spent behind a desk, no doubt. They exchanged handshakes and then both sat down.

Troy crossed his leg over his knee, drew a toothpick out of his shirt pocket and poked it into the corner of his mouth. He waited a moment, then asked, "Do you remember a while back there was a death out at the Thyme and Tide? The Beldons' bed-and-breakfast."

Roy did recall reading about it. The story was almost a classic. A stranger who'd appeared in the middle of a stormy night and booked a room, was found dead in the morning. No apparent cause. After the initial front-page article in *The Cedar Cove Chronicle* Roy hadn't heard any more about the mysterious stranger, although he recalled one additional detail. The article had stated that the man carried false identification—a driver's license that said he was James Whitcomb from somewhere in Florida.

"We still don't have a name for that John Doe." Troy frowned. "For a while, Joe Mitchell thought we might've stumbled across Dan Sherman."

"Dan? Surely someone would've recognized him."

"Our John Doe had undergone extensive cosmetic surgery. He's about the same build and coloring as Dan, which was why we brought Grace in to take a look at him. I felt bad about that. It was pretty traumatic for her, but she's a strong woman. I admire that in her."

"So it *wasn't* Dan." Roy figured he might as well state the obvious.

"Naw." Troy's gruff response lacked humor. He shifted the toothpick to the other side of his mouth. "That would've been too easy."

"What did the John Doe's fingerprints tell you?"

Troy dropped his leg and leaned forward. "Unfortunately not a damn thing. He didn't have any. Apparently he lost them in the same accident that resulted in the plastic surgery."

"Just bad luck? Or do you think he might've had them removed on purpose?" That was another possibility, although in the age of DNA, not as likely. But then, DNA technology was relatively new.

Troy raised his shoulders in a resigned shrug. "Your guess is as good as mine. All I know is that his ID was false. He comes into town, stays at a bed-and-breakfast, and then turns up dead. Autopsy hasn't determined anything conclusive. It isn't your usual run-of-the-mill scenario."

Now Roy was the one frowning. "Do you think he might be part of the Witness Protection Program?" Funny how he'd been entertaining that very notion regarding Dan Sherman a few hours earlier.

"I thought of that myself. There's only one way to find out, so I contacted the local FBI."

"They were willing to help?"

He nodded. "I gave them everything we had and they got back to me a week ago and said not."

So much for that possibility.

"What about the vehicle?"

"A rental."

"Has Mitchell got any ideas, at least, about the cause of death?"

Troy bit down on the toothpick. "Like I said, nothing in this case is coming easy. Frankly, we don't know. From everything Bob and Peggy told us, he looked perfectly healthy when he went to bed. Bob said he seemed anxious to get to his room, but Peggy attributed that to tiredness. It was late."

"So what does Mitchell think?"

"He can't pinpoint anything out of the ordinary. He's ruled out just about everything. It wasn't his heart. Not all the toxicology reports are back, but it wasn't any of the common poisons. Basically, we just don't know what killed him. Seems he was healthy one minute and dead the next."

"Time of death?"

"According to Joe, it looks like he died in his sleep shortly after he arrived at the Beldons' place."

Roy had to admit to being more than curious now; this case was downright fascinating. "I don't think you made this appointment just to discuss ideas with me. How can I help you?"

Troy Davis removed the toothpick and discarded it in the garbage can next to Roy's desk. "I can't classify this as homicide, but nothing's adding up here. He carried fake ID, but then a lot of people do." He sighed loudly. "I don't have the manpower to invest in this case. I was hoping to hire you as an independent contractor to help us identify our John Doe. And if you happen to come across any other information, so much the better. We'd be grateful to find out anything we could."

"What else can you tell me?" Roy asked. He'd already made his decision—this was the kind of assignment he savored—but thought he should know exactly what he was up against before he said yes.

"Just that our John Doe was meticulous in everything he did. His stuff was neatly packed inside his bag. It looked like something out of a military school. His clothes are the highest quality, top-of-the-line. Expensive. His raincoat was some Italian brand I can't even pronounce. Cost more than I make in a month."

"What kind of car did he rent?"

"Funny thing—you'd expect a Lexus or something, considering the expensive clothes, but it was a Ford Taurus. Interesting, eh? You'd assume he could afford to rent whatever he wanted, but he chose about as inconspicuous a vehicle as you can get."

That brought up another question. "What kind of cash did he have on him?" Roy asked.

"Just a couple hundred dollars. Nothing out of the ordinary."

"Okay," Roy said firmly. "Count me in."

"Great." Troy stood and offered Roy his hand. "If you'll stop at the office, I'll give you copies of our files, and you can go from there."

Roy could hardly wait. As Troy left, Corrie hurried into the room, her eyes questioning. "He has a case for you?"

"Not just any case," Roy said. He stood at the window, watching the sheriff step out of the building and head toward the parked patrol car. This John Doe was as intriguing as any case he'd ever handled.

Olivia had bran muffins baking in the oven—her mother's recipe—and was singing along with a tape of the Broadway musical *South Pacific* while she washed dishes. The doorbell rang, and she shook soapsuds off her hands as she went to answer it. She didn't bother to turn down the volume.

Still humming, she opened the door to find Jack Griffin on the other side. He was hours early.

"Hello, young lovers, wherever you are," she sang, pulling the door wider and motioning him in.

"*Lovers?* Did I hear someone mention the word *lovers*?" He wagged his eyebrows playfully and stepped into the house. The music swirled around them and taking Olivia by the waist he bent her dramatically over his arm, then brought her upright.

"Oh, my," she said, playing along. "You do make my heart beat fast."

Taking her by the shoulders, Jack faced her and his smile slowly faded. "I want you to go back to the word *lovers.*"

"It's *young* lovers, as in coral sands and banyan trees in the South Pacific during World War II."

"No," he said, taking her fully into his arms now. "Forget *young*. The word is simply *lovers,* as in you and me."

His eyes grew darker and more intense. Olivia realized this wasn't a joke anymore but a question that Jack—her fun-loving, anything-for-a-laugh companion—was presenting to her. "I..." All of a sudden life seemed very complicated. Jack had phoned earlier in the day and suggested they get together; he wanted to talk. He'd sounded lighthearted for the first time in months. Olivia guessed that it had something to do with Eric. A few weeks ago, Jack had mentioned that his son had requested a job transfer and would be moving out shortly. He said he'd miss the boy, but he'd sounded pleased about Eric's resolve and renewed energy—and no less pleased about having his house to himself again.

Before she was forced to reply, the timer on her oven rang, offering Olivia the perfect excuse to escape Jack and his question.

"The muffins," she said, and hurried into the kitchen. She grabbed two crocheted potholders and pulled out the tin. She set the muffins on the counter to cool.

When she turned around, Jack stood in the entryway. His eyes met hers. "Eric's moving out this weekend."

"I thought that must be it."

"I didn't mean to start off with that question about us, but you presented the perfect opening when you waltzed up to the door singing about lovers."

She'd been caught up in the song and hadn't meant to suggest they fall into bed together.

"Olivia, listen," Jack said, slowly advancing toward her. "I adore you."

She felt the same way about him, but she also felt afraid. She hadn't been with a man since her divorce, sixteen years before, and she trembled at the thought of sexual intimacy. Her hesitation frightened her, too; if she wasn't ready after all these years, then she might never be. And yet she *wanted* passion and that kind of closeness.

Feeling as though it was now or never, she threw open her arms. "Kiss me, you fool," she intoned dramatically. All at once, her life had become the lyrics to a Broadway musical—and she loved it.

Jack reached for her and their lips met in a wild and thoroughly passionate kiss. Her legs were shaky and her head was swimming. It'd been a long time since they'd kissed with such abandon, almost as if they both understood that true intimacy was irrevocable. Making love meant everything between them would change....

Jack shuddered as he wrapped her completely in his arms. The music had ended, so when his cell phone rang, it startled them both. He ignored it. Instead, he kissed her again, with the same frantic need as earlier. "Come to my house," he whispered, his voice husky. "I changed the sheets this morning."

"Jack!" This was supposed to be seductive?

"I've dreamed about us there, overlooking the Cove, making love."

The phone rang five more times before it finally stopped.

The silence seemed louder than the ringing phone. Olivia took his face between her hands and gazed deeply into his eyes. "Does this have anything to do with Stan?" she asked, needing to know.

They'd argued over Stan, and in her opinion, Jack was being utterly unreasonable. He seemed to think Stan wanted her back—which would be news to Marge, who'd been married to him for more than fifteen years.

"No," he said, kissing her. "It has to do with you and me. Leave Stan out of it."

"Why now?"

"Why *not* now?" he countered.

She wasn't sure how to reply. As she tried to think clearly, to emerge from the fog of kisses and music, the doorbell rang. Saved by the bell—again.

When she hurried to open the door she found Jack's son, looking flustered, still leaning on the doorbell. "Dad?" he shouted urgently.

"Eric, what is it?" Jack asked, appearing behind Olivia.

"Shelly. She's in labor. She doesn't have anyone."

"She phoned you?"

"No, a friend did. Her water broke last night and she's about to deliver. Could be anytime now. Her friend couldn't stay." He paused. "I should be there, don't you think? She might need me."

"True," Jack agreed.

"But she doesn't want me around, at least that's

what she said the last time we spoke.'' He splayed his fingers through his hair. ''I should be there. I *feel* it.''

''Then go.''

''I'm packed up, ready to leave for Reno.''

''Yes, I know.''

Eric seemed to be asking something and Olivia knew what it was, even if Jack didn't. ''Do you want your father to go with you?''

''Would you, Dad?''

Olivia loved Jack even more for the way he responded. He hugged his son, cast Olivia an apologetic look and said, ''Let's go.'' He turned back to her and stretched out his hand. ''Want to tag along?''

She considered it for a moment, then decided against it. ''You two go on. Call me when the babies are born.'' Pleased that Jack had placed his son's needs above his own, she took his hand in hers and gave him an encouraging squeeze.

Three hours later, her phone rang and it was Jack, calling from the hospital. ''Identical twin boys,'' he said triumphantly. ''Eric stayed with Shelly, and she was happy he came to be with her. Both boys are strong and healthy.''

''Congratulations, Grandpa.''

''I *am* their grandfather,'' he said. ''Those babies are the spitting image of Eric. No one's going to doubt who their father is again. Especially my son.''

''What's he going to do about his job?'' Eric had accepted the transfer and was expected to start at his new job in Reno in a week or so.

''I don't know, that's up to him. Fortunately he's got a few days before he has to decide.''

Seth and Justine had decided to call their restaurant The Lighthouse. Justine liked the name because it reminded her of the home where she'd grown up, on Lighthouse Road. The lighthouse at the far end of the cove was one of the community's most distinctive landmarks. Seth seconded the name because it underlined the fact that this was a seafood restaurant.

The idea of opening a restaurant had been in the back of his mind for years, but he loved fishing and the money was too good to turn down. Living aboard the sailboat, his expenses had been minimal and he'd invested wisely. After he'd married Justine, he realized that the long separations fishing demanded no longer appealed to him. Now, with a baby on the way, the time was right to start his new business.

His father agreed and offered to invest in the restaurant as a silent partner. It was a bold move on both their parts. Seth had done his research and was well aware that almost half of new restaurants failed in their first year. He was determined to minimize the risks, to do everything right. Menu, staff, prices, décor, promotion—he and Justine had thought everything through. Seth was a decent cook, but he didn't have the expertise and knowledge that running a full kitchen would require. He advertised for kitchen staff and asked other restaurant owners for advice. He soon learned that Jon Bowman had an excellent reputation. When Jon applied for the position, of chef, Seth studied his resumé, then called and asked for an interview.

On the second Friday of March, Jon Bowman arrived, walking into the ongoing construction mess.

The renovations were only partially finished. A crew of carpenters were constructing new booths while electricians hung the light fixtures. The floors had been sanded and refinished, the walls had their first coat of paint and the windows had been replaced. Seth and Justine had decided to keep the original mahogany bar, which was a classic.

Seth led Jon into the room that would be his office and gestured toward the chair. "I like what you've done," Jon said as he sat down. "When are you planning to open?"

"We're hoping for the first week in May."

Jon glanced over his shoulder as though to estimate how much still needed to be done. "Everything should be finished by then," he said confidently.

"As you know, we're looking for a chef. One who'll oversee the menu and work with us closely as we grow."

"That's why I'm here. I've been cooking at André's for the last three years. I created their menu, which has an emphasis on seafood."

"And before then?" Seth had already reviewed the resumé, but he wanted to hear the details from Jon. He and Justine had made a point of visiting André's twice to sample Jon's signature dishes.

"I was at the VFW in Olympia. I have references if you want." He handed Jon a single sheet of paper with a list of names and telephone numbers.

"Where did you get your training?" The resumé had been decidedly light on that kind of information.

He tensed a little, but that might have been Seth's imagination. "Picked it up here and there. I don't have a lot of formal education. I started out as a short-order cook for a breakfast place in Tacoma and worked my way up. It isn't like I'm going to have my own TV show soon, if that's the kind of chef you're looking for."

"It isn't," Seth assured him. He couldn't afford a

celebrity chef, anyway. He remained curious about Jon's background, but didn't press the issue. "I understand you're also a photographer."

Jon nodded. "I'm a damn good chef, but my passion is my camera."

He didn't hide his love for his work and that suited Seth.

"If you're willing to give me a chance, you won't be sorry," Jon said fervently.

Every instinct Seth possessed told him to hire the man. "I'm going to start stocking the kitchen in a month's time. Can you be ready by then?"

Jon nodded. They discussed wages, benefits, recipes and other details. When they'd finished, Seth took him around the restaurant and was pleased when Jon offered him design and decorating tips. He liked his ideas and shared them with Justine that evening.

"I had a feeling Jon Bowman was going to be the one," she told him as Seth worked in the kitchen, preparing dinner.

"I did, too."

Justine sat in their living room with her legs propped up to keep down the swelling in her ankles. At six months, the swelling was only slight, but still a concern. Seth had taken over the cooking and been inventive with eliminating salt.

"I feel like a walrus," she complained, planting her hands on the small round bulge of her abdomen.

Seth leaned over the back of the sofa and kissed her neck. "You look so beautiful," he murmured. "Not like a walrus at all—although they do have their charms."

"Get serious, Seth."

"I am serious."

She turned her face to him and they kissed, and he realized—as he did every day—how much he loved his wife.

"Tell me what you know about Jon Bowman," he said, a few minutes later as he dished up seafood fettuccine.

"Like what?"

"His background. Do you know anything about it?"

Justine needed to think. "Not much. He used to sell his pictures through the gallery on Harbor Street. Why?"

"He seemed a bit…edgy when I asked about it."

"Where did he go to school?"

"He didn't say, but I talked to two of his references. Both were managers at restaurants where he's been employed and they sang his praises."

"Have you ever seen his photographs?"

Justine moved toward the table, where Seth held out her chair. "Maryellen showed me a few of them before Christmas. They're absolutely fabulous. You can feel the emotion and the beauty."

"Hmm. Maybe we should buy a few. Hang them in the entrance. What do you think?"

"I think my brilliant husband has just had another wonderful idea."

They smiled at each other, fully satisfied with their lives.

Fifteen

Rosie had the house completely to herself. A hundred times over the years she'd yearned for a few hours alone, especially before a major holiday. Zach never understood how much work went into these family celebrations. For Easter, there was a dinner to prepare, to which they usually invited friends and other family—although things would be different this year. Then there was dyeing eggs and making up Easter baskets for the children. Although Allison and Eddie were older, Rosie felt obliged to maintain tradition.

Now that she had the time to do all this without interruption, she found herself fighting off a sense of melancholy. The children were spending the day with their father, and it went without saying that Janice Lamond would find some reason to join them.

Curious though she was, Rosie refused to drill the children about the other woman. Naturally she was dying to know if Janice and her son were at the apartment at the same time as her kids. But she refused to drag them into this divorce, no matter how tempting it was to learn what she could about the other woman's activities.

Working in the kitchen, Rosie mixed up Eddie's favorite gelatin salad and placed it in the refrigerator to set. For Easter she always served ham but only because that was what Zach preferred. Since she no longer had to accommodate her husband's likes and dislikes, she'd bought a prime rib roast. It was a small act of defiance, one that made her feel—just a bit—like an independent woman who made her own choices.

She began baking her usual Easter cake.

Her heart wasn't in it, but she persevered for the sake of her children. With the divorce in progress, they had enough upheaval in their lives without her subjecting them to more changes. The roast was enough of a deviation from tradition for this year, but next Easter they might do something completely different, such as take a trip.

The white bunny-shaped cake was Allison's favorite. Using two eight-inch round cakes, she artfully cut one layer to form ears with the center section serving as a bow tie. After frosting it, she used thin threads of licorice for the whiskers and brown M&M's for the eyes. In past years the children had helped her with the decorating.

She missed them, despite finally having the private time she'd always craved, which confused her. She was also worried about Allison and Eddie being influenced by their father's girlfriend. That wasn't jealousy, she told herself; it was a reasonable reaction.

By the time Zach dropped the children off at the house, Rosie had worked herself into a nasty temper thinking about her husband and his perfect-in-every-way office assistant. He must've been in a hurry to get rid of the kids, because he didn't stay in the driveway a moment longer than necessary, she noted resentfully, peering through the living-room window. The instant the children were out of the car, he pulled away.

"We're home," Eddie called as he came in the front

door. He shucked off his backpack and dropped it in the entryway.

Allison followed him, her ears covered by a headset as she listened to her CD player. She seemed to be doing that constantly, and Rosie disapproved. She wanted to know exactly what kind of music Allison was listening to, but she wasn't up to the challenge of confronting her. She'd finally decided that if Allison needed her CDs, she could have them, at least for the moment.

"Did you have a good time?" Rosie asked, injecting some enthusiasm into her voice.

Eddie shrugged. "We stayed at Dad's most of the day."

"What about the Easter Egg Hunt the Rotary Club held?"

"That's for juveniles," Allison informed her, removing the headphones long enough to snarl a reply. She flopped down on the sofa in the family room, and Eddie headed for his Game Boy, sprawling on the carpet in front of the television.

Okay, Rosie thought. Apparently they didn't want to talk to her. Well, that was fine, because she wasn't in a talkative mood herself.

Allison's eyes were closed and her head bobbed to the beat of her music, whatever it was. After a minute or so, she lifted the headset again and looked at her mother. "What's for dinner?"

"Your father didn't feed you?"

Her daughter looked at her as if that was the stupidest question she'd ever heard. "Dad doesn't cook."

"You spent the night with him. Do you mean to say he didn't provide you with a single meal?" And this was the man who'd criticized *her* for not making cooked-from-scratch dinners!

"We ate breakfast at McDonald's."

"Did he take you out for *every* meal?" Rosie muttered.

"Not really," Eddie told her.

Allison didn't bother to answer.

"Dad said we should eat lots of ham for him tomorrow," Eddie said, keeping his gaze on the television screen.

"We're not having ham."

Allison's eyes widened and she tore the headset off. "Did you say we aren't having ham?"

"No, I bought a roast."

"I *hate* roast," she shouted.

"Allison..."

"We have ham every Easter!"

Rosie's heart sank. "I thought we'd have roast this year, instead."

Allison leaped to her feet and scowled at Rosie. "You did that on purpose!"

"Did what?" Rosie asked, barely hanging on to her own temper.

"You know exactly what you did," Allison said and ran into her bedroom. The house reverberated with the sound of her door slamming.

Rosie looked to her son for an explanation. Eddie rolled onto his side and stared up at her. "Dad likes ham."

"But your father won't be eating with us. I thought we'd have dinner a little differently this year. I didn't think Allison cared one way or the other."

"She doesn't," Eddie told her, rolling back onto his stomach. Without a pause, he returned to his invader game. "She's just upset with you and Dad about the divorce."

Rosie sank onto the sofa.

"We had a big lunch," Eddie continued. "So we aren't really hungry for dinner."

Instantly Rosie's suspicions were aroused. "Lunch?" she asked, nearly biting her tongue in an effort to keep from asking about Janice Lamond.

"Dad took Allison, Chris and me to an all-you-can-eat pizza place."

Rosie smiled benignly through her outrage. Chris was Janice Lamond's son and if he was over at the apartment, it went without saying that his mother had accompanied him.

"I need to go out for a while," Rosie said, struggling to keep her voice even.

Eddie glanced away from the television screen and asked, "Are you going to buy a ham for Allie?"

"Yes," she said, although the idea hadn't occurred to her until Eddie mentioned it. Her destination was Zach's apartment—so she could give him a piece of her mind. On the way home, she'd stop at the Albertson's store to pick up a small canned ham in order to appease Allison.

Rosie felt as if she might explode before she reached Zach's building. Normally she left this sort of unpleasantness in her attorney's capable hands, but this couldn't wait for Sharon Castor.

No soldier marched with stronger purpose than Rosie did as she made her way from the parking lot to Zach's apartment. She braced herself, thinking Janice Lamond might be with him that very moment. She certainly wouldn't put it past him. The two of them might even be in bed together. The thought sickened her, but she didn't stop to analyze why.

When Zach opened the door to her fierce pounding, he looked stunned to see her. "Rosie! What are you doing here?"

"We need to talk," she snapped.

"Now?"

"What's the matter, Zach, do you have company?"

He moved aside, letting her into the apartment. Rosie stepped in and her stomach twisted with an expected knot of pain. His new place was sparsely furnished, but what there was had come from *their* home. Her husband had brought this other woman into his apartment to sit on furniture Rosie had shopped for, to use the very dishes she'd purchased and cherished and been forced to release.

"What do you want?" Zach asked, his voice guarded.

"As a personal favor to me," she said carefully, "I'd appreciate it if you didn't entertain your girlfriend while the children are here—at least until the divorce is final."

"What the hell are you talking about?" Zach glared at her with such ferocity that she barely recognized his face.

"Janice was with you this afternoon."

"What did you do, drill the children about my activities?" he demanded.

"No, I did not. Eddie said he didn't want dinner because of all the pizza he ate at lunch with Chris."

"And your point is?"

"I believe I've made that abundantly clear. If I need to bring up this matter with Sharon, then I will."

"Go for it," Zach said, a smirk on his face. "Make

an even bigger fool of yourself than you already have. Personally, I couldn't care less.''

Rosie refused to stand there and exchange insults with him, but it wasn't beneath her to get in one last parting shot as she turned and started for the door. ''I'd have to go a long way to top you.''

Zach slammed the door after her and she went back to the parking lot. Climbing into the car, Rosie found that her hands shook so badly she had to calm herself before driving.

Holding the steering wheel tightly, she squeezed her eyes shut in a desperate effort to keep from dissolving into tears.

Maryellen stepped into the A-line skirt and raised it over her hips only to discover she could no longer fasten the button at the waistline. She wasn't even six months pregnant, and her normal clothes had already stopped fitting. It was all too clear that she needed to buy a few maternity outfits.

''You want the whole town to know, don't you?'' she said to her baby, placing a hand over the slight mound. Her doctor was paying special attention to this pregnancy because of Maryellen's age. At thirty-five she was older than most of Dr. Abner's first-time patients.

It wasn't only her wardrobe that was about to change, but her entire life. She glanced around her home and envisioned what it would be like in a year's time. Where her bookcase stood now there'd soon be a baby swing or a playpen; she didn't know which. She'd need to find room in her compact kitchen for a high chair. Her second bedroom, which she now used as an office and craft room, would become the baby's.

A sense of excitement filled her, unlike anything she'd ever experienced. This was *her* baby, her very own child. This time she'd do everything right. This time there wasn't a man standing in the way.

High on enthusiasm, she reached for the phone and dialed her sister's number. She felt closer to Kelly than she had in years. The weekend getaway had brought them together again, all three of them. How wise her mother had been to arrange it.

"I didn't get you up, did I?" she asked when her sister answered.

Tyler bellowed in the background. "That's a joke, right?"

Maryellen smiled. "You doing anything special for lunch?"

"Nothing in particular. What do you have in mind?"

"Can you meet me at the Potbelly Deli?"

"Sure."

Kelly had the luxury of being a stay-at-home mother. Paul and Kelly had waited years for this baby and were determined to make whatever sacrifices were necessary. That option—staying with her baby—wasn't available to Maryellen. She'd have to find quality day care and wasn't sure where to even start.

Just before noon, Kelly arrived at the gallery, pushing Tyler in his stroller. At nine months, the little boy sat upright, waving his chubby hands, cooing happily and directing the world from his seat.

"Let's grab some soup from the deli and eat down by the waterfront," Kelly suggested. It was a lovely spring day after a week of rain, and the fresh air would do them all good.

"Sounds like a great idea," Maryellen told her.

Practical, too, since it would be easier to amuse Tyler at the park than in a crowded restaurant.

Maryellen phoned in their order and her sister trekked down to grab a picnic table. Several other people had the same idea, but she'd secured a table for them by the time Maryellen got there.

Sitting across from her sister, Maryellen opened her container of chicken rice soup and stirred it with a plastic spoon. Cantankerous seagulls circled overhead, squawking for a handout, but Maryellen and Kelly ignored them.

"I wanted to ask you a few things about being pregnant," she told her sister. "If you don't mind."

"Fire away." Kelly licked the back of her spoon, looking childlike and mature at the same time. She removed the plastic wrap from her oyster crackers and gave them one by one to her eager son, who instantly stuffed them in his mouth.

Maryellen didn't know what to ask first. For years she'd watched her friends marry and raise children. They all seemed so relaxed about it. So natural. She felt none of that. While excited and exhilarated about the prospect of motherhood, she shared none of their confidence. Kelly had waited years for a baby; surely she understood.

"Were you…afraid?" Maryellen asked.

"Terrified," Kelly admitted. "I read every book I could get my hands on."

"Me, too." Her mother had raided the library shelves and given Maryellen a constant supply of the most recent books regarding pregnancy and birth.

"What happened when you brought Tyler home from the hospital?"

Kelly laughed and shook her head. "Go on to the next question."

"Why?"

"Because Paul and I couldn't agree on anything."

Maryellen reached for a small cracker and chewed it. "I won't have that problem."

"Exactly. How are you doing for clothes? I have the cutest maternity tops. Would you like to borrow some?"

Maryellen nodded.

"I'll bring them over this weekend."

"That would be great." Maryellen's heart warmed toward her sister.

"What about day care? You need to start thinking about that, especially with being single and all."

That was, of course, another pressing concern. She had to think seriously about interviewing prospects and checking out centers.

"Listen," Kelly said, leaning her elbow on the picnic table. "I could do it for the first couple of years."

Maryellen was speechless. When she could talk again, she whispered, "You'd do that?"

"I need to check with Paul first, of course, but I don't see why not. Another baby couldn't possibly be that much extra work and I'm home, anyway. I'd like to help you, Maryellen. What are sisters for?"

Maryellen's eyes filled with tears. This offer was completely unexpected. She looked away, not wanting her sister to know that she was fighting back emotion.

"You know what I realized the other day?" Maryellen asked when she was certain she could keep the tears out of her voice. "I was sitting in my kitchen, reading a magazine Mom recommended, and it dawned on me that...I was happy."

Kelly reached for her hand. "I see it in you, too. I feel it."

"I want this baby so much." She pressed her palm against her midriff and closed her eyes. Lowering her head, she whispered, "I wanted my first baby, too."

Her words were met with stunned silence.

"Your *first* baby?" Kelly asked, also in a whisper.

"I...I was pregnant when Clint and I got married. Oh, Kelly, I was young and incredibly stupid. It was an accident, but we should have known it would happen because we were so careless. Still—it was a shock."

"What happened with the pregnancy?"

Maryellen looked out over the choppy blue waters of the Cove. "Clint wanted me to have an abortion. He swore he loved me, but he wasn't ready to be a father."

"How could he even suggest such a thing?"

Maryellen's throat grew thick, making speech almost impossible. "I couldn't believe he'd want to get rid of our baby, but at that time in our lives, he felt a baby was...a nuisance."

"You still married him."

Maryellen nodded, feeling sick with guilt and with regret for what she'd done. "I...I loved Clint, or I thought I did. I told him I couldn't have an abortion and that it didn't matter if we got married or not. I was going to have my baby. In retrospect, I think he was terrified of having to pay child support and so he...he suggested we get married."

"I don't understand."

"He'd marry me if I agreed to terminate the pregnancy. That was his way of proving his love, of showing me he was serious about our relationship. He insisted there'd be other pregnancies, other children." She didn't add that Clint had forced her to decide between him and the pregnancy. Either she married him right then and had the abortion, or he'd break off the relationship completely. Even now, all these years later, Maryellen couldn't bring herself to tell anyone how she'd allowed herself to be manipulated.

"So you agreed?"

Maryellen nodded, her long hair falling forward over her shoulder. "I didn't want to do it, but I loved Clint and I believed he loved me. So we ran off and immediately after a justice of the peace performed the ceremony, we drove to an abortion clinic. The whole time, Clint kept telling me this was for the best and that we were making the right decision."

"Oh, Maryellen, you must've been so torn."

"It *wasn't* the right decision for me, and even while I was at the clinic, I knew that, but I went through with it, anyway. I kept telling myself I wouldn't have the baby, but I'd have Clint." Not much later she'd realized what a poor choice she'd made. Clint was controlling and manipulative, and before her marriage was a year old, Maryellen knew she had to get out.

"I never liked Clint and now I know why," Kelly said, still holding tight to Maryellen's hand.

"That's the reason I've avoided being around children. That's why I was the first one in any group to make disparaging remarks about kids. I pretended I was too sophisticated and mature to want anything to do with them when my heart ached the whole time for what I'd done. What I'd missed..."

"I'm so sorry."

"I've carried this guilt and shame all these years."

No one else knew, not her mother, not anyone. Maryellen had successfully hidden her ugly secret.

The child she carried now was as unplanned as her first, but this time she wasn't going to repeat her mistakes. She wasn't going to involve the baby's father. Jon didn't want the child. He'd made that plain before Christmas, when he'd asked her about the possibility of a pregnancy. She'd seen the relief in his eyes when she assured him everything was all right. This time she was protecting her unborn child.

Jack sat at his desk late Thursday afternoon, reviewing an article submitted by Charlotte Jefferson for the Seniors' Page. It seemed to him that her opinions were becoming more and more political. Ever since her surgery, Charlotte had been on a mission to get a free health clinic in Cedar Cove. He had to hand it to her; she found a way to mention the need for such a clinic in every issue.

With his pencil in hand he started making the changes, cutting words, rearranging phrases for clarity and adding polish to the piece. Charlotte wasn't a natural writer but her skills had improved dramatically in the last year.

His phone buzzed and Jack absently reached for it. "Griffin," he said.

"Dad, I want you to sing into the phone."

"You want me to *what?*" His son had made some unusual requests over the past few months, but this was one of the strangest.

"Sing. Remember how you used to sing to me when I was a kid?"

As though Jack could forget. He'd sung to Eric when the boy was strapped to a hospital bed, incredibly weak from the devastation of his disease. The drugs had been experimental at the time, but they were Eric's only chance to beat leukemia.

"Just sing! We're desperate."

Jack could hear the two baby boys wailing in the background and grinned. Glancing around to make sure no one was listening, he started humming a little ditty he'd learned as a boy. "Two Irishmen, two Irishmen…"

The cries increased and Eric got back on the line. "You're no help."

"What are you doing in town?" Jack demanded.

"Shelly needed me." Tedd and Todd, too, from the sound of it. "You have no idea how much work two babies can be."

"Shouldn't you be in Reno?" His son had agonized over the decision about following through with the transfer to Nevada. As soon as his twin sons were born, Eric wanted to be with them and Shelly. He used some of his vacation time, and for two weeks he'd stayed at the apartment with Shelly and the babies, but he couldn't delay starting work any longer. Now he flew back each weekend for two days. At Shelly's insistence, the twins had gone through DNA testing, and what had been obvious to Jack the minute they were born was now official. Eric was the father.

"Dad!" He shouted to be heard above the crying twins. "Are you still there?"

"I'm here," Jack assured him.

"Do you think you could get Olivia to marry me?"

"Just a minute, son. If anyone's marrying Olivia, it'll be me."

He smiled at Eric's laughter. "So, you and Shelly have decided to get married?" he said.

"Yeah," Eric replied. "It's about time, don't you think?"

"About ten months later than it should've been, but you didn't ask my opinion."

"Shelly's getting ready to move to Reno with me."

Jack hated the thought of being separated from his son yet again, hated the thought of missing out on his grandchildren, but he very much approved of Shelly. "So you're going to take my grandsons away from me."

"You can visit anytime you want."

"Count on it," Jack told him.

They ended the conversation a few minutes later, after Jack agreed to ask Olivia about performing the ceremony for Eric and Shelly. Actually, he was grateful for such a good reason to see his favorite judge. They'd been spending a lot of time together lately, and that was a trend he wanted to continue.

As soon as he could leave the office, he headed for Olivia's house. He found her working in her rose garden in the backyard. She'd recently planted a row of bushes, which she pampered to a ludicrous degree—in his opinion, anyway. But then, he believed in plants that looked after themselves. "Like weeds?" she'd asked scornfully when he'd shared his gardening philosophy. Today she wore a large straw hat that shaded her eyes, a pair of faded jeans and a worn man's shirt. Jack stopped to admire the view of her bent over the rose bushes.

"I wish you'd spoil me as much as you do those roses of yours."

"Hush," she chastised. "I've just planted these and they need my attention."

"So do I," Jack complained.

"Stick around and I'll feed you dinner."

He grinned, glad of the invitation. His relationship with Olivia was complicated. If the twins hadn't decided to make their entrance into the world when they did, he might have coaxed her into bed with him. But when he'd returned from the hospital, she'd had time to think, time to assess whether this was the right step for them. Her decision was that, yes, eventually it should and would happen—but unlike Jack, she wasn't in a hurry.

In the weeks since, he'd done his best to shower her with love, much as she did those fancy roses she'd planted.

"I heard from Eric this afternoon," he told her. "He asked if you'd be willing to marry him and Shelly."

"Of course." Olivia reached for a large watering can and sprinkled the freshly fertilized earth. "Did he tell you when they'd like to do it?"

"No, but that's a minor detail, don't you think?"

"Seeing how long it's taken him to get to this point, I can't help agreeing." She raised her hand to her face to brush away a stray hair and in the process smeared dirt across her cheek. Jack looked down to hide a smile.

"There must be something in the air, because I heard from my son today, as well," she said casually. "James and Selina are coming for a visit next month."

"That's great. I look forward to meeting them."

"I can hardly wait to hold Isadora. Do you realize she's going to be a year old this month? I swear I don't know where the past year went. She barely knows me and Stan."

At the mention of her ex, Jack tensed. "I suppose Stan will want to see James."

"Of course!" She straightened, hands on her hips,

and glared at him in a way that made him want to squirm. "Don't tell me you're having another jealous fit?"

"Who, me?" he asked, but the fact was that he didn't like the idea of Stan being anywhere near Olivia. He could read her ex-husband more easily than a first-grade primer, and he didn't like what he saw. Stan Lockhart might be married to another woman, but he definitely had interests outside the house. Stan didn't like Jack hanging around Olivia, either. Naturally she didn't see it. Although he'd never asked, Jack had the feeling Stan had done everything he could to discourage the relationship.

"What's for dinner?" he asked, deciding to avoid the one subject that remained a sore spot.

"I was thinking of making an Oriental chicken salad."

"That's the one with the grapes and Chinese noodles I liked the last time?"

"You're easy to please," she told him, smiling.

How true that was. After years of scrounging on his own and eating far too many fast-food meals, Olivia's cooking was a treat. Still, much as he enjoyed the food, it was Olivia he came to see, Olivia he longed to be with and Olivia he loved. He hadn't actually told her how he felt. For a man who worked with words, Jack knew he was strangely inadequate at expressing his emotions. When it was a matter of political argument or moral persuasion, he could express his thoughts clearly and directly. But feelings…

"You look preoccupied," Olivia murmured pulling off her gardening gloves.

He shrugged as he followed her up the steps to the

back porch, where she kept her gardening supplies, and then into the kitchen.

"Anything special on your mind?"

"Not really," he said and realized he'd spoken too quickly.

Olivia studied him a moment as she washed her hands. When she'd dried them, she opened the refrigerator and took out a large head of lettuce.

"Anything I can do?" Jack asked, feeling like an unneeded accessory. He wanted to tell her how he felt, but he was afraid that making an announcement would be embarrassing or inappropriate; so he let it drop.

"Nothing just now, thanks," she answered.

He walked into the living room, but for the life of him couldn't stand still. He started pacing, his mind churning and his hands itching to do something, hold something. The need for a drink clawed at him. It happened like that occasionally, although such times were rare after almost eleven years' sobriety. He needed a meeting and he needed to talk to his sponsor.

"Olivia," he said, sounding more anxious than he meant to. "I can't stay after all."

"You can't?" She stood in the doorway that led from the kitchen to the formal living room, looking perplexed.

"I've got to be somewhere else—I'm sorry, I forgot. Well actually, it isn't that I forgot, it's just that I need a meeting. You don't mind, do you?"

"A meeting? Oh, you mean AA." She stepped into the living room. "Is everything all right?"

"I don't know. I think so. I apologize, but the meetings help me clear my head and get rid of 'stinkin' thinkin'.'"

"You're having negative thoughts now?"

''No, I'm thinking how good a cold beer would taste. That's 'stinkin' thinkin'' and a meeting is the best place for me to be. There's one downtown I sometimes attend. It starts in fifteen minutes.''

''Then go,'' she urged.

He was already halfway to the door. ''Thanks for understanding.''

''Jack?''

He heard her call him and stopped, his hand on the knob.

''You'll phone later?''

''Of course.''

Sixteen

Despite Maryellen's determination to keep Jon out of her life, she was curious about him. It was an unhealthy curiosity, but one that persisted. She supposed this was due mainly to his talent. Thankfully, she hadn't run into him since that unfortunate incident right before Christmas. Nor had she heard anything from him since, and she was grateful, but she also felt disappointed, which confused her completely.

The Bernard Gallery, located in Pioneer Square in downtown Seattle, sold his work now. She was sure he'd do well, and he deserved a wider audience, but the truth was, she missed his infrequent visits. She missed talking shop with him, but most of all she missed seeing his photographs. His talent was no small thing. When a notice came about a showing of his work in Seattle, Maryellen decided to attend the launch. She had no fear that Jon would be there. Experience had taught her that he avoided these events; he claimed the pretentiousness was not only unbearable but brought out the worst in him. He'd told Maryellen that comments about his "deconstruction of natural phenomena" or his "grasp of non-being" made him want to leap up and down making ape-like sounds.

The Sunday afternoon of the show was Mother's Day and it seemed fitting that Maryellen should allow herself this one indulgence. She spent the morning with her own mother and treated Grace to brunch at D.D.'s on the Cove. In a rare moment of sentimentality, Maryellen told her that she hoped to be as good a mother to her baby as Grace had been to her. Then, before heading to the ferry terminal, Maryellen dropped off a gift for Kelly.

When she arrived at the Bernard Gallery, the show was in full swing. Wearing a loose-fitting black dress with black hose and a string of white pearls she looked, in her own estimation, rather elegant. Before long, she held a wineglass filled with apple juice and made her way over to the display of Jon's work.

She found Mr. Bernard himself standing in front of Jon's photographs. He spoke to a middle-aged couple apparently enthralled with one of Jon's pictures.

"Mr. Bowman is something of a recluse," the gallery owner was saying. "I did try to persuade him to attend today's function, but unfortunately he refused."

Maryellen smiled to herself; she'd guessed right. If there'd been any chance of Jon's attending, she wouldn't have risked it. She could not allow him to learn about her pregnancy.

The Bernard Gallery had displayed his photographs by suspending them from the ceiling. The pictures were beautifully framed and matted, each one signed and numbered.

Moving from one piece to the next, she paused to admire his photographs of nature. A field of blue wildflowers blooming against the backdrop of Mt. Rainier was so intensely vivid that her breath caught in her throat. Several scenes of the snowcapped Olympics behind the pristine waters of Puget Sound revealed the thrusting strength of the mountains.

The next series of photographs showed a new side of Jon. These pictures, in black and white, were all taken in and around the marina. In one of them, an early-morning fog obliterated the Puget Sound Naval Shipyard on the other side of the Cove. Sailboats, with thinly veiled masts, rose toward an unseen sky. It was lovely and serene and mysterious.

The second photo she looked at was completely unlike anything she'd seen from Jon before. A notice taped to the corner stated this photograph was not for sale. Maryellen stopped and stared at the picture of a woman at the end of the pier, overlooking the Cove. The snowy peaks of the Olympics could be discerned in the far distance. The day was sunny and her back was to the camera. She stood on tiptoe, leaning over the railing, tossing popcorn into the air for seagulls to catch. They swarmed toward her, their wings flapping.

So Jon was taking photographs of people now. For one unchecked second, she wondered about the woman who'd captured his attention so completely and felt an unexpected and unwelcome surge of jealousy.

Wonder at his skill quickly overcame her ambivalent feelings as she studied the photograph. It wasn't necessary to see the woman's face to experience the simple joy she found in feeding the birds. Maryellen had thrown popcorn to the seagulls herself and knew how exhilarating it could be. She'd stood at the end of that very pier and—

Wait a minute!

That wasn't just any woman—that was *her*. Jon had taken a picture of her on the pier. Hurrying on to the next picture, she realized, much to her relief, that there was only one photograph in which she was the subject.

Instead of feeling uplifted, Maryellen found that her

spirits were low as she boarded the ferry for the fifty-minute sailing into Bremerton. That single photograph told her more than she wanted to know. He'd seen her at the pier without her being aware of him. When? It'd obviously been after their meeting at Christmas—probably during March, judging by the coat she was wearing. She'd gone to feed the seagulls during her lunch hour a few times, and he'd obviously caught sight of her. The fact that he'd taken this picture—his one and only photograph of a person—suggested he'd had genuine feelings for her. Maybe still did. And yet, she couldn't allow herself to respond to those feelings, nor could she act on her own deep attraction to him. She just *couldn't.*

Instead of driving directly home, Maryellen surprised herself and drove to her mother's, instead. Grace was in the kitchen, doing her weekly cooking. She'd recently gotten into the habit of preparing, freezing and storing everything she'd need for the next six days—until the following Sunday, when she'd start the whole cycle again.

"I'm trying a few new recipes," she told Maryellen, busily arranging vegetables, cans and other ingredients on the counter. "Have you had dinner?"

"Not yet. I'm still full from brunch." Her appetite was gone, but it had more to do with her churning thoughts than an empty stomach.

"What's wrong?" her mother asked.

"What makes you think anything's wrong? It's Mother's Day, and I'd like to spend some extra time with my mother. That doesn't mean anything's wrong, does it?"

Grace tore a strip of aluminum foil from the box and covered a small casserole dish she'd just withdrawn from the oven. ''If you don't mind my saying so, you sound defensive.''

''Maybe I should just go home.'' Perhaps this wasn't such a good idea, after all. Her mother could read her far too well.

''Did you see him?'' Grace shocked her by asking.

Maryellen didn't bother to ask who she meant. That was obvious. ''No,'' she said. ''No.'' For emphasis, she shook her head.

Setting the teakettle on the burner, Grace heated water. It seemed that every time they had something important to discuss, her mother made tea. It signaled that her mother considered whatever was to follow significant, something that required her daughter's close attention.

''Mom...''

''Sit down and don't argue with me,'' her mother said briskly. She pulled out the kitchen chair and gave Maryellen a slight shove in its direction.

All too soon, the tea was steeping, and the pot rested in the center of the table. ''You already know I was pregnant with you when your father and I got married.''

Maryellen knew this and wasn't interested in learning whether her parents would have married had her mother not been pregnant.

''Getting married was the thing to do in those days.''

''Times have changed,'' Maryellen felt obliged to remind her. Statistics said that a third of all children were now born outside wedlock. Other women had raised their children alone and so would she.

''He's an artist, isn't he?''

''Mom.'' The questions exasperated her. ''I've already told you I'm not answering any questions to do with the baby's father, so please don't ask."

"You're right, you're absolutely right." Grace tapped the table, as though angry with herself for meddling. "I didn't mean to do that.... Actually, I'd planned to talk about your father and me. We spent more than thirty-five years together and...well, I don't know if I was the best wife for him. I think he might've been happier with another woman. For all we know, that could be the reason he left."

"I doubt it," Maryellen said, grateful for the chance to speak honestly about her father. She couldn't do that with Kelly, who viewed him as virtually a saint, without fault. Kelly refused to recognize the truth about their father; for some reason, she was incapable of seeing him in any other way. "You know, I can hardly remember a time when Dad was happy. He went into those dark moods, and both Kelly and I knew to avoid him."

Grace nodded.

"He seemed to get so self-involved." Maryellen's memories of her father weren't all bad, but in the months since his disappearance, those were the ones that drifted to the surface. "You can't blame yourself, Mom."

"I don't," Grace said, looking flustered. "What I'm trying to say, and doing a poor job of, is this." She released a deep breath. "When it comes to the father of your baby, my advice is to follow your instincts. Don't do what everyone else thinks is best, do what your own heart tells you."

"I am, Mom, I am."

"Then that's all I can ask."

Maryellen smiled and leaned over to clasp her

mother's hand. "Thanks, Mom—I needed to hear that. Now, how about some of that pasta casserole over there? I suddenly feel hungry."

Almost a week later, on Friday afternoon, Grace was still thinking about her conversation with Maryellen. She prayed she'd said the right things. If Maryellen had decided to keep the father out of her life, there had to be a reason. At times she sensed an uncertainty in her daughter—as if she doubted her own decision—but if so, Maryellen didn't discuss it with her. After the baby was born, Maryellen might well have a change of heart.

Her assistant, Loretta Bailey, got to the library early so Grace could leave for what she'd vaguely termed an "appointment." As soon as Loretta showed up, Grace grabbed her sweater, eager to depart before she was barraged with unnecessary questions.

"Thanks, Loretta," she called back as she headed out the door.

"Oh, no problem. Are you seeing that nice man friend of yours?"

She must have something taped to her forehead, Grace thought with a sigh, because Maryellen had asked her the same thing earlier, when they'd met for lunch.

"Cliff asked me to drive him to the airport." After everything he'd done for her over the past months, it was a small thing to request. "He's taking some of the memorabilia from his grandfather's estate to a museum in Arizona."

"Oh, that's right, his grandfather was a famous Hollywood cowboy, wasn't he?"

"The Yodeling Cowboy, Tom Houston himself."

"I'm too young to remember his television show,

but I certainly remember hearing about the Yodeling Cowboy,'' Loretta said. ''My brothers used to try yodeling, and all it did was frighten the neighborhood cats.''

Grace laughed and went out to the parking lot reserved for library employees.

By the time she arrived at Cliff's place, he was packed and ready. The neighbors would be taking care of his horses and Cliff returned the favor for them when they were away.

She was a few minutes early, so Grace walked out to the paddock where several of his quarter horses grazed. As she stood by the fence, a lovely tan-colored mare trotted toward her. ''Hello, Brownie,'' she said, stroking the mare's long sleek neck.

''You could have her eating out of your hand if you wanted,'' Cliff said from behind Grace. ''Just the same as you have me.''

He said things like that just to make her blush; Grace was convinced of it. ''Ready to go?'' she asked, turning away from Brownie. It was easier to ignore the comment than respond to it.

''Anytime you are.''

He loaded his suitcase into the back of her car, then got in on the passenger side. Grace pulled out of the yard, a trail of dust behind her. Two geldings raced along the fence line with her, and she admired their speed and beauty. Grace understood why Cliff chose to live this far outside town. She felt a serenity whenever she visited his small ranch. She suddenly realized that after all the years she'd spent living in town, she wouldn't mind life in the country. She'd never expected to even consider such a thing.

"Thanks for doing this," Cliff said as she turned onto the road.

"It's the least I can do. You've done so much for me."

Without missing a beat, Cliff said, "If you feel obligated, then I suggest you think seriously about our relationship—about where we could go."

He said it in a joking way and she replied in a similar fashion. "Where we're going is the airport. Now, would you cut it out?"

"Probably not. Would you like it if I did?"

She smiled and kept her gaze focused on the road ahead. "Probably not."

Cliff chuckled. "How's Maryellen?"

"Wearing maternity clothes now. I wouldn't have wished this on her, but I'm amazed by how happy she is. She's very excited about the baby." She paused, then thinking aloud, said, "I'm pretty sure the father is one of the artists she knows." Initially she hadn't intended to, but Grace told him about the conversation she'd had with Maryellen on Sunday.

Cliff listened intently. "I admire the way you can be open and honest with your daughters."

"You aren't with Lisa?"

Cliff didn't answer right away. "Not really. We avoid the subject of her mother. It's as if Susan's a phantom woman. I think Lisa's afraid of saying something that'll hurt me, although I doubt my ex-wife has that power anymore."

"What do you mean?" Although Grace didn't want to pry, she was curious about his marriage. He'd made occasional remarks, but nothing that gave her a real picture of what his life had been like before the divorce. In a way, information about the marriages—and divorces—of others helped put her own marriage in perspective.

"I think one of the reasons you attracted me is because of Susan."

This instantly alarmed Grace. "You mean I resemble her?"

"Not in the least. You couldn't be more different. Physically, for instance. She's tall and thin, whereas you're short and...pleasingly round."

"Thanks a lot," Grace muttered under her breath. He hadn't intended to be insulting, but then a man didn't understand the effort it took to keep her weight down to "pleasingly round." Glancing over, she found him studying her with an amused look. "It's my thighs, isn't it?"

He laughed at that. "Too bad you're driving, otherwise I'd find an excuse to kiss you right now."

"You most certainly will not!"

"Not for lack of interest." He shook his head. "Don't you know how attractive I find you?"

Her hands gripped the steering wheel a bit more firmly. "Just explain that comment about Susan."

"All I meant is that you and I have a great deal in common."

"What, exactly?"

"Well, for one thing, I know what it is to have the person you love get involved with someone else. It's an emotionally damaging experience—as if every inadequacy, every doubt, I'd ever had about myself was true. If Susan had an affair, it was because there was something lacking in me."

She merged with the traffic, heading over the Narrows Bridge. She lowered her speed as she drove onto the mile-long expansion bridge. "You mean a man thinks like that, too?'' she asked, surprised by the revelation.

''Of course—but then we do what we can to compensate in other areas.''

''Such as?''

He shrugged. ''For me, I got involved with horses. I ignored what was going on behind my back, because that was the only way I could deal with it. A man isn't supposed to feel pain, you know?'' he added wryly.

''That's ridiculous!''

''Yes, well, I learned that pain comes out one way or another. I think if Susan and I had gone on as we were, it would've eventually killed me. She was braver than I was and decided to end our marriage. The funny part is, I was actually grateful.''

''What does any of this have to do with me?'' Grace asked.

''Oh, yeah—that was the point of this conversation, wasn't it?'' He grinned. ''When we met that first time—''

''You mean when you absconded with my credit card?''

''You know, I've thought about the significance of that a hundred times since.''

''Finish your original sentence,'' she said with mock sternness.

''That day I came by the library to exchange credit cards, I was strongly attracted to you. I'll admit it shook me up because I'd been divorced for five years and I wasn't interested in another relationship. And then, all at once, it was like a bomb went off and I saw the future in a totally new way.''

It didn't hurt Grace's ego any to hear this, although his interest had unsettled her in the beginning. She found herself growing more and more comfortable with it, however. For a long time she'd needed answers regarding Dan, but as the months passed, a resolution seemed increasingly unlikely and she was growing accustomed to that reality.

"I realize now what attracted me. Or, at least, part of it."

She sent him a questioning glance.

"You believe Dan's with another woman."

She nodded, swallowing down the hurt the words still evoked.

"You've dealt with the emotions felt by someone who's been betrayed in his or her marriage—what I felt about Susan's affair."

He could be right. In her heart of hearts, Grace was indeed convinced that Dan was with someone else. A woman he'd loved so much that he was willing to walk away from his entire life. So many things about his disappearance didn't add up, and she had no other answers.

Grace exited the freeway in Tacoma and took the back road into the airport. The route Dan had taught her.

"Can I tell you my theory about the mix-up with our credit cards?"he asked.

She laughed out loud. "I can't wait to hear it."

"Well, to my way of thinking, it was fate. Destiny. Call it what you will."

"The waitress at the Pancake Palace wasn't responsible?"

"She was merely the instrument of fate."

Grace was both amused and intrigued by his theory. "So, we were destined to meet."

"Without a doubt." He sounded convinced of it.

"I've come to think of our meeting as a gift. A sort of compensation for all the pain that came with the divorce."

Grace felt her throat constrict. "That's very sweet, Cliff."

"I mean it. Someday, when you're ready, I hope we can be more than sweethearts."

What an old-fashioned and rather endearing term, Grace mused. "I'd like that."

He grew quiet and looked out the window as they neared the terminal. "I know it's important that you find Dan. Or at least find out what happened to him."

"I'd like closure, but I might never have it. I accept that now. I have to get on with my life."

"Do you mean that?" The expression in his eyes revealed a vulnerability that touched her deeply. "Because if you do, then I want you to consider us being together, Grace."

"Are you talking about—" She swallowed tightly and pulled to the curb to let Cliff out. "Are you talking about us getting…serious?"

His hand was on the door handle. "Yes," he said simply.

Without another word he opened the car door; she stopped him by placing her hand on his arm. "Have a safe flight."

"Thanks."

Still, her hand lingered. She leaned toward him and he moved closer for a kiss that lasted long enough for the car behind them to honk impatiently. Cliff glanced quickly over his shoulder, then turned back to her. "Is that your answer?"

"I don't know," she said, but she smiled warmly.

"I'll think on it while you're gone."

"Do that," he said, his eyes smiling into hers.

Olivia was too excited to sit still. Stan was due any minute and with him would be James, Selina and their granddaughter, Isadora Delores Lockhart.

"What time is it?" Charlotte asked. Her mother was as excited about this visit as she was. "I don't know why you agreed to let Stan pick them up from the airport."

"Mom, it made sense. Stan lives in Seattle."

"Yes, I know, but it seems to be taking him forever," she murmured fretfully.

"They're here!" Justine cried from her perch near the front window. Stan opened the screen door, and both Olivia and Charlotte flew out to the porch. Olivia ran down the steps, her arms open to hug her son the instant he climbed out of the car. Within minutes, Olivia held a sleepy Isadora in her arms. The baby pressed her head against Olivia's shoulder, and her heart melted with love for this first grandchild.

"Grandma," James said, hugging Charlotte. "You look terrific."

"Well, I'm not dead yet," Charlotte assured him and stepped forward, waiting for an introduction to Selina. "Guess my number didn't come up."

James slid his arm around his wife's waist and introduced her. Selina's dark eyes gleamed with happiness as she hugged Charlotte and then each family member in turn.

Seth and Justine appeared as the excited greetings wound down.

"Look at you, big sister," James said, patting Justine's stomach. "Almost a mom."

"I've got months to go," she complained.

"Oh, then you're just fat."

"Be careful what you say," Seth advised under his breath. The two men exchanged a brief hug.

"Welcome to the family," James said to Seth.

"Thanks."

By the time Olivia shepherded everyone into the house, she felt weak with joy. It was so rare to have the entire family together. "Where's Marge?" she asked her ex-husband. When they'd made plans for this reunion, Olivia had included his second wife.

"Marge couldn't make it," Stan said, sounding genuinely regretful. "She sends her apologies."

"Please tell her she's welcome anytime."

"I will," Stan promised. Olivia noticed, however, that he hadn't asked about Jack. She put the observation away, to be examined later.

While Olivia and Charlotte started setting the table for dinner, Stan held Isadora. The baby nestled in his embrace and almost immediately went back to sleep. Olivia smiled to find her ex-husband sitting in her rocking chair with their granddaughter in his arms, He looked so natural and relaxed. The last time she'd seen him like that had been when James was an infant and the twins were five.... Olivia blinked away the nostalgic tears those memories brought. She hurried back to the kitchen.

"Tell me everything," she instructed her son as Selina and Justine took over the task of getting food onto the dining-room table. "Is the Navy bringing you home? I'd love it if you were stationed here in Bremerton."

"Sorry, Mom, but it looks like I've got another two-year stint in San Diego."

It was hard to disguise her disappointment, but Olivia tried. ''I'm grateful Selina's family is there.''

''My parents love James,'' her daughter-in-law told her.

''But it wasn't that way in the beginning,'' James said, patting his wife on the behind as she walked past with a large green salad.

''With good reason,'' Olivia chastised. ''You got their daughter pregnant.'' Only a month before Isadora was born had Olivia learned that James and Selina were married. She was disappointed that both her children had decided to marry without either parent present. First James, and then a few months later, Justine had eloped to Reno with Seth. Still, she believed the children had chosen their mates well, which was a source of great pleasure to her and Stan. Pleasure *and* relief.

Soon the family gathered around the table. Olivia and Charlotte had been cooking and baking for days, making certain that James had the opportunity to enjoy all his favorite dishes. There were stuffed green peppers and Caesar salad with homemade croutons, plus seafood spaghetti. James took two helpings of each.

''Save room for dessert,'' Charlotte warned.

''Grandma, did you bake me a coconut cake?'' James looked like a little boy again, excited about his favorite dessert.

''I did,'' Charlotte assured him. ''Just for you.''

''This is the cake James talks about?'' Selina asked. ''The one he told me takes three days to make? Would you be willing to share the recipe?'' The shy question was directed at Charlotte.

''First you start with a fresh coconut.''

At Selina's astonished eyes, Olivia leaned close to

her daughter-in-law and whispered, "There are shortcuts."

"But I don't take them," Charlotte told her. "Not for James, at any rate."

"He's spoiled," his wife insisted, her eyes dancing with laughter. "I can't help spoiling him, too. He's just so *cute.*"

That remark evoked a round of good-natured teasing about how cute James was.

After dinner, they sat around the table, drinking coffee, reminiscing about the old days, laughing, sharing stories. A little while later, Selina left to put the baby to bed.

Olivia showed her up to James's old room and Stan followed with the luggage.

Starting down the stairs, Stan put his hand on her shoulder and stopped Olivia. She found him studying the pictures that lined the staircase wall. Although they'd divorced many years ago, she kept their wedding photo there. Not for sentimental reasons, but because she felt it was important for their children.

Stan's gaze rested on Jordan's school photograph, taken the year he drowned. "I sometimes wonder..."

He didn't finish, but it wasn't necessary; Olivia had often entertained these same thoughts herself. She wondered what their lives would've been like if it had rained that day or if Jordan had decided to ride his bicycle instead of going to the lake with his friends.

"Mom," James called from the living room. "Grandma's doing the dishes."

"I'd like to see her try," Stan muttered, leaping down the remaining stairs. "Charlotte, sit down this instant! I'm washing the dishes."

"You?" Apparently Marge had him better-trained than Olivia ever did.

Stan paused when he saw the dining-room table, piled high with plates, cups, glasses and serving bowls. "I, uh, might need some help."

"I'll volunteer," Seth offered.

"No," Olivia insisted. "Justine's exhausted. Take her home so she won't be too worn-out for tomorrow." The grand opening of The Lighthouse was scheduled that week, and tomorrow was an Open House for the Chamber of Commerce. After spending ten hours today preparing for the Open House, the couple needed some rest. Thankfully, Justine had left her job at the bank, and Seth no longer worked at the marina.

Olivia hugged them both, and shuffled her daughter and son-in-law toward the door. James joined the little group to say goodbye. "Hey, I think it's great that you two are opening a restaurant," he said, walking out with them.

Olivia hurried to the kitchen, rolling up her long silk sleeves as she went. She saw that Stan had cleared the table, while Charlotte had picked up her knitting and begun watching "Jeopardy," her favorite television game show.

In the kitchen, Olivia discovered the sink filled with sudsy water for the pots and pans.

"You don't need to do this," she told Stan.

"I want to." He stacked plates and cutlery in the dishwasher and she put the leftovers in containers, storing them in the refrigerator.

"I'd forgotten how good your stuffed green peppers are."

"I'm glad you enjoyed them."

He grew quiet then. She found his somberness a little

unexpected after all the happy chatter during dinner and afterward.

"I guess I might as well tell you," he suddenly said, his back to her as he rinsed off dishes.

"Tell me what?" She laughed. "Marge is leaving you?" She smiled at her own joke.

"Yes—sort of." The laughter had drained from his eyes. "Marge and I are separating."

Olivia couldn't hide her shock. Her silly, flippant remark had been correct. "Oh, Stan, I'm so sorry."

"Yeah, I am too."

"Why are you—" She raised her hand. "No, it isn't necessary for me to know. I just didn't expect this."

"Neither did I." He returned his attention to the dishes. "It's been a pretty rough year for us, and we decided last week that it would be best all the way around if we took a break from each other."

Olivia couldn't think of anything to say.

Reaching for a towel, Stan wiped his hands, keeping his eyes lowered. "This evening with James and Justine here, seeing both our children so happy and so much in love—I don't know, something happened."

"Happened?"

"I'm not sure how to explain it. We're grandparents, Olivia, and we're about to become grandparents a second time."

"Yes…"

"Sitting at the table with our children made me realize how badly I wish I could undo the past. I wish you and I were a couple again."

"Oh, Stan…"

"I know, I know, I shouldn't have said that, but it's true. It hit me between the eyes at dinner. You and I always belonged together. I made a terrible mistake when I left you, and I can't help regretting it.''

A hundred times over the years, Olivia too had regretted the divorce. Had she been stronger, better able to deal with Jordan's death, she would have fought to keep the marriage, the family, together. But it was too late to recover something that now belonged to the past. Olivia recognized this, and in his heart, so did Stan. She was sure of it.

Seventeen

Maryellen was impressed with The Lighthouse. Justine and Seth had done a first-class job with the renovations to The Captain's Galley. Her mother had attended the function with her and was sipping wine, talking to Olivia in a corner of the restaurant. Apparently they had a lot to talk about, because their heads had been together from the moment Grace arrived.

The hors d'oeuvres on their silver platters were laid out on long tables draped in white linen. Anticipating a feast, Maryellen had eaten sparingly all day and was famished. Taking a salad-sized china plate, she stood in the buffet line and chatted with other members of the Chamber of Commerce.

The expression might be clichéd, but Justine truly looked radiant, Maryellen thought as she watched the husband-and-wife team greet their guests. She and Justine had talked about their pregnancies and learned they were due to deliver a few weeks apart. They'd known each other their entire lives, but other than the fact that their mothers were best friends, they didn't have a lot in common. For one thing, Maryellen was seven years older and in childhood that was significant. Justine had been in fifth grade when Maryellen graduated from high school.

In the years since, life had taken them in opposite

directions. Only now that they were both pregnant and having their babies close together had they spent any significant time together. They regularly compared notes about their pregnancies and had recently taken a day to shop for baby furniture.

Maryellen sat at one of the newly upholstered booths and made small talk with Virginia Logan, who owned the bookstore two doors down from the Harbor Street Gallery. As they discussed the town council's motion to arrange stone planters along the main streets, Justine approached.

"Maryellen," she said, holding out her hand. "And Virginia. I'm so glad you came."

"This is lovely."

"Yes, it is," Virginia added.

"So, what do you think?" Justine asked them both. "Any changes you'd suggest?" Maryellen understood how important this venture was to the young couple. Still, Justine wanted their sincere opinions, not just flattery and compliments. That was the very reason they'd decided to hold this open house.

"Everything's fabulous," Virginia said, reaching for a second crab puff. She popped it into her mouth and then closed her eyes to savor it. "The food is incredible."

Maryellen nodded agreement.

"We have our chef to thank for that. He's wonderful."

"Where did you find him?" Virginia asked.

"Word of mouth. He applied for the job, and Seth interviewed and hired him. I don't think we realized how good he really is until now. Would either of you like a tour of the kitchen?"

Virginia shook her head. "Not me, but thanks, anyway."

"I would," Maryellen said, more to be polite than from any desire to study the internal workings of the restaurant.

With Maryellen following, Justine wove her way around the people sipping wine and sampling the wide assortment of offerings. As they passed the buffet table, Maryellen grabbed a napkin and a pickled asparagus spear. She'd never been fond of asparagus until this pregnancy. These days she couldn't get enough of it. She supposed there were worse cravings.

Justine held open the swinging door to the kitchen and they stepped aside as a waitress carried out a platter displaying an artichoke cheesecake, complete with a paper-thin phyllo crust. Maryellen had tried it earlier and marveled at the unexpected blend of flavors and textures.

The kitchen sparkled with polished steel, a bevy of pans suspended from a rack above the workspace. Two men in white with tall chef's caps were working efficiently, moving about the room in an almost synchronized fashion.

"Let me introduce you to our chef," Justine said. "Jon, this is a good friend of mine, Maryellen Sherman. Maryellen, this is the chef I mentioned, Jon Bowman." She paused, frowning. "Oh, wait. You two know each other from the gallery."

If there'd been time, Maryellen would have turned tail and run. Instead she was forced to put a smile on her face and hold out her hand, praying Jon wouldn't say or do anything to embarrass her.

"Nice to see you again," Jon said but his gaze rested directly on her midsection.

"Maryellen and I are both due in the same month," Justine said as if to cover for Jon's all too-obvious attention to her pregnancy.

"I see." He met Maryellen's eyes now, his own narrowed.

She was tempted to grab onto the counter because her legs felt as though they were about to give out. "You're a very good chef," she murmured. "Um, the hors d'oeuvres are excellent."

"Thank you," he said grimly. Obviously he was no better at small talk than when she'd known him.

"Over here is Ross Porter, the pastry chef," Justine said, leading her away from Jon. "We captured him from André's too," she said with a gloating smile. "Come and check out our walk-in refrigerator. Who'd have guessed a year ago that I could get so excited about something like that?" Justine laughed.

The rest of the tour was a blur as Maryellen obediently trailed Justine around the kitchen.

"About the staff..." Too late Maryellen realized it was impossible to form a coherent question.

"Oh, you mean the staff from the old Captain's Galley?" Justine asked. "We kept a number of the waitresses and one of the hostesses. You might know her, Cecilia Randall. Her father used to work as a bartender. He moved to California shortly before we bought the restaurant."

Maryellen was only slightly acquainted with the staff from The Captain's Galley, but was pleased to hear that some of them had been retained. Her head was whirling. She'd be astonished if she managed to ask anything intelligible.

"You've done a marvelous job," she said when they

returned to the main part of the restaurant. That was the simple truth.

"Thank you," Justine said as Seth joined her. He placed his arm around his wife's waist and smiled down at her.

Maryellen was impressed with the way they'd become a real couple, a partnership in every sense. Impressed and a little envious. Investing in a restaurant was a bold move, but they seemed determined to make a go of it.

As soon as she could, Maryellen made an excuse to leave. Her heart was pounding so loudly she could barely think as she drove home. She knew without his saying anything that Jon would want to talk to her, and soon. She wanted to reassure him that she wasn't going to ask for any kind of monetary support. He obviously had no interest in the baby, and as far as she was concerned, Jon Bowman was free and clear on all counts. Once he understood that, she was sure he'd rest easier.

Maryellen hadn't been home an hour when her doorbell rang. Already? It looked as though their confrontation would occur that very evening. She certainly wasn't expecting anyone else.

He stood like an avenging angel in the doorway of her small rental home, his face dark, staring down on her when she opened the door.

"I, uh, thought you might want to talk," she said, letting him in.

He strode into the hallway. "You said there weren't any consequences from our night together."

"I lied." Her honesty seemed to unnerve him further.

"Why?"

"Because it was obvious that you were worried I

might be pregnant. You wanted an easy out and I gave it to you, so you have no reason to be angry now."

"Like hell!" he shouted.

"Please." She gestured for him to sit down. "Yelling isn't going to help. I'm sorry this came as such a shock, I really am, but there's no need to be upset."

He ignored her suggestion to take a seat. "No need to be *upset?*" he bellowed. "The hell there isn't. You're pregnant—I'm going to be a father." His scowl challenged her to deny it.

"Yes, but..." Her voice trailed off. She had no intention of pretending he *wasn't* the father of her child.

"Don't you have anything to say?" He started to pace.

"Would you kindly stand still?" Even if he wasn't going to sit down, she had a sudden need to do so. Sinking onto the sofa, she placed her hands over her stomach. "Please..."

"Please what? Please leave?"

"No... It's probably best that you know the truth."

"Probably?" The word exploded out of his mouth.

Maryellen held up her hand. "Listen—you're upset and—"

"Upset?" he repeated. "That doesn't even begin to cover what I'm feeling. You don't have a clue about me."

"A clue...?" She shook her head. "Don't bother. It doesn't really matter."

"What matters is my baby," Jon insisted.

"Would you stop pacing? You're making me dizzy."

"That's too bad, because if I stop I might do something I regret."

"Is that a threat, Jon?" She hadn't thought of him as violent, but she'd never seen him this out of control.

"A threat?" He stared at her as though he'd taken as many shocks from her as he could stand. "No, Maryellen, that isn't a threat." Then, as if he'd exhausted every ounce of energy he possessed, he collapsed into a chair.

"I apologize for this. I guess you have a right to know."

"Damn straight I do."

She was prepared to deal with his anger. It was what she'd expected and frankly what she deserved. If he'd give her a moment, she'd reassure him, tell him she didn't need his support, and then they could both continue with their lives.

"I don't want you to worry about anything," Maryellen told him. "This is *my* baby."

He frowned. "*Your* baby? Yeah—and mine."

"Jon, I don't require a thing from you. As far as I'm concerned, you're not part of this child's life. I intend to raise the baby on my own."

"Oh, no, you don't!"

"Now what?" she cried. She thought this was what he'd come to hear. She was relieving him of all obligations.

"I *want* to be part of my child's life."

"That's impossible!"

"The hell it is." He was back on his feet, fists clenched.

Maryellen got to her feet, too. "I think you should go."

"We'll see about that," he said and stormed out the door, leaving Maryellen shaken and unsure.

Why, oh, why did everything have to be so complicated? It wasn't supposed to happen like this. Yes, learning about the pregnancy must have been distressing to Jon, but once he knew, she assumed he'd feel grateful to be released from any responsibility.

Instead he was making demands—demands she wasn't prepared to consider.

This had to be one of the proudest moments of Jack Griffin's life. He stood with his son and Shelly at Colchester Park, which overlooked Puget Sound. The panoramic view of the Seattle skyline was breathing. The promise of summer was in the air; tulips lined the flowerbeds and fifty-foot-tall fir trees stood like sentries, keeping watch over all who entered the park.

Standing close to the water with her back to Puget Sound, Olivia faced the young couple, while Jack held Tedd and Todd in his arms, as proud as any grandfather had a right to be. Fortunately, the babies were fast asleep. At three months, they'd both filled out nicely and although they were identical, Jack could detect differences between them. Tedd was more active than his brother and always fell asleep last. Todd seemed content with his thumb, while Tedd preferred his pacifier. Both boys strongly reminded him of Eric as an infant, and Jack saw his son over and over again in his two grandchildren.

Jack's ex-wife hadn't been able to make the wedding. He assumed Vicki had stayed away to avoid seeing him. Bob Beldon, his AA sponsor, suggested Jack held too high an opinion of his importance to Vicki, but Jack was fairly confident he'd read his ex correctly. They hadn't parted on the best of terms, and what little relationship they'd had at the time of the divorce quickly disintegrated when he continued drinking. Alcohol had consumed his life for the next several years.

Closing his eyes, he forced himself to concentrate on the marriage vows as Eric repeated them. *Love and honor.* Jack's heart swelled with love for his son, his grandsons, his daughter-in-law—and for Judge Olivia Lockhart. Getting to know her, spending time with her, had changed his life and all for the better.

Shelly repeated her vows and then Eric's best man, a friend from work named Bill Jamison, handed him the diamond ring, which Eric slipped on Shelly's hand.

"I now pronounce you husband and wife," Olivia said and her voice echoed through the park.

In the next moment Eric and Shelly were kissing while Olivia and the friends who'd stood up with them looked on, applauding. Several people, including Shelly's maid of honor, Karen Morrison, took photographs.

With his arm around Shelly, Eric turned to Jack. "I'll bet you wondered if you'd ever see this day."

"You mean you and Shelly married, or holding my grandchildren in my arms?" It seemed to Jack he was about as blessed as any man could be, despite his faults and his past.

"Both," his son answered. Eric took Tedd out of Jack's arms and Shelly reached for Todd. Soon both infants were strapped into their carriers, and everyone was ready to depart.

"Thank you, Olivia," Eric said.

"Yes, thank you so much." Shelly impulsively hugged her and then added, "For everything. You too, Jack."

"We'd better head for the airport if you're going to make your flight," Bill said. He was the most responsible of the group, Jack noted, the one who kept them all on schedule.

"I hate to get married and rush away like this," Eric said.

Jack and Olivia walked them to the parking lot. "Go," Jack told his son and they hugged one last time. "But call me tomorrow, you hear?"

"I will, I promise." Eric strapped the two boys into the back seat of his friend's car.

Before Jack could think of a reason to detain them, the young people were off, and he was left alone with Olivia. His gaze followed Bill's car as it pulled out of the Colchester Park lot.

"I hope they'll be all right," he murmured, more to himself than Olivia.

"They will be," she assured him.

Jack brought her close, placing his arm around her shoulders. These last two weeks hadn't been good ones for them. James had come home for a visit and Olivia's time—rightly so—had been taken up with her son and his family. That was fine and good, but Jack thought her ex-husband was at her house far too often. Still, he couldn't really blame Stan for that, even if he didn't like it. James was his son, too.

"Seeing Eric and Shelly with the twins brings back a lot of memories," she told him with a wistful look.

Jack hadn't once considered that this might be difficult for Olivia. "I'm sorry," he whispered in a stricken voice. "I wasn't thinking."

"Oh, Jack, there's nothing to apologize for. I see twins all the time—right now, it's just, oh, I don't know…difficult, I guess. Having James home, and then seeing so much of Stan these last two weeks. Watching you hold the babies reminded me." She wrapped her arm around his waist, and Jack took reassurance from her closeness.

Arms still around each other, they walked back toward the waterfront. Jack wasn't ready to leave. The day was glorious and his heart was full. His son's life was on the right path now. He valued the months they'd had together, despite the irritations, which in retrospect seemed very minor.

"I feel like I haven't talked to you in ages," Olivia complained.

"And whose fault is that?" Jack enjoyed teasing her. With the mood between them so good, now might be the time to declare his feelings, but again he hesitated. He'd put it off for so long that whenever he thought about it, he experienced a feeling of panic.

"As much as I loved having James and everyone at the house," she was saying, "I'm grateful to have my own life back."

"I'm grateful to have *you* back," he said. "I don't want to sound selfish, but I missed you."

"I missed you, too." She turned her head and her lips grazed his cheek.

Jack's heart accelerated. "You mean that?"

Olivia laughed, the sound light and sweet. "Of course." They continued to stroll arm in arm, oblivious to others around them. He loved having Olivia all to himself, and despite what he'd said, he didn't feel the least bit selfish.

"Stan's confided something in me," she suddenly told him.

Jack frowned; the last person he wanted to discuss was her ex-husband. "Oh?" he said, doing his best to appear interested.

"Apparently he and Marge are having problems."

Jack could understand that. The man was cagy. Okay, so Jack was prejudiced but he disliked Stan Lockhart, and with good reason. "He's not getting a divorce, is he?"

"I hope not."

"Me, too." Alarm bells rang in Jack's head. Bob had suggested Jack was making more of this ex-husband situation than warranted. His gut told him otherwise.

"I'm worried about him," Olivia went on to say.

"Worried about Stan?" Jack made that sound like a waste of time. "He's a big boy—he can take care of himself."

"Yes, I know he can, but this has really thrown him."

"Marital problems are never easy." Jack strove to seem wise and mature, generous too, in his assessment of the other man's troubles. He didn't wish Stan ill, but he wanted one thing made clear: Olivia was off-limits.

"Poor Stan," she murmured, shaking her head.

Jack turned her into his arms. "If you want to feel sympathy for anyone, let it be me."

"*You* need my sympathy?"

"Yes." He grinned. "I twisted my ankle this morning and the pain is so bad." He started to walk with an exaggerated limp.

"Jack!" She broke away and slugged his shoulder. "You're a fake if ever I saw one."

"Ouch." He rubbed his upper arm. "That hurt."

"Good. It's what you deserve."

"If you give Stan sympathy, then you have to give me some, too."

Olivia laughed. "It's not a competition."

"Listen, I'm serious. It wouldn't surprise me if Stan wanted you to help him through this."

"Jack, you're being ridiculous."

"I don't think so." The playfulness left him and he shoved his hands deep inside his pockets. "What would you say if I confessed that I've fallen in love with you?" he asked.

Olivia didn't answer for a long while. Jack stopped walking and turned to study her. She looked at him steadily. "I'd say you sound like an insecure little boy and that you're trying to score points in some imaginary contest with my ex-husband."

Jack clenched his jaw. "That's what I thought." Then, because he didn't feel it would do any good to continue this conversation, he asked, "Are you ready to leave now?"

"If you are."

"I am," he said. In fact, he was more than ready.

Grace dug the pitchfork into the soft earth and turned the sod. She hadn't planted a garden in years. Where she'd once tended zucchini and tomatoes had long since been transformed into lawn. Cliff had offered to rototill the patch, and now she was digging up the turf so he could prepare the soil.

Buttercup, who was busily chasing butterflies behind her, barked when Troy Davis's patrol car turned into the driveway. Grace stood, removing her garden gloves before she walked over to the gate to greet him.

"Hello, Troy," she called.

"Grace." He touched the rim of his patrol cap. "You got a moment?"

"Of course. Come inside." Her stomach churned with anticipation. She wanted to ask if this visit had anything to do with Dan, but she'd already been through that earlier in the year. ''Do you have another body you want me to look at?'' she said, trying to make light of the incident.

''Not this time.''

''Coffee?'' she asked.

Troy shook his head and took a seat in the living room. ''Sit down, Grace.''

The seriousness of his tone told her something was terribly wrong. She sat nervously on the edge of the sofa cushion. ''Is it Dan?''

Troy nodded. ''We got a report from a couple of hikers about a trailer up high in the woods.

''Dan's trailer? Is he there?''

''Dan's body is. He committed suicide.''

Grace gasped and her breath froze in her lungs. For a long moment she couldn't breathe. She should've been prepared for news such as this, but nothing could have diminished the shock of learning that her husband was dead.

''He left a letter addressed to you.'' Troy reached inside his shirt pocket and brought out an envelope, which he handed to her.

''Suicide—but when?''

''Best we can figure, he's been dead more than a year. He shot himself last April.''

''But that's not possible!'' she argued. ''John Malcom spotted him in May, don't you remember? So it *can't* be Dan's body. I'm sure of it.'' She was desperate to prove the body was that of someone else. This had to be an elaborate hoax. It simply wasn't possible that the dead man could be her husband.

''Grace, the letter is dated....''

''It couldn't be April,'' she continued to argue. ''He

was back in the house last spring—I knew it the moment I came home from work. I sensed it. Don't you remember me telling you how the house smelled of evergreen? When Dan worked in the woods, he always smelled like a Christmas tree…I recognized the scent. He was in this house.''

''He probably was back. Before April thirtieth… I'm sorry. But I'm afraid there's no doubt. It's him.''

She was shaking now, so badly that she didn't trust herself to stand.

''Is there someone you want me to call?''

Grace stared up at him, unable to respond.

''Olivia?''

Grace nodded, then covered her face with her hands as she struggled to hold back the tears. All these months she'd assumed Dan had run off with another woman. How could John Malcom have been mistaken? He worked with Dan; surely he'd recognize him.

Troy went into the kitchen and used the phone there. He was gone several minutes and when he returned he pushed the ottoman over and sat down in front of her. ''I'm sorry, Grace. Real sorry.''

She had withdrawn and barely heard him. She saw his lips move but no words registered.

''Olivia's on her way.''

She nodded, although she didn't understand what he'd said.

''Do you want me to call the girls?''

She just stared at him.

Troy patted her hand. ''Don't worry about any of that yet. I'll talk to Olivia and see what she thinks is best, all right?''

Again she nodded, without knowing what she'd agreed to.

Buttercup wanted inside the house, and Troy stood and opened the door for the golden retriever. The dog ran immediately to Grace and nudged her hands. Grace wrapped her arms around Buttercup's neck.

While Troy went outside to meet Olivia, Grace picked up the letter. Where she found the courage to open it, she didn't know.

April 30th

My dearest Grace,

I'm sorry. Sorrier than you'll ever know. If there'd been a way to spare you the horror of this, I would have done it. I swear I would've done anything. I did try, but there's no escape from the hell my life has become. I can't carry the burden of my guilt another day. I tried to forget, tried to put the war behind me, but the memories have pressed in on all sides and there's no longer any hope of escape.

Years ago while I was on patrol in Nam, we took enemy fire. In the aftermath, a few of us got separated from the unit. Desperate to find our way back to base, we stumbled into a small village. What happened afterward has haunted me all these years. A young woman and her baby stepped out of the shadows. Her infant daughter was clutched in her arms but I thought she was hiding a grenade. Only there wasn't a weapon. All she had was her child. Instinct took over and I fired. I murdered a mother and her baby in my desperation to survive the war—my desperation to get home alive. I watched her fall, watched the horror come over her face and heard the screams of her family. Then there was more gunfire and more mothers and children and the shooting just never seemed to stop. Almost forty years now, and it's never gone away. I hear their screams in the night. I hear those screams in my sleep, cursing me, hating me. The irony is that they could never hate me more than I hate myself

There's no forgiveness for me, Grace. Nothing can absolve me from my sins. Not you, not our daughters and sure as hell not God.

I'm sorry, but it's better for everyone involved if it ends here and now. I didn't write Maryellen and Kelly. I couldn't. I was never the husband you deserved and I wasn't any kind of father. I love you. I always have.

Dan

Grace read the letter a second time, letting her eyes rest on each word, one by one, as she tried to assimilate what he was saying. By the time she'd finished, the knot in her throat made it impossible to speak and tears slid down her face.

"It's Dan," she told Olivia who knelt in front of her. Then, her cries surging from deep inside her, she started to wail. Huge sobs racked her shoulders, sobs that shook the very core of her being.

She'd wanted answers, sought resolution, but not *this.* Never this. Dan's death from a self-inflicted gunshot wound wasn't even close to what she'd expected. He'd been alone, trapped in a private hell. He'd been caught in a time warp, tangled in guilt and shame created by a war he'd never wanted to fight.

The tears flowed until there were none left inside her. "The girls..."

"Troy's gone to get them for you," Olivia told her. "They'll be here any minute."

"I thought he was with another woman."

"I know." Olivia stroked her hair as Grace leaned into her friend's comforting arms.

"All this time he's been dead."

"Yes."

"Almost from the first."

"So it seems."

"He left that one night and then he came back, remember?"

"Apparently he changed his mind."

Grace sobbed. "He came back because he couldn't make himself do it." She recalled how angry he'd been, how Dan had lashed out at her and claimed he'd been in hell for the last thirty-five years. She'd assumed he was talking about their marriage when all along it had been the war.

So many things began to fall into place.

"Troy found his wallet and his wedding ring in the trailer."

Grace lifted her head. "He left his wedding band at home." She'd found it the night she'd thrown all his clothes out of the house. Finding the ring was what had triggered her tantrum. She'd believed at the time that he'd *wanted* her to discover it. She'd believed Dan had wanted to flaunt his new love. How wrong she'd been.

"That was the ring he charged on the VISA card," Grace whispered.

When Dan disappeared a second time, Grace had returned home and found the bedroom a shambles. He was gone and he hadn't taken anything with him, but he'd emptied the drawers, torn the room apart. What she didn't understand then was that he'd been on a search. What he sought, she realized now, had been his wedding band. When he couldn't find it, he'd gone into

Berghoff's and purchased another. For some confused reason—loyalty? guilt? both?—he'd wanted his wedding ring on his finger when he blew out his brains.

"Mom!" Kelly rushed into the room with Paul and the baby. Her daughter's sobs tore at her heart, and Grace held out her arms. Maryellen was only a few moments behind. Together they formed a circle, arms around one another, weeping, sobbing, hugging. Then Grace kissed each one in turn and whispered, "We need to make burial arrangements. It's time we laid your father to rest."

Eighteen

Daniel Sherman was buried three days later in a private service with only family and a few friends in attendance. Bob Beldon, a childhood friend of Dan's, gave the eulogy. The two men had been on the high school football team together and then following graduation they'd enlisted in the Army on the buddy program. Maryellen hadn't realized how close Dan and Bob had once been. After Vietnam her father had let that friendship and all the others slide as he became immersed in his own hell.

Maryellen returned from the memorial, physically and emotionally exhausted. Needing time to think through the events of the past year, she parked near the gallery, then walked down to the waterfront.

The gazebo area, where the Concerts on the Cove were held each Thursday night during summer, was deserted. Sitting halfway up in the stands, Maryellen stared straight ahead as she considered the complex relationship she'd had with her father. He'd loved her, she knew now, as much as he was capable of loving anyone. Kelly, too—perhaps more. And he'd loved their mother.

Grace had taken his death hard. Maryellen attributed her mother's intense grief to the fact that she hadn't been prepared for the shock of it. For her, it'd been easier to believe that Dan was with another woman—easier to accept, in some ways, than the knowledge that he'd taken his own life.

As to her own feelings, Maryellen was confused. This was her father, and she loved him, but she'd learned early in life to avoid Dan whenever the darkness came over him. As a five-year-old, she'd come up with that term. "The darkness." It all made sense now. Her father had been haunted by guilt since the war, guilt he couldn't drive off and couldn't share.

Maryellen understood that, since she, too, lived with regret and pain. She, too, struggled with the past. All this time, she'd believed she had nothing in common with her father and without knowing it, they'd been more alike than she could possibly have guessed.

A tear fell onto her cheek, and then another, catching her unawares. Maryellen wasn't emotional; she refused to be. Couldn't afford to be. She'd locked away her emotions when she walked away from her marriage. Emotions were too costly.

The sound of someone approaching made her straighten and wipe the tears from her face. Somehow, she wasn't surprised to see that the intruder was Jon.

"I read about your father. I'm sorry." He stood some distance from her, down by the gazebo, and looked out over the water. The sky was an azure cloudless blue, and the wind was still.

"Thank you." The foot ferry that traveled between Bremerton and Cedar Cove lumbered toward the pier. Maryellen concentrated on that instead of Jon. He didn't leave and she wanted to be alone. If she didn't pick up the conversation, maybe he'd get the hint and go away.

"I'm sorry to talk to you about this now—"

"Then don't," she pleaded.

"You've taken that choice away from me." To his credit, he did sound apologetic. "If you'd told me about the baby we could've—"

"We could've what?" she shouted. "Gotten rid of it?"

Her anger appeared to shock him. He stiffened and then dashed up the aisle so that he stood directly in front of her. "No, Maryellen, we could've talked this out like civilized human beings. Instead, you deceived me. You let me think everything was perfectly fine and it wasn't."

She lowered her head and stared at her feet. "You're wrong. Everything *is* fine. I'm going to have my baby."

"That's where you're wrong. This isn't your baby, it's *our* baby."

"No." A chill ran down her spine, a niggling fear.

"A father has rights, too."

Maryellen went cold inside. "How much is this going to cost me?"

"What?" He frowned, obviously confused.

"How much money will it take for you to leave me and my—me and the baby alone?" she demanded.

He stared at her for a long, heart-stopping moment. "You want to pay me to stay out of my child's life? Is that what you're suggesting?"

She nodded.

"No way!" He sounded angry and disgusted. Then he completely bewildered her by asking, "Who told you?"

"Told me what?" There seemed to be something she could use against him.

"If you don't know, then I'll be damned before I hand you another weapon."

Her mind raced with what she knew about him, which was little. He worked as a chef, was a talented photographer and had inherited an incredible piece of land from his grandfather. That was the sum total of everything she'd learned about him—with one small sidebar. He was a fabulous lover. This last thought made her stomach tense.

"When did you take the photo of me?"

He didn't answer, but stood his ground.

"I saw it in Seattle. That *is* me, Jon. Did you think I wouldn't recognize myself?" She wasn't the only one who'd been deceptive.

When she glanced up, she saw that he looked chagrined, as though embarrassed that she'd seen something he'd never intended her to know about. Well, she did know and she didn't like it.

"I didn't think you'd ever see that," he admitted, his hands in his pockets.

"Of course you didn't. Did you follow me around, Jon? When did you take that photograph?"

He lowered himself onto the bench several feet away from her. He kept his eyes focused on the waterfront and the jagged peaks of Olympic Mountains in the background. "We're both adults. We should be able to come to an agreement regarding the baby."

"If you don't want money, what *do* you want?"

"My son," he told her. "Or my daughter."

"Why? Why does my baby matter to you? Is it some sort of male pride? Or vengeance? Or what?"

He shook his head. "A child is a child, and that's a hell of a lot more than I ever expected out of life." His voice was rigid with anger. "I've given up a lot over the years, but I'm not walking away from my own flesh and blood.''

Maryellen was beginning to feel truly frightened. His interest in the child wasn't something she'd anticipated. She'd completely misread him that time before Christmas. Based on his reaction and on her own past experience, she'd believed he wouldn't want anything to do with their child.

''All right,'' she said reluctantly, ''let's talk about this. How involved do you expect to be?''

''I want joint custody.''

''Not on your life!'' Her reaction was strong and immediate. ''I can't do that.''

''Why not?''

''What do you know about taking care of an infant?''

He shrugged. ''About as much as you.''

''You work nights,'' she argued.

''You work days. It's a perfect set-up. Our child will be with one of his or her parents at all times.''

By now Maryellen's stomach was twisted in tight knots. ''That's too difficult—we'd constantly be shuffling the baby from one house to the other.''

''You asked what I want, so I'll tell you,'' Jon continued. ''Joint custody is number one on the list, but I also want to be at the hospital when the baby's born.''

''You want to be there? For what possible reason?''

He ignored her question. ''Have you chosen a birthing partner yet?''

''My mother.''

''Fine, have your mother go in with you. But after the baby's born, I want to be the first one to hold him or her.''

''No.'' This was getting far too complicated, far too

unreasonable. She longed for him to simply leave her alone. She'd already been through one traumatic experience today and she wasn't prepared to deal with another. "Anything else you want?" she asked with weary sarcasm.

"Oh yes, there are several more items on my list."

"I was afraid of that."

"And your response is likely to be the same, isn't it?"

In retrospect she'd been naive to think he'd be like Clint and demand she get rid of the baby. She'd been even more naive not to consider that Jon might actually wish to be involved in the baby's life.

"Why can't you be like other men?" she muttered irritably. *Like Clint, for example.*

"Me?" he challenged. "Why can't you be like other women who use a child as a meal ticket and a way to manipulate men?"

"You have a rather jaded view of the female population."

"No more jaded than your view of men."

He had her there. "Touché."

He let the conversation drop a moment, and then turned to her. "Can we compromise, Maryellen? Will you voluntarily allow me to be a part of my baby's life? To be a father to my child?"

That he would ask her this on the very day she'd buried her own father was an irony she'd never forget. "Do I have to make that decision right now?"

"Yes, I'm afraid so."

"Why?"

"Because I've been to see an attorney. If we can't work this out between the two of us, then I'm going to take you to court."

* * *

The day Grace laid her husband to rest, she'd stood with her daughters at the gravesite and gathered them close so the three of them could bid Dan farewell. The nightmare was over. She had the answers she needed. What she hadn't anticipated was the aching regret that accompanied them. For three days, she'd suffered from nightmares. The questions and doubts that had plagued her constantly since his disappearance had been dispelled by his letter; she knew now that she wasn't to blame for his misery or for his final choice. But she'd discovered that the answers were as haunting as the questions.

Dan had chosen to take his own life. He'd chosen to die rather than confront the past, rather than deal with the future, rather than seek professional help. What Dan wrote in his letter explained his dark moods, but it didn't offer the expiation she sought. It didn't explain why her husband hadn't been able to turn to her. She'd failed him, failed their marriage. Dan was never the same person after Vietnam; she'd known that and she should've gotten him help.

With friends and family at her side these last few days, it had been easy to push the nagging questions out of her mind, but she was alone now. The girls were both in their own homes. They had made peace with their father and gone back to their lives. But Grace wasn't sure she could ever do that. Dan's last act had changed the way she saw her whole marriage—her whole life.

She boiled water and then left a pot of tea to steep while she changed out of her suit and into slacks and a sleeveless top. Her eyes stung from the tears she'd shed, but they were dry now. No sooner had she poured her tea than the doorbell rang. Grace half expected Olivia and would have welcomed her dearest friend. Her feelings were contradictory; she didn't want to be alone, but she didn't want company, either. Olivia would understand that.

But it was Cliff Harding who stood at her door, a bouquet of perfect yellow rosebuds in his hand.

She blinked, stunned to see him, and instantly, to her utter embarrassment, dissolved into tears. Covering her face with both hands, she wept aloud. Cliff opened the screen door and stepped inside, and immediately took her into his arms.

Grace clung to him. She felt the roses press against her back, the tiny thorns tearing the material of her blouse, and still she clung to him weeping and sobbing, her cries echoing in the empty house.

Cliff led her to the sofa. His arms encompassed her as her body shook with sobs.

She didn't know how much time had passed, but when the tears were spent, she lifted her head and between deep breaths apologized. "I didn't…mean to… do that."

"I'm glad you did," he said quietly.

Not understanding the comment, she raised questioning eyes to him.

"It feels good to be needed. No one's needed me in a very long time."

Grace pressed her head to Cliff's shoulder and exhaled a wobbly breath. She gloried in his warmth, his solid strength. "I never expected it to end like this," she whispered.

"I know you didn't." He wrapped his arm around her shoulder and kissed the top of her head. "I'm sorry, Grace, sorrier than you'll ever know."

"He wrote me a letter…. It helped explain. All the

years I believed… I thought there was someone else, some other woman who could make him happy."

His hand stroked her hair. "What about the friend who spotted him in town?"

"According to the sheriff, it couldn't have been Dan."

"A case of mistaken identity?"

Grace nodded. "It must be." She blew her nose in a tissue, thinking she must look dreadful. "It explains the mangled Christmas gifts I found, too." That was a sign of the depths his depression had reached. He felt unworthy of anything good in his life, to the point that he'd destroyed anything he loved, including the gifts his family gave him. His world was a bleak, black void. He felt trapped in the darkness and couldn't find his way out.

"Did you learn where he got the cash to buy the trailer?"

"That I don't know. We never had thirteen thousand dollars in all the time we were married. With Dan only working part of the year, we often went for months living on one paycheck, scrimping, going from payday to payday. We had to take out loans to pay for the girls' schooling. I don't understand how he managed to put that kind of money aside."

"He must have planned this for years."

Grace had thought that, too. "I don't know if he intended to kill himself right away…. I think he just wanted to escape. Dan loved the forest. He felt more at peace there than anywhere else. His moods got much worse after he lost his job as a logger. I just assumed…"

"You assumed the depression was caused by the loss of his job, which is only natural."

"I did," she said. "I realize now that he lost whatever sense of peace he had when he left the forest. That's why he bought the trailer. He intended to live there for a while, I think, mull over his life..." She sighed. "I'd *like* to think that, but how true it is I have no way of knowing. He returned to the house once. I'm positive of that." Still, Grace didn't understand why he'd come home so briefly. She felt a wave of pity for him and wished again that she'd been more perceptive.

"Can I do anything for you?" Cliff asked.

Grace shook her head. "I'm so tired. I haven't slept more than two or three hours at a stretch since Dan was found."

He grazed her temple with his lips. "Sleep now," he urged.

She reached for his hand and held it. "I don't want you to leave."

"I won't. I'll be here when you wake up."

"Promise." That was important to her for reasons she didn't want to analyze.

"I promise." He led her into the bedroom, and when she lay down on the bed, he covered her with a blanket, leaned over and kissed her cheek. Then he crept from the bedroom and turned off the light.

Grace closed her eyes and heard the door to her room close with a soft click. While sleep was tempting, all she really needed was to rest her eyes for a moment. But she instantly drifted off. Three hours later, when she woke, night had settled in and darkness surrounded her.

As she took a moment to orient herself, she heard someone in her kitchen. Tossing aside the afghan Cliff had spread over her, she climbed off the bed and came into the hallway.

"Cliff?"

"I'm here." He appeared, wearing her apron along with an enticing grin. "I've made us dinner."

"You cook?"

He shrugged. "Don't expect anything fancy."

The table was set, with everything neatly in place. A tantalizing scent wafted from the oven. He'd put the roses in a vase on the table and had used her best china and linen. His care sent a feeling of warmth surging through her.

"Olivia phoned," Cliff told her. "We spoke for a while. Maryellen checked in, too. You might want to give her a call later."

"What about Olivia? Should I return her call?"

"Only if you want. She was more concerned that you not be by yourself, but I assured her I was here for you. I'm not going anywhere, Grace."

His words comforted her. She'd felt so desperately alone since the discovery of Dan's body. Even after he'd disappeared, she hadn't experienced this cold loneliness in quite the same way.

Reaching for the pot holders, Cliff withdrew a casserole dish from the oven. "I hope you like shepherd's pie?"

She didn't feel like eating, but nodded. Since he'd gone to so much trouble, the least she could do was make an effort to show her appreciation. Only when she actually sat down to eat did she realize how hungry she was.

"You're an excellent cook."

"Thank you." He smiled, apparently pleased by her praise. "My repertoire is pretty basic, though."

When they'd finished with the meal, they lingered over coffee and then, because she needed to do something with her hands, she started clearing away dishes. Cliff insisted on helping and wouldn't take no for an answer.

"I meant what I told Olivia," Cliff said as he set a dinner plate inside the dishwasher.

"What do you mean?"

"I'm not leaving you. Don't worry, I'm not going to set up camp in your living room, but I want you to know I'm here for the long haul." He leaned against the counter and sighed. "Today, the day you've buried your husband, probably isn't the right time to tell you this, but I care deeply about you, Grace."

His words hung in the air between them.

"I care about you, too," she said quietly. She knew that Cliff was meant to be in her life as surely as the sun shone in the sky.

"You feel the same way?"

"Don't sound so surprised."

"It's just that—damn, you can't say that to a man when he has a dishtowel in his hand."

"Sure I can," she teased, "and do you know why? Because I don't plan on leaving *you* anytime soon, either."

Then they were in each other's arms again. They didn't kiss; the day of Dan's funeral was too soon for that. But the time *would* come again and they'd both know when it did.

"Are you sure your boyfriend won't mind me stealing you on a Friday night?" Stan asked Olivia as they stood in line at the six-plex theater.

"Jack's busy." He'd phoned and invited her to come with him to the school board meeting, but she'd declined. Because Jack was so paranoid about Stan, she didn't mention that she was going to an early movie with her ex-husband. She would tell him, though; she just didn't want a big discussion about it.

"This is almost like old times," Stan said.

"Not quite. Are you buying the popcorn or am I?"

"You are," he said.

"Well, in that way, I guess, it *is* like old times." With three young children, a night out for them had been infrequent. Going to a movie every six months was a big deal. In order to save time, Stan generally bought the tickets while she stood in line at the snack bar.

"Where is Clark Kent, anyway?" Stan asked as they walked into the theater.

He certainly was curious. "He had a meeting to attend."

"Are you going to tell him about this? Because I don't want to be a source of trouble between you two."

"Of course I'll tell him." She wasn't one who kept secrets, and Stan should know that. His questions irritated her.

They sat in the back of the theater, and as soon as they were settled in, Olivia took a handful of popcorn.

"You actually like this guy, don't you?"

With her mouth full, she simply nodded. The truth of it was, she did. Jack was intelligent and argumentative and he had a sense of humor; he challenged her and he made her laugh. He was a bit insecure, too, but she was willing to look past that.

Stan seemed about to ask her another question when the previews started, for which Olivia was grateful. She didn't want to spend the evening discussing her personal relationships.

After the movie, they stopped for coffee and dessert

at the Pancake Palace. That had also been part of their date-night routine. But as they sat in the booth across from each other, Olivia was determined not to let Stan sidetrack her, either with nostalgic references or with questions about Jack. He'd contacted her, wanting advice about his marriage. So that was going to be the subject of their conversation.

"Are you and Jack—"

"Wait a minute." Olivia raised her hand. "Is tonight about you or me?"

Stan lowered his eyes. "Defeat has never come easy to me."

Olivia had to bite her tongue to keep from reminding him that he'd been the one to pack up and move out of their home. He'd been the one to file for divorce and the one who insisted their marriage was over.

"What happened?" she asked.

He shook his head. "Marge wants out."

"Why?"

"She says she doesn't love me anymore—that we had something special once but we don't now. She's already filed for divorce."

"How do you feel about that?"

Stan refused to meet her eyes. "It hurts like hell."

Then, because her own experience had given her some insight into Marge, Olivia asked, "Do you think she's met someone else?"

Stan's gaze shot to hers as he slowly nodded. "I've thought that for some time."

Olivia didn't feel any sense of vindication at being right. She felt sadness for both her ex-husband and his second wife. Stan and Marge had once had a solid marriage, but apparently old patterns had reasserted themselves. She recalled that Marge, too, had been married when she'd met Stan.

"I'm sorry."

He tried to make light of it, but Olivia knew him well enough to recognize the pain in his eyes. For the first time, she looked at him and didn't see the strikingly attractive man he'd once been. Stan seemed old and somehow, worn-out, his skin sallow and lined.

They talked for nearly an hour and she was astonished to see that it was almost nine by the time they paid for their coffee and pie.

"I haven't been sleeping well," he confessed as they drove back to the house on Lighthouse Road. "I have to tell you, Olivia, this divorce business has really got me down."

She patted his hand. "Life has a way of working everything out. Don't give up on Marge yet."

Stan pulled over to the side of the road. The sun was just setting, and the last threads of light cast a golden glow across the shimmering waters of the Cove. "I've always loved the view of the house from here," he said, leaving the engine to idle.

Olivia did, too. She remembered when she'd first seen that old house with the For Sale sign in the front yard. She'd felt chills go down her spine. She didn't even need to tour the inside to know this was the home she wanted for her family. Although the price had been a stretch for them, together they'd managed to come up with the down payment and get a loan. The twins had been four then, and it was the first time they'd had their own rooms. Unfortunately the house hadn't been enough to hold their family together after the loss of Jordan. Yet in many ways Olivia viewed it as a symbol of everything that was best about their marriage.

''Marge moved out last weekend,'' Stan admitted.

Olivia hadn't known that. ''I'm so sorry, Stan.''

He sighed and looked away. ''Thank you for not gloating. This is what I deserve, isn't it?''

''We've been divorced a lot of years.''

''Yes, I know, but you've been decent about it, Liv, really decent.''

She wasn't sure that was entirely true.

''I don't think I can face going home. Not tonight,'' he said, sounding broken and tired.

''What are you going to do?''

''I'll just get a hotel room.''

Olivia knew this could just be a ploy, but she did feel bad for him, and she understood his not wanting to go back to an empty house. ''There's no need to do that. You can sleep in James's old room and drive to Seattle in the morning.''

Some of the stress left his face. ''You wouldn't mind?''

''No, but I do have an appointment tomorrow. I should leave by nine.'' She and Jack were going to Sol Duc Hot Springs so he could do research for a travel article. Since she had the better car, she was picking him up.

''No problem, I'll be on the road by eight. Sooner if you want.''

''Any time before nine will be okay.''

Stan parked his BMW in the back by the garage and before he went upstairs, Olivia gave him a fresh set of towels.

This was the first time they'd slept in the same house since their divorce. As she readied for bed, she wondered if she'd done the right thing by inviting him to stay.

In the morning, her doubts disappeared. She was awake at seven and while she brewed coffee she heard the shower running upstairs. Humming to herself, she was surprised to hear someone ringing her doorbell.

She ran to answer it.

"J-Jack?" she stammered, instantly afraid he'd hear Stan and assume the worst.

"I come bearing gifts." He held two containers of coffee and a white bakery sack. "Maple bars," he said enticingly. "Your favorite. I thought we'd have breakfast here before we head out."

"I—"

"Olivia," Stan called as he bounded down the stairs. He stopped cold when he saw Jack. He wore one of Justine's old housecoats and a pair of her fuzzy slippers.

"You remember Stan, don't you?" she muttered, which was probably the most inane thing she could have said.

"Oh yes, I remember Stan." Jack's eyes were cold and narrow.

Stan, doing his best to appear dignified, wrapped the silky housecoat more securely around him. "Obviously, my timing couldn't have been worse."

"On the contrary," Jack said. "Your timing couldn't have been better."

"Sorry." Stan cast an apologetic look at Olivia and hurried back up the stairs.

Jack and Olivia faced each other. "You can't believe that Stan and I...slept together." Surely Jack had more faith in her than that!

"Whatever, Olivia."

This was such a juvenile response she didn't know how to react.

"He wants you back."

She'd heard that before. But Jack didn't know how badly Stan was hurting. This *wasn't* what it looked like!

"You can believe me or not," Jack continued. "That's completely up to you. But I'll tell you something. It's either him or me. You decide."

"You want me to tell my ex-husband that I won't see him again?"

Surely even Jack must realize he had no right to make such a demand.

"That's exactly what I want, or we're through."

"I don't deal well with ultimatums," Olivia told him.

Jack set the coffee and the maple bars on the dining room table. "That tells me everything I need to know." He turned and headed out the door.

Olivia was so shocked she didn't know what to do. Shocked and then angry. It took her a full ten seconds to decide to chase after him. By then Jack had reached his dilapidated old car.

"You say Stan wants me back?"

"He's made that plain for months." Jack's hand was on his door.

How dare he just walk away like this! If what he said *was* true, then the least he could do was show some gumption.

"Jack Griffin, do you care about me at all?" she cried.

He turned around and glared at her. "It's him or me. You have to decide."

So Mr. Hotshot was still playing that game. "You're wrong. I'm not the one making the decisions here, it's you. You're the one who's running away with your tail between your legs. You're the one who's tossing out ultimatums."

"What do you want me to do?"

Finally a question she could answer. "What I want, Jack Griffin, is for you to *fight* for me. Prove to me that you're worthy of all the faith I have in you."

Nineteen

Maryellen felt about as pregnant as she could get. It was hard to believe that she had another six weeks to go before her baby was due. She hadn't heard from Jon since mid-June, the afternoon she'd buried her father. She wasn't foolish enough to believe he'd relented and wouldn't follow through with legal action. In the three weeks since, she'd been constantly alert, waiting for him to make good on his threats.

With summer in full swing, Maryellen had been busy with the steady stream of tourists. The gallery was doing well, but several of her summer customers were disappointed to find she no longer carried Jon's work. She'd heard, via the grapevine, that he was selling exceptionally well at the Bernard Gallery in Seattle. Word had it that his prints sold out almost as soon as he delivered them. The problem was the same as when she'd carried his work; his deliveries were sporadic and demand far outweighed supply. She appreciated the reasons in a way she hadn't before. He used to cook at André's and now worked five long days a week at The Lighthouse, which was quickly gaining a reputation as one of the area's finest restaurants. Seth and Justine's new venture appeared to be thriving with Jon at the helm.

Maryellen was pleased for the couple's success.

What bothered her, what downright irritated her, was Jon's golden touch. He was too perfect, too good. Talent spilled out of him like water from an overfilled glass. He designed and built his own home, took brilliant photographs and was a talented chef. Other than his lack of minor social skills—which could, in fact, be seen as evidence of his sincerity and therefore a plus—the man had no flaws. If he did take her to court over shared custody of their child, there was every likelihood he'd win. Unless she was able to dig up some dirt in his past… She'd sensed secrets about him and he'd as much as admitted there was something to use against him.

The thought unsettled her. Battling for custody in a courtroom wasn't the way she wanted it. The plan had been to raise her child alone. She'd assumed that when and if Jon ever learned of the baby, he'd be relieved she hadn't involved him. But—as with so much else in her life—she'd been wrong.

By closing time, Maryellen was tired and out of sorts. Her feet hurt, she felt fat and ungainly, and the last thing she felt like doing was fixing dinner. Fish and chips appealed to her, so she stopped at a small café near Colchester Park that served some of the best.

She sat at an outside table, across the street from the water, with the Seattle skyline in the distance. Elevating her feet on the opposite bench, she set the cardboard container on the table and then licked her fingers, savoring the salty taste of hot chips. A pickup pulled into the lot, one she instantly recognized, and Maryellen froze. *No, please, no.* Jon should be at The Lighthouse, he should be taking photographs or working on his house. He should be anywhere except here.

Jon seemed equally surprised to see her. He climbed

out and stood beside his truck for a moment, appearing uncertain as to whether he should acknowledge her.

"I didn't follow you if that's what you're thinking," he said in an expressionless voice.

"I know." She refused to allow him to ruin her meal and reached for the saltshaker.

"Justine's having all kinds of water retention problems because of salt," he said, frowning. "Should you be using it?"

"I'm completely healthy." How like a man to try to tell her what to do. Her irritation flared up and just as quickly died.

"And the baby?" He focused on her stomach.

"She's developing nicely."

"She?"

Maryellen nodded. "I've had periodic ultrasounds because of my age."

"You knew all along?"

"No—I had them tell me just recently."

"A girl." He said it as if in absolute awe. "Have you picked out names yet?"

"I was thinking of Catherine Grace."

His face softened. "My mother's name was Katie. She'd be very pleased if she knew."

"You can tell her." She didn't think he intended to keep the baby a secret. Perhaps this small concession on her part would convince him of her good faith.

"My mother's been dead fifteen years."

"I'm sorry." Maryellen instantly regretted saying anything.

"I want my daughter in my life," Jon said, his voice firm.

"Perhaps we could reach a compromise." It hadn't

been part of her plan, but she didn't want to drag this through the courts, either.

"Such as?"

"Weekends?" she suggested.

His face as void of emotion as he considered her offer.

"I don't want to shuffle the baby back and forth—days with you, nights with me," she explained nervously. "I want her life to be stable and full of love. Please try to understand."

His reluctant nod followed. "All right. But my weekends sometimes aren't the same as yours."

"We can work around that."

"Then we're in agreement about the baby and me?" he asked, as though he wanted to be sure there was no misunderstanding. "She'll be with me two nights a week."

"Yes."

"Thank you." He seemed relieved and perhaps even moved by her compromise. "I plan on being a good father." He turned toward his truck, his reason for stopping at the café apparently forgotten. "Go easy on the salt, you hear."

"Yes, sir." Maryellen gave a mock salute and smiled, and to her astonishment, Jon smiled back. He got into his truck and drove off, but as his vehicle disappeared from view she realized that she'd done Jon Bowman a disservice. He genuinely cared for their unborn child—and for her. Throughout this ordeal he'd been honorable and kind. She was the one who'd mistreated him.

Maryellen's appetite vanished, and she pushed her meal away. The baby fidgeted inside her, stretching and kicking as if to remind her that every child deserved a mother *and* a father.

"All in due course, Catherine Grace," she murmured, rubbing her abdomen, "all in due course."

For five months Roy McAfee had searched for information on the John Doe who'd died at the Beldons' bed-and-breakfast. So far, he'd learned that the airline ticket had come from a small town in southern Florida. This same town was where "James Whitcomb" had lived, according to his counterfeit ID. Roy had traveled there, showed the man's picture to authorities in the area and come back with nothing.

His next angle had been to contact plastic surgeons in Florida, but none recognized the work or knew of the case. One physician suggested it seemed to have been done twenty or thirty years ago, as techniques had changed over time. While that was interesting, it wasn't especially helpful.

Six months after his death, the John Doe had yet to be identified. And despite the days and nights he'd logged on this case, Roy was no further ahead. The toxicology report had revealed nothing to unravel the mystery. Because of budget restraints, Troy Davis hadn't ordered more extensive tests.

Roy knew the county didn't have a lot of extra cash—and curiosity was definitely not an item in their budget. With no clear evidence of foul play, there was nothing to investigate.

Corrie came into the office carrying a cup of freshly brewed coffee. "You're thinking about the dead guy again." Because they still didn't have a name for him, his wife referred to him as "the dead guy."

Roy growled something unintelligible under his breath. "I'm not dropping it."

"Troy doesn't have the money to continue funding the investigation."

"You don't need to remind me of that." After his last report, in which he had little information to add, Davis had said to let it go. Roy didn't like hearing that, but there were plenty of other cases that needed his attention. Still, this one nagged at him, much the same way Dan Sherman's disappearance had.

"We've already put out more money than we've taken in."

Roy had heard that before, as well. From the beginning, Corrie hadn't been keen on his delving into this investigation. He didn't think she could explain her reasoning any more than he could rationalize the time and expense he'd poured into the case.

"I can't stop thinking the dead guy came to Cedar Cove for a specific reason," Roy murmured, turning the puzzle around in his mind. He didn't believe for a moment that this was a random visit. Something else that had bothered him was how the man knew about Thyme and Tide. The bed-and-breakfast wasn't on a main road. He had to go off the freeway and down several side roads in order to find it.

Either the John Doe had gotten completely lost in the storm, or he'd specifically chosen the Beldons' place. If so, why?

"Maybe he's a hit man," Corrie suggested, then shook her head. "I've been reading too many mysteries."

Roy had thought of that possibility himself. "In which case, he would've been carrying a weapon and he wasn't."

"Unless it was being planted for him." Corrie shrugged. "It happens that way in the movies."

"Hit men carry their own pieces."

Corrie leaned against the edge of his desk. "When's the last time you spoke to Bob Beldon?"

Roy had to think about that. "A couple of months ago, I think." His wife had a gift for asking the right questions. "He swears he'd never seen the man before that night," he said slowly.

"Yes, but I remember you telling me that something about his reaction was slightly off."

That niggling feeling came every now and then. Roy didn't suspect Bob of anything underhanded, nor did he believe the other man was withholding information, but often people weren't even aware of what they knew. Bob most likely had some vague sense of recognition—so vague he didn't consider it worth mentioning. Maybe he'd met the dead guy in his previous job or on a vacation.

"I think I'll pay Bob and Peggy a visit," Roy said.

Corrie grinned knowingly. "I figured you might think that was a good idea."

Peggy was working in her herb garden when he pulled into the driveway. He could see her with her straw hat and a large basket, snipping and gathering. Getting out of the car, he waved to her; she waved cheerfully back. Although the couple was around the same age as Corrie and him, they hadn't socialized. He wasn't sure why.

Roy saw another car parked in the driveway, one he didn't recognize. Probably belonged to a guest. The front door opened before he could ring the bell and Pastor Dave Flemming stepped onto the porch. Dave served as a Methodist minister and was a likeable guy;

Roy had met him on a number of occasions. He knew that Pastor Dave had officiated at Dan Sherman's funeral, which had been small and private, and had met with Grace a couple of times since, helping her deal with the tragedy.

"Roy, how are you?" Pastor Dave said, extending his hand. "Good to see you."

"You, too."

"You're popular today, Bob," Dave said on his way out the door.

"You here to see me?" Bob asked.

"If you've got a minute."

"Sure thing." He held the screen door open and invited Roy inside. "Pastor Dave asked me to coach a church basketball team."

"I didn't know you were interested in sports."

"I haven't played in years," Bob said as he led Roy into the kitchen. He offered him a glass of iced tea, which Roy declined with a shake of his head.

They sat across the table from each other. "Apparently Grace mentioned to him that Dan and I were local sports heroes a hundred years ago," Bob murmured.

"You and Dan went to school together?"

Bob nodded. "We were good friends at one time. In fact, we enrolled in the Army on the buddy plan and took our training together."

As long as Roy had lived in Cedar Cove, he couldn't remember the two men having more than a nodding acquaintance.

"I don't think you came by to ask me about Dan, now did you?" Bob said.

"No. I'm still trying to find out who your visitor was."

"You learn anything?" Bob leaned forward slightly.

Roy shook his head. "I know you've gone over the details of that night a number of times."

"With you and with Troy." Bob sounded bored.

"I appreciate your cooperation."

Bob nodded. "No problem."

"Tell me your impressions again."

"Let me think." Bob leaned back in the chair and closed his eyes. "It was late. The news was over and Leno was just coming on. I saw the car's headlights from the window and asked Peggy if we had any guests down on the books. She said we didn't."

"What was your first reaction when you saw him?" Roy asked.

His eyes remained closed. "Hey—you know what? I thought he seemed familiar, which is odd because I didn't get a good look at his face. I'd kind of forgotten about that, with all the commotion the next morning."

"Familiar?" Roy pressed. "In what way?"

Bob frowned. "I don't know. Nothing definite."

"His walk? The way he carried himself?"

"Maybe."

"What else?"

Bob opened his eyes and shook his head. "I had…an uneasy feeling."

"Define uneasy," Roy probed.

Bob thought a moment and then shrugged. "It was like a gut reaction—that this man meant trouble."

"Trouble," Roy repeated.

"I guess I was partially right, seeing that he turned up dead in the morning." Bob sighed loudly and shook his head. "Sorry I can't help you more."

"You have," Roy said, which seemed to surprise Bob.

"How?"

"I'm beginning to think you *did* know this man. I want you to sleep on it. Let it work in your mind and get back to me if something else occurs to you."

"You think he was here because of me?" Bob sounded shocked.

"Yes, Bob, I do."

Finally Rosie was to have her day in court. She'd waited almost six months for this. Sharon Castor, her attorney, walked next to her as they approached the front of the courtroom and sat down.

"We have Judge Lockhart," Sharon whispered.

Having a female judge reassured Rosie, since another woman would understand her position more clearly than a man. Although he continued to deny it, Zach was involved with Janice Lamond. If he'd been honest about the affair, the divorce would have been over months ago. She blamed him for the delays, blamed him for everything. He, of course, blamed *her*. He accused Rosie of dragging things out and being unreasonable. She accused him of lying. On and on it went.

"That's good, isn't it?" Rosie whispered, leaning her head close to Sharon's.

"Lockhart's fair, if a bit unorthodox."

That wasn't what Rosie wanted to hear. She wanted this procedure to be quick and straighforward. After six months of haggling over every detail, she was ready for the divorce to be done. Ready to make a new life for herself and put the bitterness and ill will behind her.

Zach approached the table, his attorney at his side.

Rosie didn't look at Zach, but she felt his gaze burn through her. She stiffened her spine and refused to acknowledge him. Her eyes stung from lack of sleep. Her head throbbed with the worst headache in ten years and she felt she might be physically ill. Zach would never know any of this, however. She'd keel over in a dead faint before she'd let him know what his affair had done to her sense of worth, her dignity and her heart. This divorce had just about destroyed her emotionally.

The judge was announced and all the people in the courtroom briefly rose and then immediately reclaimed their seats.

"Good morning, Your Honor," Sharon Castor said, rising to her feet once more.

"Good morning." Judge Lockhart flipped through the pages of the brief, scanning the details. "I see you've reached a settlement in the matter of alimony."

"We have, Your Honor."

"I've read through the parenting plan."

Rosie caught her breath. She'd held out as long as she could on the issue of joint custody. It wasn't what she wanted. She assumed, from the amount of time Janice and Chris spent with Zach, that he intended to make them part of his life and thus part of her children's lives. Knowing that, she fought him with everything she could. Their fights had grown ugly and vengeful. Rosie regretted the things they'd said and done, but in the heat of her anger, the venom had flowed out of her. She hadn't known she was capable of behaving this way. Hadn't known Zach was capable of treating her with such contempt.

"It appears that you've agreed to joint custody."

"Yes, Your Honor."

Judge Lockhart gestured at the document. "It states here that the children, ages fifteen and nine, are to live with their father three days a week in the first and third week of each month and four days a week in the second and fourth week. Is that correct?''

''Yes, Your Honor.''

''They are to pack up their belongings and transfer from their house to his apartment—and back—every three or four days. Isn't that a lot of moving about for these children?'' the judge asked, frowning.

''Your Honor.'' Zach's attorney stood. ''It's important to my client that he share custody of his children.''

''I have no squabbles with his motivation or the concept of shared custody,'' Judge Lockhart said, ''but to my way of thinking, it isn't the parents who need a stable home life, it's the children.''

''My client couldn't agree with you more,'' Otto Benson said, and Zach nodded.

''Ms. Castor, is your client in agreement as well?''

Sharon looked at Rosie, who stood. She spoke directly to the judge. ''I want what's best for my children.''

Judge Lockhart studied both Zach and Rosie. ''The family home is at 311 Pelican Court. How long have you lived at this address?''

''Three years, Your Honor.''

''You intend to keep the home?''

''Yes, Your Honor,'' Sharon answered on Rosie's behalf.

The judge set aside the paperwork and sighed heavily. ''That being the case, I'm going to put your word to the test. Both of you have stated that your main concern in this divorce is your two children. That's what I want to hear. Both of you seem determined to stay in their lives and I commend you for that. I hope you mean it. I agree to accept all conditions and terms as submitted to this court with one exception: joint custody."

"Your Honor!" Zach roared to his feet.

"Hear me out, Mr. Cox," the judge ordered and Zach sat back down.

Smugly Rosie crossed her arms, pleased that this insightful judge had seen through her husband.

"As I stated earlier, it's important for the children to have a stable home. You two—not the children—are the ones who've decided to end this marriage. Therefore, the children are to remain in the house and the parents are the ones who'll be moving in and out every few days."

"But Your Honor—"

"These are my terms. Either accept them now or delay the divorce."

Horrified, Rosie looked at Zach. How could they go along with this after they'd struggled over every single detail?

"Have you made a decision?" the judge asked.

Zach and his attorney were whispering. Soon afterward Otto stood. "Your Honor, my client agrees."

Sharon glanced at Rosie and she too nodded. "My client agrees also."

"Very well," Judge Lockhart said, "the marriage is dissolved. I hope you can make this work, for the sake of your children."

Rosie hoped so, too.

"Call him," Charlotte urged Olivia. "He's miserable and so are you."

"No, Mother." Olivia put her teacup down. "Not this time." She was still furious with Jack, and she refused to approach him. If he could so easily give up on her, then she considered herself better off without him. But she asked, "How do you know he's miserable?"

Her mother set aside her knitting and reached for the teapot in the middle of the kitchen table. She replenished her cup and then Olivia's. "He asks about you every week when I drop off my column."

That was encouraging. Still, Olivia had seen no actual evidence of his concern. If Jack cared for her as much as he *said* he did, then he should take her advice and fight for her.

The phone rang, and Olivia absently reached for it. "Hello."

"It's Seth." Her son-in-law didn't sound like himself. "Justine's water just broke and her labor's started. We're leaving for the hospital now."

"But it's early," Olivia cried. Three and a half weeks early, and that couldn't be good for Justine or the baby.

"No one bothered to tell the baby that."

What she heard in Seth's voice was a sense of panic. "I'm leaving now," she assured him. "Everything's going to be fine. Babies are born early every day."

"Yes, I know. This just caught me off guard. Can you call Stan for me?"

"Of course. Take a deep breath and I'll meet you at the hospital."

As soon as Seth was gone, Olivia punched out Stan's work number and was put through immediately. "Stan Lockhart."

"Hello, Grandpa," she said, bubbling over with mingled excitement and concern. "Justine's in labor and on her way to the hospital. Do you want to meet us there?"

Stan laughed, sounding delighted and equally thrilled. "I wouldn't miss it for the world. Tell her I'll see her soon, Grandma."

"No need to rush," her mother said as Olivia set the portable phone in its base. "These things take time."

So spoke the wisdom of age, but Olivia knew she'd be hopeless anyplace but at the hospital. A baby was about to be born into their family, and she felt too much joy to hold inside. She couldn't sit still, and began pacing compulsively through the house.

"Go," Charlotte advised a few minutes later. "I'll take care of everything here. Call me later."

"Thanks, Mom." Olivia kissed her mother's cheek, grabbed her purse and car keys and was out the door.

For nearly an hour she sat alone in the waiting area. Seth came out to give her bits of information every now and then; so far, everything was going smoothly. Stan arrived, looking frazzled, two hours later. They sat and drank coffee and chatted.

"Remember the night James was born?"

"I don't think I could forget that." She gave an exaggerated shudder. "We barely made it to the hospital."

Soon they were laughing, caught up in memories of the early years of their marriage.

"Remember the Christmas Eve you decided to assemble Jordan's bicycle?" she asked.

"Don't remind me," Stan groaned. "As I recall, the instructions were in Japanese and you were the one who said assembling a bike couldn't possibly be that difficult."

"My mistake."

"What about the time you decided to teach Justine how to bake bread?"

Olivia rolled her eyes at the memory. In an effort to be helpful, Justine had picked up—and dropped—a ten-pound bag of flour that exploded on impact. For years afterward, Olivia found traces of the powdery substance all over the kitchen—beneath the sink, behind the refrigerator, in the backs of drawers.

The hours passed with barely a notice as they immersed themselves in laughter and memories.

At close to nine, Seth appeared, wearing the biggest grin Olivia had ever seen. She'd almost forgotten the reason they were at the hospital. She leaped to her feet, ready for the news.

"We have a son," Seth announced. "Leif Jordan Gunderson. He's a big boy for arriving early. Six pounds, two ounces. The doctor said he's a mite premature, but his lungs sound like they're working just fine."

Olivia promptly burst into tears.

By the time Olivia got home, she was happy but exhausted. Her mother had left a note on the kitchen table.

Think about what I said.
Jack misses you.
Call him.
Mom

Jack. Olivia hadn't give him a thought since she'd left for the hospital. In fact, she'd had a perfectly wonderful time reminiscing with Stan. All of a sudden she wasn't sure what she wanted anymore. All of a sudden there was more to think about than she'd realized. If her ex-husband wanted back in her life, then maybe she should let him. Maybe she should consider *all* her options. Maybe it *wasn't* too late for her and Stan....

Getting ready for bed, Olivia thought about her divorce, and the couple she'd seen earlier that morning came to mind. Her decision to take them at their word and force them to put their children first had been a bold one. The kids were to stay in the home, and the parents would move in and out. Everyone who lived at 311 Pelican Court would be going through a big adjustment and for the sake of their children, she sincerely hoped they could make it work.

As for her...well, Olivia would watch and wait. She'd see how things went at 311 Pelican Court—and she'd be keeping an eye on events at 204 Rosewood Lane, too. Just making sure that Grace continued to regain her confidence, her emotional equilibrium.

And with two men in her own life, who could tell what might happen at 16 Lighthouse Road?